VESSEL FOR THY POWER

BOOK 1:
PART 1

S.J. AUTHORITY

DIVINITY UNIVERSE

Dedication

I dedicate this book to my parents, who, despite going against the culture, supported my dreams of being a writer; to my brother and sister, who would talk all things fantasy and sci-fi with me and supported me through just about every good and bad time I could think of. And, of course, I dedicate this book to the Holy Spirit, who helped me write this book in the first place! Love you, H.S., you're a real one.

Acknowledgments

I want to thank my parents, Kayode and Ola Peter, for their invaluable support, and especially my father, who told me to write a book in the first place.

I want to thank my siblings, Faith and Joshua. Joshua, my brother, designed my book cover and page break icons. Faith, my sister, who fed my love for stories by being an avid reader herself.

I cannot forget to acknowledge my friend D, who, when I was a fledgling writer, encouraged me to keep on going and who became a notable rival to help me get better. Though this is a formal acknowledgment, I do want to say, "Ha, I got my book out first!"

I would also like to thank my editor, Yvonne J. Medley of Medley Management and Prose, a seasoned writer in her own right, who gave me the necessary feedback and eye-openers that I needed to get this book to where it is now. Her help not only included editing but also gave me other important information that has saved me heartache and headaches.

I also acknowledge my friend, Naysa Barnes, a childhood friend of mine, who was a supporting drive of my book. Not only that, but this is also the friend who keeps egging me about my social media presence. If it's good, thank her. If it's not, I didn't follow her instructions clearly.

I want to acknowledge another childhood friend, Jarred Walker, who, being the youngest of our five-man group, keeps us grounded. His presence not only serves as an inspiration for several characters over the course of a few works but also a reminder that our village are our greatest protagonists.

I want to acknowledge my friend, Joshua Wilbanks, who is not only a good friend but also my boss at my part-time job. He's a great boss who gave me a steady working environment, especially since he let me write on the job.

I cannot forget to bring up my original fan and mentor, Rachel Heinhorst, she's an English professor at the community college I went to. I entered college at a young age, and she was one of the people who helped nurture my writing gift while I was there. I don't think my work would have been as refined nor do I think I would have been as motivated in college without her.

I cannot leave my acknowledgments without thanking the Holy Spirit—the one who helped me when I got stuck, the one who helped me with the themes of the characters, and the one who told me to split the book in two. Words cannot properly describe the incredible help that was given to me by this Helper and Advocate.

Table of Contents

CALENDAR

The calendar system in Vessel works a bit differently than it does in the real world. There are key words that need to be established before this could be fully understood:

Year(s) – Xantus/Xantem

Winter—Shiffraim

Spring—Blossom

Summer—Hestus

Autumn—Aumir

Each xantus has a governing star in which it was named: Elerf Star, Night Star, Destuan Star, Sunrise Star, Orben Star, Day Star, Hoffler Star, and Sundown Star.

The stars are split between the seasons:

Elerf Star, Night Star, and Destuan Star are in the Shiffraim season

Sunrise Star is the sole star in the Blossom Season

Orben Star, Day Star, and Hoffler Star are in the Hestus season

Sundown Star is the sole star in the Aumir season

Glossary

(The) Abode—The legendary and mythical home of Yehowehel and his spiritual children, the Vehem. A place that sits in a realm far above the other realms and overlooks several spiritual planes as well as the physical plane. It is said that a small hole in the ground of the Abode provides light to the entire universe.

Amoran—One of the primary houses of Setas-Li and the royal house. Amoran was the name of the ship that carried the bulk of the first Setas-Lisian settlers to Dominius. It was led by a philosopher warrior who led the people and was unanimously named the first king of Setas-Li.

(Seplechuran) Berserker—A type of dark warrior less than Umbran Sovs. They possess dark powers albeit weaker than their Sov counterparts. They also have special abilities and are more closely related to Shades.

Bhall-Duraht—The self-proclaimed free town on the southernmost part of the continent. It sits in the old territory of the desert kingdom that disbanded into small nomadic tribes.

Blades of the Legendary Vehem—The sacred Blades, over which the war was started. Seen as symbols of power and keys to the Holy City of Leruam Pol, these enigmatic weapons were said to have fallen to the world of man due to a great conflict in the Abode.

Blinkblade—Known as Amoran Style: Blinkblade or, more commonly known as, Blink. A special ability known only to the Amoran clan. The ability allows them to see the White Rail, a straight, ethereal line, and latch onto it to do a high-speed attack. The best practitioners are said to be able to manipulate the White Rail, but some think that's myth.

Borealis—One of the primary houses of Delfizcan. The bulk of the tribe lives at the base of Mount Borealis by which their tribe is named. They are the strongest and most prominent warrior tribe who have access to the mysterious power—the Borealis Rage.

Borealis Rage—A special ability of the Delfizcani of Mount Borealis. A green glow shines in their eyes, amplifying their physical prowess in every aspect and numbs them to physical pain. However, when the glow fades, the pain they were numb to pays them back with a vengeance.

Burnwinter—A creature of an old Seplechuran folktale. Burnwinter is the commontongue name for the great serpent, the actual name is Draaktel Hernviinter which translates to Monster (or Abomination) of Fire and Ice. Its body was said to be so long it stretched from Seplechurus to Kuto. In the myth, it was killed by a legendary spear that pierced the serpent's heart.

Camerus—A tribe from an unknown continent. The only known member is Caesar Camerus and his two sons, Jace and Aidan. The tribe is known for their exceptional strength and durability, far stronger than any normal person on Dominius. Camerus are known for their thick dreadlocks and their love for cloaks and jackets.

Chyber—A small four-eyed rodent the size of a watermelon. They have pointed ears with curled inner ears, along with a zigzag tail that makes a unique "chy" whipping sound. Their eyes are big and adorable and are often used as pets. They are found in the Utopian and Termas regions.

Day of Nissi—When the ancient Setas-Lisians first tried to settle on the continent, they were met with Seplechuran resistance. With the help of one of the local independent tribes, the Setas-Lisians made a daring attack on the mountain regions on the East Coast of the continent, winning against Seplechurus and establishing themselves as a kingdom. The local tribe became House Phillian, one of the founding houses of Setas-Li.

Delfizcan—The northernmost kingdom that is formed from the various cities and towns built around mountains. Like many nations, Delfizcan is the home of settlers who moved to Dominius after civil unrest on their home continent. The people formed a nation, albeit, more peacefully than Setas-Li.

Delfizcani-Setas-Lisian Conflict—In times past, Delfizcani warriors were able warriors and laborers. In several different conflicts, those who had the Delfizcani usually won the day, and in most of those several conflicts Setas-Li was the enemy. This bred animosity between the sides as the Setas-Lisians saw Delfizcani as mindless savages and the Delfizcani saw Setas-Lisians as pompous warmongers with a god complex. This eventually devolved into Setas-Lisians capturing Delfizcani for their slave trade. And that act single-handedly pushed Delfizcan into Seplechurus's hands.

Elyssi—The official Utopian language. The original language of the first Utopian tribes before the occupation of Setas-Li and Seplechurus. It nearly died out but an effort by one of the Utopian kings brought the language back.

Galvan—A special ability unique to the members of Setas-Lisian's Phillian clan. It allows them to harden surfaces in front of them. Training can increase the range, length, and durability of the hardening.

Great War in the Abode—An event shrouded in mystery. Seen by the prophets of various nations, it became the catalyst for the fall of the Blades that sparked the war.

Seplechurus—The largest and oldest territory on Dominius. Formed to consolidate the power of the northern region, Seplechurus was originally a group of indigenous tribes that banded together to survive a harsh Shiffraim season that claimed thousands of lives. It eventually became an empire that accepted any person or territory willing to join it.

Sez-Maraness—A nation formed on the western region of Dominius. As of 1149, it is the only republic to exist on Dominius. It is mostly aquatic land filled with beaches, peninsulas, and fjords.

Shade—A mysterious, dark entity made from darkness. Generally thought to be formed when dark powers bind to the fleeing spirits of human hosts. Emperor Ras describes them as "simple reflections of greater sources."

Shatersus—A nation of the earth. Shatersian cities are built into mountains and fissures and are all connected through underground paths. Gems and other earth materials are commodities of the land and have greatly influenced the physiology of the people.

Hometrees—Offspring of the Jireh Tree, also known as jeerihat. It has become Utopian tradition to have a hometree through one's home as a symbol of the family within. It is the job of the head of the household to maintain the tree because it is indicative of the family within. If one dies, it sometimes takes decades for someone to receive another.

Hericon—An old name for the region before the land was split among the nations. It is a simple ancient word meaning north. It eventually became the name of the northern faction.

Ignisium—A special ore that came from a meteor that fell in Sepelchuran territory. It is highly volatile. It is used as explosives due to its ability to turn friction into a powerful reaction.

Illisia—An old name for the region before the land was split among the nations. It a simple ancient word meaning south. It eventually became the name of the southern faction.

Iquan—Quadruped creatures that resemble a mix between a horse and big cats. Fiercely intelligent, loyal, and adaptable, iquans are used primarily as war mounts or guard steeds. They are found in every region, sporting different colors and manes. Despite resembling horses and big cats, they are genetically related to neither.

Jireh Tree—The mythical tree of Utopia. It is a giant tree that pierces the clouds. It is said that its roots spread throughout all the territory of Utopia, nourishing the land, hence why Utopia has so many unique animals and vegetation. Legend has it that it was planted by Yehowehel to celebrate the creation of the world. It is the parent tree to all Hometrees, and its nutrients are so unique that certain plants cannot grow without it. It also acts as the Hometree for the Utopian Castle.

Kcauss (Voshkovik)—The rose-bearing sub-tribe of the Voshkovik clan. Kcauss translates directly as rose in commmontongue. They were the first to bear the name Voshkovik, thus bear great influence in their greater tribe and in all of Seplechurus.

Kcauss Flowers—An ability unique to some members of the Kcauss Voshkovik tribe. This ability gives them the power to manipulate specialized roses to for combat. However, all roses can turn dead opponents into rosebushes.

Kojcut—A name for Utopians who have Seplechuran blood, more specifically, those who have ancestral blood from the Seplechuran occupation.

Treated better than the Pachra, due to the nature of the Seplechuran occupation, Kojcut are given higher priority when it comes to land and jobs. They maintain their Seplechuran pale skin and eyeshadow but keep their brown hair and hazel or green eyes of Utopia.

Keerie O' Theos—Meaning god wielder in the ancient tongue. A Keerie meant many things in mythology. The Keerie were thought to be an angelic sect between principalities and powers. However, some myth concludes that these are humans who were chosen to be deities or Vehem. Some say, they hold unimaginable power that could level mountains and destroy or create continents. While many do not believe that the Keerie would resurface, some people have hope that they would walk among man again.

Kromopha—Legendary patron Vehem of Forgiveness and Diplomacy was said to be a grieving woman who lost her sons and her husband to war. It is said that, instead of seeking revenge, she journeyed to the kings of the warring kingdoms and convinced them to stop the war. Even after being stabbed by one of the kings, she still brokered for peace. She was, fortunately, successful. When she died, she achieved Vehemhood. Her constellation is two crucifix shapes with a star in between them. It is argued to this day if she was ancient Utopian or Seplechuran.

Kuto—A series of islands make up the land of Kuto. It is a beach-laden territory that boasts the most aquatic diversity of any land. Each island holds a tribe with different specializations and crafts.

Leroza—One of the primary houses of Setas-Li. Leroza was named after the merchant ship that carried most of the goods of the first Setas-Lisian settlers. The woman who was the wisest with the funds during the settling effort became the first leader of House Leroza. In current day, House Leroza is in charge of fiscal affairs.

Leruam Pol—The legendary Holy City of Leruam Pol, said to be a special city in the middle of the continent of Dominius that is inaccessible through normal means. Legends say that once the city is entered it will grant power and eternal life to all who enter.

Mate Tree—A special tree that thrives from the nutrients of the Jireh Tree. Two trees that grow evenly apart from one another. Their branches grow opposite each other as if one tree. Many rare species of bird and flower make their home in or near the trees.

Pachra—A name for Utopians who have Setas-Lisian blood, more specifically, those who have ancestral blood from the Setas-Lisian occupation. They are considered second-class citizens and less than pureblooded Utopians. They tend to have noticeable blond hair and/or blue eyes while maintaining the olivine skin tone of Utopia.

Phillian—One of the primary houses of Setas-Li. An indigenous tribe of hunters on Dominius that had no allegiance to Seplechurus or Utopia. They befriended the Setas-Lisian settlers and, after believing in their visions for the future, helped them establish themselves on the continent. After the Day of Nissi, they were given the name Phillian which translated to protectors.

Songlua—A tribe from an unknown continent. The only known member is Roselyn Songlua Camerus and her two sons, Jace and Aidan. The tribe is known for their exceptional eyesight that allows them to see much farther than the average person, much deeper colors than the average person, and to see better at night.

Sov Degit—The Seplechuran government uses a tally system to make decisions. While most officials get one tally, the emperor/empress gets three during all matters, Umbran Sovs get two during war matters. What can be considered a "war matter" is up for debate.

Umbran Sov—A title meaning Dark Sovereign in Seplechuran. In times past, Umbran Sovs were covert military leaders who specialized in night raids following the night ambush by the ancient Setas-Lisians. Now, they are the names given to Emperor Ras's generals to whom he granted dark powers. They are also known simply as Sovs.

Uniket—The common Delfizcani language. Born when the first Delfizcani settlers moved from their arctic island home to Dominius. To solidify their new life on the continent, they combined their tribal languages with some commontongue to make Uniket.

Utopia—A relatively young kingdom formed from many of the indigenous tribes of Dominius. It is the southernmost kingdom that boasts in dense and luscious forests, exotic animals, and unique flora. It, at different points in time in its infancy, was occupied by both Setas-Li and Seplechurus.

Utopian Occupations—Utopia was the longest occupied territory. It was occupied by Setas-Li after they first settled on the land after the Day of Nissi. The Utopians were liberated by the Seplechurans. Decades later, the Seplechurans forcibly occupied them to protect them from Setas-Li while also getting back at the settlers. After Utopia aligned with Setas-Li, due to some political happenings, Seplechurus willingly left.

Vehem—Legends say Vehem are humans who, through great works, ascended to the Abode to become children of Yehowehel. Each Vehem is a paragon of a specific concept or entity, and they manage that power from above. While Vehem are not worshipped, their names are invoked, and their stories become legend.

Voshkovik—One of the primary houses of Seplechurus and the largest. The Voshkovik tribe is made up of five sub-tribes. When the first Kcauss Voshkovik was saved by his blood sister, who also commanded flowers, he formed a pact with her to be one tribe. Later, several other tribes formed blood pacts and became what is known as the Voshkovik tribe.

Vurhsan Stag—An elusive creature from Utopian Myth. It was said to be birthed from the dying forests of Utopia during the many occupations in the past. Some say it is the spirit of the forest given form to watch the indigenous people and protect them during hardships. Seeing it is a sign of good luck, but if it runs from you in a panic that's bad luck (since it smiles upon those who protects the forest and are in love with nature). It is made from roots, vines, bark, and bushes with horns that extend to the skies.

War for the Holy City—The unofficial name of the conflict that set the continent of Dominius ablaze. It started when a great event shook the continent of Dominius. Then, the prophets from various nations prophesied of the Great War in the Abode that allowed the Blades to fall to the physical plane. What should have been a group effort to find the Blades turned into conflicts that eventually escalated into full-on war.

Waritutu—A very adaptable fish that is in Delfizcan. It is a beefy, four-eyed fish that uses its special organs to regulate its temperature. It is a common fish in the cold regions of Delfizcan. But, if carefully transferred, it can live anywhere.

Yehowehel—The god of Dominius and the creator of all things. Yehowehel was said to be the planet itself however seeing the corruption of man, he forsook his body and watched the people from his new home in the Abode. It is said he steers the direction of all living things and those who obey him intently become Vehem, patron deities who hold a portion of his power.

PART ONE

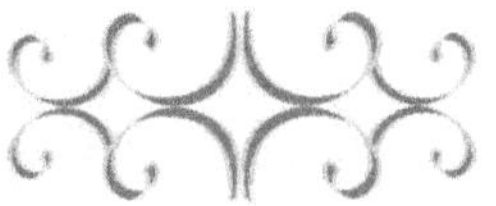

LIBERATION

Prologue

DIVINITY. A CHANCE for mortals to play god and attempt to mimic their creator. In the Abode, the home of the god Yehowehel, there was a great war that fractured the very heavens. Legends say that a Great Sword broke apart, bearing the spirits of mighty Vehem warriors, and fell to the physical plane. Prophets all over the continent of Dominius prophesied that the fractured Blade served as keys to Leruam Pol, the hidden gate in the inaccessible center of the continent.

Each of the great countries came together to discuss the possibility of finding them together. At the table was the Illisia, the southern region of the continent, which consisted of Setas-Li, the regional leader; Utopia, Shatersus, and Zaberas. Along with the Illisians were the Hericons, the northern countries: Seplechurus, their regional leader; Delfizcan, Sez-Maraness, and Kuto.

While the majority of the Illisan countries wanted to band together and search for the Keys together, the Hericonian countries wished to gather the Divinity for themselves, hoping to fight prior transgressions. The Illisia, soon following the same method, engaged in an all-out war with their northern neighbors. The peaceful breezes of Dominius regressed into the torrential wails of battle. Open, beautiful fields became graves, gardens became battlefields, and havens became workplaces for the healers.

But while the nations raged against one another. A smaller, personal story was unfolding. Jace and his brother, Aidan, had their lives completely ripped away. The war found its way to the south, to the small, independent town of Bhall-Duraht. In the event so aptly named the Massacre of Bhall-Duraht, Jace and Aidan found out their small town was not so independent and far from the war as they thought. Their parents' fate was unknown: they either burned to death along with some of the screaming villagers or beaten and taken as slaves to be used as pawns in the mindless game of the nations. So many fates were unknown, including that of their beloved friend Serenity, who was a sickly outcast with a heart of gold. The brothers, unknowing of the fates of their family and friends, have sworn on their lives to find out, and to avenge all who have already dearly suffered the savagery of war, now spreading across the continent. Unbeknownst to them, their parents, Caesar and Roselyn, had already trained them for such a time as this. Now, the time has arrived. And they must deliver.

1

THE ORPHANS

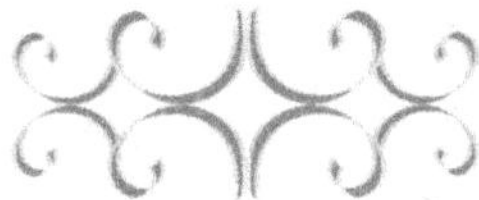

Nobody cared about Bhall-Duraht until somebody did.
—The Protector

"YOU'RE GOING TO need to try harder than that," Jace said with a flip of his scabbard.

Aidan flourished his blades. "I find it humorous that you think I was trying yet."

Even though this all started much before 1149, it only mattered until then. The Illisian and Hericonian nations were at war. Not for resources or land, not this time; this time, it was for Divinity itself. The sky split one day, and the morning sun grew dark. A barrage of lights scattered about, signaling something prophesied for many xantem—The Aftermath of the Abode. The Vehem, the deities of Dominius, had finished their war, and mankind now had its reward—the Keys to the holy city of Leruam Pol. The Illisia and the Hericonian, the two factions, waged war for these divine treasures, hoping to ascend to godhood. But that didn't matter.

Even though this all started much before 1149, it only mattered until then. Because that's when the Seplechurans, leaders of the

Hericonian faction, attacked and massacred the small, free desert town of Bhall-Duraht.

It was an attack, for which they would soon pay dearly—with interest.

But for this moment, it was another morning, another day in the training field—an open space filled with trees that captured the lukewarm morning dew on their emerald leaves. An aromatic smell wafted through the morning, as well as the distinct smell of steel.

Jace always found something entertaining about fighting his younger brother Aidan, who was energetic, limber, and unorthodox. The strength of a sword in both his hands was just about equal, making Aidan a valuable sparring partner.

Jace kept his sheathed sword close to him, his powerful legs spread apart, feet grinding against the grass, and his center of gravity low. The flash of Aidan's blades came at him again, but Jace simply swiped with his scabbard.

Aidan dropped his hands in a pout, "Come on, Jace, at least do something else, other than dodging and blocking! I thought we were fighting. You're less fun than our last contract."

Jace retorted, "If I were to do that, I would break my stance, idiot." He goaded, "Besides, didn't you say you can force me? Come on and try."

Aidan began to hop, the soft grass muffling his steps. That look of determination on his face was exactly what Jace wanted. Aidan was always a mischievous little beast; this meant he was going to get resourceful. He grinned. "Oh, let's give 'em a show."

The sunlight piercing through the thick forest canopy started to shift as the sun woke from its slumber, creating formless patches of light on the forest floor. Jace surmised to himself: *He's going to try and blind me by using a light patch on the ground.*

Aidan bolted up a tree, lodging one of his swords midway. He swung from the sword to several other branches, and he kept on swinging.

Watching, Jace shouted a taunt, "Who's not fighting now?"

"Patience, dear brother." Aidan launched himself at Jace from one of the branches, bearing that impish grin he usually carried.

Jace blocked the attack. Aidan harnessed the momentum to flip to another tree. He repeated the tactic, keeping to the trees only to descend for one strike. This was uncharacteristically predictable. Jace kept his eyes on his brother as he jumped across branches.

"Aidan, this is getting …" Just then, Jace's eyes forced shut, shielding himself from the light.

All Jace heard was the sound of breaking wood and the snarky voice of Aidan, "I win."

The smell of steel filled Jace's nostrils before his eyes opened; Aidan had a blade to his older brother's throat.

Jace tilted his head upward, the light passing over the blade that Aidan had lodged a moment ago. "I wasn't expecting that."

"It was a tactic from one of the books Mother left us."

"She left us only fairytales and language books."

"Fairytales have action in them," Aidan grew a smile. "Chalk another win for me."

"A tie," countered Jace.

"Why?"

Jace motioned down, then up again with his eyes while clearing his throat. He watched the defeat materialize on Aidan's face as he noticed the scabbard pointing at his pelvic area.

Aidan sighed, "Dang it."

Both warriors retreated their weapons. It was then, Jace noticed his shortness of breath and broken sweats. Despite looking as if he were chiseled from stone, he didn't feel that way. His heart thrummed with energy, but his knees felt like jelly. He told himself he wouldn't train long, but that lie was a mantra by now.

"We're actually doing this, taking back our home from the Seplechurans?" Aidan asked.

Jace shut his eyes, remembering everything from that day. Ten xantem ago, when he was the ripe age of eleven, the Seplechurans took their home in the dead of the night.

It all started with the yelling. Was someone hurt, he thought? Were people fighting in the streets again? He looked out the window, seeing the very stars fall in a fiery burst of explosions.

"Catapults!" one of his neighbors yelled.

Bells and alarms rang; people called to their neighbors and loved ones. Jace leaned out the window, trying to piece together the events. It didn't make sense then. The violence and death were unnatural. It was foreign. The pieces started to all make sense as one of the stars headed for him.

Something tugged at the hem of his shirt, pulling him with impressive strength. He was dragged from his room, pulled under the person's weight as the star crashed.

It was so loud! A loud, high-pitched hum overpowered every sound, including that of his mother's voice.

"Jace!" She yelled; her maroon, braided hair was a mess. "Get up now!"

He shook his head, his mother's words finally reaching his mind. Flat on the floor, he asked, "Where's Aidan?!"

"Your father has him. We need to go!"

His mother grabbed him, kicking down their front door. To this day, Jace asked himself, how did his mother ignore everything? Because when he saw it—it broke him. Adobe homes were completely shattered, battered corpses were burned under the flaming boulders from the catapults. People yelled in agony as they realized they were the last surviving family members; their parents, siblings, and children—screaming from their homes until there was nothing but silence.

Jace ran, but he didn't feel his legs move.

"No! Honey, look at me." His mother stopped to kneel, grabbing his shoulders. He tried to turn his head, but she pulled him back. "Don't look at them. Look at me."

He did as he was told, focusing on his mother's beautiful brown eyes so filled with lashes, her cocoa skin that matched his at the time, and her hair, a dark maroon, a symbol of her home.

"That's it. Use your eyes. Focus on me. Observe only me." She stood up. "Let's go."

He followed her instructions. He focused on her as they ran, but his ears captured the rest.

Jace blinked back the tears. Clenching his fist, Jace replied, "Yes. We're taking it all back."

Aidan grinned. "We're going to let them have it. I honestly can't wait."

Jace smirked at his little brother, "When aren't you excited about causing trouble?"

"Oh! You're funny," Aidan retorted flatly.

Jace clapped his brother on the shoulder and shepherded him a few meters to the drapery of vines that covered their home cave. "Let's get ready." He spread the vines open, tucking them under a rock to hold them still. Jace and Aidan had quickly become excellent hunters. So, that took care of their daily sustenance; inside that cave, all they had to survive on, for the past ten xantem, were books, threads, weapons, and medicines. All that had been stockpiled by their parents long ago in case something were to occur. Later, they used those tools to begin hunting and then to start work as mercenaries to train, to prepare, to strategize—and to temper themselves.

"Did you finish my weapons?" asked Aidan.

"Yeah." He let a second swoop by before lobbing back his question. "How about the clothes?"

"Of course," Aidan gave a slight performative bow, "my perfection is boundless." Then, he reached for one of the many crates in the corner of the cave. Aidan was surprisingly organized, keeping all his creations in proper order. After moving a few things, he handed a crate to Jace.

"Mine?" Jace took the weighted crate under his arm as if it were a small child.

"Yours." Aidan turned to heave his crate. "Change outside," he motioned with his quick nod. "I left a mirror out there from one of my solo contracts."

Jace halted. "You took on a contract without me?"

Without even looking back at his brother, Aidan quipped, "It was a small one, relax."

Jace sighed exasperatedly, not wanting to have *another* conversation on the topic. He just went outside, searching for the slab of glass, finding it near a bush. He brushed the stray branches and grass along with some water before setting the crate down and opening it. He got dressed methodically, admiring every aspect of the outfit. The design, he noted to himself, was immaculate; the sleeveless vest shone with a glittery blue thread, the edges of it adorned with white. It was a proper contrast to his now chestnut skin, which manifested at puberty like most of his father's clan, and his ebon hair and eyes. It was honestly a nice touch, Jace felt. But white wasn't the best color for the desert, he conceded. Regardless, Jace reached into the crate to pull out a pair of shimmery white pants, which had a golden buckle to hold the look together. He brought his dreads forward to obscure his face. Taking it all in, he couldn't help the quiver in his lips and the sinking of his eyes; his arms rattled as if he saw a ghost.

Aidan appeared from the mouth of the cave. Aidan shivered. "You look like Father."

"I … know," Jace awed.

He'd heard it many times before from the townsfolk back in his town, but it didn't really mean much until now. The man he admired so much was staring back at him in the mirror, looking as if he was going to speak those quiet words of wisdom. "Though I don't look entirely like him, all I'm missing is a coat. You know how much Father loved his coats."

Aidan muffled a chuckle because at least he could remember that. "You're in luck, my friend." Aidan quickly ran into the cave, returning with something that Jace had wanted for so long—a coat. "Surprise!"

Jace paused a moment before taking it from Aidan's hand. The colors were inverse, a stunning white cloak with blue linen sewn into the edges of the fabric. Despite hating working with gold, Aidan managed to sew golden plates on the shoulders and golden buckles on the wide lapels. Jace knew his brother was an amazing seamster, just like their seamstress mother, but to think his skills improved this much was simply impressive.

Their father was a quiet man from another continent who spoke little and even littler of his home. However, he mentioned that a large coat was a sign of power and leadership. To finally have one himself, Jace stared at his father's image through his own reflection; he had no words.

It was the morning of the Massacre. A young, six-xantus-old, Aidan was snoring on his brother's bed, so Jace wanted to distance himself from the noise. He heard movement from his parents' room, so he decided to investigate. Jace would never forget what he saw.

His father stood in front of the footrest of his bed, staring at himself in a mirror with a grim expression, adorned with a jade coat, gold with thin patterns sewn into the fabric of it. The flared lapels nearly hid his father's face, so Jace decided to step closer to get a good look, but the wooden floors creaked, and his father turned to him quickly. His father's expression softened, and he beckoned Jace closer.

"Father?" A young Jace asked then, struggling with his long, unruly hair.

"Jace," his voice crackled and reverberated with deepness. "I thought you were sleeping."

"That's Aidan," Jace chuckled. "He's loud even when he sleeps."

His father didn't smile much, but Jace knew that joke amused him.

Jace, studying his father's finery, wondered if his mother had made that for him. Upon closer inspection, it was beautiful but older; some battle scars were in it that were not resewn. He knew that his mother would never allow that to stand.

"It's a symbol from my home," his father's foreign bass accent grew deeper. "Coats, long ones as these, were symbols of power and leadership." His father turned to him, staring not into his eyes but into his soul, possibly his future. "You will earn yours one day."

It almost felt, Jace had concluded, that his father knew, he knew that the world—*his world*—was going to end. That coat wasn't just a symbol of power and leadership. It was a declaration of war.

"How does it feel?" Aidan placed an observant finger over his lips, breaking Jace from his trance.

"It looks great." Jace cleared his throat, pushing down the memory.

Aidan scoffed, giving a sharp, disregarding gesture. "It's made by me; I know it looks good. How does it *feel*?"

Jace rolled his eyes, but he knew Aidan wasn't wrong. He stretched the sleeves a little to get the feel of length, and he moved a little to get the feel of movement. Aidan's work was flawless—their mother would be proud.

"It feels good, very natural," Jace's eyes glued to the coat; it was so simplistic yet keen.

Aidan nodded appreciatively, doing that annoying thing where he feigned a tear in his eye. Jace sighed, shaking his head, but his words were to his clothes, lost for his feelings.

"I shall now adorn myself with my artwork," Aidan took a bow. "Please, continue to bask in my sovereignty of the needle."

Aidan disappeared into the cave, leaving Jace to finish his surprise. While his brother specialized in the needle, Jace spent his time studying the art of the forge. It brought back so many memories as Jace hit an anvil, the days when he would be beside his father, watching the metal mold by his strength. Using the smaller caves, Jace was able to simulate his childhood memories. It required a xantus for him to tunnel through the rock to make a proper forge, but he did it, and the weapons he made were astonishing. He laid his best works in an ornate golden crate that he stole from the Seplechurans during a raid.

He ambled over to the crate to peek at the two black scabbards embellished with golden vine detail. He picked up one, brushing his thumb over the blackened cross guard, then the hilt, then the pommel.

"Ready?" Aidan asked.

Jace dropped the scabbard back into the box, hoping that Aidan hadn't seen his surprise. Starting a quest with a gift was sort of a tradition, he knew. So, it would be disappointing to let it spoil. Jace responded to his brother's question placidly. "Yes, I am." He turned around, expecting some exuberant and theatrical outfit like his brother's personality, but to his surprise, it wasn't. Aidan wore a basic, sleeveless, black shirt that seemed a little tight on the skin; it was adorned with similar golden vines—like the scabbards. "You peeked," Jace leered.

"Of course, I peeked, I wanted to be matching," Aidan sassed with another one of those impish grins. He brushed some lint off his harem pants; then he rushed over to his blades. He rubbed his hands together, like a gnat in front of a meal, expecting Jace to just bestow him with a sword. He apparently didn't take to tradition as much as his brother did. "Oh, come on," Aidan pouted, "I just looked at the scabbard; I didn't unsheathe the blade or anything."

Jace frowned, making his eyes even narrower than they already were.

"Is that your natural scowl, or are you mad?" Aidan asked.

Jace groaned because Aidan could be a pest sometimes. But he knew he would be lying if he said he didn't look at his brother's work either, though the coat caught him by surprise. "Just take the blades, don't open them. We don't want to lose any light."

Aidan shivered in excitement. "We're leaving now?"

Jace picked up the third and final blade inside the golden crate. It was wrapped in sackcloth bandages. Even Jace nearly forgot how the blade looked, but he knew of its lethality, and that's all that mattered.

He swung the sword buckle over his shoulder, nodding to Aidan. His energetic sibling put on his own sword buckles, ready to go.

"Alright, Bhall-Duraht, here we come."

2

The Thief

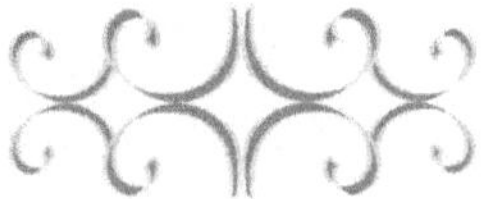

Catch me if ya can, laddies …
—The Thief

Bhall-Duraht, Xantem 1159

"I THOUGHT YA SEPLECHURANS were supposed to be tough!" She taunted, knowing they were too far to hear her.

The warriors of Seplechurus, the so-called Undefeated Empire, were supposed to be something.

They were known for their ferocity, but most importantly, their numbers since they were the first, in fact, to have men and women in their ranks. It was a shame their numbers meant so little to strategy.

It was said that their helms were fashioned after the *aquadrig*, the fabled underwater sea dragon of the frigid north. It was the very same one that adorned their banners and shields. The creature was known for its large horns on the side of its skull and a fin on the top of its head. It was a real shame it wasn't fashioned after a sand dragon because the north couldn't help them here.

Here—was a different battlefield; this wasn't the forest where the Utopians ruled, nor the mountainous fields of the Setas-Lisian kingdom—this was the desert. While the Seplechurans had to fear armored soldiers in the other kingdoms, in the shifting sands, they had an entirely different opponent. *Me.*

"*Stuvuh zveri!*" A soldier yelled, halt, in his native tongue.

But that couldn't stop the girl from running; after all, the Seplechurans hadn't caught her before, so there was no point in stopping now. She slipped into a narrow alley, the mob of soldiers not too far behind. On the other side, she saw a ladder leading to a roof with some barrels on top. *Perfect.* The girl climbed the ladder and then repositioned it right in front of the alley.

"Wait for it," she whispered confidently to herself.

As she saw one of the soldiers make it through the alley, she tipped a barrel down the ladder, watching it roll into the soldiers, toppling them like dominoes.

She sat on the edge of the roof, shouting a hearty laugh as she saw the soldiers struggling to get back to their feet. She laughed so hard; her sand-colored hood revealed a small bit of her reddish locks.

In her hand, she flipped around a dagger with dangerous skill. "Ha! Armor is not that helpful in the desert, is it?" the hooded figure laughed, boisterous and proud.

As the girl laughed, two soldiers made their advance behind her, sliding out their curved, crescent-shaped blades from their sheaths. Being in the desert for so long, certain sounds stood out more than others; metal boots crushing grains of sand might have been a faint one, but she had detected it. Still, these soldiers were stealthier than most. They had those special discreet sheaths, sligek, as they were called, were made for quiet, easy unsheathing; one side was entirely removed to allow the blade to slide out, soundless, so they could sneak up on their prey. But who could truly sneak up on *her*?

She feigned obliviousness, shouting more and more insults at the Seplechurans, who tumbled over. But when the shadow of a blade rose over her head, it was time for action.

The hooded figure dodged to the side as the sword of her assailant was brought down. She quickly got to her feet, dodging another attack. She knelt, grabbing another knife from her other boot. With a dash, she fought between the two soldiers, tactfully using her cloak to obscure the one she didn't face. One soldier desperately went for a stab, but the figure dodged with a sidestep forcing that soldier to impale the other. She kicked the blade from the stabber's hand and swept him under his feet. Upon hearing the thud, she breathed through her teeth; Seplechuran helmets were not great at protecting against falls.

"*Da bur tov?*" the stabbed soldier asked. "Who are you?" she repeated in commontongue.

Time for the reveal, she thought. The figure removed her hood, letting curly locks fall onto her shoulders. She still wondered how so much of her hair fit inside the hood. With a playful skip, she stared at the soldier's *aquadrig*-themed helmet with her own shadowy brown eyes.

She saw the soldier's surprise; most soldiers had the same look. "You're not from the desert," they would say. She honestly wondered what gave it away. Was it her brownish-red locks, the warm beige skin, or maybe her accent of the Hericonian north? Delfizcani inflections were very distinct. She heard some Delfizcani made it down to Bhall-Duraht, but she was never one of them.

"Ya're new here, aren't ya?" the figure asked, then she repeated in Seplechuran when the soldier looked confused.

The soldier nodded, terrified at how close the dagger was to her neck. "Yes."

"Well, after that little display, surely ya know now, dontcha?" The figure asked in Seplechuran. Again, the soldier affirmed with a nod. She added, "You are Grim Reaper of Bhall-Duraht, She Who is Fused with her Shadow." The soldier continued this time in commontongue. "Aurora, Thief."

The freckles on Aurora's face danced as she smirked. Hearing the fear in the Seplechuran's voice was well deserved. She moved into town seven xantem after the infamous Bhall-Durahti Massacre. The town looked horrific when she first arrived. Injured people being thrown on iquan and camels, only to die before they were transferred to the forests further north. The adobe houses that took so long to build were shattered in an instant. If she looked hard enough, she could still see the blood from the aftermath of that day.

While the Seplechurans were no architects, after gathering a few slaves who lived in the formerly free town of Bhall-Duraht, they were able to rebuild most of what was lost. She loved adobe houses because narrow alleys between them allowed her small frame to pass through with ease, while most of those burly Seps needed to run in single-file lines. At least they tried, like they tried to revitalize some of the trade, even then, however, that was mostly Seplechurus and the northern countries. Good thing, Aurora thought, that the gold found its way to *another* northerner.

Back then, she was nothing but a pest. But now—she basked in how much her name had grown. Her name was branded on the lips of every citizen, official, and officer in the Seplechuran army, but she enjoyed being too far away to deal with. Seplechurus was too far north and much too busy with the war to send someone to the deserts down south to deal with her. Even if they tried, they couldn't even catch her, still.

"That's right, lassie." Aurora pressed the dagger closer to the Seplechuran's fair skin. "Now, tell me where the slave caravans are, and I *might* show ya where the best healer in town is."

The sounds of soldiers running up the ladders interrupted her interrogation. She had honestly forgotten about them.

"I'll be back." She said as she flipped off the building and landed safely on the sands. Soldiers spotted her and immediately tried to chase her down.

The soldiers chased her, but she could see that their hearts weren't into it. There was a reason she was called The Grim Reaper; she didn't just kill quickly; she did it quietly. One wouldn't know they were dead until they were at the doorstep of the Abode. She was a ghost; she moved as such. She glided on the sands. They saw her but couldn't hear her.

Aurora vaulted off a barrel, lodging two of her knives into two throats of oncoming soldiers who probably should have worn their helmets. She snatched the daggers and kept going. She pushed through the herds of citizens who were buying and selling, making herself flow with the crowds. The remaining soldiers who chased her lacked finesse, pushing and barreling through the crowds. They ran ahead while she slipped in an alley with hands filled with gold and other trinkets from the crowd.

"Love to play this game all day," Aurora said, watching them stupidly race beyond her, "but I have a meeting to attend to with a stabbed soldier," she muttered, sinking deeper into the darkness of the alley, only to rear her head unexpectedly—like death.

3

THE TRAITOR

I will bear that title to help them.
—The Rose

WHAT REALLY MADE her a traitor? Was it the betrayal of ideals and morals, or was it the betrayal of those who held them? Some people saw it as synonymous, but not Natalie; she saw them as separate entities. To betray is to forsake, to forsake is to abandon, and she never abandoned her home.

Tree bark prickled under her calloused fingers as she watched a flame flicker below. The faint lights danced on nearby trees, providing warmth in the dreariness of the night. It reflected the dark purple armors of the scale-clad Seplechurans. The flame offered a pale reminiscence of the colors she once wore.

Below her, a single soldier stood guard, probably praying to Yehowehel that they weren't followed. But Natalie knew his prayers were moot as she kept looking at him from her perch, eyes of an owl. She removed a small stone from her pouch, flicking it to a nearby tree. The soldier below scrambled his head, looking for the source of the noise, only to rest moments after.

It was a true shame the light didn't reach higher.

Natalie wanted to shed a tear; in her heart, she knew she should be sleeping in locked arms with her people. Not stalking them in the dark. She could try to convert them to see her light, but what good would that do? She tugged on her espionage clothing; even in the dark, she could see the Jireh Tree emblazoned on her chest. The symbol of Utopia, the site of her defection. Her arms quivered; she should be wearing the dark purple of her people.

But there was a reason she left.

The emperor had gone too far: enslaving people, burning the homes of innocents. Not even that desert town in the warm south was safe.

The Utopians intercepted a few of the Seplechuran contrabands, holding the people hostage like they were animals. Their eyes, lifeless, lacking hope; their skin burned or beaten.

The war started so many terrors, and it was her people who started the war. She had to abandon her role as Head Kcauss, heir to the rose-bearing Voshkoviks, just to make her statement known. She could not stand on the side of tyranny. Not anymore. This was the reason why she could beat back the tears for her people, because the faster she ended the war—the less her people would die.

She descended from the trees, making the littlest of noises. Every movement she could not hide, she simply distracted the guard on duty with a rock. She could see the soldier in terror, but he was so quiet about it, an admirable Seplechuran quality.

Her feet touched upon the soft Utopian grass, caressing her soles with verdant bristles. That was one thing Seplechurus lacked, one thing that made her stay welcoming.

As she peered behind the tree, she noticed the soldier started to mutter to himself, no, hum, "*Vaza häs uva meri, zudem Yehowehel a sol …* (When the night descends, trust in Yehowehel the strong …)" It was the old Seplechuran folksong that was passed down from parent to child; it got them through the harshest winters and bitterest of wars. It was a song she loved to sing around campfires with her best friend, her sister, Pasha. Now, she questioned if Pasha would even look at her in the same light.

She exhaled, wanting to sing the song herself. But instead, her tongue was bitten, and her voice silenced—hushed as it sounded in her home, hushed as it sounded in Utopia, once the region became a war zone. She threw another rock.

"It was all in my head," he whispered in Seplechuran with a sigh of relief.

"Wrong."

A cutlass slowly made its way to the front of his neck as a hand clasped over his mouth. His deranged muffling woke one soldier, who woke the rest. Soon, all their weapons were unsheathed and pointed right at Natalie.

"*Tov! Judavek!* (You! Traitor!)"

That word again, *Traitor*. The word that she heard over again. It scratched at her mind and broke her heart. To hear it in her native tongue was even worse. It made her body feel weak, withering her slowly. "Me … I know," she replied flatly. With the butt of her cutlass, she knocked out the soldier in her grasp. She walked closer to the firelight, letting it illuminate her features. Fair-skinned, long black hair, smoky pupils, and a faint blackness around the eyes—a mark of her Seplechuran heritage without a doubt. "I urge you all to surrender," she spoke in commontongue.

"You abandoned your country, now your own tongue?!" One of the soldiers yelled in Seplechuran. "*Judavek!*"

Her face was apathetic, her eyes distant. The skill she had honed more than fighting with the blade was how to fight her emotions. Only if she could tell them that she knew of the emperor's lust for power, the way he sends them like sheep to the slaughter, or how their home in the north has become colder in heart than it has in weather. She could say it, but it would be the same as the others. Disbelieving, they would spit in her face and curse her name. "I abandoned nothing," She spoke in her native tongue. "It is you who forget Seplechurus's history."

"Do not lecture us about Seplechurus when you wear the colors of another kingdom!"

It was true, she had no right to speak in her cloth. However, their ears were deaf when she wore her motherland's armor, but now, she stood out. They would have to turn their faces to her. She was the Seplechuran that walked the path alone.

"Your parents would be disappointed," another mocked, "the only heir Kcauss Voshkovik—a traitor."

Now the rage made it to her eyes. She readied her blade for combat, uttering no words. She had no more words—for the people who abandoned her first. The battlefield went mute as she took a deep breath in and breathed out. She'd fought so many of her people before this that the sounds of battle couldn't reach her ears properly. Instead, all she saw was the chaos of rose thorns that wrapped around her weapon and the bodies of those who berated her on the nature-floor.

They were not dead, she was grateful, but each one who lived killed her inside. Their words were a blade to her heart, yes, but they were also a constant reminder of why she fought; each of them had a family, a home, something to go back to. She felt compelled to honor that. She massaged her temples as someone approached her from behind. Too busy fighting a headache, she spoke without facing them. "What is it?"

"Natalie," a man wearing all black linen spoke to the back of her muscular figure. All the convoys have been intercepted. What would you have us do?"

She sighed, body still. "Jail them. I want none killed."

The man spat, "These are murderers and marauders; it does not matter if they are your people."

She turned her head. "Do you question me?"

"Yes," he hissed, "the king will not be happy to hear of this."

"Just do as I say."

The man turned. "Utopia will tire of you; sooner or later, they will turn on you."

He left. Once again, she had to admit the truth. It was a hard world she was in, a world where she was unwelcomed by both sides. She knew what would happen when she defected, but the pain of not being accepted, of not being loved anywhere she went. She wanted to explode. Natalie dropped to her knees, unable to hold back the tears any longer. But she knew that was the price she had to bear—the branding of being a traitor and trustless.

"Hold fast, Natalie," she spoke to herself, "they *will* know the truth ..." She silently finished the final part of her conviction ... *but when?* She held herself, humming, "*Vaza häs uva meri, zudem El a sol ... ort hech tev praed.* (When the night descends, trust in Yehowehel the strong ... with him, I blossom ...)"

4

THE PRINCE

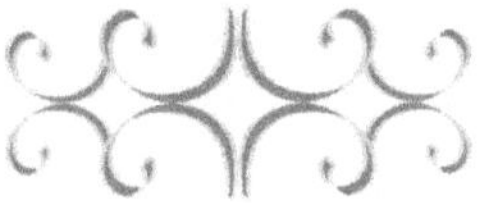

It will be me. It must be me.
—The Prince

1159 Setas-Lisian Castle, Study Wing

PRINCE NICKLAUS LAMENTED his lack of answers, exclaiming to himself, "Something must be here!"

War was such an enigma, and there wasn't a single way to solve it, he felt. It was as chaotic and as individualistic as the people who had taken part in it, each of their reasons was different than the next. *Their answer for this war is here; I must find it.*

Nicklaus was determined to be the one to find the answer. Some people enjoyed the war for the bloodshed, others for the glory, for money, and some even forgot why they fought in the first place. For him, it was the Blades; it has always been about the Blades. Most countries, including his own, started to use the war to settle their own personal vendettas with each other. It blinded them so much that if a Blade appeared before them, they would ignore it just to murder their neighbor. *That is why no one is worthy, except me, of course.*

The young man grew tired of the feeling of parchment; the crackling fragility in his hands was almost sickening, but someone had to search for it. He backed up his chair from the desk of scattered papers. He bathed in the light of the oculus, hoping it would give him some clarity on the situation, but all it did was reveal the dust mites clouding his study. He tapped his fingers on his wooden desk that was shadowed by the picture on the wall of one of his great ancestors, Setois the Wise. The one who started the grand, cavernous library Nicklaus now called his study. White, square-tiled floors undergirded the thirty rows of bookshelves on each side. Murals of scholars from each clan adorned the ceiling around the oculus. Large windows adorned both sides of Setois to grant light and, superstitiously, wisdom to those who sat in the seat in front of the desk.

He parted his golden locks to reveal weary blue eyes surrounded by a plethora of red veins. He carried his chair forward, determined to find some answers. At least a clue, *one* clue concerning the whereabouts of the Blades. He would wield it and put an end to the war.

He scanned through the papers, glancing at one only to throw it away when the pieces didn't fit in his mind. He brought his fist down on the papers, scattering the poor parchments while trapping some under his veiny fist. With a pinch of his temples, he sighed in his native tongue, "*Gohri perç du horr. (Great love of the kings.)*"

He knew he had to calm down. If his anger got the better of him, he could miss crucial data. But even with all his resources, could he truly find the answer? He wondered. Could he see the people laughing outside again like they used to? Could he—would he—find out why he should be the next reigning monarch of Setas-Li?

He descended in his chair, frustrated. Rubbing the bags under his eyes. Was he really to be king? He pondered. He didn't have an answer, just more questions. He had little problem becoming a monarch, but the question for him was, why? *Why should I be a monarch?* He badgered himself once again as he did every day. What could he bring to the table that no other monarch had? He knew that if he had a Blade, the answer would be obvious.

He picked up the papers again; the different languages were mostly gibberish to him because his translations were spotty. His vision started to blur; he rubbed his eyes only for them to worsen. His hands cramped with writing and mind-aching theories. He needed rest.

"Yehowehel," Nicklaus called out to the deity, "please, a sign." The young man leaned back in his chair, defeated. His sleepless days only grew worse, and the neglect of his body had taken a toll on his mind. He rubbed his eyes again before looking at the pages, but the words continued to be incomprehensible. They were already confusing in their different languages, but now he couldn't even see them. Nicklaus sighed. "Perhaps a break is in order, as long as my mother doesn't –"

A grating, high-pitched squeal of the giant metal doors broke his concentration. Honestly, if he didn't have that squeal to prevent him from being snuck up on, he would have it oiled at once. The steps were paced and loud, a failed imitation of grace echoing throughout the hardwood floors of the study to the back where the young man conducted his research. The large shelves slid by as the regal figure approached. *Yehowehel, preserve me.*

He stood, trying his best to look composed, brushing his golden doublet and trousers. But if his horrific odor didn't give him away, unkempt strands and the red surrounding the blue of his pupils would.

"Nicklaus," the deceitfully calm voice called, "I came to inform you that—*gohri horr* ..." She paused mid-sentence, sniffing around with flared nostrils, investigating. "... What is that smell?"

The red boiled to his face. "I ... have not left here in three days, Mother."

She rolled her blue eyes, which matched his, and kept her nose pinched between her pale, slender fingers. With a brush of her shoulder-length brunette hair, she spoke a demeaning tint to every word. "You call yourself a prince? You disdain fighting, and now it seems bathing has even left your mind. Just go and wash up. Suitors will be here momentarily."

It was always suitors with her. The world was at stake, and all she could think about was marriage. She wanted Nicklaus to get married, not because of love, but for status and appearance, and of course, grandchildren. Nicklaus dreaded children. They were always so loud, unbearable, snotty, and disrespectful, among other things. His mother wanted grandchildren before she grew old, yet she bore not a single speckle or wrinkle on her face.

"Suitors, mother?" He attempted to mask his anger. "Should we not be focusing on more pressing matters?"

Her brows furrowed, "Now what, in the name of Yehowehel, is more important than continuing the royal lineage?"

"Ensuring there is a country for my children to rule," Nicklaus hissed.

His mother paused to think, shaking her head, disdaining any bit of understanding. "Just do as I say." She walked off, her steps not as steady as they were before.

Nicklaus sighed, sinking back into his seat. It was frustrating to argue with his mother, his queen, but their squabbles had increased as of late. With his father too busy with the war, no one could possibly mediate for them.

He sniffed his clothing. He did smell putrid, and after feeling his muscles, he noticed how his once-toned frame had begun to soften quite a bit. "Maybe … a shower will clear my mind, no?"

He weakly pushed himself from his desk, his weary palms nearly slipping off a paper that fell to the floor in his stead. He looked at the papers, staring at their linguistic complexities.

If he wanted his answers, he could not stay in his study mode forever. He must journey into the open. Many of his papers made reference to the desert kingdoms south of Utopia. Minuscule news reached him in the castle, so he needed to travel to a place where he could get his answers.

The young prince stood, packing some of his papers. He would need a plan because his destination was—Utopia.

5

It Begins

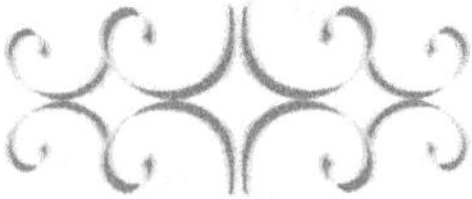

This is where the fun begins!
—The Wildcard

THE SUN WAS shining, the grass was green, and a town was about to be liberated; what was not to love? Aidan strode through the dirt-paved roads, flashing an occasional dance move to showcase his excitement. He knew it was annoying Jace who concentrated more on the plan, but how could he stop dancing now? Everything in Bhall-Duraht filled him with a level of hope he hadn't felt in xantem. The hope to see his old friends, his townsfolk, and maybe—just maybe—their parents. They couldn't be dead; they were so much stronger than that.

Aidan grew up on his mother's stories, told to him before the massacre. His mother would hush him to sleep with the tales of her and her husband's fantastical heroism. While Jace dismissed them as petty stories, Aidan knew if they were true, his parents were amazing.

Galvanized by the mere thought of his mother's epics, Aidan slid across the ground, giving a twirl in a patch of light that pierced the treetops. In this world, everything was a stage, and he needed to perform.

Everything relied on it, including his fighting style. Two swords, twice the impression.

"Can you please stop doing that?" Jace groaned.

"Can't," Aidan slid once more, "life's a game of cards, and I'm the wild, my friend. The stage needs its hero." He watched Jace groan and keep to himself without comment. And that was okay for Aidan, for he knew that he only just needed to keep moving and keep smiling. He had to, his mother said so. In the final moments of the Massacre, Aidan was given three instructions that he swore to live by for as long as he drew breath. The first two instructions from his mother were, "Keep smiling and keep moving forward."

Aidan didn't quite remember all that happened before the massacre, even as Aidan strained to recall his memories, he couldn't. He was so mad that he couldn't remember the most pivotal moment of his life, but he remembered the pain—the aching pain of fire that forced him to yell as his father fought soldiers to protect him.

He arched his back, tears welling in his eyes. A piece of debris broke off from the catapult boulder, pinning him under it as he made his escape with his father. It was one of the first times he saw genuine fear in his father's face, the face of a man who didn't want to lose his youngest son. The soldiers were drawn to Aidan's screaming. His father drudged toward him, soldiers piling on him and arrows and swords sticking from his back, and yet his father did not stop moving. However, Aidan remembered it vividly, the next part, *a soldier raised a sword at him, and his father's face physically contorted in anger, and everything and everyone just died as if a god raised an invisible hand and sundered them in two. His father didn't explain; he simply threw the boulder off his son, picking him up and comforting him.*

"It is alright, Aidan." He stated determinedly. "I am here." His touch soothed the burns, and soon Aidan stopped crying.

He couldn't remember what happened after that, just that his mother finally showed up with Jace in hand. She caressed his cheek. *"Keep moving forward," she said with tears welling up in her eyes, "and keep smiling."* She looked as if she wanted to say more but didn't. Her words after that just jumbled, murky as muddy water. Yet, he knew, that's what he needed to hear at the time.

His mother was his guiding grace. He learned everything from her, and she favored him more. While his father admired Jace's physical capabilities and knack for the forge, Aidan's mother saw the intricate hands of a seamster in him. And judging by Jace's reaction to the clothes, their mother was right.

Aidan calmed his dancing down slightly, giving Jace some peace of mind. "So, what's the plan?"

"We don't know what they've done to the town, so we should go in secretly, know their numbers, and then we strike."

"Makes sense. Hopefully not much has changed since you stopped visiting a few seasons back."

"Agreed."

Aidan sighed, weighing his words, "Do you … think we'll find Serenity?"

For the first time in xantem, Aidan saw his brother freeze up. That name always rattled him, and he tried his best not to speak it, but Serenity was their best friend, and the girl that Jace loved.

Jace looked on, face unreadable. "Aidan, you know that she can't be alive."

"You don't know that."

"I *do* know that, for a fact. I've been going back for xantem, and I haven't seen her."

Aidan's shoulder dropped, and the skip in his step slowed to a walk. Jace had told Aidan that he returned every day for four xantem, hoping that he would see his friend. During Jace's absences, Aidan observed that his brother looked more and more hopeless, to the point where he looked completely drained. One day, Jace just waited at the mouth of the cave, not even bothering to leave. That day, Aidan never mentioned Serenity or going back. The only reason why Aidan had hope was because the last Seplechuran wagon he raided spoke of slaves from the massacre, something that Jace refused to believe.

"We should still hold out—wait." Aidan stopped his brother.

"What is it?"

The road seemed clear, and in the case of a normal person, it would be, but Aidan wasn't a normal person. There was another reason why he was his mother's favorite: his eyes. His mother came from a clan of warriors that had immensely elevated eyesight (they also saw color better); though Aidan could not see as far as his mother, he could see twice as far as the average man, maybe even more. There was a reason why he lived by the third saying from his father, "Always be your brother's eyes," and knowing their father, there was a double meaning to that. Those were the last words his father said before they all parted—he wanted to take that and the other two slivers of guidance as seriously as he could.

"I see a wagon, a couple of soldiers."

"Arms?"

Aidan squinted. "Just swords, nothing we can't handle."

"Perfect warm-up, we'll practice our ambushing."

Aidan nodded with a smile, "They'll never see us coming."

Following plans was not Aidan's strong point. He could make them, but he relied too much on his instincts that he nearly forgot what the word, plan, meant. However, those were the moments when he relied on Jace the most; it was a time when he never felt closer to his brother. His brother always had his back. One could easily understand the attachment being surrounded by the enemy. "Quite the predicament we have gotten ourselves into," Aidan chuckled as he flourished his blades.

"'We?' You're the one who attacked them," Jace seethed through his teeth.

"You're the one who told me to attack them!"

"I clearly mouthed 'don't attack.'"

"Oh! I thought you said 'go, attack!'"

"You have mother's eyes, how did you possibly see 'go, attack'?"

"I … I don't know."

"Aidan?"

"Yes?"

"You're an idiot …"

The soldiers moved closer, not giving the brothers room to operate. From their xantem of experience, Aidan and Jace learned one thing about Seplechurans: they fight like bullies, only attacking after cornering their prey. That sparked a simple yet brilliant idea. "Want me to make up for it?" Aidan asked.

"Do you want me to throw you?" growled Jace.

Aidan grinned. "Actually, yes."

It took a second for Jace, but it clicked. While Aidan inherited more of his mother's eyes, Jace inherited more of their father's unnatural strength.

Aidan sheathed one of his two blades and quickly grabbed hold of his brother's hand. With a heave, Jace sent him flying over the enemies that surrounded them. Impatient as ever, Aidan noticed, Jace began bashing the soldiers before Aidan even had time to touch the ground. Once Aidan landed, he bowed.

While Jace loved being such a barbarian, Aidan settled for finesse. The play had started, and its main character had arrived; now the curtains rose. His excitement was palpable. In the books that he read, the curtains would open at his moment, ready for him to make his theatrical debut.

He spun, letting his opponents take in the glow of his red sword, forged from *ignisium,* an explosive material that resembled scarlet-tinted glass. Making swords out of them was unheard of, but Jace somehow turned explosives into a sharp weapon that could sunder steel. The best part, ignisium is mined in Seplechurus, the irony that Aidan lived for.

He unsheathed the other blade. "Let's give 'em a show."

The soldiers took to all sides, readying themselves for whatever Aidan had to bring, but that was the joke, the great twist in his masterpiece; no one could predict what was coming.

The five soldiers yelled something before attacking. Aidan lowered his stance slightly, his eyes focused. He dodged with precision, slashing at the soldiers' armor as he ducked from their blows, and instead of waiting, he jumped at them before they could recover. He launched a powerful kick, knocking one soldier into another. *That's two!*

Before he could stand, two soldiers slashed at him from both sides; he blocked them, one blade to one opponent. "Quite the predicament … again." He rose slowly, knowing very well he could overpower them. *Actually, no, that's no fun.* So, in a single motion, Aidan hooked one soldier's foot and parried the strike. Unintentionally, the other soldier overextended themselves and fell forward when Aidan moved, knocking himself out. *That's one more … I guess.* "You slash with your hands, not your body. You put *way* too much power in that." Aidan quipped. He seemed genuinely confused about how she didn't know better. "Who taught you?"

"I don't like you," the only female soldier hissed.

Aidan shrugged. "Not everyone has good taste, sweetheart."

She roared as she closed the gap, signaling the fifth, and last, of her conscious companions to follow suit.

Aidan dodged their strikes, critiquing their form with a huff. This didn't make for a good show. So, he settled for the Jace approach and kicked his opponent hard into a nearby tree, knocking one of them out, leaving the lady soldier. Aidan slowly retracted his foot. "Seplechuran armor has an impact weakness; you'd think someone would fix that." He shrugged. "I guess that leaves you."

"You're an unskilled child," she blasted in Aidan's direction. Then she picked up her comrade's weapons. She made her stout declaration to Aidan, "I will teach you manners!"

"Oh *ho,* look who's talking! I'm gonna enjoy shutting you up; that's the only thing your friends there did right." This time, Aidan moved forward, keeping both his swords level in front of him. He avoided power strikes, using one blade to attack and another close to him for defense. He kept the widest smile on his face, still remembering that the best part had not come into play yet. He continued his strikes, letting his *ignisium* blades seethe; they replicated how he felt—fired up.

The soldier left herself open by doing a double overhead strike. Aidan chuckled at how he could attack her there, but what was the point when the end was near? He retaliated with his own slash, and to the surprise of his opponent, his blades seared clean through hers.

"What?!" she yelled

"I know!" Aidan exclaimed excitedly.

Aidan swept her feet, pointing his blade at her throat before she could rise. She steadied her tired breaths, hoping that her skin would not meet the same fate as her blades.

"I'm defeated, kill me."

Aidan's face went solemn. The absolute first lesson he learned from Jace was mercy. There was always strength in mercy. "Only kill if necessary, only if they're a threat," he remembered Jace telling him. Aidan trained himself for that reason—to overpower his enemies so he wouldn't perceive them as a threat. That lesson was the hardest to learn for Aidan. *Why have mercy on the people who took everything from them?* The answer didn't come from Jace this time; it came from their father. He preached mercy more than anything else, saying that those without mercy are weak because they give in to their lust for death. Turning his attention back to the soldier, he responded, "I'd love to kill you, but this planet needs you for something besides fertilizer."

"What?" She subtly sighed in relief.

"Eh, I don't make the rules, I just follow them … or break them when I'm bored." Aidan kicked the woman before she could utter more words. He looked around, smiling at his work. Not bad for his first official battle to take back his home, he bragged to himself.

Zero, and that's the show.

6

THE PIECES OF HOME

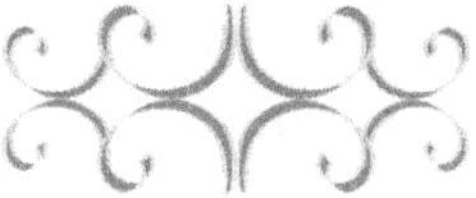

Obstacles will not halt me.
—The Protector

J ACE COULD FEEL his brother messing around on the battlefield. Aidan's obsession with the theater always baffled him because Aidan never saw the darn things and yet he was hooked; *maybe he would be an actor if all of this wasn't happening.*

Jace stepped over the soldiers that he had already defeated, keeping his thoughts his own. Unlike his brother, Jace preferred to keep his motivations and excitements in his mind; there was little reason for him to show them to the enemy. This proved to be unnerving for his opponents, like the swordsman in front of him now, who kept on shouting the same word over and over. "*Draaktel! Draaktel!*"

Jace's Seplechuran was sloppy, but the word was something he had heard before in the little novels he read to Aidan when they first moved into the cave. *Draaktel* was the name the Seplechurans called the creature in the series *The Legend of Burnwinter;* the only book Jace liked. Though he looked nothing like the serpentine creature, it was apparent they shared one similar quality—they both were monsters. While Aidan inherited more of the eyes of the Songlua from their mother's clan, Jace inherited more of the strength of the Camerus from his father; it was the power to stand against any foe, the power of a boulder, and the durability of a mountain. Though a slight exaggeration, these Seplechurans clearly did not know the extent of Jace's capabilities as their helmets lay crushed by Jace's bare hands, and their swords lay snapped. "Give me the keys to the wagon, and there will be no trouble."

Immediately contradicting himself in his thoughts, he boasted, *Yes, there will.* Mercy was the path that he would tread for as long as he lived. However, he felt that his opponents should beg for death before he was merciful. They needed to be broken but not removed.

He approached, his cloak fluttering in the small breeze that kicked up, making him a regal nightmare, fading all to black as he wore white. "My patience is being tried," he hissed when the soldier did not respond. Just then, Jace heard the rattle of armor. The poor thing was scared. *I guess a broken spirit will have to do.* Jace simply reached for the keys, leaving the soldier to contemplate if he should change his undergarments now or later.

The wagon was quite large, larger than any wagon he'd yet to see, and it had a blue tarp instead of purple. Purple was for soldiers and cargo, but blue was new to him. A wagon of that size didn't make much sense if it wasn't carrying people or supplies. *Why so large?* He questioned in his thoughts, finalizing that it had to be an animal, some sort of war beast.

The lock felt cold as he reached for it. He shoved the key inside, turning it slowly until he heard the click. He readied himself for the beast. With a steady breath, he opened the door, and what he saw forced his eyes to widen. He was right; *Aidan was right …*

"Jace! What did you find?" Aidan hopped to his side, but he, too, froze, seeing what was inside.

Slaves, about twenty, sat folded up, shackled, and beaten with bags over their heads. *Why weren't there any windows? No seats? A war beast would be treated with more care*—both brothers surmised without words.

Jace picked up the rattled soldier, the one he nabbed the keys from earlier, ripping off his helmet to look him in the eyes. The fear in those eyes was something Jace knew too well. After all, he did bear that look when his home was taken. "Where are these people from?" Jace roared.

"*Te b'rugh*! (I don't know!)" The rattled soldier replied.

The red veins pulsed within his eyes, pupils shrinking as much as his patience. His veiny hands grabbed the soldier by the face, shoving him into the tree behind him. He could feel his breaths chopping and a strong desire to rip the man's head clean from its shoulders.

The young man fell, cowering in the face of death. He was going to definitely die if he kept breathing like that, but his body settled for a closer option—unconsciousness. Jace slapped the boy, but he didn't get up. With a roar, Jace punched a mark in the tree, then ripped his hand from the splinters.

"Pardon me," Aidan crooned.

"What?!"

"Hey, calm down, I'm on your side." Aidan sheathed his swords. "Why don't we ask them?" he motioned to the slaves.

Jace closed his eyes, pacing his breaths. "Breathe ..." he muttered his mantra, letting it loose with every exhale. It was the word that calmed him during fits of rage or burdening anxiety. He stomped into the wagon, ripping chains off with his bare hands. The people were too tired to resist as he guided them outside. Aidan gingerly slid the sacks off their heads.

The captives shielded their eyes from the sun, letting their weary pupils adjust. One man blinked several times before his eyes fully adapted to the light. "C-Caesar?" He spoke.

Jace shivered. That name—it was seldom on his lips but was weighed on his mind. A name that felt more like a stranger's legend than a father's solace.

"Not exactly," Aidan spoke up for his brother.

When Jace realized how he had completely paused upon hearing the name. The other slaves stared at him with the same awe; some stared with fear. He cleared his throat. "No, I'm Jace."

The man squinted. "As I live and breathe … you, did, survive."

"You *two*," Aidan corrected.

The man looked over to Aidan, eyes filling with realization. "I don't believe it! You boys are alive!"

"I'm sorry, but who are you?" Jace asked as he used one of the bags to wipe his hands.

"It's me! Mr. Yaveer, the baker!"

The brothers blinked. Mr. Yaveer was an old Mareenian man and was quite rotund back in the day. The fact that he was so bone-stricken dry was horrific. He looked at their faces, letting his smile falter only a little. "It's been tough in Bhall-Duraht, but I'm glad I can still count myself among the living."

Aidan piped up, his hopefulness renewed, "Are there more survivors?"

"Lots. The Seplechurans killed a good number of us to make an example, but most were taken to Seplechurus as prisoners, some of us were shipped back to Bhall-Duraht as workers."

Aidan jabbed his brother in the side, and for once, Jace felt the need to smile. He knew Aidan wasn't going to let him live this down, but maybe he had the right to, maybe their parents were alive, maybe Serenity.

Jace continued his conversation with Mr. Yaveer while Aidan ran his mouth to the others; his jolly nature kept their minds at ease.

In the corner of Jace's eye, he noticed two more people inside. Two children, no more than thirteen-xantem-old, shivered in fear as they hung back. Jace tapped his brother; they shared a look before addressing the children. "You should go with the others," Jace advised, his voice as nice as he could make it.

The children didn't respond; they remained huddled in the corner, taking refuge in the darkness. Aidan hopped inside the wagon, nearly hitting his head up against its roof as he did so. The children cowered at his approach. With some effort, he pulled apart the chains as Jace had done earlier. "There we go, you're all safe now."

One of the children, a little boy, had reddish hair that awkwardly formed like a bowl on his head; the signs of torture and sleep deprivation made him look older. "Thank you," he mumbled.

"Don't mention it, now let's get you two out of here, aye?" Aidan stretched out his hand to the boy, and the young one happily accepted. The little girl beside him quickly followed.

"Our sister is in town." The girl blurted, though her voice was a whisper. "I miss my sister."

"We're heading to the town; we can bring her here," Aidan leaned down, ruffling the little girl's hair.

Jace glanced at the girl: pale white skin, ebon eyes, and a shadowy look around the eyes, it was obvious she was Seplechuran, at least in part. *So, they're enslaving their own now? What exactly is going on in this war?*

"No, we need to go back," she pleaded.

Jace crossed his arms, grumbling his thoughts. The children mistook his grumblings as being directed at them; they quickly hid behind Aidan.

"Jace, you're scaring the kids."

Jace, startled slightly, realized his error. "What? Oh, sorry. I was just thinking."

Taking the children back to the place where they were enslaved would be terrible for them, but they could provide valuable information. *But to use children as such?* Jace questioned himself. Was he better than the Seplechurans? Only if they were willing would he do it, Jace decided. Besides, Bhall-Duraht probably had changed since the last time they were there. Jace grumbled again, "Do you two know your way around the town?"

The boy spoke, "Yes, we run the streets all the time."

"Do you think you can help us get in undetected?"

"Definitely."

Jace looked toward Aidan, hoping to see some sort of assurance in his eyes. Fortunately, Aidan nodded. Jace looked back at the children, silently praying that he was not making a mistake. "Good, then we'll take you with us."

"Forgetting something?" Aidan interjected. He not-so-subtly hinted to the soldiers on the ground.

"Let's give them a taste of their own medicine."

Aidan smiled impishly. "Great!"

Jace was unsure if leaving the fate of the Seplechuran soldiers to Mr. Yaveer was a wise idea. He was always violent and sometimes spiteful, though it may not be right to say that, since it was Aidan and Jace who were stealing his pastries back then, but it was out of their hands now. What he could control was what was lying in front of him. He honestly did not know if trusting children with such a daunting task was right, but he needed them. He watched from the back, looking at them, and they were intimidated. From the hands of tyrants to people they didn't know. But Jace knew what desperation, hopelessness, and weakness could do—and things it forces one not to do.

"So, what's your sister like?" Aidan asked.

The children were fairly hushed, almost as quiet as the forest, strange to believe a fight even took place. "She's amazing," the girl replied.

Aidan glanced at Jace before flashing his signature smile, reaching inside his pockets, before turning around to face the children. Jace nearly wanted to smirk, knowing fully well what his brother was about to do. "Take a look at these." Aidan pulled out two golden chains about three links long, the shortest they've been.

"What are those?" The girl asked.

"These two are Chuckle and Snark, they're my friends."

The boy raised an eyebrow. "Two chains?"

Right after he said that, the two pieces of golden metal sprang to life. It surprised Jace, too, when he first saw them. Chuckle was the more energetic one, chiming in high-pitched noises when "seeing" the children. Snark, Jace's least favorite, was not as animated.

"WOAH!" The two children exclaimed.

The girl grabbed Chuckle, letting it crawl on her face as if it were a caterpillar. Snark stayed on Aidan's shoulder, hissing in a low, shackling sound when the children got near.

"Don't mind him; Snark is like Jace; he's cranky, but he means well sometimes."

Of course, he uses this moment to insult me. But Jace could hardly mind, with the children distracted, he could think, and after meeting Mr. Yaveer and some of their old neighbors, maybe he had some hope that Serenity was alive after all; maybe their parents were, too. Regardless, he had to remain skeptical; the Seplechurans had still killed a lot of people in the Massacre. But that little boy, that small eleven-xantem-old boy that was still in Jace, untouched by the Massacre, wanted to believe, and believe he would. He felt something was going to happen in Bhall-Duraht, something spectacular.

Jace hushed the now jovial children when they finally approached Bracklyn Pass, the mountainous, cauldron-like swath of land that surrounded the desert. While Aidan and the children were distracted by the chains, Jace noticed the trees started to vanish, with the rocks taking over most of the view. They had one path in, the sole pathway through Bracklyn Pass to the desert—their home.

"Everyone ready?" Jace asked resolutely.

Aidan and the children nodded. They seemed a lot happier than he felt, but it was comforting to have that level of innocence around. It kept him hopeful.

He smirked, nodding to them as well. "Let's go."

7

THE ORPHANS AND THE THIEF

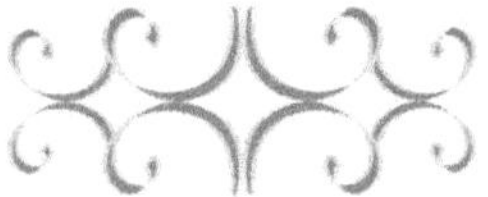

I have to find them.
—The Thief

THE DESERT PASSED in a blur. It was no Delfizcan, but the air still cooled Aurora. However, nothing could cool her temper.

She infiltrated the healer's office and interrogated the soldier at knifepoint; the slave wagon had already left the desert; she could be too late. The worst part, it had new slavers, people whose schedules she didn't memorize.

She leapt from one building to another, ducking under clotheslines, somersaulting over rooftop crates. Her cloak resembled a murder of crows as she whipped by, keeping to the rooftops of houses and the darkness of alleys. She had to make her way back to Natasha. *She'll know what to do*, she thought.

Aurora stopped, resting atop an old adobe house, watching slaves, merchants, and soldiers below. The muscles in her brow instinctively stiffened. She would love to stick a dagger into every Seplechuran guard right now, but she had to maintain her covertness. Natasha always told her that humans were the planet's greatest resource, good or bad, and people needed each other; thus, slavery was inevitable, especially in wartime. The Illisia spat at the fact that Seplechurans had them, and yet the hypocrites wasted their breath.

Aurora shook her head; now wasn't the time to be political. Right now, she needed to find that wagon. She could use the old underground paths she'd been living in, but she'd been trying to use them less. The Seplechurans had been curious about how she'd been disappearing for xantem; now was not the time to give them a reason to get too serious about killing her.

She dashed over to an old wooden house, hiding on its slanted roof. Soldiers came and went like the wind. She nearly bolted off the roof, but her eyes caught something. From the old well, *her old well*, a boy, wearing the most beautiful white cloak she had ever seen, and it was stitched with golden plates and a buckle on the right lapel. The pen in her mind wrote away as it added one more thing she needed to steal. But just by looking at him, she could tell that he was tough, and not Seplechuran-tough—stronger—much stronger. He had a towering, unrelenting stance about him, and the look in his eyes lacked a certain light.

What followed was even better. She could never forget that goofy bowl-shaped hair of the boy and the innocently round eyes of that girl. *Arundel and Lulia,* she nearly shouted. In a moment of glee, she wanted to embrace them, then yell, but something was off. They were nervous.

Her fingers slipped down into her custom-made black boots, revealing a bloody glint of steel. She rolled the daggers in her hands. There was a good chance she was going to get hurt, but better her than Arundel and Lulia. She maneuvered around the house to get a better vantage point, but then she noticed something else. Another person exited the well; he seemed closer to her in age. He lacked the modesty of the frowning man, revealing his arms so unnecessarily. His arms were impressive and chiseled, but not as bulky as the other man's. However, it didn't matter; exposed arms were just another weak point, just another vein.

"I'll take care of them, then I'll meet up with you later," she heard the younger one say. She observed the sleeveless boy grabbing Arundel and Lulia and racing toward the meeting house. Aurora immediately thought, *Are those two aware of Natasha's involvement? The children could be bait.*

She followed intently, waiting for the precise moment. There was a road that Arundel and Lulia knew very well; that's where she'd strike, and they could run for it. She made sure she was soundless as she ran atop the adobe homes.

She jumped into an alley, hiding in the darkness, intently peeking through the ebon-blanket of the shade. But something was wrong. The immodest boy stood still, focused. He had the gleam in his eyes of a fight. Arundel and Lulia were running away, and Aurora only heard the boy say, "So, are you going to hide there, or are you going to come out and play?" He looked in her direction, smiling. "I don't bite." *He knew I was here? Who is this laddie?*

Slowly and cautiously, Aurora emerged from the alley, juggling her daggers playfully to hide her surprise. Up close, she didn't see anything special, just two swords and some chains that'd fetch quite the price. The boy had such feminine eyes, contrary to his frame. She tried to observe his weak points, but she couldn't get past his skin and hair. Where was he from? she pondered. *Sez-Maraness? No, Mareenians are either as light as sand or as dark as bronze, and that hairstyle is much too long.* "You got me, laddie," she hummed, flipping her daggers. She observed her surroundings, knowing that if a fight were to ensue, she needed the advantage. She was in the quiet part of town. Seplechurans wouldn't come here until the dinner bell. Meaning that if she killed the immodest man in front of her, he wouldn't be found until later in the evening.

"Who are you?" He asked as he paced. One of his swords was out-stretched and cautious.

"I'm Aurora the Thief, the Seps also call me the Grim Reaper," she bragged. Her eyes carefully watched him as he paced around her, daggers prowling about in her hands, waiting for a throat to slit.

"Thief, I believe, but Grim Reaper? Really? You're a couple inches shy of being a child."

Aurora stomped, her face lit up like a red bulb as she faced him with rage and her daggers clutched in her palms.

"Who ya calling short ya dumb laddie?!" Aurora held her tongue, knowing there could be stray soldiers skulking about.

The boy just smiled, "Laddie? What is that, a kid? I only see one child here." He raised his hand horizontally to about his chin. "What are you? Like, to my lip? Maybe that's too much height."

Oh, that's it. In a flash, Aurora moved with the speed and accuracy of a hummingbird, dashing past the boy before he could unsheathe the second sword. Aurora held out her hand; his other sheath was settled in her palm.

His insults stopped, but the dobber (old Delfizcan for idiot) kept a smile. He changed his stride, hands up. "Aww, did I hit a nerve? Sorry about that. Now, you wanna hand me my blade back?"

Waving the scabbard, Aurora taunted. "If ya want this back, yer going to have to take it." She expected some curses in Seplechuran, maybe a call to the guards.

However, he just stood there, silently accepting her challenge. His knuckles cracked as he flexed his fingers one by one. "Is that a challenge?"

Aurora shrugged. Keeping this boy occupied would help Arundel and Lulia get to Natasha—and maybe give herself some entertainment. "Maybe," she winked, "but I gotta warn ya, no one can catch me." The boy dramatically sheathed his sword before taking a bow. This was a game to him, she'd decided; *he couldn't be Seplechuran—much too playful.* With a challenging grin, he returned her wink as he crouched into a running position. She rolled her hazel brown eyes. *It's time to put this laddie in his place.*

"On your mark," he started.

Despite his being the child, she had to admit, his excitement was contagious. She crouched as well. "Get set."

"Go," Aidan yelled. In a flash, both the boy and Aurora sprinted up a nearby building, vaulting to another one to reach the rooftops. He was pretty good. He dodged and dived, easily maneuvering around crates. The boy's grin never left his face as his legs pushed him further and further. Aurora could tell that he had trained well, but he was no match for her; no one was—and he noticed. "Wow," he huffed from fatigue mixed with excitement, "you really are fast."

She didn't reply; she simply jumped into the people below, seamlessly blending into the crowd like birds flocking together. Aurora grinned as she thought, *Ha, that little dobber ran ahead.* She quickly diverged into another alley, scaling the buildings to return to the rooftops, her running partner nowhere to be seen. "Heh, the laddie ran on ahead. Quickness is not only in yer feet."

After carefully observing the area, she sat down and unsheathed his sword, admiring the glassy red glow of the blade. She removed her hood, shaking loose her curly locks. The blade was surprisingly heavy, and yet the boy carried two of them. "Maybe he should have invested more time training his speed than his strength," she mocked under her breath to her newly acquired prize. Her shadowy hazel pupils followed the glint of the gold chain on the pommel; she caressed it with her fingers, feeling its strange hardness under her calluses. "What is this?" And then it suddenly burst out, growing and wrapping around her all at the same time. In a matter of seconds, she was encased in a golden coffin. She struggled and whispered pointedly and urgently for it to let her go. This, somehow sentient, chain only gripped her harder.

"Good job, Snark," the familiar voice praised as he jumped on top of the building. He walked beside the bound Aurora, pointing his blade at her. I believe that's checkmate, Grim Reaper."

"Neat trick," Aurora struggled to say.

Noticing, the boy spoke to the chain, "Snark, loosen up." The chain, presumably Snark, loosened its grip as the boy commanded; Aurora started to wiggle around some more and took deep breaths.

"You're faster than me, I admit." He looked nearly disappointed to acknowledge. "But I win."

Aurora sat herself up as the chains allowed. She moved in the boy's shadow since the sun beat down harshly on top of the house they stood on. It was rare for her to stay still in the wide-open space.

"Alright, alright, ya got me." Aurora sighed, looking slightly distraught. *That's a first.* Her head fell. "So, are ya the one who's finally gonna put me out of my misery?"

He unsheathed his blade, placing the tip under her chin; it almost burned her. He tilted her chin up, winking.

She finally got a proper look at him as he paused to think. He had the strangest thick hair, much different from anything she'd seen. Though it was black, in the sunlight, she could almost see a red tint. *Is he from Kuto? No,* she finalized. They didn't have that warm brown skin he had, nor did they wear small ponytails. *Breaks tradition.*

"I know what to do with you," He broke her evaluation. The boy smirked. He snapped his fingers, and then the golden chain released her instantly.

Befuddled, she asked, "What is this?"

"Um, mercy? I don't know." He grabbed his stolen sheath and placed it in his belt before grabbing his other blade. He sheathed both swords. "I think the world would benefit if such a beautiful girl is kept alive." He winked again.

Aurora's face flushed a bright red as she looked away from him. "Don't even go there." She stood up stretching her back. Snark's grip was tighter than she'd imagined.

"Aurora! Mr. Aidan!" Lulia yelled from below.

"Aidan?" Aurora asked.

He looked at Aurora with an obvious face of realization and a strange recognition. "You're the little ones' sister."

Aurora looked slightly taken aback.

Aidan quickly explained everything that happened with the slave traders and the children.

Aurora's eyes widened at the story. "Oh, I apologize," she muttered, "I was so worked up. I didn't want to lose them."

Aidan nodded, his eyes darting around. Aurora realized it, too. They were on a building where anyone could hear them; maybe it was time to go.

"No problem, that was an understandable reaction. Though, if you want to talk further, we might need to leave here."

Aurora started to walk away before she motioned to Aidan. "I know a place."

Aurora dashed away, Aidan in tow. She smiled when she looked back at him, and he couldn't help but wink, which made her flush with redness again. But, when she turned away, her smile faded at the sound of two words she replayed in her mind: *Not again.*

8

Lost Heart

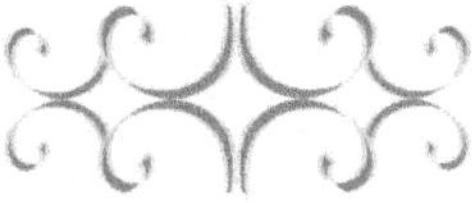

Hope like this is for children.
—The Protector

THE FAMILIAR DESERT heat greeted him, and so did the sights of his home. Adobe brick houses, so packed together that they left little room for the sun, had clotheslines stretched across the houses to provide shade for those walking the streets. The sound of the nearby merchant district became a nostalgic cacophony, with tents and covers varying from every color under the desert sky. Even barrels and wheelbarrows still cluttered the front of houses. Jace chuckled to himself, *Not even the Seplechurans could clean that up.*

Nothing felt heavier than the heart, especially at this moment. His heartbeat pounded twice as fast, his legs shook with each step, and the sweat—that was from the heat, *yeah, the heat.*

His home was as he left it. The buildings restored from the catapult wounds, the sands undisturbed by war and blood, it was all so familiar—and free, so beautiful in a way he couldn't explain.

He thought the first place he was going to visit was his home, but after seeing Mr. Yaveer and the other slaves, he had to know if Serenity was still there. A part of him wanted to abandon such a far-fetched quest; how could Serenity be alive? He questioned. Everyone in Bhall-Duraht who didn't escape either died or was thrown into slavery. That voice ordered him to turn back and address the mission. That part of him was loud and brutal as it told him to spare his heart. But there was a smaller voice, a childlike voice in the back of his mind, one telling him to move forward and have hope. His heartbeat was so fast he needed to grab his chest to slow it down. *Think,* he told himself. If Serenity was there, what would he say to her? Could he even speak at all? But what about if she wasn't there? He massaged his temples. So many questions flooded Jace's mind, but everything, every scenario could be answered by just going to her house.

He left the quiet area, walking past slaves and soldiers, the former looking at him for some semblance of hope, the latter eyeing him with skepticism. *Not now, Jace, soon.* The Seplechurans eyed him but moved along, presumably, he figured, thinking that he was a mercenary their higher-ups hired.

He pushed through the crowds of people still haggling with travelers; however, soldiers lined every shop, holding their weapons when someone, a traveler, argued a price. He thought aggressively, *must they regulate everything?*

Many came to Bhall-Duraht to start over, to leave behind the war and their old lives; it was a land for those to escape. Bhall-Duraht *was* freedom. Yet, for it to turn into this—unacceptable.

Jace pressed on; he couldn't be hasty, especially after lecturing Aidan not to be. He simply moved, and eventually, he made it through; he made it to her. There, he stood in front of Serenity's home, one of the two wooden houses built in Bhall-Duraht. It made him chuckle hollowly because he could imagine his younger self asking Serenity to come play outside. He always brought his carving knife to make flutes, something he hadn't done for xantem.

His younger self knocked and out came Serenity: withering pale white skin from her disease, grayed hair from her roots, and her strange angular eyes, which Jace had only seen in Serenity's mother.

Would she answer now? He wondered.

Knock.

No answer. Jace wanted to give up. But Serenity was a frail girl, he reasoned during the silence. Maybe she was taking her time to get to the door.

Knock, Knock. Jace knocked again, harder to make sure someone heard. His hands wanted to stop knocking on the door, but his desperate heart wanted to hear an answer.

Knock, Knock, Knock.

The door opened. A middle-aged Seplechuran woman appeared. Her appearance immediately reminded him of open tongs. Her raven-black hair cascaded over one eye while the other inspected the Camerus giant thoroughly.

"May I be of help to you?" The woman asked, her voice a low commanding tone. "If this is about my husband's approach, I know very well he is arriving."

Jace didn't answer her, his mouth opened, but words did not escape it. He sighed once more, sorrow moving every muscle in his face. *She's really gone.*

"Are you mute, boy?" The woman asked, rubbing her temples.

Jace, with all his power, mustered a fragile smile that was breaking fast like brittle glass. He placed a hand on his pommel, then bowed low before the lady. "I'm sorry to have bothered you; I have the wrong house."

The woman stared a moment longer before retreating into her house. A purple cloth and a lavender scent stayed in her wake along with the sound of jewelry shackling her steps. "I am reduced to being called by sellswords? One would assume I would get more respect, being wife of Umbran Sov, hm?" The door closed.

Jace stopped in his tracks. His body grew cold against the heat of the desert. *Umbran Sov.* A title that shook anyone to their core. Jace returned to the door, knocking frantically. The sound of chiming jewelry answered the door before the woman did. Her face screamed with annoyance. "Yes?" Her voice dragged.

Jace stood up straight, but his voice gave out to his fear, "Your husband is an Umbran Sov? When is he supposed to arrive?"

The woman measured Jace's reaction, her gray eyes scanning him extensively before answering. "Later this afternoon."

Jace gripped the pommel of his blade and bowed again. A dew of sweat that he only wished was from the heat fell from his face. "Thank you."

This was not good; an Umbran Sov would be a great threat to their plans. They were prepared to fight regular soldiers, not one of the emperor's personal elites. *Umbran Sov* was a word that had no true commontongue equivalent. The closest commontongue translations were Sovereign's Shadows or Dark Tamers, which, if rumors were true, had taken on a more literal meaning. They were rumored to have led the new attacks on the major Illisian kingdoms with the power to single-handedly fell an army. Jace didn't believe such rumors, but one couldn't be too careful. To deal with such a threat would not just be impossible, it would be—suicidal.

Jace spun. He needed to find Aidan before he somehow got himself into trouble. However, Jace beat his brother to the trouble as a small frame crashed into him. "Watch it," Jace growled impatiently.

"Why can't ya watch where ya goin' ya hulking dobber!" The girl exclaimed.

Jace cocked a brow, shuffling his arms in annoyance. The little girl stood, brushing the sand off her bum before she intimidatingly stepped closer to Jace. *She can't be serious. Does she really want to fight?* A Delfizcani by the look of her, Jace studied, with those mud spots littering her entire face, top to bottom. The hair's a bit browner than he'd remembered.

"Well, I see you two have met," Aidan laughed, clapping his hands amusingly.

Jace scoffed, "You know her?" *Of course, Aidan would know her.*

Aidan shrugged. "Yes and no; I came here to figure that out."

Behind him, Jace saw the Seplechuran woman watching this with a tad bit of familiarity. Trouble always associated with trouble, and somehow Aidan managed to join in.

"You rarely bring guests, Aurora," she started, "do you want to bring them inside before everyone finds out?"

Aurora nodded. "Yer right." Aurora motioned to everyone. "Inside, *now*, we need to have a wee discussion."

Aidan and the children hurried inside, but Jace did not. Some random, disrespectful brat wasn't about to tell him what to do, not here, not in his home. He folded his arms in defiance, narrowing his eyes at the girl and the woman.

"Even ya," she hissed.

Jace glanced at his surroundings. Now would be the worst time to get caught by the Seplechurans, he surmised. As much as he hated it, the little thing was right. He walked inside, shutting the door. *Hopefully, I'll know what this is about.*

9

PLANS OF A RECKONING

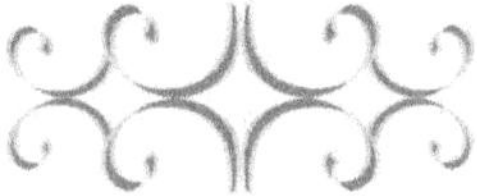

He's taking this harder than I thought.
—The Wildcard

NOTHING HERE RESEMBLED the likes of Ms. River and her daughter, Serenity—nothing at all. The wooden beams still held the loft that overlooked the entrance, the windows across allowed the morning light to get in, but it felt so dark, so absent. Aidan couldn't begin to understand how Jace felt; he tracked his brother's eyes narrow and scan the room where Ms. River held memorabilia, only for him to glare then shift them away. Jace tried hard to look tough as he posted himself on the farthest wooden beam from the rest of the group, arms crossed and eyes leering, yet Aidan observed mist glinting in his eyes. This was why Jace hated to hope. It made him feel like a building erected on sand that is surprised when a storm blows it away.

Jace continued to scan the room and managed to get trapped by Aidan's sympathetic gaze, only for the older brother to avert and stare at Natasha. "So, introductions or answers first?" he pushed. "I would like some information."

Aidan, upset with Jace's disdain, decided to address the situation at hand, yet as he saw the eyes of Lulia, she drew an honest smile out of him, but he couldn't overcome the feeling of guilt that stirred up in his gut. *I did this. I made him hope.*

"Honored to business, yes?" The woman's words drawled toward Jace's attention. "Good." Her accent was a bit different from that of other Seplechurans, Aidan encountered. Her h's were softer; his guess—she was from a different region. She had the grayest eyes, which gave Jace the once-over. It was obvious she was incredibly observant. The woman's eyes then turned to Aidan, who received a shorter appraisal.

Interrupting the woman's observance of Aidan, Aurora walked over, glaring daggers at Jace as she handed the Seplechuran a cup of tea. The woman sniffed the tea in a savory fashion before taking a sip. Looking up, she said, "Thank you, Aurora." She took another sip, then turned her attention to the brothers. "I suppose we can start with introductions. Since Aurora brought you here, I will start." She stood, clutching her tea tightly, her eyes revealed no emotion, and her face was as flawless as her demeanor. "I am Natasha Voshkovik, Seplechuran strategist and overseer of the assimilation of Bhall-Duraht into the Seplechuran Empire."

Aidan quickly glanced at his brother. The word *assimilation* forced him to cringe slightly, but otherwise, he took it well. Aidan honestly didn't know how much his brother could take standing in this building. Whatever Natasha is about to tell them must be good. Responding to Natasha, Aidan yielded a slight nod and said, "A pleasure."

"This is Lulia Voshkovik," Natasha continued. "Her parents were Seplechuran merchants who were murdered by bandits in the desert; Aurora rescued her, and I adopted her when we met."

Aidan gave her a warm smile, pulling out Chuckle and Snark to play with her. "Lulia is a pretty name."

She grinned at Aidan before playing with the chains.

He returned his gaze to Natasha, who was looking at the chains intriguingly. Surprisingly, she said nothing. Even Jace was looking again, suppressing a smile.

Natasha continued, "The boy is Arundel, another orphan and Aurora's student."

Arundel waved to both Aidan and Jace. Though he muttered a few words that Aidan couldn't quite catch, Aidan inclined his head anyway. Eagerly waiting for an introduction to his new friend, he slipped her a coy look, trying not to make it obvious. He hoped his face wasn't getting red and hoped even more that no one was watching him. *Crap, she might be looking.* He glanced around only to find Natasha watching.

She smiled, "This warrior is Aurora." She looked intently at Aidan. "Young man, I was told you caught her. Impressive."

Aurora scoffed dismissively. "He cheated."

"I was cunning."

"Ya tricked me."

"I played to my strengths; you played to yours. Mine were better."

"Aurora," Natasha interjected, "we did not finish introductions." Aurora grumbled, sitting on the armrest of the couch.

Honestly, Aidan didn't know if she was mad at him or not. Some things don't go the way people intend, and he had to learn that. His intentions were mostly pure, but his mouth was always another thing. He sighed, dismissing the thought. "I'm Aidan Camerus, that's my brother Jace. This town was once our home."

Natasha sipped her tea, "Camerus? Hmm."

Aidan knew that look immediately. She recognized the name, and she was from Seplechurus—maybe their parents were there after all, he wondered. But Jace was already so hurt over Serenity, Aidan didn't want to give him something else to worry about.

"You two lived here before massacre, yes?" Aidan nodded. She then turned to Jace, and her eyes gave him that appraising look again. She was looking for something. "And you, what can you do?"

Jace lifted his foot and stomped with enough force to shake the building. Lulia gave a small squeal while Aurora instinctively drew her daggers so fast Aidan didn't catch where they came from. The elder Camerus only mocked Aurora with his eyes before returning to the beam, unmoved.

"So, yer a monster," growled Aurora.

"*Draaktel*," Jace replied. The others raised their brows a bit. To which, Jace replied, "When you've been fighting Seplechurans for a decade, you tend to pick up a word or two."

Of course, those two would go at it now; Aidan could already tell. However, strangely enough, Natasha wasn't trying to diffuse anything. She just watched with the faintest of smiles on her face. "Enough, you two," she called out, "it seems we all want same thing."

"How so?" Jace growled.

"You want your home back, and I do not want Seplechurus to have it."

"Oh? A twist in the story." Both Aurora and Natasha stared at him. He chuckled nervously, waving off his comment. "Uh, never mind. What were you saying?"

"To start from beginning, I opposed vote for assimilation of Bhall-Duraht. We would have victory if one of our Sov's didn't cast Sov degit."

"A … what?" Aidan asked.

Aurora answered absentmindedly, "Sorry, Seplechurans don't use participles. Sov's get a double vote in war matters; it's called a Sov *degit*."

Natasha continued, "I spent xantem trying to get this position so I can undermine this assimilation. Our current emperor acts like child, and I will treat him as such."

Aidan didn't know much about Seplechuran politics, but he knew something didn't add up. Natasha having power in the government sounded incredulous to him. Seplechurus wouldn't assign her to that position because she was the wife of a Sov, *would they?* "Who, exactly, are you?"

"Very good question. I am High Strategist for Seplechuran Military."

Oh … Oh. A High Strategist in Seplechurus held much power. They were equivalent to princes and princesses in other countries, authority-wise. Meaning that if the emperor, his children, and the Sovs were to die or abdicate, *she* would rule. "That's … intense," Aidan awed.

Jace nodded. "You have my attention."

She turned to Jace. "I thought that would." Natasha kept explaining the details with a little more vigor; it seemed she was waiting for Jace to jump on board. Aidan used the plan all the time: butter Jace up with something he wanted to hear before delivering a great question or, usually, an absurd request.

"I want you three to defeat my husband when he arrives."

And there it is. Aidan leaned forward. "He's a Sov, an Umbran Sov; we can't fight that."

Natasha stood, bearing the slightest cringe on her face as she paced slowly. She drew in a deep breath. "Did you not say you fought Seplechurans for decade?"

"He said that." Aidan gestured to Jace.

"But were you not with him? Three of you have gifts that will allow for victory. This path should be made straight, yes?"

In that moment, Aidan looked to Jace, who seemed deep in thought. Then Jace looked up from his brooding; the word Umbran Sov was the smelling salts to his sleeping vengeance. "How do we beat him?" he asked.

Natasha smiled slightly again. "*Now*, you are asking right questions." She finished her tea, handing the cup to Lulia, who dashed for the kitchen.

"My husband is poor excuse for man, but he is still Seplechuran general." Natasha stood, her hands clasped behind her back; though her voice remained calm, her posture and presence gave off something more ferocious. One could only be in attention as she spoke, hoping not to miss a single word. She commanded respect, and she held authority, and quite frankly, it was easy to see how she held such a high position. "Regardless, every warrior has their weakness, and we will exploit it." Natasha paused to let her words sink in.

"So, what's the plan, lassie?" Aurora cut her silence. "We can't fight him head-on."

"Dear Aurora," Natasha began to explain, "how long must I be with you for you to understand that I already have plan?"

"Alright, sorry," Aurora chuckled, "let us hear it."

Natasha moved her observant eyes to Aurora, then to Jace, and then, finally, to Aidan. She saw something in them that would light the fires of liberation; it was enviable how quickly she knew so much about people she had just met. When she opened her mouth, her words came out like a quake. She was just as determined as they were. "Now listen closely." Her eyes narrowed. "I do hate to repeat myself."

10

Plan in Motion I

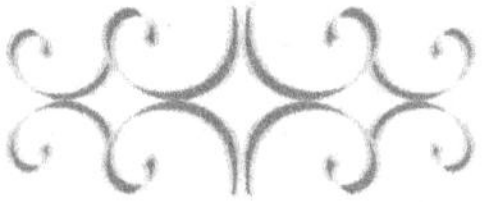

All who smile are not the same.
—The Thief

SAND KICKED UP in the gust of wind, and tiny grains swarmed like bees in a patch of flowers. Atop the highest building overlooking the entrance of Bhall-Duraht, Aidan and Aurora waited, their sun-kissed faces ripened from the heat. Below, a small contingent of soldiers baked along with them. Banners bearing the emblem of Seplechurus flapped in the wind, which were the only other noises they heard. "I hope this plan works," Aidan whispered to Aurora, "even Natasha said that he could be unpredictable in battle." She could understand why he was so nervous: he'd never worked with Natasha before this, and she remembered how daunting it was taking orders from a Sep. "I learned that her plans are always effective; it is just the execution."

Aidan's breathing slowed, but his face remained still. Aurora got the feeling that it wasn't normal for him. His eyes were glued to the horizon as if he could see all the way that far. She released a dry chuckle. *It wouldn't surprise me if he could.* Because he was full of tricks like those golden chains on his shoulders.

"I hope you're right," Aidan said, almost muttering. "I hope you're right." Aurora reached for her hood to shade her but remembered that she couldn't wear it since it made too much noise. She felt safer with it on; she felt as if she was an actual reaper, but now, she wasn't so sure. Minutes turned into hours, and Aurora was tempted to go back for her cloak. Below, she saw the soldiers shift uncomfortably. One of the merchants gave them water every now and then, and a part of her wanted to snag it, but she hated stealing liquids; they were much too loud.

"Sorry about Jace," Aidan blurted. "He's normally not like this."

"Yer kin, he's a hotheaded one, ain't he?" She folded her arms as she laid on the floor. She soon turned around due to the sand raiding her eyes.

"Normally, under most circumstances, I'm the hotheaded one," Aidan sighed painfully. "But the girl he loved, our friend, his best friend—she used to live in the house Natasha is in."

Loved. Aurora could guess what happened to her. A bit of guilt arose in her; she knew exactly how losing a lover felt. They disappear and take a piece of the heart with them.

Even Aidan looked so serious; it was hard to believe that only a few hours ago, he flirted and made jokes. Now, he looked more like his kin than anything else. "It all hit him harder," Aidan continued, "I feel like he lost the most. People liked him; he was friends with everyone; Serenity was a different case, though he …" He chuckled ruefully. "… Never mind, let's skip the bad things, no time for that now." Then he smiled as if nothing happened. "Hard to smile when you're talking about sad things, yeah?"

But the pain was still evident in the back of his eyes. *What exactly did they lose?* She wasn't in the mood to press him out loud, though; besides, most knew how that felt in wartime—even her.

Changing the subject further, Aidan said, "I have a question: why do Arundel and Lulia call each other siblings if they're not family? I mean, they referred to you as 'our sister', so I found that odd."

Aurora cocked a brow, they should be watching the horizon for the Sov, but it was an innocent question, right? "Seplechuran culture; close friends are considered family."

"That's really amazing. I never thought of it that way."

He looked at the horizon again, still smiling at what he'd just learned. He did that a lot—smile. It was honestly weird, but not for reasons that one would think. Aurora stole from different kinds of people to disrupt Seplechuran trade. She'd seen so many fake smiles it was sickening, but on Aidan, she somehow knew it was genuine. The last time she saw someone smile that easily, it was Ruben.

"You alright?" Aidan asked her.

Aurora shook her head, noticing the tears on her cheek, she batted them away. "It's hot. I'm not used to staying in one place."

He removed a band from his thick dreadlocks. It was tied in the same pattern as his kin's but some parts had braided areas. He pushed the band in her direction with another smile. "It's the hair; it heats you up if you leave it down."

She eyed the band, flicking her eyes between it and his smiling visage. She took the band, her eyes not leaving his for a moment. *He's trying to buy my trust, clearly.* Aurora bunched up her hair with her hand to bind. *I won't let him get to me.*

"You look good," Aidan complimented.

Aurora averted her eyes, mostly focusing on corralling her hair.

Aidan held his mouth to muffle his laughter, and even those two chains started to laugh—if that's what they called laughing. "Not much of a talker, are you?"

"Ya tend to normalize when people are trying to kill ya all the time." The laddie got a little silent after that, and Aurora honestly thought she said something wrong.

Before she could muster another apology, he spoke up again. "Well, I don't plan on killing you; let's get that out of the way. How about you tell me where you're from?" Aidan asked. "I've never heard your regional accent before."

Is he okay? Does *he really care to know me? What person would fraternize with a thief, knowing of their profession? One of the most punishable offenses in wartime? He is so strange.* "Delfizcan," she answered as she wiped the sweat from her brow. "Mount Borealis."

"Ah, that makes sense. In the books I've read, the Delfizcani characters had their 'f's' changed to 'v's' because of their accents."

Aurora touched her lips, then sounded the word 'forever' even quieter than in her already whispered voice. She blinked before staring back at him with the epiphany settling in. "I had no idea we did that."

Aidan chuckled, happy to see someone enlightened by his knowledge. He sat up, bowing in a dramatic fashion, which Aurora assumed was normal for someone like him. "You're welcome, I … " He paused.

He looked out to the horizon, his body started to tremble, and Aurora didn't know why. She looked in his direction and saw nothing, but when she moved to the front of him, she saw a strange dilation in his pupils. *Can he actually see that far? How far?*

"Aurora," he called out to her, unmoving. "He's here." The sand kicked up wildly in the distance, and the shaking earth followed it. Thumping hooves grew ever louder as they approached, and with it came a feeling of dread and malice. Aidan and Aurora, along with the soldiers below them, watched in anticipation as the figure approached. It was a chariot of purple-coated metal and the astounding six strange animals that drew it. A peculiar cross between a large feline and an equine, the creatures roar-neighed into the town, halting at the behest of the driver. The wheels were replaced with flat boards, letting the chariot glide with ease across the sands. On it, one man with scarred muscles glistened in the sweat brought on thoroughly by the heat. A red cloak flew at his back, symbolizing the rank of a mighty warrior. The soldiers below welcomed the Sov with a harsh Seplechuran salute that consisted of a pump of their fist and a stomp of their feet. One wearing a white cloak stood out and greeted him. "Lord Umbran Sov," he saluted, "we welcome you to Bhall-Duraht."

The Sov's large frame hopped off his chariot; the earth shook when his feet met the ground. His height was as intimidating as his size; he was a goliath in every physical aspect. "Where is my wife?" His raspy voice was identical to his appearance, large and intimidating.

The white-cloaked soldier replied, "Several soldiers informed her of your coming."

The Sov growled, "Stubborn wench." He flicked his cape to the side, walking through the saluting soldiers with a commanding presence. He paused as he passed through the last of his soldiers. With a hiss, he spoke, "Idiots." He ripped his massive bardiche from his back and spun it in his hands. To the surprise of Aidan and Aurora, a darkness enveloped it, causing the blade to grow into a horn.

Aidan suddenly grabbed her wrist. "Move!"

The laddie called his strange chains for help, and the two of them jumped off as the Sov swung his bardiche through the building. The ground shuddered, and the sand started to hide. His mounts fled for their lives, and the soldiers followed suit. After one blow, one of the largest buildings crumpled under the weight of the darkness.

Aidan crashed harshly onto another building. The chains hardly found any bearing to cushion their summoner's fall. Aurora, however, landed gracefully with a tumble.

They had little time to register their predicament before the Sov leaped onto the building they were resting on. *He's a beast … he's not human anymore.*

He heaved his bardiche over his shoulder. With three words, he let his intentions be known—and let the dread truly sink in, "Time to die."

11

Plan in Motion II

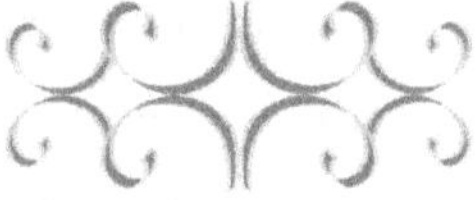

This better be worth the trouble.
—The Protector

JACE COULD HEAR the fighting from where he was; it nearly drowned out his own battle of fisticuffs as he downed two soldiers. However, compared to what he had heard, he could only imagine what the battle was doing to the terrain. "Stay down," Jace warned. These warriors were not worthy of death.

He approached a very familiar building, one of the few structures that he had seen before the massacre: the old community kitchen. How dreadful it was that the smell of meat and herbs was replaced with the smell of sweat and steel. The beautiful building now served as a depot, holding their various weapons and war machines, but more importantly, it held their ignisium ore.

The wooden building was as he left it many xantem ago, the pavilion still intact, but the well had a Seplechuran banner hanging off it, which he promptly ripped off.

He had a feeling that Natasha's tactics were sound, but something still scared him about it all. This was an Umbran Sov; they were as much myth as reality. With such power, such fury, why would they set their sights on a small town like this? Maybe one of the legendary weapons was here; the sands always held great mysteries.

Jace rushed inside, hoping to find the stores with minimal resistance. His knowledge of the community kitchen became helpful as he turned the corners of his childhood. Boots stomped against the hardwood as he passed the old drying racks, which the Seplechurans now used for weapons. His father created those. The last time the young Camerus stepped foot in the area, his father finished butchering meat, and they had a large feast where Serenity and Ms. River were invited. Now, it was infested with hope-breakers and friend-killers.

He stood resolute as five of them stood between him and the salt storeroom in the back, which according to Natasha, was where the ignisium was stored. "Stand down, and I promise to spare you," he cautioned angrily. At first, he wanted to minimize the violence, but the more he looked around, the more he wanted them to attack him. The banners that lined the windows were gone, country flags that marked unity among the Bhall-Durahti people were all replaced with shields bearing what he assumed were Seplechuran clan crests.

"*Tjak!* (Attack!)" One of the soldiers yelled.

Yes. Jace made sure to savor the next few moments. He could feel the pull of his ancestry, guiding every attack. His strength broke through their petty armor. Their helmets were designed to scare, yet he grabbed the beast's jaw, throwing helpless bodies around. When his heart finally began pumping, he realized his adversaries were all defeated. He scoffed; he was mixed with confusion and disappointment. There was no way Seplechurans were that easy. Where was the challenge he'd promised himself? Jace pondered. He scowled at them groaning on the floor, daring them to get up as he passed by. "I highly encourage you all to leave. This place will explode soon," he spoke absentmindedly.

The soldiers' groaning thickened. They were unable to move. He looked back, knowing full well they weren't going to evacuate in time. That wasn't his problem—was it? He could leave them there; *the less Seplechurans, the better*. He worked to finish them off in his thoughts. He clenched his fist, unsure of what to do.

"*Save them,*" an ethereal voice echoed in his mind that wasn't quite his own. *Why should I?* In his thoughts, Jace challenged the voice. No answer.

Jace continued to the salt room, and there they were. The glowing ores blinked with the solidified power of the sun. These batches were much more unstable than what he used for Aidan's swords. Before he entered, he looked over at the soldiers. They were still hurt. There was a moment of hesitation, then a groan. He marched over to the soldiers, picking one of them up with his abnormal strength.

"W-What are you doing?" The soldier cowered, his accent much harder than Natasha's, but Jace understood.

"I'm getting you all out of here," Jace replied, trying to convince himself more than anything. "Be grateful for your weakness. I'm only doing this out of pity."

Jace carried the soldiers outside, laying them in an area where they could avoid the damage. One by one, Jace moved each soldier out of the building with impressive speed. Each of them grew more perplexed at Jace's actions, and as he jogged back and forth, he questioned: *What the hell am I doing?*

He ran inside once more, reaching into his cloak and thanking Aidan for pockets, pulling out a long fuse. After setting up the fuse and lighting it, Jace wasted no time in his exit, barreling through the window and rendezvousing with the soldiers he saved.

BOOM!

The entire building erupted with smoke and flames. Chunks of the building were now cinders, and a pile of ash, fire, and blackness rose, clouding the arid air. Jace and the soldiers watched from a steady distance as the entire area burned. With his part done, Jace left; there was no reason to stay. The soldiers didn't thank him, and he would spit at their gratitude anyway. Jace walked, still curious—*what was that voice?*

Regardless, he didn't have to worry anymore; the rest was up to Natasha and the children. Now, Jace ran toward the Sov, hoping this battle would be far more glorious than the one before.

12

A Threat Far Greater

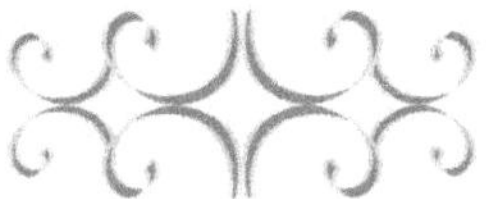

Time for the fun to start.
—The Wildcard

THERE WERE TIMES when Aidan cursed his own words when he thought he would say something that would anger a belligerent ruler and be sent to the guillotine, forced to die as a martyr for the cause of comedy and his own amusement. It wasn't the blaze of glory moment Jace craved, but it was okay.

"I can't believe ya said that to him!" Aurora yelled, nearly breathless. "The goal is to survive!"

"It just came out!" Aidan kept pace with her, as the paths grew shorter and shorter.

"How does 'ya look like the offspring of a mangy ox and a flea-bitten cur who died after intercourse' just come out!?"

She had a point. "My mind is a brutal place."

The Sov landed in front of them, kicking up sand in a rumble. Aidan and Aurora slid to a halt, eyes dilated and muscles quivering. The ox-cur swung his bardiche after releasing a guttural roar that was only amplified by his helmet. They began to slowly back up while the Sov kept a steady, menacing pace forward.

Aidan lifted his hands pleadingly. "I am very sorry I upset you; I just—I just thought you already knew you looked like that."

"AIDAN!"

There were times when Aidan cursed his words. The Sov used his monstrous strength to send the barrels and wheelbarrows flying in their direction. Aidan unsheathed his weapons and cut cleanly through them with his swords, heat pulsing after every slash. He couldn't help the smile, which he tried to hide.

Aurora probably wanted to rip him to shreds, but surely, she must've known that having two people against the Sov was better than one. But he could tell she even doubted that. "Can ya just shut yer mouth for a second?!"

"But who else is going to tell him that at least his mother thinks he's a handsome gem?"

"I'm gonna stab ya myself!"

The Sov approached, holding his bardiche for an overhead strike. Aidan pushed Aurora out of the way, readying himself for the attack. Yes, there were times when Aidan cursed his own words—but not right now.

The Sov swiped at nothing but the air; Aidan fluidly moved around his attacks, leaving Aurora to find an opening. The best opponent was an angry opponent, they were the most predictable no matter how smart they were, and Aidan had a gift for annoying people.

The minute the Sov missed, Aidan locked eyes with Aurora, and in that moment, she adopted his smile. *Now, she gets it.* Aidan began to analyze his opponent. *Big, stupid, and angry.* However, the Sov had strength that rivaled Jace, meaning fighting him head-on would be dumber than anything he said prior.

"You worm!" The Sov yelled.

The Sov brought his bardiche around, catching Aidan mid-dodge. Despite what Aidan mentally cautioned himself about, he attempted to block the Sov's attack, but it proved fruitless as he crashed through the walls of a home. "I'm okay!" Making light of what the Sov had just done as he coughed the adobe dust from his lungs.

The Sov yelled, "You will die under the might of Seplechurus!" The Sov raised his arms again for another strike; it honestly seemed that was the only attack he could do.

Before the bardiche could be brought down, the Sov grunted as he found a dagger lodged in his hamstring. He spun around, angrily staring at Aurora who was flipping a dagger in her hand.

"Fergot about someone, didn't ya?"

Aidan promptly made his escape out a nearby window while the Sov engaged Aurora in a small duel, which was more of a dodge and retaliation on her part. Her fighting style was very reliant on speed and agility, the fawn-like dashes, the graceful aerials, and flips. She was dancing around the man. She stung like a scorpionhawk at his hamstrings before deftly retreating.

Aidan was captivated by her fluency; she was something to behold. After seeing her work, he could maybe, *maybe,* believe that she was some Grim Reaper.

Aidan readied himself to join in, but he glanced away, smiling, then returned to the fight. He mimicked Aurora's strategy, using his heated blades to weaken his opponent. The Sov was just such an angry person, and each strike made him more so. This was Aidan's ideal opponent, a volatile and slow warrior.

"Enough of you!" He lifted his weapon to the sky, roaring at the top of his lungs. A wave of violent blackness radiated from him, knocking both Aidan and Aurora aside.

"What the …?" Aidan awed.

So, this was the power that fell an army, the strange, dark power that Natasha warned the trio about. Even she was a bit wary about throwing them into a situation she knew little about. She'd only seen her husband, the Sov, coat his weapon with it during training; she admitted to them how little she knew about his other abilities.

Aidan recouped himself, and Aurora did the same. That shockwave didn't send them far, but Aidan blinked his eyes, watching the little lights dance around in his vision, the sand swaying like the sea, but somehow still. His fingers couldn't curl around his weapon properly as their touch became foreign. "What … did you do to me?" He shook his head, but his vision grew worse.

He could see shadows growing. He put his guard up as he was launched into another home; this time, blood accompanied the dust. He tried to lift himself, but he felt the Sov grab his leg and launch him into the sand before throwing him, unintentionally, into the arms of Aurora.

"If you wanted me so badly, Aurora—," chuckled Aidan.

Aurora interrupted, "Not the time. What did the laddie do to us?"

"Not sure. I'm seeing two of everything, including you, not that I'm complaining." Double the Aurora meant double the eye roll: he could see that fine. He wanted to clean the blood dripping from his nose, but the battle would prevent it.

"Focus on the battle, laddie, before—,"

Aidan cut her off. "Hold that thought." He looked at the Sov. "Hey, ox-cur, the sand hits harder than you."

The Sov came closer, seemingly faster than before. Aidan whispered to his chains, "Do you two feel alright?" Chuckle and Snark gave very energetic replies.

"Great." Aidan stumbled to his feet, shaking his head to at least be able to perceive the looming giant. He walked almost drunkenly before charging into a sprint. The Sov swung his bardiche, but Chuckle yelled to Aidan. The young Camerus slid between the Sov's legs, and the two chains wrapped around him.

With all his might, Aidan swung the Sov around as the chains grew longer and longer. With one loud yell, Aidan launched the Sov upward, however, not as far as he hoped. "Up top!"

The afternoon sky sun was blocked by a shadow, one that flew the greatest coat ever made. "Aurora, move!" Aidan yelled. The two of them scurried right as the shadow revealed itself to be Jace who was midair gearing for a powerful attack. With a yell, he delivered a devastating punch to the Sov, forcing him to the ground faster than he ascended. Aidan reached out with his chains to grab Jace midair, bringing him to his side.

"Are you alright?" Jace asked.

"Yes," Aidan snarked, "I'm bleeding out of my nose and covered in adobe because I'm having the time of my life."

Jace's eyes rolled. "You're fine." He looked at Aurora. "Thief?"

"Ya don't care," she huffed.

"I don't, but for the sake of our town, I will act like I do."

Aidan brushed his clothes down, revealing a little bit more of the golden vines of his garb. *Still looks good, perfect.*

Jace smacked his brother on the shoulder. "Aidan, focus." He glared at the Sov. "What can that bastard do?"

Aidan rolled his shoulder. "Simple version: he hits really hard, *insanely* hard, and he lets out some kind of wave that messes with your senses."

Concerned, Jace asked, "Are you still affected?"

Aidan looked at Aurora, then back to Jace, and nodded. "A little, but I'll live. You have a plan?"

"Barely. Are Chuckle and Snark affected?"

Aidan flexed his fingers. "Nope, it messes with my sight and a little of my touch, and as you probably know, they don't see and touch—at least not like we do."

The two chains shook with excitement, letting out small chimes to convey such. Aidan knew they were his best bet, but they couldn't do much except grab.

Aurora pointed to the sand crater. "Hey, not trying to rush ya laddies, but he's getting up."

The Sov emerged from the sands, helmet falling from his face. He didn't look like an ox-cur, but he did look terrible. His face was covered in bruises and scars as if he had been burned. His hair completely receded, and by the looks of the marks, not by choice.

"Oh wow," Aidan breathed through his teeth, "he looks hideous. He's married to Natasha? That lucky beast."

"I need to gag ya," Aurora sighed.

"Aidan, did you notice?" Jace interrupted.

"Left eye?"

Aurora looked between the brothers. She couldn't see much without Songluan sight, but she seemed to understand. "Natasha said he had a wee problem with his eye."

"Not a wee problem," Aidan commented, "he's blind in one eye."

Aurora placed her hand on her waist. "That's why he didn't see my dagger coming."

Aidan smiled, looking at Jace. "Plan?"

"Plan."

The poor Sov's lungs were expanding like the bloody patch that outlined his head. Jace always hit hard, but that burial site held a new record.

Jace didn't have time to divulge his entire plan before the Sov ran at them again. Moments like this were when Aidan shined; a place where instinct took control and regimented thought was cast aside.

"Let's move," Jace gave the order.

"WOO!" Aidan used Chuckle and Snark to latch onto a building, swinging right into the Sov. The Sov slashed, and Aidan quickly vaulted off his weapon, retaliating with a swipe, burning the Sov's armor.

He must've learned his lesson, because now the Sov used horizontal strikes, leaving himself less open. But the problem with his bardiche, dark energy or not, was that it was two-handed. Meaning, he was always open.

Daggers soared through the air, and Aurora hit with pinpoint accuracy at the Sov's joint. She hid in the nearby buildings, attacking through the windows on the Sov's left side.

He yelled, "Cowards! Can you not fight me man-to-man?"

"You should be honored," Aidan sassed, dodging a blow. "We know we can't beat you up front. Well, he can."

Aidan soared over the Sov right as Jace ran in for another strike, this time for the ears. The Sov staggered, shaking his head, giving Jace time to kick him aside.

The Sov tried to get up, but he kept to the ground. Knowing how hard Jace hit him, he probably couldn't hear.

"Y-you cannot defeat Sov ..." He stood.

This guy is a monster! Aidan readied his swords.

The Sov raised his bardiche, and Aidan's eyes flickered to Jace. "Here it comes!"

Aidan stood in front of Jace, then Chuckle and Snark swirled together, forming a shield.

What they were expecting never came; instead, Aidan felt a sizzling snap in the air before he was knocked backward with Jace at his back.

Jace halted much of the push, but Aidan clutched his arms as he fell to his knees. The excitement drained from his face, and his skin started to pale; his lips quivered.

It was just ten xantem ago, when everything fell around him, when fear and fire were the only things he could see and feel.

Aidan rocked himself. "It burns … it burns."

Jace yelled, "Aidan! Get ahold of yourself!"

"Laddies!" Aurora warned.

Aidan blinked back to reality, seeing the shadow of the Sov peering over them. Jace moved to the front, blocking the strike, but immediately fell under the dizzying spell of the Sov.

Aidan tried to move, but the Sov pushed Jace into him, trapping his leg. Aidan clenched his teeth, then looked up, seeing Aurora coming in close behind the Sov. However, Aidan didn't know if it was her shadow or the fact that the Sov could hear again, but he pushed Jace into a building and caught Aurora by the neck.

"You … I know who you are. You have been thorn in Seplechurus' side for too long; I was sent here to kill you before I routed my armies against Utopia."

"Glad to …," Aurora choked on her words. The Sov squeezed harder, forcing the red to rise in her face. "Put me … down … ya bloke!" The Sov started to chuckle to himself; it almost sounded like strange gurgling. Aurora continued to thrash about, and her anger continued to rise. She gritted her teeth as her next words came out as a snarl, "I said. Put. Me. Down!"

A strange glow flickered in Aurora's hazel eyes; it radiated a strange green, mysterious but absolutely furious. It blinked like a dying flame, but in the swift moment her eyes shone green, she threw her dagger with all her might. The Sov laughed. A throw like that wouldn't hurt him—or so he thought. Aurora's dagger pierced his armor, hitting him in the neck.

Something about that green flare forced Aidan to move; he caught Aurora with his chains, then he proceeded to slash at the Sov with his heated blades as his armor started to wear down.

"Aidan, move!" Jace yelled.

Aidan flipped away, and Jace ducked down into a powerful blow to the exposed part of the Sov's lower chest, and with a great yell, he delivered a vicious uppercut.

The Sov stood still, and the others waited with bated breath. But, like many monsters before him, he toppled over, unmoving.

The trio waited for a second, holding their breaths, but per usual, Aidan was the first to speak, "Is he …?"

"He's alive, surprisingly." Jace huffed, "That dark power must increase his resilience; that would have killed a normal person."

Aurora walked over to Aidan, jabbing him in the side. "Dontcha go freezing up like that, ya could've gotten yerrself killed."

"Sorry, I …" Tightness welled up inside him, inside all of them. A deep sense of dread started to rise in them that they couldn't explain, almost as if it was alive.

"You should have killed me …" The Sov smashed his weapon into the ground, encasing himself in a strange gooey blackness. The rounded sphere seemed to absorb all light as it grew and grew until it was taller than any of the buildings in Bhall-Duraht. Brief flashes of light emitted inside that cocoon, and what they saw the Sov morph into was something that was no longer human.

As they stood in terror, Aidan could only think of one thing to say, "I'm not being paid enough for this."

13

Frozen in Fear

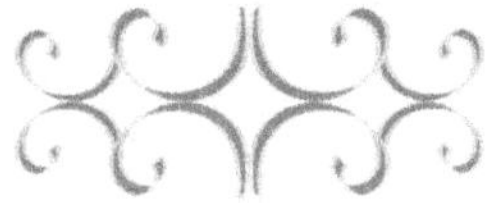

Courageous, I will stand, someone has to.
—The Protector

THAT MORNING, JACE didn't know what to expect: not the slaves, not the thief, not Natasha, not the Sov, and certainly not whatever this was. Before him, an egg made of pure blackness flashed images of a large beast with a horn of a bardiche's blade. *The Sovs fell an army together,* he thought. *Now I know how.*

The wind started to kick up as all three of them stared in awe at what they were about to face. Nothing could have prepared them for this. Nothing.

"We have to run," the thief recommended. "We can't beat that, not without a miracle."

"That's cowardice," Jace retorted, though he felt the need to agree.

"It's not about cowardice, ya idiot! We *cannot* fight that!"

"We won't make it far," Aidan choked. "He's turning into a quadruped, you know, four legs, he'll catch us."

It was a quick evaluation, but all options came to the same conclusion—they were dead. Jace looked at Aidan, whose eyes couldn't leave the forming creature. That fool was trying to smile, yet it stopped somewhere in between. Even the thief dropped to her knees, skin paled like Seplechurans.

The town was lost, they couldn't take it back, it was pointless. They were stupid to even hope that they could; everything about the plan was foolish. All for what? To die? They could have moved on, but the past was hard to let go, wasn't it? *He* couldn't let the past go. Now he dragged Aidan into this mess, all because he couldn't be the bigger person and move on. If his parents could see the disappointment that he was to their legacy.

"*Encourage them,*" the voice from the ignisium depot spoke, "*Victory is yours.*"

Jace swallowed a lump. He was hearing voices again. There was no reason to fight, but there was no reason to flee either. For a moment, Jace had to believe. Even Natasha, a random Seplechuran woman, had faith they could succeed. The person whom he should have hated the most had the most faith.

"We have to fight …" Jace spoke lowly.

"What?! Why?" Aurora yelled.

That was a good question, but her asking it made the answer clear.

"Natasha, the children, the people."

The thief drew her dagger, a petty object for a petty thief. She pointed at his neck, hoping to deter him. "Don't ya DARE use them like that!"

Jace brushed the dagger to the side. "Listen, we may not have a prayer, but they have a head start. If the explosions rattled them and if she managed to convince everyone that an army was coming here, they all left."

"… but not fast enough," Aidan finished. He stared at Aurora. "Aurora, we have to."

The dagger shook in her hand, the red catching her face as the realization got to her eyes. She knew, and the sheathing of her dagger proved it.

"We need to give the laddies more time than just running around in circles."

Jace nodded. "Then we'll give it to them. We'll protect them."

The thief nodded, Aidan nodded, all determined faces. The timing couldn't have been better.

The egg began to shatter.

The attention immediately returned to that thing. Jace felt the emotion rise to his eyes, the terror in his bones, and the smell of death wafting around them.

He placed a hand on Aidan's shoulder, "For mother and father."

He returned the gesture, "For mother and father."

A fissure spread down the egg before webbing across to all sides. Everything felt so quiet, even the breaking of the sphere.

Jace stared at the silvery sheen on his sword. He chuckled hollowly, so poetic, as Aidan would say: the first time he would see his sword in a long time, would be the last day he used it.

The spots of silver blazed through, adorned with the slightest hint of blue. A beautiful scabbard made for an ugly occasion. A white line painted vertically, with an intricately carved arrow tip at the end. *The Songluan Arrow, a gift that the tip always aimed true.*

"Ready?"

"Aye," the thief replied.

Aidan sighed, "Surprisingly, yes."

The three of them readied their weapons.

Then the roar. A horrendous gust of wind threatened to knock the trio off their feet. Jace heard the sound of Chuckle before feeling his brother grab onto him. He creased his eyes as he looked at the thief holding onto his brother for dear life. Shards of the ebon albumen hurled through the town along with the sea of sand that blinded him. He could only imagine how Aidan was feeling with his sight so impaired. But then it stopped. The sand didn't know the wind had ceased, leaving Jace to brush it aside. But he soon wished he hadn't.

He was first met with a thick, gray, leathery hide, the creature's neck and body seemed to have merged. The only notable border between the two was the face covered in strange black fur and feathers. Staring into the leonine eyes and that large bardiche horn, Jace knew the fight was going to be unlike anything he had faced before. The Sov truly didn't resemble a human anymore, he looked chimeric; something out of *The Legend of Burnwinter.* "YOU SHOULD HAVE KILLED ME," He roared. "NOW YOU WILL FACE THE MIGHT OF SEPLECHURUS!"

"Move!" Jace instinctively shouted, unable to remove the shakiness in his voice.

The Sov charged through the streets of Bhall-Duraht, trampling every piece of Jace's childhood underfoot. The monster kept going with no regard for anything, swinging its horn with such carelessness. Was this what made Seplechurans happy, Jace ruminated with angst, destroying what should be preserved, what should be protected?

Jace ducked through the streets, hiding among the alleys as he pondered on Natasha's words, *The emperor is child, and I will treat him as such.* His memory echoed with her voice. The emperor must have surrounded himself with children as well.

The sound of adobe being crushed and trampled hurt more than the debris crashing into him. The Sov just destroyed the town, looking for them, the little mice were unable to fight back. For however many minutes they could, the three of them scattered around the town, hoping, praying not to get trampled.

The eldest Camerus dove into a building as the adobe crashed all around him. Even Camerus skin wasn't strong enough to counter such pain, and despite that, he could only think how the others were fairing. Jace wanted to lie there, hoping the Sov would think they were dead. However, he would not take kindly to Natasha's betrayal if he ever found out.

With a faint growl, Jace tried to push himself up, but the building was far too heavy, even for his strength. Maybe that was it; maybe Jace could finally rest there. No one else would know as long as everyone kept still.

"Hey ox-cur!" He heard Aidan yell.

El, please tell me I'm dreaming. Please tell me that's not Aidan.

"I think I forgot to use an animal to describe you."

No, no, no Aidan! Jace lifted himself off the ground, arms shaking when he faltered.

Aidan was so stupid sometimes, always picking fights he couldn't win. He never thought things through, always relying on Jace to bail him out of most problems. *He is so ... wait ...* Maybe that was it, all along, Jace thought. Maybe Aidan was reckless because he knew Jace was there, because he knew he could rely on his brother. He was confident because he knew there was a backup plan, and yet Jace laid there, thinking of cowardice.

"Over here, you ugly sea rhino!" Aidan yelled, his voice a lot more distant.

He's trying to lead him away. Jace clenched his fists, yelling with all his might to lift the rubble from his body. He emerged, sending the debris flying all around him. He panted, body smothered in dust and sand. He still had a reason to fight.

The earth still rumbled beneath the beast's steps; the air was still putrid with its foul stench. Jace could only see the destruction wrought across his town. Emotion welled up in his face as he glared at the beast chasing his brother.

There was so much relying on him now, not just Aidan, not just every person who was in Bhall-Duraht, but those who were out there as well. Natasha, the children, the memory of those loved, and those who still lived relied on Jace to take a stand. *Now.* Even if he couldn't win, he would still fight; someone always had to. "HEY!" He yelled at the top of his lungs.

The Sov spun around; a dark smile twisted into a serrated grin. Jace held out his arms, "YOU WANT A CHALLENGE?" He beat his chest. "I'LL GIVE YOU ONE."

The Sov's voice rumbled through his grotesque mouth, "You?" He gurgled. "You cannot scratch me! I'll trample you like I did this town!"

The Sov charged, but Jace, he stood still. Aidan was probably scared out of his mind, and to be frank, Jace was too; his heart stammered, and his legs felt like jelly. However, he knew, courage wasn't about experiencing fearlessness; it was standing tall as one looked fear in the eyes.

"Voice," Jace invoked mentally, "you told me you'll give me the victory, but I wish to define that. I don't want a victory where everyone around me is dead; I want a victory where I can smile with those who trust me to protect them. I stand here and now. It's either victory or death."

The Sov grew closer, just a couple more steps, and the creature would crush him, but there was a calm. Amid his pain, his heart slowed its pace; his breath became that of a Blossom breeze.

Jace inhaled, then exhaled with a whisper, "Breathe."

His mind drifted to another world. He floated like he was underwater, his breath coldly still. It was dark all around him, except for one blue orb of light that shone before him. His eyes were closed, as if he were in a lucid dream. All that was heard was a booming voice that sounded distant, powerful, yet comforting. It spoke in a somewhat whisper yet at a perfect volume, its language was mysterious, yet the words started to make sense the more it was heard. It said,

"Stand firm, O protector borne, for your winter cometh. The darkness thought it could advance, but you stopped them cold. The statues still adorn the lands of their first stand.

The wind answers your howl.

You stood rigid, not to be stubborn, but to shield. To your foes, you were unstoppable, to your allies, unmovable.

You led armies into battle and fought valiantly when all hope seemed lost.

A warrior fit to my design.

You, leader-borne, pure as snow, guided all through the tundra, for your domain bows to no one else.

Not much remains eternal; however, cold, winter, night—you—will never cease. My chosen who embodies all the winter summons, This is Thy Name:

Nevrence

Tell me—what is the vessel for thy power?"

Instinctively, Jace felt the need to raise his sword to the sky. The little blue ball nearly blinded him as it got closer, circling him before crashing into his blade.

At first, nothing happened, and he thought he had made a mistake. But then, a strange force of power coursed through his veins; it caused him to shiver. Then light jutted from his eyes and mouth. Then the real world.

Jace opened his eyes as the Sov leaped in the air. He had no time to question whether his vision was delusion or truth. He had time to say his final words—maybe just one—and he chose wisely. "NEVRENCE!!!"

The clouds grew dark, and the eruptive wind swarmed Jace, enveloping him in a torrent of sleet and snow. Instantly, the Sov was blown away by the sheer power of the wind.

Power swelled up in Jace like never before. The well in his stomach exploded, for his spirit had synchronized with his body.

Energy tingled his muscles and touched his bones, he felt the cold chill surround him, sending its force for miles all around. Blue light filtered about as the physical chains were removed, and the spirit took charge.

Inside, Jace saw the light crack through his weapon, filling his eyes with the light of a sky blue. It felt as if his weapon was a cocoon for something far greater.

It was. For when the last shattered the visage of bronze, it became the most beautifully crafted weapon he had ever seen.

A strange, unrecognizable, cold sheath made from something close to glass, diamond, and crystal, radiating and reflecting hues of blue and white. As he pulled the weapon, the wind parted for its new master. Holding his blade of pure, sharpened, clear ignisium-like substance that reflected light in fractals. The handle was made of a beautiful, navy leathery material. But the most stunning part was the six wings made of snow. The center of the blade filled his eyes with a stunning luster as the blue orb hummed to life, marking that its master was ready to end all evil.

That morning, he didn't know what to expect: not the slaves, not the thief, not Natasha, not the Sov, not the monster, and certainly—not this.

14

BREATH OF EL

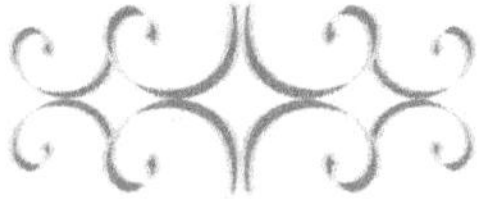

Breathe.
—The Immovable Iceberg

I *FEEL LIKE A god; I feel like El.* Jace couldn't understand what was happening, if it was truly happening at all. The surreal moment that happened in the last minutes? Seconds? Not even time could hold this wondrous moment.

He flexed his fingers, a shock coursed through his veins, causing his body to tremble; it felt like excitement, but less tangible. All his injuries could not compare to the well in the pit of his stomach that sent a wave of healing energy to his muscles and joints. He felt the need to move, as if staying still would cause him pain.

A smile crept on his face as he realized it all: the legend, the war, the prophecies. This was one of the Legendary Blades. In his hand? How was that possible? Could he really be chosen to wield such an impressive weapon?

He stared at his weapon once more, the shimmering Blade. It reflected his emotion. Tears streamed from his eyes, freezing up before flying away like dust. *The craftsmanship, the art …* he couldn't help but to admire it.

But something else, something far more malicious, lingered around him; a deep wave of inertia swaying him off his feet. An energy, a power, in direct opposition to his own; a counterforce with an intent to disrupt his peace.

"SO, ONE OF THE LEGENDARY BLADES WAS HERE AFTER ALL. I WILL KILL YOU AND TAKE THAT BLADE." The Sov yelled, stumbling to his feet.

Him—that must be the darkness I'm feeling. Jace rolled his shoulders.

The Sov bore his serrated teeth, failing to intimidate a determined Jace who simply walked forward to meet the challenge. He almost wanted to repeat the Sov's words from earlier, *you should have killed me,* but added his own, *because now, I cannot be matched.*

Jace whipped his Blade to the side, causing a gust of wind to sunder the sand. He breathed; his breath was visible in front of him. He paused, amazed; he'd never seen it before.

He inhaled, exhaling his mantra, "Breathe …"

The Sov charged, waving his horn. Jace felt what he could do, but his mind and body were not as one. This may have been what Aidan always talked about: feeling something without knowing what would happen. But he did know this: something welled up in him, a surety in his spirit; whatever it was, he focused it on his hand. And his Blade responded.

Jace smashed the ground with a roar, and more of that clear ignisium came from the ground in a wave, raising spikes as they met the Sov's horn.

Jace's eyes shuddered a moment before he touched the spikes he had just created. They chilled his fingers but refreshed him as well. He had heard about this. "This isn't clear ignisium. Is this … ice?" Then, above him, the sky started to weep small fragments of soft fractals. On descent, they kissed his face, forcing a smile to return to his lips. "Snow …? This is only the second time I …"

Jace held a fractal, watching the whiteness glow in his palm, untouched by the desert heat. The spirit-well in his belly reached the fractal in his hand, causing it to grow and harden, its fractal edges were sharp enough to cut with.

Without hesitation, he launched the weapon at the Sov, piercing his hide. He yelped with pain and cursed in Seplechuran. Jace breathed again, watching his breath flutter before him. "It's time to see what else I can do."

Jace started to run. The wind brushed his face with an intensity he'd never experienced before. He slid across the sand as he found himself passing the Sov. And this Ice Warrior made a mental note of his newfound speed, but the question now was simple: How strong was he?

He started to circle the Sov. Jace sent ice to one side of the creature, distracting him before barreling right into the Sov's back legs—toppling him.

Jace's eyes widened. He was now sure he was a god, or at least this is how he pictured gods to be: powerful, fast, sovereign.

He clenched his fist, and the wind howled in reply. With wide arcs he circled his Blade, causing a snowstorm to circle above him. Each particle of snow started to glow like heated ignisium but with the hue of a clear sky. He brought his Blade down, and the wind just encased the monster. The Sov thrashed about, as the small bits of hardened ice cut at him helplessly.

Once his experiment was over, Jace slashed away the snow. The Sov shook his hide; he looked more annoyed than damaged. Whatever he was, he had to be just as strong as Jace.

"Now to …" Jace fell to one knee, part of that inner excitement disappearing as fast as it came. He stared at his Blade; one of the wings of snow faded away. "Darn, the wings are a sort of hourglass, counting down to … maybe my reversion?"

The Sov rose, bloodied but far angrier than before. He didn't seem tired; maybe he'd practiced transforming. Either way, the battle needed to end.

Another sensation pulled at Jace; he gave in to it as the second wing started to grow dull. He sheathed his Blade and then held it forward. Ice projected from his scabbard, growing large enough for him to combat the Sov's horn. Instinctively, he tested the weight. It was balanced with his new strength.

The Sov roared, spilling gooey, putrid-smelling saliva on the sands. Jace roared, commanding the wind to amplify his voice.

With a shake of his hide, bone thorns emerged from the Sov's body. They fired off in Jace's direction. Jace conjured an ice barrier that halted the spikes. He leapt over to meet the Sov in combat.

Each swing they took started to spread the sands further. Adobe houses became nothing more than tumbleweeds. As Jace figured, the Sov was just as matched, and far more experienced in his form than Jace was in his. He held the monster in deadlock, trying to force his strength against his opponent's, but he lacked the mass to push his body forward enough to halt the Sov.

The second wing faded.

Jace fell to his knee, the fatigue hitting harder than it had before. Then he realized something: his body couldn't take the power; he was inexperienced, he was a human. If the power was of the Abode, he couldn't wield it for too long.

Jace needed a solution; he needed someone; he needed—"HEY, OX-CUR!" That was a voice to be missed. Jace couldn't see them, but he heard Chuckle and Snark rushing to his aid. The Sov's hind legs were bound, causing the monster to fall over and lose the deadlock. "Let's fix this, shall we?" Jace yelled as he slashed at the Sov's eyeball.

The Sov flailed with an unearthly roar. His blood splattered across the sands, coating it with a strange, inky black. His teeth gaped in rage as he turned to see Aidan, casually, ruefully taunting.

Jace made distance between the Sov, feeling the fatigue kick in. *Not quite a god, it seems.* Jace stood, watching the Sov brushing his feet in the sand.

The Sov kept his horn low to the ground, yelling at Aidan, "I WILL RUN YOU THROUGH!"

Aidan taunted, "You'll try!"

Jace tried to stand but fell. His body shook slightly, and his breath seemed much more uncontrollable than before. The gray skies began to part, allowing the sun to peek at the battle. He knew he needed to end this.

The Sov charged, and Jace could barely move. He had to find a way to minimize his movement and his ability usage while somehow delivering a fatal blow. *But how?*

Jace looked up, hoping to ask the Voice for more guidance, but his words caught in his mouth when he saw his opportunity—sunlight.

Without any hesitation, he plunged his Blade into the sands below, turning the sea of grains into a lake of ice. The wave caught the Sov, forcing him to slip away as Aidan used one of his chains to escape.

The third wing faded.

Roaring, the Sov released a rain of bone-thorns to attack the fleeing Aidan. While he dodged most of them, one bone grazed his side. Even from an immense distance, Jace could hear his brother yell. Another bone was headed toward him, and Jace mustered the strength to lift his Blade. "Aidan!" He yelled. The power reached his fingertips, but he halted his blast when a sandy blur swept across the sands, picking Aidan up and moving him just in time. *The Thief!* Jace nearly forgot about her. She really was a Reaper.

The Sov roared about in annoyance, turning his attention to Jace, who was far less mobile. Jace was easy prey, both of them knew it. He rose, gathering the last of his strength. *This will end—now.* Jace pointed his Blade to the ice path he created, then raised it as the Sov came in for a charge; spears of ice erupted from the path to impale the Sov with needles of ice rivaling his thorns. The Sov slowed but was not deterred.

The fourth wing faded.

Jace ran forth, calling to all his strength. He leaped in the air, dodging the Sov's ram. Before he landed, he summoned small platforms to catch him. Now the Sov was still, waving his mighty horn to catch Jace as he leaped from one platform to another.

Even with one eye, the Sov was formidable, nearly catching Jace as he leaped from the platforms.

The small footholds cost Jace his fifth wing, and his fatigue made him feel heavy. But he was not done. He summoned his last foothold to the sky, the Sov's eye followed. And the light blinded his darkness.

The sunlight stared at the Sov through its frozen looking glass, but the Sov could not stare back. Jace summoned his ice extension once more as he fell to the earth. He literally had one shot. With a roar of pain and power, the ice spear plunged through the Sov's blade, sending the power of ice through his body. The Sov's body was like that of the Voice's saying—a statue. His roars barely made it through the crystallizing process.

Jace wasted no time punching the Sov's frozen body, shattering him into millions of small pieces.

The sixth wing faded.

As Jace guessed, the heightened strength and the sovereignty over ice faded, and his blade was normal once more. He fell with the Sov's shattered remains.

The world shifted into a wavy blur; the sand's coarseness became that of pillows. Even the sky dropped slowly as the darkness crept into the corner of his narrow, smoky eyes. One more smile crept on his face as he couldn't help some words pass from his lips, "Heh, just like we practiced."

The desert felt hot again, the sky was bright, and everything around him felt real once more.

15

THE NEXT STEP

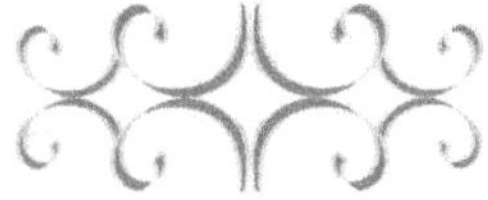

Bhall-Duraht was never the same.
—The Wildcard

AIDAN'S MEMORY WAS vivid.

Somehow, he returned where it all started, back where his pain originated. His body was small again, but that meant the world became so much bigger. He looked at himself from far-watching eyes, yet through his own. The world shifted around him strangely.

He kept on running, watching as his world bore the orange smile of death, but what he saw next stopped him to the core.

"Mother, Father?" His little voice squeaked.

His father's sword swept across the chests of the Seplechurans who attacked him, leaving them for dune crows. Beside him, Aidan's mother, with flourishing maroon hair, nocked an arrow, firing with expert precision and grace. Aidan impulsed a smile that he couldn't help but muster because his parents were amazing fighters. But something was wrong. Someone else was there.

Suddenly, an orange blaze erupted from the center of the town. In it,

Aidan saw something: shadowy teeth that stretched in unnatural angles; with the gape of its mouth, it released the most bone-chilling roar. Fire rained from the sky at its command, engulfing more and more things.

"MOTHER, FATHER, LOOK OUT!" Aidan yelled.

But it was no good; the fires engulfed them. But they weren't dying. They just burned endlessly, yelling for their lives in sounds Aidan couldn't properly comprehend. Tears strolled down his face as he watched his parents beg for death's sweet release. He clapped his hands over his eyes, and yet he could still see them burn. He could see his mother reaching for him, skin dripping off her bones. Then with clarity he heard her scream, "Aidan!"

He looked up; a ball of flame headed for him. He couldn't move. His eyes could only witness as the ball grew closer and closer, and …

"Laddie …?"

His eyes shot open; the tears were still so real on his face, but his environment was far different.

"A-Aurora?" groaned Aidan, "Where am I?"

He tried getting up, but his body ached sorely. Aurora lightly pressed her hand against Aidan's chest, "Yer safe," Aurora sniffled, "yer still in Bhall-Duraht."

Aidan laid back down, taking in the faintest breath of relief. *It was just a nightmare.* The hollow building gave credence to what Seplechurus could do. Despite beating the Sov, a simple look around told him that they couldn't save the town. But, for some reason, the pain didn't sink in properly. His head rested on an extremely comfy pillow, and his onyx eyes met Aurora, a playful smile at his lips. "Well, I'm glad to have woken up to such a pretty sight."

Cheap tin filled his ears as Aurora drenched the cloth and reapplied it to his head, "I see that the heat pitch didn't damper yer mouth. Good."

Aidan winked. "Missed my charm—wait, heat pitch?"

Aurora chuckled slightly. She sat on the side of Aidan's bed, her freckles lighting up in the afternoon sun. "Heat pitch, ya know, a fever."

"Oh. I had a fever?"

"Aye. Ya were burning like the sun. Had to patch up yer wound first, but ya kept flailing."

Aurora smiled softly; her hands pressed upon her legs in masked relief. She took a deep breath before continuing. "But yer fine now, that's what matters." Her eyes fell slightly, and she was clutching her knees tightly. She must've been anxious, he felt. As tempting as it was for him to flirt, Aidan resisted because he had seen that same anxiety on Jace's face before. He reached out, clutching her hand. "Thank you. I guess you saved my life, huh?"

For the first time, she smiled sweetly. "I guess I did, but I guess it was repayment. Yer kin saved us all, though I don't want to admit it. What is he anyway?"

Aidan shut his eyes for a moment, thinking back to the brief images that he saw of Jace fighting with ice and snow. He observed Jace using the elements to his whim as if he were some divine being. He thought *it was exciting and awe-inspiring, but when did Jace learn he could do something like that?* He could only come up with a simple solution, "He's my brother—with a very cold sword."

Aurora rolled her eyes playfully. "I think I can guess that."

Aidan shrugged, wincing as he clutched his side. "That's all I can guess; he's never done anything like that before."

Aurora pressed the cloth on Aidan's forehead. After a moment, she removed it, the slight breeze chilling the water on his head.

After she squeezed it and put it back on his head, he said, "Thanks." He smiled. "I'm not complaining, though; I've never seen snow before."

"You haven't?" Aurora cocked her eyebrow.

"Nope! I've lived here all my life, and it never snows in the desert. It gets frigid, but not to the point of snow."

Aurora smiled with a slight smugness. "It snows all the time in Delfizcan, well, mostly in the highlands."

Aidan's eyes glowed with excitement. "Really? You got to show me one day."

She looked at him questioningly, a bit surprised. She simply shrugged. "Maybe." She stood up, wiping her hands together before brushing her bound hair with her fingers.

"Where are you going?" Aidan asked.

"I have to check on yer kin; Natasha is looking after 'em."

"She's back?" Aidan jerked his body, only to feel more pain.

Aurora pressed a soft hand on him to keep Aidan down. "Aye, her plan worked perfectly, but when they heard all the commotion, they returned: slaves, soldiers, and all."

Aidan breathed through his teeth. "How were their reactions? They probably were shaken up by all the destruction." He was expecting Aurora to tell him that the Seplechurans were ready to rampage from here all the way to the north, but she didn't; she simply hid a small grin that Aidan had already come to enjoy.

"Well, they were shaken."

"Aurora the Thief, are you hiding something from me?" Aidan slyly asked.

She motioned with her head. "Think ya can stand? We can visit yer kin together; then I'll show ya something."

Surprises were something Aidan had always longed to see; the excitement of the unknown swelling within him felt better than the actual surprise. Jace was never exceptional at surprises; it was either a new training regiment, or it was something he simply couldn't hide. There was nothing Aidan couldn't see coming; that's why his brother's sudden mastery over ice struck him as odd.

Aidan slowly lifted his body, clutching his side as he sharply winced. After a quick breath, he slowly turned to face the door, what was left of it, anyway; and then he finally stood. "You could help me," he clenched his abdomen with a chuckle.

Aurora leaned on the door. "No, no, watching ya struggle is so much fun."

Aidan stood up straighter. "Yes, and watching you squirm like a caterpillar was breathtaking."

"Ya cheated." She grumbled.

He smiled smugly. "You lost."

"Don't make me take my bandages back."

Aidan opened his mouth, but he knew better than to question a girl titled the Grim Reaper of Bhall-Duraht.

"Thought so."

Aurora reached for Aidan's arm, throwing it over her shoulder and sliding her hand around his waist. She met his eyes—rolling her own when she noticed his smirk.

My charms are working. Aidan thought.

The two stepped in unison, avoiding the fallen debris and shattered furniture. A faint smell of wine hung in the air, which horribly mixed with the scents of sweat and steel.

The hall narrowed out, but the broken side gave it more room; however, it sacrificed the beauty to ruination.

Aidan felt his steps to be much more careful. Though his side was injured, his right foot felt numb. He wasn't sure if it was loss of blood or maybe that "heat pitch." It wasn't a complete negative, as an anxious Arundel stepped on his foot upon entry into the hall.

"Mr. Aidan, sorry!"

"I can't feel my foot …" Arundel's face paled, but Aidan's laughter broke the little boy's fear. "Relax, it's from my injuries, I didn't feel a thing."

Aurora rolled her eyes. "Is his kin awake?"

"Yup, he's talking with Auntie Sha. I'm fetching some food … if I can find any."

Arundel gave a Seplechuran soldier salute before running off. Aidan knocked twice on the door, shoving it open before he heard permission to come in.

"Something told me you were awake," Jace groaned.

"Since Arundel literally shouted my name, I'm going to take that as an obvious test that your ears still work."

Jace cocked a brow. "It seems near-death couldn't shut you up."

"Eh, death couldn't do it."

A silence hung over them for a moment.

Jace smiled. "I'm glad you're alive."

"I'm glad *we're* alive. Camerus brothers stay together." Aidan limped to his brother's side, grabbing him in a light hug.

Aurora stood by Natasha, who was at Jace's bedside. The Seplechuran whispered something to Aurora, which drew a chuckle out of the Delfizcani.

Natasha spoke as if continuing, "You are in time; *Yace* was telling me about Blade."

"It's Jace."

Aurora scoffed. "It's Seplechuran dialect, just deal with it … *Yace*"

Aidan could see the horrible memories flooding in for Jace. A Seplechuran family in old Bhall-Duraht would butcher his name constantly due to their accents, and he absolutely hated it. Aidan, however, remembered tricking them to say things with j's in them just to get a laugh.

"You heard voice at depot, yes?" Natasha asked, interrupting Aidan's thoughts.

Jace nodded. "Yeah."

For the next few moments, Aidan heard some of the best storytelling ever uttered from his brother's mouth. An enigmatic voice, Jace's mercy, the tale of encouragement, and, best of all—snow in the desert.

Jace was always a good storyteller; he just lacked the motivation to read stories and talk-less write them. When he was finished, Aidan was left wide-eyed, mouth agape. "Can you do it again?"

"Probably, the feeling seems …" Jace looked at his fist. "… suppressed, not gone. I would have to research the effects."

Natasha nodded; her fingers cupped her chin. "So far, diagnosis is extreme fatigue and hunger, but he shows no signs of deterioration, but I am not medic."

Aurora folded her arms, thinking before piping up, "So, the laddie needs to use it more."

Natasha nodded in agreement. There was a brief silence that fell, and everyone was lost in their own thoughts. Aidan, he could only think of the amazing lore that was written in the desert. Where would such a power lead them if they were to travel? Would they explore the unknown that is Dominius, or would they stay here? That battle left Bhall-Duraht in bad shape.

Jace broke the silence. "Do the Seplechurans have more knowledge on the Blades?"

"No," Natasha exclaimed with visible anger on her features. "That is why this war is pointless; we know nothing!"

Natasha cleared her throat, taking steady breaths to collect herself. The redness in her pale skin started to rise, Songluan sight unneeded. Aidan didn't think about it before, how much this war hurt her. She was forced to send people into a war with little information and motive. As a strategist, she must've felt that her hands were stained, too.

"My … apologies. It is clear you will not find answers in sands; I suggest Utopia."

Utopia, the fabled land of flora; the people there were said to be one with the forest. The trees there were unlike anything that was imagined before. Aidan and Jace had been close to the border before; a couple of their contracts needed work up there. Though they'd never been in the heart of it; well, Jace had, but he was a baby.

Aidan exchanged a happy glance with his brother, who seemed less than amused.

"Why?" Jace asked, more in defiance than in curiosity.

"It doesn't matter why!" Aidan interjected, "It's Utopia! We can travel!"

Jace held up a silencing hand, which only made Aidan roll his eyes and huff. Seeing the silence, Natasha spoke, "Utopia was former colony of Setas-Li then of Seplechurus, giving them extensive knowledge." She rubbed her temples. "Also, that is where my … daughter defected."

Aurora placed a hand on Natasha's shoulder, and yet, the Seplechuran woman didn't even move.

"Natasha, are you okay?" Aidan couldn't help asking.

She looked up, the mist building in her eyes. With a catlike slowness, she blinked away.

"If you go to Utopia, you can convince them to inhabit this town, as safeguard from my people." She continued, ignoring Aidan's question.

Aidan sighed in his head. *Of course, she's not going to tell me.* He looked to Jace, shrugging in agreement. *Natasha's plan seems brilliant. As Aurora said, it's all about execution.*

Jace sighed out loud, "I have no reason to doubt you. We leave after we recover."

Aidan pumped a fist. "YES! We're going to Utopia!"

The little plan of liberation evolved into something much more. Aidan couldn't help making the connections between them and the warriors in his novels. He was going to travel for the purpose of saving the world! *What could possibly be better? The answer? Nothing.*

16

Broken Long Before

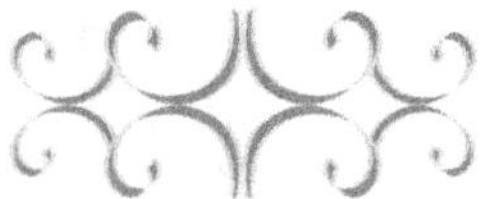

Some things are unexpected even when one prepares.
—The Seplechuran Strategist

Y*ACE WAS FAR more compliant now; he appeared to be man of results.* Natasha clasped her hands on her lap, bracing herself with steady breaths. She looked at Aurora, whose hand was still on her shoulder.

The brothers chatted away, forming plans without including a vital member. Natasha knew the youngest wouldn't seem to mind, but the older one, *Yace,* would need convincing, but she had planned this from the beginning. "I want you to take Aurora."

"What?!" Aurora, Jace, and Aidan all yelled in different tones.

As predicted, Jace asked, "Why should we do that?"

"Answer is obvious now, is it not?" Natasha breathed out her words. "You need her."

Jace objected with a brisk stand. "No, we don't. We're fine all on our own."

"You brothers are exceptional warriors, but what world experience do you have?"

Jace sighed. "We were mercenaries for the better half of a decade; that's experience enough." He groaned, massaging his temples. "Natasha—*Ms. Natasha*—I respect you enough to—"

Natasha cut him off, "Then adhere to what I say. Aurora's knowledge of shadows and hidden stratagems can be of use. Your experience is limited to bartering and deal-making."

Jace remained stubborn, but he couldn't deny Aurora's strength, honestly, no one could. Natasha kept her gaze steady, her face not leaning toward any emotion.

Jace grumbled. "We'll—"

Aurora cut Jace's sentence short when she stormed out without a word. Only the erratic kick of dust marked her exit.

"Give me time." Natasha followed her.

So afraid of change, that one, but she had such lust for adventure, for companionship that she could not quite understand. Natasha sighed at her own thoughts. The brothers may have thought she came up with a brilliant plan to utilize all their abilities, but it was the simple fact that they were acquainted with Aurora. Natasha didn't need to rely on her own judgment for this plan; anyone Aurora called an ally, or even a powerful adversary, was worth their weight in gold. "Aurora," Natasha called.

"There's no point in joining them lassie, they don't want me." Aurora explained, her small frame sinking into a split couch in complete exhaustion, her hands covering her eyes.

Natasha held her own elbows, letting out a troubled groan. She knew this would be an issue. "Aurora, I know enough of your past, I know you are afraid of getting hurt—"

Aurora abruptly slashed that notion. "Stop." Stabbing the air with her pointer finger, she raged, "Ya don't know me. Stop actin' like you know me, ya got it?"

Natasha tipped her chin slightly, glaring at Aurora. Aurora moved her hand. "Whatever," she groaned.

Natasha stomped. "Aurora."

Aurora sat up, grumbling to herself. "Fine! I don't wanna get attached again, okay? Is that what ya wanted to hear?"

That pain, Natasha knew, stayed with everyone no matter how much one tried to admit they were over it. Pain lingers—the pain of abandonment always lingers.

Natasha sat down beside Aurora, wrapping her in a sudden hug that made Aurora flinch uncomfortably. Natasha looked awkward as she tried; the thought of physical comfort was foreign to her.

"I am … unfamiliar with this, so I do apologize," Natasha relayed almost humorously yet still deadpanned.

Aurora stifled a laugh. "Ya'll *still* don't have a word for it in your language, aye?"

Natasha smiled softly.

Aurora succumbed to Natasha's embrace, and the Seplechuran hadn't felt such a daughterly love in such a long time. It felt as if an inner ember started to ignite, filling the body with enough energy to carry on. It somehow opened the gates of her eyes, letting tears flow.

Natasha stroked Aurora's hair, long and curly as it was. Her manicured fingers caressed every strand. "Aurora, I want you to be happy. Do not let one bad person ruin your outlook on people. Your former friend, he acts like the loud one, does he not?"

Aurora looked away a little. "I never told you that."

"Your odd reluctance gives you away." Natasha leaned back, lightly pushing Aurora from her. "Be happy, go with them. Form new bonds."

Aurora swiftly hugged Natasha, the Seplechuran returned the gesture, surer of herself this time.

"Thank ya," Aurora sobbed.

Natasha leaned in. She didn't want to divide her little family; if anything, she wanted to keep Aurora in the desert, but something about that girl couldn't stay in the desert.

"You are welcome, Aurora." Natasha smiled to herself.

A few moments passed before Natasha escorted Aurora to her new companions. It seems that the brothers were wiser than most, seeing as they agreed to allow her to join. It was admirable, something Natasha could relate to. They fought for their home, they fought for answers.

She only hoped that these two would be kinder than her previous companions.

The discussion with the boys lasted a short while; honestly, if it weren't for Aidan, it would not have been a conversation at all. Fortunately, their personalities balanced each other, *Aurora should fit right in*, Natasha thought.

"Laddie, ya want to see that surprise I mentioned?" Aurora lightly tapped Aidan.

Aidan grinned. "I'm always ready for surprises. *Yace*, you coming?"

The older one folded his arms, glaring at his younger brother. The latter smiled in such a refreshing way, even though he was in pain.

"This does concern you somewhat," Natasha stated. "You can return to bed after."

There was a large, rumbling groan before the bed screeched under the weight of Jace's shifting body. Natasha inspected the bandages before she let him take a step.

Aurora looked to Jace. "Hey laddie, hold yer kin, will ya?"

"Tired of me already, Aurora?" scoffed Aidan.

She hesitated, but she eventually said, "No."

Together, they all journeyed through the devastation of Bhall-Duraht, the buildings now indistinguishable from the sands on which they stood. Those that weren't dust looked more like ruins of the old world. Natasha didn't stay in Bhall-Duraht long but felt pity. She searched the brothers' eyes; they were trying to look away. However, their faces started to change when they heard the laughter.

"What's going on over there?" Aidan asked.

"Arundel, getting distracted from bringing your food, I assume," Natasha answered.

They all turned the corner, and she watched as the brothers' faces lit up brighter than the sun. Who could blame them? It was not every day that one played with snow in the sandy desert.

Children, adults, soldiers, and slaves put aside whatever differences they bore and started to throw snowballs at one another. Arundel skillfully dove under a strike and planted two snowballs in the face of a soldier in the same action; Natasha nodded in pride, seeing that his training was coming quite well.

"What is this?" Jace asked.

"The Seplechuran Resistance." Natasha replied.

Yace finally understood. "That's why you wanted them distracted and not killed. If we took out a Sov—"

"—they'll naturally follow the next chain of leadership," Aidan finished.

Natasha smirked. "Slow to catch on, but you are correct."

The two Camerus looked on in awe, as it seemed everyone forgot who they were for a moment. It was glorious but, most of all, inspiring.

"*Yace,* you do not simply hold power to fight, you hold power to inspire. You have gained ability to bring hope to world longing for it."

Aidan gasped. "I just thought of it, it snows all the time up north, right?"

Natasha and Aurora nodded.

Aidan continued, turning to his brother, "You just brought a bit of their home to them, Jace."

He understands. "Some soldiers here have not seen snow in xantem." Natasha huffed tiredly. "I have not seen it for some time. This war has taken so much from us. Even memories of our home," she paused, taking in a shaky breath, letting her next words sink in. "You have been given gift. Cherish it."

So many gifts have been squandered for so long, so much potential snuffed out by a single war. Natasha could not plan for the losses; she could only mitigate the pains.

The playing people saw them, and they tried to pull *Yace* in for a snowball fight. Natasha couldn't help the chuckle on her lips—a snow-ball fight, in the desert. Even Aidan's strange chains were playing with everyone; the only way for them to leave Aidan's side.

She had to ensure this was maintained. There will be no slaves, no soldiers, only the free and the willing. If she weren't the High Strategist— maybe she would have moved here with her daughter and husband all those xantem ago.

Natasha faded into the back, as the others pulled the trio into a fight, Aidan frowning as he could barely move to play. Natasha nearly joined herself. However, she would make a war out of it all.

She journeyed alone, hands clasped in front of her, gown dragging in the sand. Regal as she was, powerful as she was, she felt so hollow. She prepared for so much, and yet it never made things easier.

Then the glint of metal caught her eye.

Like a crow, she couldn't help the gleam. She walked over, knowing the steel well. With a tug, she pulled Brand's bardiche—the bardiche she and her daughter gifted him—from the sands. His shattered corpse, now a white dust on the ground, slowly melting away.

She couldn't hold it in.

Natasha clutched the bardiche, letting the emotion fall from her eyes—letting the tears flow down the silvery metal. With all her foresight, all her planning, and cunning, nothing could properly prepare her for the experience of the war.

17

Impenetrable Thief

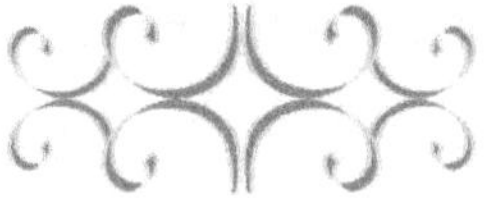

Where's the snow?
—The Thief

THE SUN ROSE and fell for two weeks, and the boys were recovering nicely with the passing of each day. One would think things would go back to normal, but things changed—for the better. The Seplechurans realized Natasha's dream of peace. It was no surprise that everyone wanted the war to end. Especially since the Seplechurans stationed there were younger and much more hopeful.

No one was more excited than Aurora. She didn't have to skulk around alleys and dark corners to get around. Some soldiers eyed her suspiciously, but no one made a move against her. The former slaves were too busy fawning over the brothers. However, some of them, in fact, did recognize them. Survivors, those two were.

Now, Aurora was tasked with packing the sacs for their trip, and she couldn't wait. At any moment she could be seeing the world again, though part of that scared her. The world was a dangerous place; she knew that firsthand. But it became much better when there were people to see it with; she only hoped they were better than Ruben and Mira. She couldn't remember the last time she thought about them. Were they still together, she wondered. Did they find another poor sap to befriend only to betray them later? Was Ruben still deceiving people with that smile? She didn't notice how much the questions stung until they did. But it was fine, she could defend herself now, she wouldn't fall prey to the same things. If history repeated itself, she was ready.

Aurora was at the edge of the town, not too far from where she and the Camerus brothers fought the Sov. She wiped her hands as she finished triple-checking what she needed.

"Thief," Jace called from behind her.

She stopped in front of him, dropping the sac at his feet. With a roll of her shoulder, she answered, "Dobber."

He narrowed his eyes, picking up his sac then looking away. "Where's Aidan?"

She shrugged. "He told me he had things to do."

He returned his sight to her. "What kind of things?"

She placed a hand on her hip, shifting her weight. "He's yer kin, ya tell me."

"You were supposed to be with him."

"Correction: the laddie was supposed to be with me."

The big dobber folded his arms in a huff, growling words under his breath.

"What was that?" Aurora asked pointedly.

Jace ignored her, keeping his eyes on the town.

He's insufferable! He's like a big child! Aurora yelled in her mind. She knew if he were the only person she traveled with, she would have stayed in the desert. But there was a relief in being hated outright instead of hiding behind fancy words that left one guessing. However, it didn't make his behavior tolerable. "If ya got a problem with me, better say it before we get to open road. Out there, yer stuck with me."

"You're a thief," he bellowed.

"And?" she scoffed, jerking her head. "Yer a mercenary, you kill others for sport and pay."

Jace's eyes narrowed as veins popped up from his fists. "We don't simply kill anyone. We have morals. You, on the other hand, take everyone's hard earnings, work, profession, and livelihood because you couldn't make it yourself, then you justify your actions by who you steal from."

"Oh, so that's yer problem? I take from 'hard-working' people, eh? Ya think I asked fer this?!"

His eyes met hers for a moment, then they both turned away. Silence overtook them, just like that. Aurora knew he would not understand; there was no point in telling him. She would be sacrificing too much anyway, she knew; it was either be understood and be vulnerable or be invulnerable and misunderstood. She would settle for the latter.

Moments later, Aurora moved to the canopy that the people set up in the few weeks of rebuilding. It was crude, but it provided shade just the same. Even the dobber was not stupid enough to stay out in the heat, and there was enough space for him to stay a good enough distance away from her. As much as she wanted to start conversation, she knew it would end in some sort of argument. But there was much she wanted to ask: living in a cave for ten xantem was not something she would like, especially after Galcks. Fortunately, Aidan arrived just in time. He tried to catch his breath right as he dropped a crate on the floor. "I know, I know, sorry," he pleaded.

"Where have you been?" the dobber asked.

"I asked Natasha and some of our old neighbors for some materials I—" he paused, contemplating, "—didn't want to go home, not until we got back, until we deserved it."

Jace nodded, mimicking Aidan's grim expression. "Yes, you told me, that's how you mended our clothes."

Aidan's mood picked back up. "But what I didn't tell you is that I managed to make a new outfit," He waved his hands dramatically. "I call it The Sunset Warrior."

The dobber looked exceptionally confused. "Why do you need another outfit?"

"I don't. It's part of my *female* collection."

Aurora raised her brow. Aidan shared her glance, dropping the crate in her hands, forcing her to fall forward. He smiled as if he were unaware of what he did. "Get dressed."

Aurora, with a heave, lifted the crate and tromped over to a destroyed, old building that had enough walls to give her some privacy. She opened the crate, seeing a blast of sunset-orange filling her vision. It was a beautifully seamed kirtle filled with faint, pale diamond patterns. *Sunset Warrior, I get it now.* The sleeves were a daring yellow that flowed well from the orange of the body. Aidan's eye for color may have been more impressive than his mouth; her innards giggled. She brushed the shirt aside and saw the breeches; they were the same orange and had the same design, each thread immaculately made. However, if the diamond-shaped cleavage window had been any lower, she might have had to stab him.

She tried it on, feeling the soft but sturdy fabrics under her fingertips. The kirtle was form-fitting enough to outline her small frame but loose enough to let her move; the breeches were the same. There were even some boots in there, but Aurora had to pass; she was quite sure Aidan did not leave a space for her daggers and lockpicks.

If she was grateful for anything, it was the fact that the sleeves were long enough.

She turned the corner to see the brothers in conversation, but when they saw her, they paused. Even the dobber looked impressed.

Aidan whistled flirtatiously. "My, my, who is that?"

Aurora rolled her eyes, pressing her yellow slit skirt. This time, she couldn't hide her giggle. The gift could have been another ploy, or maybe he was acting out of emotion; they did slay a beast a few weeks ago. Regardless, the outfit was beautifully sewn, so with the creator present, she had to ask, "Do ya think it looks good on me?"

Aidan said nothing as he meticulously scoured his creation, muttering to himself as he nitpicked color and checked for mistakes. Aurora huffed, crossing her arms—only for Aidan to lightly slap them back down so he could observe the outfit. She tapped her foot. This was unbelievable. She was having a moment, but his eyes weren't even on her. "Excuse me!" she yelled.

"Oh," Aidan looked up, "did you say something, Aurora?"

"I asked if ya thought it looked good on me!"

He dismissed her with a wave. "Of course, Aurora, I made it."

Jace sighed from the back, "You have no idea how to talk to women."

Aurora picked up her old cloak and threw it at Aidan's face. The laddie stumbled on his arse, allowing Aurora to promptly throw Aidan's sac at his face. At first, she thought that Aidan sewed clothing because he wanted to lure her in, but now she was sure he didn't—he was far too dense for that.

An hour passed; thankfully, the winds were calm that day.

It was good, too; it made it easier to get through the large dunes that covered the landscape. Aurora remembered the journey inside the town; she never thought she would leave the place again. Her younger self hated it, the way her mouth would get dry so quickly, the lack of water, and the sand nesting in her hair.

Speaking of hair, Aidan let her keep his hair tie, which made the desert trip bearable enough, but not quite.

She wanted to thank him at least, but there was an unspoken rule in the desert: don't speak. That's probably why it remained unspoken for so long—she'd come to that conclusion later. All the energy talking was better spent climbing the dunes and chasing off giant two-tailed scorpions. To Aurora's absolute amusement, she found out Aidan could stay quiet for long periods. Maybe that gave credence to how daunting the trek was, she assumed.

Two more hours passed. Aurora dreamed of the sweet, snowy mountains of Delfizcan, of home. She never got tired of the endless amounts of ale in the taverns or the townsfolk singing *Jæggur ton Førchet,* Break the Invaders, the anthem of the people. She could almost feel the snow falling on her face when she hummed it. The mirages danced to her favorite tune but lacked the flute.

"Land ho!" Aidan yelled.

Finally

"Mirage," The dobber corrected.

No ...

Aidan slumped as he kept on walking, but strangely, the dobber seemed just fine, as if he couldn't feel the heat at all. Probably hoarding that ice Blade to keep him cool. She could try and swipe it, but she didn't really know how it worked. *It'll probably kill me,* she sarcastically thought, but quickly reevaluated. *Maybe I should try it.*

She picked up her pace, keeping her feet as steady as she could on the shifting sands. With a quick lunge, it would be as good as hers. She crouched low as she started to approach, but an arm suddenly stopped her.

"Don't try it," Aidan whispered. "You're already on his bad side."

"I'm not trying anything."

He winked. "Oh, come on, Aurora, I thought of it first."

"Aidan," Jace called. "How far can you see?"

Aidan left her side, standing atop a large dune. In a moment, he dropped to his knees, raising his arms.

"Land?" his kindred asked.

"Land."

"Then let's go."

Aidan brushed his knees and jogged down the dune, his kin close behind. Aurora shook her head. "That laddie is so weird," she smiled. "Aye."

It was far, but eventually, Aurora saw the entrance to the pass. She didn't really know how Aidan could have seen it, but she was thankful for some hope.

Bracklyn Pass, the large stone road carved centuries ago by the first inhabitants of the desert so they could make their home anew in the forest areas of Utopia, or that's what Natasha told her, at least.

The trio stopped at the entrance of the pass, emptying their shoes of sand and cleaning their clothes before Aidan threw a fit. His chains started to stretch, like they had even done anything.

"So, we'll rest here for a moment, then we'll get through the pass and make camp on the other side." The dobber commanded.

Aidan groaned. "Aww, come on Jace, a moment? My legs are killing me."

"You would be better if you had trained more," retorted Jace.

"Yeah, like anything'll train me for walking hours in the desert."

"You always complain about something, Aidan. If Father were here, he'd train you even harder.

Aidan yawned, shedding an imaginary tear from his eye. "Please, go on; I yawn when I'm listening, I swear."

Ugh, Jace sounds like a Setas-Lisian. Protocol this, training that, the dobber was such a bore. Probably didn't know how to lighten up if Yehowehel himself came down from on high and told him to. Aurora rested herself on a boulder as the brothers continued to argue. Aurora simply sharpened her blades, listing the kill count of each before she put them in her boot. But as she got to one dagger, she paused. Dried blood rested simply on the upper curve, the rest of it untouched. She looked up; the brothers didn't notice. She wiped the blade with the inside of her skirt, then sheathed it in her boot.

That was a secret she didn't want to tell anyone, something that went deeper than any wound of hers. In fact, it was an accumulation. But with her, it was just two options: be understood and vulnerable, or be misunderstood and invulnerable, and she perfectly preferred the latter.

18

Reprieve

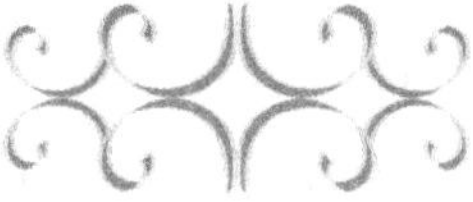

Rest, at last.
—The Rose

Utopia, finally. It had been a fortnight since she had rested; her eyes felt puffy and heavy as she barely had time to behold the root gate that acted as the entrance to Utopia. People yelled and cheered at the triumphant return of Natalie's soldiers, while her subordinates basked in the glory. She could not. She rubbed her temples, sighing to herself. She could slip through the crowd not because she was stealthy; no, it was because no one cared for her there. Utopia was only a utopia for those who were Utopians.

She turned her iquan, Votich, to the left of the gate, leaving behind the gawking crowds and the egotistical soldiers. She just needed to head home, rest, and then interrogate the prisoners that she had.

"Rose," one of her subordinates called to her. That type of disrespect would not be received well in Seplechurus, and it would have been customary for her to slap him if she were further north. She halted Votich, who growled as the man approached. He warily stopped his advance, staring at her iquan but speaking to her. "What shall we do with the prisoners."

I could have sworn I said this already. "Jail them. I want to interrogate them personally. There are too many Seplechuran units in these forests; I want to know why."

The soldier nodded, still staring at Votich. Still, after all these xantem, she felt as if Votich got more recognition than she did.

She pet her steed's lavender mane, running her hand over his striped fur, causing him to purr lowly. "Come." She led him away.

Every day, she questioned why she defected. The Utopians were as deaf as the Seplechurans, but she needed them to listen, somehow. The Utopians needed an edge in the Illisian alliance, and she needed an opening; it was a fragile alliance, but it worked.

She couldn't endure the voices of her people screaming profanities at her in her mother tongue or the sound of their bones cracking as the Utopians forced their mouths shut. And, of course, there is the reason why so many Seplechurans were in Utopian forests in the first place: were they planning an attack? Or were they reinforcing a position she didn't know they had?

The Utopian's "expert" on Sepelchuran movements was just as stumped as the Utopians.

Votich hiss-neighed, grabbing Natalie's attention. She didn't realize it yet, but she was home. Two tree yurts, the size of two normal Utopian homes, had flowers budding up the ladder she would need to climb. She hopped off Votich, patting him on the side as he trotted over to his small canopy where he slept.

Touching the ground, no matter how soft that grass was, made her legs shake as if she were chained again. The ladder that she had climbed constantly became that of a blur, fading to black, then to the orange of the sunset.

She didn't need to see to climb. Once atop, she crossed the sturdy wooden bridge to her "living yurt" where her bed and her kitchen sat. Everything sat in an orderly fashion, from the table and chair in the middle of the room, aptly decorated with rose vines, to her bed, which was smoothed out to perfection. Weapons hung with rose thorns decorated her wall, but of course, sitting across her bed was her favorite possession: her cutlass, her first cutlass commissioned by her father when she survived her training on Konkev Mountain. Every moment she entered her room, she stared at it—a reminder of simpler times, a reminder of what she wanted back. "I miss these days," she muttered, her fingers grazing the cold steel.

Fatigue reminded her that it was very much still present. She disrobed, much too tired to even wash up. However, would she really want to fill her bed with forest dirt and mush? She bristled, *of course.*

She threw on her sleepwear and flopped on her bed. Without even a second passing, sleep took her.

Shake

 Jingle

 Rattle

Natalie's eyes flicked open; someone was there. *Another protester?* Maybe someone who didn't like her leadership. Either way, their first mistake was attacking her at night—Seplechurans rule the night.

One of the benefits of sleeping diagonally was that it gave her attackers the false sense that she was too tired to be alert. The second benefit was that her hanging arms could easily reach for the dagger under her bed.

She counted. *1 ... 2 ...*

"Lass, are you awake?" The voice of her superior called.

She slowly moved her hand away from the dagger. "Great General?" she called out, "Why are you skulking in shadow?"

He gave a boisterous laugh, one that hurt her head right after waking. "I couldn't find a lamp, lass. I was hoping you would have one up."

"I positioned my lamps so darkness would take algae at certain time."

As if by divine word, the algae in her lamp started to glow, filling her room with a pale blue light. It lit the many wrinkles that covered the Great General's pale sandy face, as well as his thinning gray hair that was prevalent on his head and his arms.

"Well, I suppose I was worried for nothing then." He held her by the shoulders. "It's rare to see you immediately sleep after getting home. Is something troubling you?"

Natalie sighed but kept her shoulders resolute. "It all troubles me, I will not lie. However, I can keep my opinions to myself. What concerns me is why we are seeing pockets of my people in Utopian forests—especially on southern side ..." Natalie pinched her chin to think, her eyes darting around to make sense of it. "Wait, what is most profitable thing in south ...?"

The Great General furrowed his brows, but this was different—he wasn't thinking; no, that face seemed more akin to sorrow. "Bhall-Duraht, that's the only thing that would have any worth that far south."

Natalie nodded. "I will organize a team to go south immediately. It is possible my people did not settle for destruction; they could be rebuilding to work as southern branch for operations."

The Great General nodded. "It would explain the scouts ... get on it, lass."

19

Through the Pass

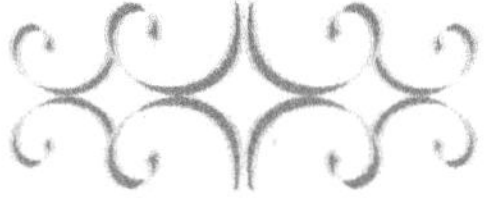

It seems fate defies what we expect, quite often.
—The Protector

IN LIFE, IT was natural to have expectations. Certain things were born just to spite the expectations held by people. Be it fate, divine providence, or some other third force he couldn't explain, Jace found himself among the people whose expectations were casually defied.

He remembered the final days of Bhall-Duraht quite differently from Aidan. While his younger brother focused on the action, Jace focused on the words. His parents instructed him to be a leader to not only Aidan but also to others, a call of maturity that no one else could answer. However, could someone call him immature or even selfish for wanting to stay a child a little longer? It was a question he knew he had no right to pose to anyone who depended on him.

Now, the voice of Yehowehel thrusted upon him another task, one far greater than he could imagine. Him—a young orphan boy with little to no actual real-life experience. In his hand, he possessed a weapon sought after by so many; it started the very same war that took everything from him.

Aidan danced, carefree as ever. His little brother always had someone to look up to, and he was someone that Jace didn't want to fail. And how could he forget the people? The smiling faces of everyone, past and present—he took responsibility for them. It all made his heart beat faster and caused his head to float on air, but if Yehowehel chose him, his mind argued, that meant he could do it, right?

The trio made their final trudge through the pass just as quietly as they walked through the desert, save for the scuff sounds of Aidan's dancing. Although the pass had constantly shifting grain and inconsistent footing, it was winding, and the drop could be treacherous. Despite this, Aidan decided to do flips.

Jace shook his head as he kept on going, the wind sputtering his cloak as he stood unmoved by the breeze. What he could conjure would put this breeze to shame.

A few desert-brown deer ran from them; other animals such as goats, chybers, (chunky rodents known for their four eyes and good meat), and other grass-eating mammals made their trek through the pass easily. Bracklyn had little vegetation, well, not until they made it beyond the ridge.

Jade grasses, calm wintery air, and colorfully adorned trees. The branches of the nearby flora grew in spirals, branches reaching the heavens in a strange way. Jace mustered a smile, his brother beside him bearing the same reaction. The scene was beautiful, no matter how many times he saw it.

They continued on in silence, but the elder Camerus could sense the agitation of his brother. He wished to speak.

"So, Aurora …" Aidan started.

She spun her head, "Aye?"

"You want to … ask some questions about us? Just to make sure you know us."

Oh great. Jace dropped his shoulders as he continued to look at the scenery, feeling the smoothness of the roads compared to the sandy ones they'd just left.

"Ya … right, I don't know much about ya. Actually, ya'll don't know much about me."

"That's for sure," Jace added.

"Oh, hush you," Aidan silenced. Aurora stuck out her tongue at Jace; Aidan poked her in the forehead. "Stop."

Rubbing her forehead, the thief asked, "Well, what do ya want to know?"

How long you plan on staying, and when are you leaving? Jace promptly thought.

"When did you get to Bhall-Duraht?" Aidan asked, but Jace liked his unspoken questions better.

"Hitched a ride on a shipment caravan eight xantem ago, never left."

So, that meant she had arrived two xantem after the massacre, right after hell broke loose. Jace couldn't help but think about how she would have fared if she had arrived any earlier.

"Interesting, that's good you came after the Massacre."

Is it? Jace grumbled.

"Well, since we're on the topic of the massacre, laddies, how did ya two escape? Natasha said no one should have left there alive without shackles."

Aidan, as usual, flourished himself before taking a bow, halting their progress. With a brush of his scarlet-tinted black locks, he said, "Well, even as a young lad, I charmed the lady soldiers with my good looks."

Jace snorted, "Oh. Please."

"Oh yes, thank you, Jace," Aidan feigned insult.

The thief started laughing beside him, clutching her gut. "Oh, please, that's just … Oh, my stomach!"

"Aidan, the truth, please." Jace wiped a tear from his eyes. "No more lies."

Aidan gave an exaggerated sad expression. "You don't think I'm charming?"

"You're as charming as a snake," Jace said flatly.

Aidan narrowed his eyes. "Says the man so cold and charmless that a blade of ice manifested in the desert of all places."

"HA!" The thief cackled with a clap. "He got ya with that one!"

Jace rolled his eyes, folded his arms, and shook his head.

Aidan smirked triumphantly. "Yeah, thought so. Anyway, what I meant to say was that our parents—fended the soldiers off to help us escape."

It grew solemn so fast that even the wind started to calm, listening intently. Jace unfolded his arms, paying his own silent respects to his parents. "We escaped down an old well," Jace explained absently. "While they distracted the soldiers." That may have been more information than he needed to tell her, but she needed to know the reason why they were so intent on finishing this quest. It's not just that their home was taken, but their *everything* was taken. They were entrusted to take back their home for their parents, for their friends, for those who live, and for those who died. And it seemed that she knew it. Her face spoke it without words.

"Oh," she muttered.

Jace continued, "Our parents stocked an old cave with supplies in the East Durahti Forest—"

"—if we took one of the other paths in Bracklyn we would've passed it," Aidan interjected.

Undeterred by Aidan's interruption, Jace further explained, "—it was for emergencies. When the supplies were running low, I took up mercenary work; Aidan joined not too long after."

Aurora glanced at Jace. She quickly changed the subject. "Ya must've been pretty famous given yer strength."

Aidan shrugged, brushing his strands. "Eh, not really. Being a mercenary with morals isn't really that profitable. Not only that, we couldn't stray too far from the cave since it became a Seplechuran smuggle route, and we needed to watch their movements."

Aurora cocked her head, standing as her eyes rolled to one side in thought.

The brothers stopped. "What?" Jace asked, annoyed.

"Wait, did you all destroy field camps at all and raid shipments along that route?"

"When we couldn't get work, yes," Aidan answered.

Aurora stomped. "What! They blamed me fer that! I had to go into hiding fer days, if not weeks, when you two did that!"

The brothers shared a glance, their growing smiles blossoming into laughs.

"Why ya—" She cut her words short. Each of them glanced to the side, ears monitoring the sounds of the road. Something rumbled in the distance.

"Do you hear that?" Jace asked.

Aidan nodded. "Yeah. Aurora?"

"Aye."

The trio ducked behind the trees, keeping a steady eye out. Per Aidan's training, he leapt into the trees, hiding among the branches. He kept his keen eyes locked on the lookout. Jace awaited the information, but Aidan looked baffled, which immediately drew concern.

"What's wrong?" Jace called out.

"They're Utopians."

"Here?"

The thief chimed in, "That can't be right. Is it an army or a wagon?"

"Wagon," Aidan replied.

That made even less sense. Utopians wouldn't travel this far south for no reason; they must be after something in the desert or maybe to cut a deal with the Seplechurans, if they knew that, they were there.

"Allow me," the thief pushed by Jace.

"What are you doing?" he asked.

She gave an Aidan-like smirk. "I'm going to apply that experience Natasha was talking about, watch and learn. And wait fer my signal, okay, dobber?"

She went to the main road, walking normally. In time, the wagon crossed paths with her. She stopped in front of them; they stopped in front of her. Then she busted out in a Seplechuran folk song, "*Sud evot eveket lum!*"

The soldier paused, then joined her in the theme, fluent Seplechuran accents radiating from the seafoam green, stag-themed helmets.

The thief yelled a more vigorous verse, grabbing a soldier and locking arms with them. The two danced while the others clapped their hands enthusiastically, even Aidan was moving to the theme.

Jace noted the song had a nice tune to it, and the thief didn't sound bad. However, she didn't need to continue the farce. Clearly, they were Seplechuran; what was she waiting for?

The iquan that pulled the caravan became agitated with the singing, pawing at the floor and whipping its head around. The driver beat it with a stick before carrying on with the song. Jace grumbled at the mistreatment but kept his eyes mobile.

He nearly jumped at the wagon until he saw the gleam of jewelry in the corner of his vision. An avaricious-looking merchant jovially jumped out of the wagon to join the festivities. Jace could see the Seplechuran pale skin from where he was. A gleam shone in the thief's eye now, and seemingly the final act of proof that this was secretly a Seplechuran vessel. Jace nodded. *Clever, little beast.*

She swung around, dancing with the merchant woman, and everyone started clapping. Then, one swift motion later, she grabbed the merchant and placed a dagger to her neck.

"Oh laddies, come out and play."

Distracted, Jace, Aidan, Chuckle, and Snark made quick work of the soldiers and tied them up with some rope in the wagon. The trio gathered around the wagon, looking intently at the cargo.

"Look at all this stuff, laddies!" Aurora exclaimed.

"This is unreal, Jace," Aidan yelled, opening the crates of sewing material. "The goods back here are incredible! We never have to take another contract ever again!"

Jace didn't want to admit it, but El-above, this horde was quite the catch. These were probably used to curry favor with the Sov and fund the campaign. At least it will be funding *someone's* campaign.

"What are we going to do with all that food? There's no way we can eat all of it," Aidan exclaimed more.

The thief nearly drooled at the second barrel. "Hmm, I dunno about the food, but I'm definitely keeping some of these daggers. Shatersian daggers have great edges."

Aidan piped up again. "And some of the sewing material could be useful to me; can't say I will use all of it, but the merchant has taste, at least." Aidan spun his head. His eyes widened. "OH!" He picked up a golden ring of sorts, and he slipped it on his right bicep, giving it a once-over. "Chuckle, Snark, does it look like a cousin or what?"

The two chains came to life, shimmering with excitement at Aidan's new attire. The thief even gave him a compliment, too. There was no mistaking the red on Aidan's face.

Jace rolled his eyes, walking over to one of the soldiers, freeing him. "Go into the desert and call for help; they'll supply you with another wagon if any are available."

"They will come for you," the soldier seethed. "You should have killed me."

"The last person who said that to me is dead, so don't tempt me."

The soldier went his way, looking back every now and then. Once he was far enough away, Jace went to grab the reins. However, that's when the problem arose. "Great, an iquan."

It was one of the ficklest and most intelligent creatures of the mid-North to North regions. They resembled a horse with the fur of a large cat, the stripes of a tiger, the mane of a lion, and a face mixed with all three, and judging by its lavender coloring, it was from Seplechurus. This one, however, lacked the mane, meaning it had to be female. Jace further observed the purple fur with light purple stripes; *what did Aidan call that color again?* Regardless, the hooves were splayed into three parts, the nails manicured and elongated. The tail was the same light purple color as the stripes but thin and wavy. The face was what made it a true Seplechuran breed; it was not as long as a horse's face, and the teeth were sticking out the front. Its pupils were sharp but big. The whiskers didn't stick out; instead, they bent downward.

For once, Jace didn't need to read a book for this animal; his parents had two when he was growing up, and they hated him. Iquan usually listened to their owners and, strangely enough, chose their owners. If it chose one of the soldiers, they would have to pick up *another* stray. He grabbed the reins, only for the beast to pull away. Jace growled, only for it to hiss and then eat the grass. "Listen," Jace tried to reason with it, "I'm not going to beat you or anything; just move."

The iquan stared at Jace before looking away, hissing.

He pinched the bridge of his nose, sighing deeply. Aidan tapped him on the shoulder. "Is there a problem?"

"The dang beast won't move."

The beast looked offended, whipping its scruffy tail in a haughty manner. Aidan shook his head and then began stroking it. "Who's a good iquan? That's right, you," He spoke in a childish cooing voice. "You don't like the mean Jace and Seplechurans, do you? You just want some belly wubs." Aidan continued speaking in a childish manner while stroking the beast, and somehow, it began warming up to him. It stared at Aidan, and after a few seconds, it butted its head with Aidan's before laying its head on his shoulder. Even the Seplechurans were shocked at how well Aidan got along with it. "All it takes is some love, Jace."

Jace rolled his eyes.

Aidan continued to stroke the beast then, started speaking with it. The last time Jace saw this level of animal mastery, his parents were still alive. It seems it wasn't just their mother's sight that Aidan inherited. However, this meant something else important. Jace clapped Aidan on the shoulder. "That means you're driving."

Aidan frowned, but then he started to smile. An already bad omen. He returned the gesture. "That means you're stuck with Aurora in the back."

Jace wanted to reconsider, but the iquan made sure to mark its territory by striking the ground. He wasn't going to ride the beast at all. *This is going to be a long journey.*

20

Companionship is the Best Medicine

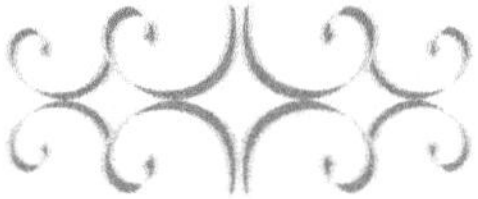

A journey is best with loved ones, right?
—The Wildcard

THIS IS EXACTLY what he was born for. Aidan held the reins on the iquan with excitement, journeying with his companions to seek out adventure and reputation. He wondered what things he would learn and what people they would see. Will they be friend or foe? Where would they hail from? Such questions filled his mind, and he couldn't resist a smile.

El only knew what awaited them in Utopia; what would it be like? He heard the stories of the vast and dense forests filled with glowing springs. Strange fruits and plants grew only in the nearby towns, and, of course, the capital city (conveniently named Utopia Capital) was designed like rings of a tree trunk. But the thing that excited him the most was a Vurhsan Stag. A rare stag made from roots and plants but still bled like a normal animal. Aidan almost wanted to cry; *what a beautiful union between plant and beast!* The book he read even had a picture, but it was half-finished since the stag scampered before the artist could complete it. *The mystery, the intrigue!* "I can't believe it! Utopia's only a few days away!" He received no reply. "Hey, you two haven't killed each other yet, have you?"

Aidan glanced through the window. Jace and Aurora were glaring at each other. It was almost as if one was waiting for the other to react. They were two dormant volcanoes, waiting for the smallest reaction so they could burst.

"You two do realize that we're going to be stuck together for a long time," Aidan said with a sigh.

Jace huffed, "This journey won't be that long."

"Yeah," Aidan added some deviousness to his voice, "but we're all going back to Bhall-Duraht. To live there. *Forever.*"

Jace became silent again. Aidan was not sure if that was a good sign or a bad one, but knowing his older brother, he was probably thinking. "C'mon guys, at least pretend to like each other."

"No," they both replied.

"Aww, see, there we go; you two idiots can agree on something."

"I think you need to focus on the road, Aidan," growled Jace.

Aidan chuckled, "Bold of you to assume I care what you think." That was false as much as it was funny. However, Jace never grew out of his rough mindset, and it just grew with him. Aidan let go of his past with hope, and Jace held onto it with vengeance.

"Just focus, okay?" Jace replied exasperatedly.

"Aye, what the laddie said," Aurora hesitantly agreed with Jace.

"Oh look, the thief is stealing my brother's words." Aidan looked back, seeing Aurora's surprised reaction. His usual instinct to smirk activated. "Oh, what? Just because I think you're cute doesn't mean you're free from my sarcasm. It's my natural defense against getting bored, so I better hear some conversation."

Chuckle and Snark laughed from their blades, mocking the others as much as Aidan did. Though annoying, Aidan couldn't help his words; he was built for annoyance, built for distraction, but most importantly, he was built for entertainment, even if the audience solely included himself. He didn't know if he could talk all day, but he was sure to try. They needed to come to an understanding, especially if they wanted to work together against Seplechurus. Aidan may not have been their most intelligent member, but even he knew this: companionship was half the journey. It made the bad times good and the good times even more so, but they were so stuck in some strange hatred for one another that they hadn't noticed the obvious.

Besides, making friends was one of the things his mother stressed. She knew the power of companionship, saying it showed her what it truly meant to live. Aidan didn't know how long it would take for Aurora and Jace to build a friendship; maybe it was later, maybe it was soon. Either way, he was the one who had to deal with them, and it was going to be glorious.

The night fell faster than he'd noticed. The two enemies in the back drifted off to sleep a few minutes ago, but Aidan was staring intently at the colors of purple, orange, blue, and pink that swarmed the skies above him. The mixture of colors lit something in his soul, filling him with a vibrance that couldn't be explained. Being born with Songluan eyes was such a privilege; his mother told him that people could not see color as beautifully as they did. He couldn't imagine seeing the world in such a dull state. He needed something that captured that vibrancy.

"Hey iquan, want to sleep off?" He asked as he noticed the slowed movement. "You rode all day; you must be tired."

There was a strange sound that was a mix between a neigh and a roar followed by a wide yawn.

"Jace, we're going to stop tonight," Aidan stated.

He heard his brother murmur awake. "You're right; the iquan is probably tired; you must be too."

"Kind of." Aidan shrugged.

"Don't be modest; you need rest. I'm not going to let you push yourself, okay?"

Aidan saluted. "Aye-aye, captain."

Camp was set up quickly after they stopped. Aidan unlatched the iquan from the wagon and allowed her to stretch out her tired legs. Afterward, Aidan led her to a nearby stream to drink. Jace set up the fire while Aurora handled the small meal. The forest made few sounds, an occasional bug here and there, but otherwise, nothing. Nothing until the firewood crackled harshly as the fire consumed it whole, soon to turn the wood to ashes.

"This is good, Aurora." Aidan licked his lips. "What is this?"

"Jerky stew, the wagon had some ingredients fer it."

Aidan swallowed the stew whole, including the floating chunks of meat, then held out his bowl for another serving. Aurora poured more into his bowl before filling her own.

"Where did you learn how to cook? Natasha doesn't seem like the type." Aidan stopped, realizing how rude that may have sounded.

Aurora swirled the spoon in her stew, playing with the meaty chunks, dunking them in the stew before they resurfaced. "My ma ..." she replied hollowly.

Aidan's eyes fell; he could already tell by her reaction what had happened. Jace, too, kept his eyes on his bowl, eating slowly.

"I'm, uh, sorry," apologized Aidan.

"It's alright. It happened a long time ago, laddie." Aurora finally took a sip of her stew. "Apologies won't bring her back."

Aidan slid in closer. "But they will make you feel better; the apologies aren't for her; they're for you."

She grew silent, and Aidan was sure he had said something wrong. The pain of loss is a strange beast; even he, who still hoped his parents were alive, had to come to terms with the fact that he might be wrong. But at least he knew he had a measure of hope. How much more devastating is it for someone who had no hope?

Abruptly, he finished with his soup. His appetite had flung away, gone with the breeze.

Jace, however, got up, fetching more of the soup for himself, not looking at anyone as he did so. Before sitting down beside the fire, he looked back. "Good recipe."

Was he trying to cheer her up? Yeesh, he was terrible at it, like an iquan kit trying to swim in a horrible storm, terrible. But Aidan had to commend the fact that Jace tried; maybe he was warming up to her. However, seeing how pessimistic he was about their parents' mortality, maybe that was sympathy. The quandary went back and forth in his mind.

"Well, I'm off to bed." Aidan groaned as he stood. "Thanks for the food, Aurora. It beats Jace's cooking." He knew Jace agreed.

"Yer welcome."

"Who has the first shift?" Aidan asked.

"Me," Jace said flatly, "you get some rest."

Aidan yawned with a stretch, looking from branch to branch, finding a thick one where he could lay his head. Though with most of them swirled to the sky, it would be difficult for him to find one. He eventually settled for the iquan's fur. It was comfortable. He drifted into a deep, deep slumber—

No.

His mind was a fallen branch drifting into the chaotic sea. His thoughts were clouded with black smoke, suffocating his optimism and burning down his mental shields.

It's the nightmare again.

He had to be asleep; how seamless the transition was from fatigue to nightmare. His home stared at him through burning eyes and smoke-dripped skin. This time, no parents, no people, just him—and that thing.

He couldn't move this time; in fact, he couldn't speak either. It was just him and the roaring flames engulfing his town. The soft, shifty sands stiffened like grained corpses, losing their luster and their flexibility of form. There was only fear and fire.

Aidan held his throat, trying to speak, but something caught his words. A large fireball started to pour from the flame wall. It was blinding, scorching. The heat tore at his skin until he could feel nothing. Then, it sought to consume him.

Aidan startled awake, drenched in sweat just like Bhall-Duraht. The iquan nudged him, brushing the sweat from his brow. He quietly apologized; his rising temperature probably made the beast extremely uncomfortable. "Great, now my clothes stink." Aidan stood, and the iquan stood with him. He comforted her, telling her to stay put. He walked silently by Jace.

Snap!

He leapt. The firewood sizzled quietly, and then it snapped again. Aidan swallowed a lump, clutching his chest, only to feel his heart trying to escape. He softened his breath, continuing to where he got water for his mount.

Though it was dark, he could perceive the smallest lights with his special eyes, including the light of the occasional fireflies.

He rubbed his temples. "That nightmare again. What was that thing?"

Aidan brushed off the ideas from his head. It seemed that returning to Bhall-Duraht must have triggered some dormant memories, but it was concerning why Jace wasn't in them. "Guess I'll say something in the morning—"

He halted. There was a glint of daggers in the faint moonlight, the shape he knew; those were Aurora's. Now that he thought about it, she should've been on watch if Jace was asleep, but by the looks of it, she was freshening up. The novels he read told him that approaching her could end in two ways: there would be a beautiful night in his future or the most brutal slap he'll ever receive.

Aurora's personality was telling enough. He decided to move further upstream; maybe she wouldn't hear him.

After he washed himself and his clothes, he returned to bed, praying to El that his dreams would no longer be plagued with nightmares. El answered.

21

Now, The Green

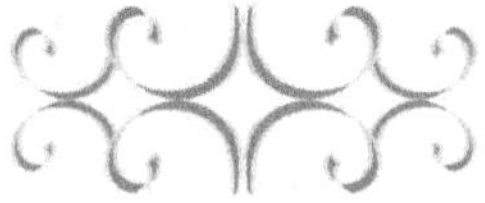

The wild doesn't feel as peaceful anymore.
—The Thief

SHE FOUND IT a lot more challenging to sleep in the wild. The air didn't sit right in her lungs, the ground didn't tremble under her feet, and the space—anything could attack from anywhere. Waking in the four walls of a building provided her with a lot more security than she had hoped to admit. The wild had no such protection. Wondrously scary, it was so much freedom that she didn't know what to do with it. Xantem ago, she would curse herself for thinking in such a way, now, not so much.

She stretched her arms, the orange light peeking through her eyelids. The pop in her shoulder told her to stop stretching and take in her environment. Aidan still slept, the iquan was sleeping soundly beside him. She didn't need to look for the dobber. A harsh breeze startled her with its wintry bite.

She rubbed her hazel eyes and then made her way over to him, *might as well see how he is fairing with his new toy.* The closer she got, the air grew colder, sharper. Honestly, it refreshed her; it reminded her of home.

Now, snow started to tickle her warm beige skin, greeting her to the winter land that was the dobber's domain.

Her eyes were greeted by large pillars of ice, five of them standing as tall as the trees. The dobber was in the middle, channeling the wind to his command. It started to dance through the leaves and branches, making them hum an unnatural tune. At first, it seemed unintentional, but Aurora noticed small holes in each of the pillars, *the laddie's making music.* But that wasn't the strange part; it was that he was smiling widely. He conjured the wind again, letting the snow-filled gales pass through the pillars with impressive control, that is, until he saw her. The wind notes fell flat, and the snow became drearier than it had been before. His smile was replaced with a scowl, and Aurora remembered why she hated him so much.

"Thief." He sheathed his Blade, sending a forceful wind that shattered the pillars of ice. They fell with a deafening rumble causing her to shield her ears.

"Dobber." She rubbed her ears.

"Where were you last night?" He stomped toward her.

Aurora shuddered. *He noticed I was gone?* She took a step back, averting her eyes, but she felt his glare. As that mountain of a man inched closer and closer, her legs quaked, and her hands began to move on their own.

"I was just washing up." That wasn't technically a lie.

"Do you think you can lie to me? You were supposed to be on watch."

She clutched her arms while inching back. Her legs rattled; it could have been the Blade, at least, that's the excuse she wanted to admit. "I'm not lying!"

"Then why do you look so guilty, thief?"

She finally made eye contact to yell, "Because ya have that ice thing in yer hand! Who wouldn't feel just a bit intimidated by that?"

His voice became a low growl, "You better not be doing anything that'll impede our progress."

She looked defiantly into his eyes, staring him down though she couldn't match his scary height. "I wasn't doing anything to hurt yer little quest."

His eyes narrowed, then he scoffed, reverting his Blade back to its normal form. "Listen, I don't trust you. The only reason you're here is because of Aidan and Natasha."

The redness rose to her face, her frown turning into a scowl. "Ya have been nothing but a stupid, controlling dobber since I met ya! Ya act like yer somebody's master!"

She bit her tongue; she said too much. A different shade of redness rose in her cheeks, one much drearier, clouding her heart with stormy visions.

His expression softened. "I'm not anybody's master; I just want to protect what I care about." He stepped closer. "So, if you do anything that hurts Aidan or my town—" he poked her shoulder. "—I'll deal with you myself."

She clenched her fist as he walked by. Everything he did made her feel less human. He was a reminder of what she hated about those stern, authoritative types.

She reached inside her boot, grabbing her dagger, and he knew; he turned on his heel, scabbard in hand. The flash of blade and scabbard glinted in the morning sun, the clouds above eager to see how it would turn out. But then she heard the chimes.

Snark grabbed her, chiming lowly in a mocking tone. Chuckle grabbed Jace, wrapping both his arms.

Aidan sauntered over, still yawning, but with both his blades drawn. "Ladies, please. What did I tell you two about going outside without your chaperone?"

Aurora gasped. Something about being bound made her feel so weak that she struggled, but Snark only tightened his grip. Her breaths became heavy, and her heart stuttered to motion. She had no idea if the fear reached her eyes, but it was enough for Aidan to let them both go. She eased a little, and her shoulders fell like her heavy breaths.

"I leave you two alone for one night, and you're trying to kill each other," he sheathed a blade to press a dramatic hand to his chest. "Without me? I'm appalled."

The corner of her lips lifted slightly; even the dobber's did too, but when they locked eyes, the scowls returned.

"Oh, stop it," he pushed both of them away from one another. "Jace, you're driving Zania, Aurora, you're in the back.

"Zania?" Jace asked with a quirked brow.

"Yeah, I named the iquan. It was kind of tiring calling her 'the iquan.'"

"She's not going to let me on the reins."

"I know, that's why you're going to cut a tree and use your dormant carpentry skills to make a wider seat. We should have some fasteners in the back. You're staying with me since I can't trust you two to play nice."

Somehow, he diffused the problem, just like Ruben did. It was strange for Aurora to see someone talk down a problem she would have otherwise solved with a dagger, but maybe that's why they were kin, and maybe that's what Natasha saw in him. She couldn't trust the smile too much; she knew she couldn't, but he kept reeling her in. It wasn't what he did but how he did it.

"Aurora," Aidan called.

"Aye?"

"Sorry about the chains. I'm sure it's not fun being wrapped up."

She simply nodded, clutching her wrists. He took it as his cue to leave. Aurora stood there, still massaging her wrists, remembering the feeling of being bound. "Never again," she muttered.

After a small breakfast with the local fruits, the team began to move again. The new seat in front was done crudely, but Aidan did mention that Jace's skills were dormant. Aurora didn't complain; however, the entire wagon was hers save for the barrels of goods they had, and without the dobber taking up so much space along with the barrels, she had room to stretch.

The next couple of days were much the same as the previous: she would fight with Aidan's kin, Aidan could break it up, and they all journeyed in silence. It grew tiring, and she could see Aidan slowly losing more and more of his smile. She couldn't imagine how Aidan felt breaking up her fights all the time. He always had a smile, but she could feel his sanity slowly slipping away. A part of her wanted to see his breaking point, to see where the smiles would fade away like dust—*no—I shouldn't think like that*, but she couldn't help it. His kin's breaking point was apparent, or maybe something deeper troubled him, but she wouldn't like to find that out. She wondered if Aidan was worse; the nicer ones tended to have darker emotions. Hopefully, that was something she didn't have to see; begrudgingly or not, she liked him just the way he was.

Utopian Traffic, ugh. They finally made it to the central trade routes, but as expected, the roads were crowded and noisy. The cacophony of iquan and horses was deafening, ruining whatever sleep she desired, but the merchants were even more annoying, stopping wagons at every turn just to sell something. It was funny to see the laddies unable to speak properly to a merchant despite growing up in Bhall-Duraht. While they haggled well, some of the merchants got the better of them with things they knew nothing about. They made some horrible purchases, but Aurora had no problem stealing back the coin when no one was watching. The wagons eventually moved at a slow pace, but the team finally realized why the traffic was so intense.

"Darn it, a toll," Aidan said; he looked to his kin, "Do we have any gold left?"

The dobber reached into a small coin purse, and the faint jingling disturbed Aurora's ears. That was a sound she was not used to. One must always have their coin purse full when traveling. It was such an essential rule.

The laddies approached the toll gate, scared out of their heads. The Utopian soldier spoke up, "*Flarion end dublet.*" She repeated in common-tongue. "Toll and search."

"How much?" Aidan asked rather calmly.

"Depends on your cargo," she motioned for the guards to search. They carefully inspected every part of the wagon. The seafoam green-clad warriors were nearly startled when they saw Aurora in the back. She winked, putting up her hands to prove she didn't have any weapons. They squinted, seeing a Hericonian, but fortunately, the Seplechurans they had stolen the wagon from had outfitted it for Utopian merchants, so they were sure to let them slide. The soldiers simply checked around her, looking at the barrels and such. One reached over her; the horrible stench of sweat filled her nostrils. She wanted to gasp for air, but instead, she smiled sweetly when he finished their search.

The soldiers retreated to their presumably commanding officer and then whispered something to her. She approached the brothers, saying, rather worriedly, "Are you aware there is a Delfizcani girl in your wagon?" She enunciated her words with the banner in hand.

Jace sighed, "Unfortunately."

Aidan smiled. "Yes."

There was a brief pause; maybe the officer was expecting something else, but she somehow didn't get it. There was an exasperated sigh before she delivered the price, "Fifty-five coin."

Aurora watched humorously as the laddies couldn't produce the coin. They sifted through the air of the purse, hoping that El would drop coin from the Abode. After a moment of contained red-faced glee, Aurora produced another coin purse, "Oh, laddies, ya fergot yer other coin purse, back here."

Aidan played along perfectly. "Oh, there it is; I thought we were stolen from."

Aidan handed the proper coin, and the team was off.

Once they were far enough, Jace spoke, "Thief, explain."

"Ya got swindled with all those merchants; I just took some of yer coin back; yer welcome. Ya'll are from Bhall-Duraht AND are mercenaries; how did ya let that happen?"

"I knew the price for that fruit case was really high! They were supposed to be exotic!" Aidan exclaimed.

The older Camerus sighed once again, "That still doesn't make it right."

"Hey, I just evened the deal. I didn't steal what was his."

Either out of fatigue or admittance, Aurora noticed Jace said nothing. She saw Aidan sigh with relief as the disagreement didn't turn into another fight. Even Aurora was too tired to go at the laddie again.

The day was long, but Utopia Capital was only an hour away, and soon their trip was going to end. Aurora was less than thrilled; all she did was cook and argue, nothing was genuinely as exciting as she had hoped. Once they returned to Bhall-Duraht, it would be the same old; maybe she would steal from fewer people, and she might mess with the Utopians more if they say yes to the proposal. But those were plans for later, she decided. Right now, she needed to drift off to sleep.

22

CHANGE OF PLANS

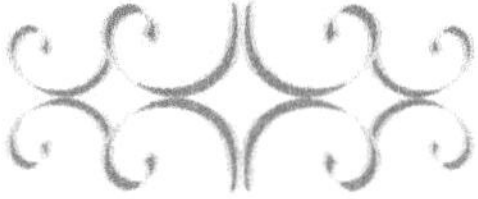

It is expedient that we move quickly.
—The Rose

IT MADE SENSE now, the reason why the Seplechurans were moving south. Natalie knew her people wouldn't just settle for destruction; the town of Bhall-Duraht had too much strategic significance. Most people thought the Seplechurans destroyed Bhall-Duraht because the storytellers knew where the Blades were, or at the very least, they had the most lore and stories containing them.

In truth, she pitied the town despite not agreeing with its creation. Bhall-Duraht touted itself as a haven for people who wanted to escape the politics and control of the kingdoms, a place where everyone, no matter their background, could start over.

Truthfully, Natalie loved that sentiment, a place where people didn't have to be held down by lineage or past. However, as much as she loved second chances, she couldn't agree with that town. The people that gathered there were cowards or lawless blights. She couldn't help but think that those people simply were escaping the rules and cultures that built them up. She heard people abandoning their names, their clans, their families for this *second life*. That town didn't give hope to those who wanted second chances; no, it simply bred cowardice. Those people ran from their lives; they were shameful in every facet—yet even they didn't deserve what happened xantem ago.

Natalie opened her eyes; she sat quietly in the foyer before the great doors that led to the throne room. She rarely got to visit the castle for reasons incredibly obvious to her, but that did not stop her from admiring its beauty.

As with all homes, Utopian houses had *Jeerihat,* a hometree, in commontongue, growing in the middle of the structure. The largest of these, the Jireh Tree, the largest tree on the continent, grew in the middle of the castle. Its roots lined and strengthened the corners of the walls. Flowers sprouted on the roots; ones that released a calming scent. Several times Natalie had to fight the lustful touch of sleep.

The Jireh Tree *is* Utopia; even with Natalie's own roses, she could feel the life that surged beneath her feet. Utopia was beautiful, inside and out—only if all its people were the same.

"Utopian Rose," a soldier approached, his stag helmet saddled at his side. He flipped his dark brown hair, revealing a blinded left eye. He seemed much too young for scars, but war can be unforgiving. He appeared to be Kojcut, a name for Utopians who have Seplechuran blood in them, many xantem ago when the Seplechuran empire extended this far south.

"Soldier," she greeted by standing, "is Great General Johannus ready for me?"

"Almost." He straightened his posture. "He is reading some missives; it appears that one of them has him troubled."

Natalie crossed her arms. "Is it from war front?"

The man shook his head. "I don't think it's that kind of concern … but I'm sure he will tell you." The man moved in closer. "The missive had the Setas-Lisian royal seal. You know the Great General's reaction to those."

Natalie nodded but subtly hinted for the man to step back. She needn't look around to feel the eyes on them.

The man chuckled, "You fight and nearly die several times, you would think the suspicions would end."

"Princess sympathizers … *dugavka*."

The man smiled. "Watch your tongue, Rose. You don't want to get us in trouble."

Moments like these were why Natalie hated politics and the culture surrounding it. Instead of passing the crown to the next son as in normal kingdoms, Utopian royalty must campaign for the crown if there is more than one capable heir. This often led to heightened tensions in the streets. While the campaign trail had slowed down because of the war, many people still argued the main points: the prince wanted new clans to form, especially ones for the Kojcut and Pachra, whereas the princess did not, in hopes of preserving old traditions.

"I do not care who wins," Natalie said sternly. "As long as it does not get us killed."

The man rolled his eyes with a laugh, but his voice dropped in exasperation. "Spoken like someone who is *not* going to stay in Utopia after the war."

"Leaving has crossed my mind …"

"Well—" the man's words were cut off as he turned his head for a moment, then turned to face her. "The roots have spoken. The Great General is ready for you."

"Thank you."

The man inclined his head. "See you on the war front, Utopian Rose."

"Same with you, soldier."

The man walked down the right hall, while she walked forward from where he had come. A slight smile on her face came and went. Natalie quickly made her way down to the hall, where a smaller yet still imposing metal door, covered in vines, stood. The Vurhsan Stag was emblazoned on the front, equal on both sides of the door. The soldiers in front pressed their antler pikes into the ground before opening the door.

Natalie smoothed her gambeson and stood straighter. She placed a hand on the butt of her cutlass, standing resolutely as the wind from the door battered her. With a nod to the soldiers, she walked in. The Great General's whitened brows were knit, the creases from his brow merging perfectly with the wrinkles on the rest of his frame.

"Lass, belay your journey south," he commanded without looking at her. He laid the missive softly on his wooden, well-curved desk that oddly stood in the middle of the room.

"May I ask why?" she questioned softly.

He motioned for her to sit in one of the seats in front of his desk, and she obliged.

"As you know, Seplechuran units have been moving around the southern edge of the continent. What you don't know is that the king wants to move in full force to the south, but he needed your espionage team to give accurate assessments."

The king? Requested for her directly? She was flabbergasted, knowing that this was much more recognition than she'd received from the Utopian monarchy in such a long time. *Did Utopian crown think situation that dire?* "What has changed?" she asked. The Great General handed her the missive, with eyes wide. She realized the problem. "Nicklaus—is coming here?"

"To see Bhall-Duraht, no less. He suspects the secret of the Blades is down there."

Natalie's brow knitted in the same way as Johannus's did as the contemplation began to set in. "If my people are really there—they may have already found …"

"Indeed. Nicklaus is a scholar on the Blades—an expert on these matters. If he's going, we might already be too late."

Natalie continued to read, her knit brow raised in confusion. "Then why is he requesting dinner?"

Johannus leaned forward. "He does not know the gravity of what Utopia has been dealing with. I will use this dinner to inform him and suggest that he request aid from his father if the situation is as dire as we fear."

"That is wise."

The Great General rubbed the small of his neck, his knit features softening, a smudge of red underlay his features. "I was—hoping you could join us."

"Of course, I will join."

The Great General cleared his throat. "It's a formal dinner."

Oh no. "Please, Great General, do not make me do this."

He put out his hands pleadingly. "It's the prince," he whispered.

Natalie closed her eyes, inhaling slowly. She could not believe this betrayal; she could already hear the other soldiers—and Nicklaus.

"Very well." She got up, not even waiting for the Great General to thank her. It was her worst nightmare. She had to put on a dress—with a bow.

23

A Princely Arrival

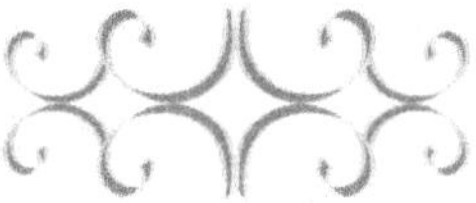

It took so long to even escape that prison.
—The Prince

HAVING GILDED WALLS didn't make it any less of a jail. The hatred of knowledge in the Setas-Lisian castle made Nicklaus's stomach churn. *In these perilous days, people needed to seek the truth instead of each other's throats,* he surmised.

Nicklaus rode into the forest city wearing the drabbest of robes he could find, a white doublet with golden breeches. He kept his rapier at his side; the basket hilt design and ruby-studded gems may have been a bit much, but he had an excuse for why he had it. The only giveaway to his identity was his flowing blond hair, which he had trouble hiding, though he made a small ponytail to fall with the rest of his hair, so instead, he settled for spectacles, also to aid his sore vision and further hide his identity. He thought he blended in with the peasantry nicely, especially since he was able to run away before his guards could assemble. His guards' disdain for knowledge and their otherwise stern presence would have made his journey to the sands much harder than it needed to be.

"It seems we have arrived Jacques," he said to his chestnut horse.

The city of Utopia Capital was as beautiful as he had remembered it, the hardwood homes arranged in circular patterns around the castle. Roots growing over the houses, flowers budding from each one, and of course, the shaved grass pathways, but the best aspect was the Hometrees, the giant trees that grew in the center of every home, symbolizing the flourishing family within. Though Nicklaus was no Utopian, he endeavored to have one for his own home one day. "We must find Uncle Johannus; he will grant us safe passage through the desert."

Jacques seemingly neighed in reply. Nicklaus petted him as he kept riding through the city.

The people of Utopia always had a wondrous commotion about them: women stirring up stories as they prepared food for their families, men trading advice as they tended to their gardens; it was all so very charming; however, there were certain sounds that felt out of place. Three travelers, wearing rather exquisite clothing, were filled with smiles and awe as they looked around the great city. Though one of them was much larger than the prince, it didn't stop the childlike wonder streaming from his eyes like stardust. The other smaller, male's smile couldn't be hidden or contained. They were probably diplomats from the desert, Nicklaus pondered; maybe Bhall-Duraht was not as uncivilized as he had previously thought. He took it upon himself to educate them, of course, as a more knowledgeable sort. "Hello," he approached with a princely smile, hopping off Jacques. "Is this your first time here?"

The trio focused their eyes on him, and at once, he made his observations. The large one in the cloak was very muscular, far too muscular for a diplomat; maybe his occupation lies in protection. He held his weapon with such force. Despite his wonder, he was ready for war. He answered, "Yes, we are here on an important task."

"Ah, so you must be diplomats." Nicklaus huffed with pride at his seemingly correct assumption.

The sleeveless one spoke, "Yes! It is actually more of a military matter."

Nicklaus quickly noticed that the younger one possessed two blades and bore little problem flaunting his build with that immodest outfit. He couldn't have been a diplomat, but his charisma betrayed his weaponry.

Nicklaus smiled. "A military matter? Has the desert come to its senses to choose a side?"

The large man grumbled, clutching his sword tighter. Nicklaus pretended to ignore it, such a protective nature, especially over his home. Such patriotism would be better served for Setas-Li, but if they eventually chose to be allies, Nicklaus could possibly have his aid.

"The desert wishes to provide resources; such is the reason we came with a wagon of goods," the immodest one answered. "Such immaculate kingdoms such as Utopia—" he paused with a bigger smile, "—and even the great Setas-Li deserve such resources."

Such diplomacy! The desert is truly evolving into a cultured society. Nicklaus was determined to visit to help them in their pursuit of culture. He could possibly provide books for their education. But he needed to hurry there first. He had matters to attend to. "If it is military matters you seek, then it would be wise to consult the Great General. I was on my way to see him now."

"That would be helpful if you could get us an audience," the white-cloaked one spoke, releasing the strong grip from the pommel of his sword.

The immodest one yawned, "Now? No way, we just got here; let's find an inn, then look around. Business can wait until later."

What diplomat pushes their duties until later? Maybe the trip is simply that perilous. Nicklaus wanted to shake his head, but he kept his nice smile throughout as the two similarly looking diplomats quarreled.

The large one demanded with a grumble, "I say we consult the general now."

The immodest one replied with a cross of his arms, "Says the person who didn't drive the full way."

Exasperated, the bigger one replied, "I would've if I could've."

"But you still didn't drive."

"Laddies!" the Delfizcani girl yelled, "let's just settle fer the inn."

The white-cloaked one frowned. "I don't take orders from you."

The small girl stood in the face of opposition, glaring at her opponent as her people did to Nicklaus's own. "Yer kin is tired, he decides," she finally spoke.

"That settles it," the immodest one clapped, "we're heading to the inn."

Nicklaus interjected, "If you are pursuing that venture, then here." He reached into his horse satchel and pulled out three tickets. "These are passes for Jireh Inn. They will provide all your needs for free."

The Delfizcani raised a brow. "Ya have these how …?"

"I'm," Nicklaus coughed, "a scholar; my other companions were to accompany me, but they grew ill."

If the Royal Court has taught Nicklaus anything, it was to lie, fake smiles, and use sweet words. He did not need to tell them anything; he just needed the desert. Their arrival was ordained by Yehowehel. Nicklaus now just needed to keep them in Utopia.

The immodest one took them with a smile. "Aurora, please, don't look a gift iquan in the mouth, yes?" He turned to Nicklaus. "Graciousness upon graciousness, you Setas-Lisians are amazing. Thank you—?"

"Nicklaus," he blurted. He mentally cursed at himself for using his real name.

The immodest diplomat lifted a hand. "Well, Nicklaus, I'm Aidan, this mountain is my brother Jace, and this is our companion, Aurora. I would introduce you to Zania, but she is with the wagon."

Nicklaus shook Aidan's hand, noting the firmness and strength it had. He was most definitely a warrior. "Charmed. It is really a pleasure to see diplomats. I hope your dealings come through."

"Yours too, scholar."

Nicklaus mounted Jacques once more, then followed the path he memorized from his youth. Each Ring of Utopia had a checkpoint that required a thorough search to pass. Once he confirmed his intentions multiple times, he finally reached his destination, a small gate on the outskirts of the inner wall.

Two guards stood in front of the Jireh root fence that protected the home of the Great General. Nicklaus dismounted Jacques, smiling once more.

"Name?" the guard asked.

Nicklaus removed his glasses and unfurled his hair, giving the guards seconds to recognize him. They fell to the floor immediately; their stag helmets which they wore, now placed beside their bowed heads. "Our apologies, your highness."

"Not so loud. Is my elfather home?"

"Nicklaus." A voice above him made his heart leap. He nearly tipped over at the sight of Raven, his pet name for Natalie, sitting on one of the support pillars of the fence. Her legs crossed, hands resting comfortably on her knees. The sun silhouetted her, but Nicklaus knew the crow-black eyes were staring down at him.

"Natalie! You startled me."

"It is not hard. You never look up."

He did not notice his hand clutching his heart, but once he did, he did not bother to remove it. She gracefully jumped off the pillar with a twirl, landing behind him with a flourish of her ominously dark locks. "Uncle Johannus is here, but he is preparing dinner with Aunt Eleanor."

Nicklaus finally put his hand down, but his heart remained unaware. He turned to face Johannus' house, then turned back to Natalie. "That will take a while. I wish to not be delayed, but it seems Yehowehel has other plans." Nicklaus pondered that he could settle in the Jireh Inn, but perhaps it could be wiser to head to the library to find some solace. Maybe, he further thought, the diplomats would be there; the Utopian Library was known for holding many bits of knowledge.

"Anything I can help you with?" Natalie asked.

"*Non, everé o vel.* (No, everything is well.) I will not trouble you."

She bowed, eyes focused away from him. He'd only seen her like that a handful of times—those were most definitely her worried eyes.

"Does something trouble you, Raven?" he asked.

She faced him with a faint smile. "It has been a while since you have called me Raven."

He smiled softly. "You have not been listening. But, I would like my question addressed."

She sighed, keeping her eyes on his. "What concerns me should not bother you, so I will not let it."

"Is it the dress?" He teased flatly.

She squinted, inclining her head seconds later before disappearing into the darkness of the nearby trees. The way she melted in the darkness made even the shadows jealous. Her reputation earned her many names, but she did not respond to many of them. It was an honor he felt that she not only acknowledged his name for her but responded to it. It was truly hard to believe that they were antagonistic to one another at one point. Though, he may rekindle that if she truly was wearing a dress.

Nicklaus shook his head, refusing to get lost in his own thoughts. He decided to seclude himself in the library, despite the pleasantries, despite the friends; he needed to pursue his goal.

The voice of his father rang in his mind, telling him how he was prophesied to be the king who would lead Setas-Li into a new golden age. He remembered the promises of grandeur, of an amazing future that he would trailblaze, but in order for that to come to pass, for Setas-Li to seek triumph not only in this war but also in history, he needed a Blade from Yehowehel—and he would stop at nothing to retrieve it.

24

Mend Thy Torn Kin

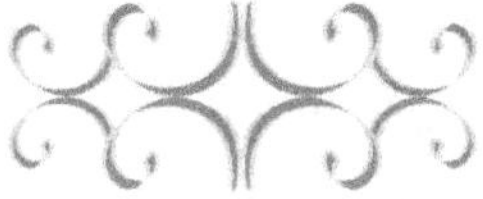

Not sure how long I can keep this up.
—The Wildcard

AIDAN DID NOT know how long he could play mediator between the two; they made it hard for him even to think about or enjoy the scenery of Utopia. Though it wasn't his job to make them friends, he thought it would be better if they were. The way they glared at each other was so spiteful, as if they'd held a vendetta against each other for xantem. The white-hot hatred between them had to be something deeper, something Aidan had to figure out before they returned to Bhall-Duraht.

"I can't believe you flattered that Setas-Lisian," growled Jace.

"Hey, Setas-Lisians like their egos stroked. Do that and they're as obedient as dogs." He waved the tickets in his brother's face. "See what I mean? But uh … anyone else think it's bad that we don't know where Jireh Inn is?"

Jace groaned. "Well, we wouldn't have this problem if you just asked him instead of acting."

Aurora piped up to Aidan's defense. She took the passes from him and shook them in front of Jace. "Well, what would ya have him do? He got us a place to stay and some food, what did *ya* do?"

Jace glared at Aurora, probably thinking of the ways he could ice her. "I didn't ask for your opinion, thief."

"I wasn't waiting fer yer permission."

Aidan groaned. "Can we push off the fighting to later?" But the human fires at his sides were stoking more and more; he felt their presence burn him—and he didn't like how fire felt. The glares went through his head as they locked each other down with heated looks, waiting for the first move as an excuse to devour.

Jace exclaimed, "You're a disrespectful, lawless cretin. I don't even know how Aidan and Natasha convinced me to bring you along."

Aurora stopped to point a finger at Jace. "Oh? I'm lawless, eh? Ya didn't say anything when I stole back that coin fer the toll."

Jace stomped his foot. "That's all you do, steal! What do you actually do for yourself? You can't make a living leeching off others!"

Aidan put up a finger in an attempt to interject. "Um, guys."

People all around started to stare, and even the soldiers looked as if they were ready to pounce on them at any moment.

"The entire 'leeching-off-of-others' thing again?" Aurora yelled. "Are ya running out of reasons to hate me, or are you making it up as ya go?"

Focused on her, Aidan made a split-second mental note: *Oh, I need to write that one down.* Out loud, he interjected to both Aurora and Jace, "Can we please calm down? People are watching." Aidan pressed a hand on both their shoulders.

Their steps toward one another ceased, but their sinister glares did not. Aidan tried to press harder for them to create some space, but it wasn't much use, well, not without hurting Aurora.

Jace continued to yell. "The fact that you take leeching with no reverence at all means you would have no problem hurting others to get what you want."

Aurora shot back. "I would never—"

"—then what were you doing the other night?" Jace interjected. "Clearly, you weren't watching the wagon for wild animals."

Aurora stepped back, unable to fix her eyes on Jace. Aidan noticed the small tremble in her fingers, her pupils began to dilate, and her legs weren't as sturdy with defiance as they once were. Her eyes were frighteningly identical to the look she made the other day when Aidan wrapped the two of them. It seemed to paralyze her. This was something deeper. He turned to his brother, pushing him a bit harder. "Jace, stop. That's enough."

Jace clenched his teeth, grinding them like steel. He slapped Aidan's hands away before pointing a finger at him. "You're taking her side?! We're supposed to be brothers, Aidan."

Aidan stomped his foot, pointing a rage-filled finger at his brother. "Don't. You. Dare. I have been *nothing* but a brother to you!"

"So, being a brother means taking her side over mine?"

People started to gather, parents holding their children back. Families were slightly scared by the tone of the heated argument.

Aidan spoke through clenched teeth, trying to restrain his anger. "Why is it always sides with you? Why is it always about you?! 'I'm the leader-this', 'I'm the leader-that', so, what am I? Your slave?!"

Jace physically jerked when he heard the word slave; his face changed for a moment, but just for a few seconds. "Don't change the subject, this is about her. She was helpful in the Bhall-Duraht fight, but other than that, that girl is useless!"

Aidan tried to convince himself that the words weren't directed at him; he knew it, yet a hollow void filled his chest. Those words were crushing, soul-shattering even. He could only look at Aurora and she didn't even seem present. Her body shook as she started to take some steps back, lips trembling before the tears started to set in. Again, she began to clutch her wrists. Aidan caught sight of the pain in her eyes and finally understood that distant look. She threw the passes at Jace, her small freckles drowned in the redness. "Fine! Take yer stupid passes! I hated both of ya anyway!"

"Aurora, wait!" Aidan called, but before he could step forward, she mustered some newfound speed and ran off. The crowd was so thick that Aidan lost sight of her nearly immediately. He picked up the passes, staring at them with glittering eyes coiled with redness and steam. "You can be an idiot, you know that?" Aidan clenched the passes, shaking them tightly, "You want to be some great leader, but you lack trust for anyone." He faced Aurora's direction, but before he moved further, he turned, spite forming in his eyes. Jace, for once, seemed almost regretful, but Aidan didn't care. "Mother and Father would be *so* proud of the leader you've become." With that, Aidan threw one pass at Jace. It weakly smacked off his chest and fell to the floor. Aidan hoped that he left Jace with something to think about because this problem would cost him all that he attempted to be.

Aidan tried tracking Aurora, but she left no trace. Sometimes, she seemed like a ghost, with how fast and quietly she moved. Everywhere Aidan looked, he couldn't find her. He had some pride in being able to find anything he wanted due to his Songluan eyes, yet this proved to be a challenge. "Where could she be?!" Aidan stood on a building talking to himself. His eyes searched around; she was nowhere to be seen. Aidan fell to his knees, defeated. He smacked his forehead several times before settling with a sigh. "Sorry, Aurora." Aidan bathed in the sun's warm rays; he shielded his eyes as he stared at it, remembering the last time he felt so helpless:

His mind drifted to many xantem ago, when he was training with his brother for the liberation of Bhall-Duraht. Everything Jace could do, Aidan couldn't. Anything Jace could lift, Aidan couldn't. He wanted to give up. He called himself a failure—a useless son. But in the back of his mind, in his heart really, he heard his mother cheering him on. From then on, he tried, and he found what he was good at. He found *Aidan*. That's why he couldn't believe his parents were gone; he wanted to show them—*him*.

Everyone needed that person in life, Aidan learned. Aurora needed that person in her life. Aidan concluded it in his heart. "I have to find her." Aidan scoured the city as fast as he could, surely a Delfizcani girl so far from home couldn't be too hard to find.

He paused in the middle of the street; running around a city he was unfamiliar with would be useless. No, he needed to *know* Aurora to find her. Now, he was scouring his mind: What did she like that would give him a clue? She's fond of thieving, daggers, and breaking into places, but that wouldn't help. She was fond of her home, but that wouldn't do her any good.

Aidan growled at his latest revelation; he'd been attracted to this woman for a few weeks now, but he never got to know *her*, not the one who steals, but the one who lies beneath that. She didn't make it easy, he conceded, but was he trying hard enough? Aidan cursed at himself. *Maybe I should've approached her at the lake. Wait, lake.* "Excuse me," Aidan stopped a passing man. "Do you know where the nearby lake is?"

"Oh, some lakes, right?" His accent—light and breathy. "We have some washing areas in the south side of the city. Since it's afternoon light, it'll be where most of the lasses are leaving, holding pottage, mind you. Ya can't miss it."

"Thank you!"

Aidan rushed to the southern part of the city ring, following the man's instructions. The need to rectify things found itself to be the driver of Aidan's movements. His parents told him to be his brother's eyes, and sometimes Jace couldn't see where he was wrong; now was a time to change it.

Aidan halted in front of an area with large, overwhelming trees, and, like the man had said, women were leaving there by the dozen, holding pottage—mind him. The trees were marked with some words, but Aidan could only make out *freshe*, which meant clean. *Good enough.*

The washing areas were neatly positioned with their own alcoves, surrounded by trees that blocked the sun and showed off the glowing waters.

He walked deeper, enchanted by the glowing leaves in the small area. They hid the sunlight to produce their own light, slightly hopeful, slightly ominous. He was so entranced by the leaves, he didn't notice Aurora's frame slam into his.

"Oh, sorry," he reached out his hand.

Aurora pushed it aside, standing herself and brushing her garbs. "What are ye doing here laddie?"

"I just wanted to check on you. I know Jace can be—harsh."

"Don't worry about it," she cut off any further words, "I'm fine."

She wasn't. He could tell she finished crying; he could see the red in her eyes slowly fading away. Her pupils were scattered, too, always looking away when she peeked at him.

"Aurora, it's okay to admit you were hurt."

"I'm not hurt! Just leave me alone!"

She tried to brush past him, but he caught her arm before she could leave. In a scattered moment, she reached for a dagger and slashed at him in a singular motion, "Don't touch me!"

Aidan brushed his wound with his thumb; luckily, she hadn't slashed that deep.

Her hand was trembling, but the dagger was still in a defensive position. Her eyes were pained, and angry, and very scattered, too. She wanted to run away; her feet were ready for a fine sprint.

"Sorry," he found himself saying, "I just wanted you to feel comfortable here."

She breathed out, loosening her stance only slightly. "Why?"

Isn't it obvious? "We're friends, aren't we?"

"We are *not* friends."

A sharp pang ripped through Aidan's chest. They saved the town together, didn't they? Why was it so hard for both Jace and Aurora to see that? It was as if they hated each other for no reason. "Then why are you here? I thought you liked us, at least."

She took a moment to think; maybe she didn't know, or maybe she had a hard time putting everything into words. "I wanted to take a chance on something," her shoulders relaxed a little, "but after what yer kin said, I think I lost my bet."

"On us? Aurora, you can trust us." He handed her one of the passes to the inn.

She stared at it for a minute before taking it, and yet her body grew tense again, and her eyes narrowed. She shook her head. "Trust is not that easy, Aidan."

Aidan caught her hand before she moved. "Can we at least make it easy?"

She looked into his eyes while the wind howled through their hair for a moment. She swallowed deeply, shaking her head once more. "Nothing about me is easy."

"How fast you move looks easy," he joked.

She snatched her hand, muttering her next words, "… and yet it's hard to be on time."

She bolted so fast that the wind didn't even know she was gone. Aidan clenched his fist in frustration, feeling something weird on his fingers. *Blood*? He stared in Aurora's direction, rubbing the thick liquid between his fingers.

25

LEADER

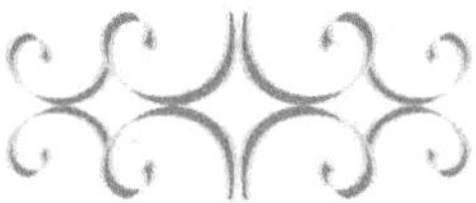

Yehowehel couldn't be wrong, could he?
—The Protector

THE DOOR SWUNG open, then it slammed with a loud thud. Jace threw his cloak on the chair in the corner while he, himself, fell on the bed. The wooden floor of his room groaned, but not as loudly as he did. His fists were cemented on his knees, clenched in a jumble of mixed emotions. Anger. Sadness. Realization.

"What am I doing wrong? Father made being the leader look so easy." Jace sighed, trying to lean back on his bed, but his blade stopped him. He unbuckled his belt, looking at it in his hands. He unfurled the clothed art, giving it a solid stare. He unsheathed it, the glinting silver, the sharp edge; a true piece of work, but what about the *other* Blade? As Jace thought about uttering the words, his breath grew cold, chilling the air around him. "Nevrence," he muttered.

The blade transformed, without the dramatic sounds and the freezing winds, just a brilliant shine that filled his room. Mimicking Jace's mood: the strong winds, a whisper, the cold chills, a shiver. Jace raised his eyes to the Abode, looking for some sign in the presence of his ice-bladed weapon. "You called me a leader … didn't you?"

A knock on the door interrupted Jace's waverings; with a simple closing of his eyes, the Blade reverted to its normal state with the same blue shine. With weary knees and a heavy heart, Jace opened the door.

"Hello?" A small maid stood nervously on the other side. The look of shock on her face when she beheld Jace's height would've made him chuckle if he weren't so dreary. His eyes narrowed at her, waiting for her to speak; his tapping foot started the timer.

"Bah-nuvel traveler," she continued.

Jace inclined his head slightly, seeing as Bah-nuvel is a common greeting in Utopia. "Bah-nuvel," he greeted.

"Afternoon lunch will be prepared shortly; we hope you will join us."

Jace sighed disinterestedly. "No, thank you. We will be having food later." *I hope.*

Hearing the word, *we*, the maid, scanned Jace's room, only seeing his cloak and his sword. A questioning eyebrow was raised. He sighed, "They're … out."

The girl nodded her head, stepping back from the door; this was a cue for her to leave. Utopians didn't have a word for "bye" in their native language, and they rarely used the common language to part ways; it was always a "see you soon in this life or the next." It was strange to Jace, but he read enough about their customs to understand.

He closed the door, his body instinctively returned to his bed and to his blade. His onyx eyes scoured the shivering steel for some type of answer, but the sword provided none. Mysteries swelled in his mind, and doubt crept at his door. *Maybe Yehowehel chose wrong?* "Did I get this Blade out of desperation, or did I earn it?"

Jace sheathed his blade, the silent sound of the blade running through the scabbard reflected the quietness of his answers. He let out one more loud breath, leaning on his bed, blocking whatever noise he could from his mind. That's what his father did. He hushed his breaths, keeping his inside as quiet as the outside, but the outside soon betrayed.

"What?!" The voice of the maid rang out. "I gotta do it again myself?"

"Ma and Pa wanted you to make the food," a second voice rang out, "they said you make it special."

A loud groan was only muffled by the walls of Jace's room. "Everyone likes my cakes, but no one wants to help. Yehowehel preserve me." Two sets of feet walked downstairs, one less enthused than the other. With that out of the way, Jace closed his eyes, his muscles relaxed in his newfound quiet. It was only a second, maybe two, before his eyes shot open.

"Finished cake? Like, the result of a process …" Jace sat up; he briskly picked up his blade and unsheathed it, looking at his reflection. "Maybe it's not who I am but … who I could be." He sheathed his blade, leaning it against the wall. He grabbed his cloak and rushed out the door. He knew what he needed to do.

26

ALMOST

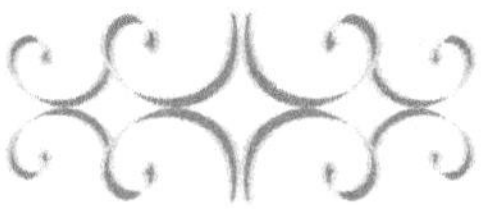

I just need some space ...
—The Thief

AURORA HELD HER hands to her face, unable to stomach the feeling of everything. Because everything felt so close, like a monster lingering in the dark that inched closer and closer to the light. The fact that she was nearly caught made it worse. *I need to return to my room.* Too many eyes, too many people watching. It was too open, far too open; she needed doors, she needed to hide. She wiped her eyes for the tenth time, making sure no tears were shed. When she could, she sank into the shadows, carefully making her way to the inn. The outdoors of Utopia was far too bright; she just needed her room; she needed to recoup. *Almost there.*

The door to the inn was right there. Her hand reached out to what was believed to be her salvation, then—the devil appeared.

Honestly, she hadn't truly noticed the difference in their height as much as she had now. He was like a tower, head reaching into the clouds, ready to pull down divine punishment like an overzealous god.

"Aurora," Jace called, his hand still on the door's iron latch.

She growled yet didn't look him in the eyes. "I'm not talking to you; out of my way." She wanted to push him away, but El knew that she could break her hand by even touching him. When she finally eyeballed him, she held captive his gaze as she subtly reached for a dagger.

He sighed, pinching the bridge of his nose. He moved aside. "Where's Aidan? He went looking for you."

She shrugged, wanting to keep the conversation brief. Despite her lack of an answer, she observed how he didn't say anything to stop her. She wondered if he planned to trick her or if he actually felt guilty for his behavior. *A little late fer regrets, and honestly,* she wasn't in the mood for excuses. She wanted to be alone in the comfort of her own company—like it always had been. She scurried up the stairs, slamming the door shut upon entering. She leaned on the door, sliding into a sitting position on the floor. Her head burrowed in her hands as she fought back tears while her body shook. She managed to pull her head from her hands, squeezing her arms. That's when she felt it. A small patch of blood oozed from her skin. She rubbed it between her fingers, both curious and terrified.

Did Aidan see? Did anyone else see? Her arms started to tremble; her voice was shallow, and even the voice inside her head was a whisper.

She didn't think her problems would outrun her again. Everything happened so fast, she felt like the slow one. Again. No speed meant no control. She buried her head into her legs again, holding herself a bit tighter. She scoffed between her sobs, wanting to laugh at the fact that she thought she had a chance for control.

27

An Invitation

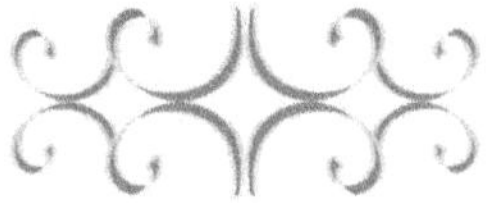

How could this go bad so fast?
—The Wildcard

AIDAN OPENED THE door, weary of everything that had transpired. He knew things would end up like this if Jace and Aurora didn't stop fighting, but he didn't expect it to be so soon. Jace's always been bullheaded, and Aurora clearly had a problem Aidan couldn't figure out. He knew she wouldn't tell him if he asked nicely, but he was hoping that something miraculous would happen.

The pain of uselessness—he knew it all too well. Compared to Jace, Aidan felt inferior for most of his life, not until he read a book that opened his eyes. The character was wingless, unlike its other brethren who had wings, but later discovered that it could swim, while the others couldn't. They had the entire sea to themselves.

Aidan tried so hard to be Jace, but he found out he was always going to fail, so he had to find the undeniable *Aidan*. There wasn't any control in feeling like someone else, quite frankly, he'd never been freer than he had been now.

He walked the halls of the inn, passing by Aurora's room. Should he knock? No, she didn't want to talk to him before, *I'm sure a few minutes isn't going to change her mind.*

Aidan entered his room, closing the door with an exasperated sigh. On cue, his chains started to crawl over him as he crashed on the bed. Chuckle seemed to be the most concerned, while Snark held back. "Hey, you two, sorry, I'm not in a talking mood right now." Snark laughed lowly, causing Chuckle to body slam straight into it. *Looks like everyone is fighting today.* Aidan propped up his leg, hands pillowing his head. If only he could get those two to talk, his mind tortured.

Aidan yawned, still tired from the trip. The exhaustion of everything made him crave sleep; *maybe it was a bad dream. Things couldn't be going this badly so fast, could it?* Playing mediator was not what he signed up for when he embarked on this quest.

Knock, knock.

"Aurora?" Aidan's head shot up.

Chuckle and Snark gasped, wrapping themselves on Aidan's blades before staying completely still.

"Not quite." Jace's voice sighed from the other side.

Aidan didn't even feel like opening the door, but leaving his brother outside would only make things worse. "Brother." He opened the door apathetically.

"Aidan …" Jace sounded tired. "Can we talk?"

"That depends, are you going to be nice now? I can only take so much brooding."

Jace silently nodded, taking a seat at the singular desk that seemed to be placed in all the rooms. He sighed, "I was wrong."

Aidan held his shock; he questioned if their father had to say those words, if he said them to their mother or someone else. If he did, maybe

Jace, who tried so hard to emulate their father, wouldn't have a problem saying it. "You don't say?" Aidan mocked.

"Let me finish, please."

Aidan rolled his eyes but motioned for Jace to continue.

"I wanted to be a leader so bad; I really did. I got so much of an ego, too, when I got the Blade." Jace ran his hand through his hair in frustration. Aidan could see Jace trying to make sense of his words at the same time as speaking. "I thought being a leader was barking orders and putting everything under intense scrutiny," Jace took a deep breath in, choking halfway through it. "I was wrong."

Definitely sounds like father, at least in part, Aidan nearly laughed. Their father was most definitely the-barking-orders type, and the definition of stern would have his face beside it in the lexicons, but people respected their father and listened to him greatly. Aidan could see that Jace was lacking something—the full picture. *Maybe he'll get there.* Aidan shook his head. "I'm not the one you should be telling that to."

Jace groaned. "I saw her at the entrance to the inn; she didn't want to talk with me."

"No surprise there."

Jace rubbed his temples. "I also went to her room, but she didn't answer, clearly."

Aidan propped up his leg again, then subtly turned to his brother. "Do you think she'll leave?"

Jace sighed with a shake of his head, leaning back in his chair. "What reason does she have to stay?"

Aidan stopped the joke in his throat, simply replacing it with a sigh. Jace was right, she's probably not answering because she's already gone. Natasha wasn't going to be happy about it, especially after everything.

"However, we can't dwell on that now," Jace added, "Bhall-Duraht is our priority. When Aurora's ready to talk, we'll deal with it then."

Cold, but correct. Aidan couldn't push the idea of a sulking Aurora outside his head, but they did come there with a purpose. "What did that scholar say? About a Great General?"

"Johannus." Jace leaned forward, elbows digging into his thighs, fingers laced in thought, "Mother and Father mentioned him. Apparently, they were good friends."

Aidan sat up. "Do you think he'll owe us? Or do we owe him?"

"If they were as good friends as they said, we wouldn't owe him anything."

Back to business, that's Jace. The fact of the matter became apparent enough; now they needed to find this general. If only they followed that scholar.

Knock, Knock.

Aidan chuckled, "Two guests in one day? I must be famous." He raised his voice, "Who is it?"

Nicklaus asked from the other side of the door. "Hello, ambassadors?"

Aidan and Jace exchanged glances. The former flipped himself out of the bed and then opened the door with a pseudo-energetic smile. "Scholar! I must thank you for these rooms." Aidan realized he was laying it on thick. "Please, come in."

The blond Setas-Lisian raised a hand. After a flick of his golden locks from his glasses, he then spoke. "No, no. We will commune soon. I wanted to extend an invitation to you all. I am having dinner with the Great General. You will be my guests, no?"

Thank you, Yehowehel. "We wouldn't miss it, however, our other companion is ill, so she won't be joining us."

The scholar looked away, but Aidan couldn't miss that subtle sigh of—relief? Setas-Lisians and Delfizcani were on opposite sides of the war, maybe he felt uncomfortable seeing her.

"That will be fine. Well, I will take my leave. I have many books to indulge myself in, prior to our dining. We have until sundown; a soldier should come and meet you then. *Beskie*."

"*Beskie*," Aidan replied in his best Setas-Lisian accent. He shut the door, silently pumping his fist. "That was easy."

"Of course." Jace's expression grew serious. "What we say will be harder."

Aidan shrugged with a sigh. "Always gotta spoil the victories, huh, Jace?"

"I'm practical."

"You're no fun."

Jace sighed. "Regardless, we should rest."

Aidan nodded, feeling his bones turn to jelly anyway. He escorted his brother out, watching him enter his room with another heavy sigh.

Aidan nearly closed the door, but there was something he wanted to check. He knocked on Aurora's door again, and once more, no reply. His chest squeezed tight, and his arms were still weak; *did we really messed something up?* This was much her journey as it was theirs, and now it seemed to be ruined so easily. Aidan returned to his room, giving one more lasting look at Aurora's room before entering his own.

28

SOUR INTRODUCTIONS

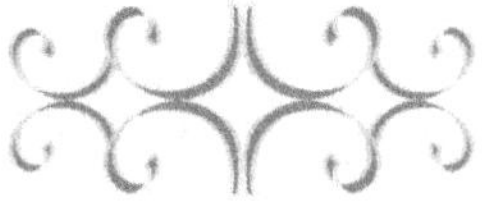

How can nobles wear such things?
—The Rose

NATALIE ALWAYS HATED how prissy dinners were. In Seplechurus, as long as one wore pants and a shirt, they were okay.

Natalie tugged at the blue fabric that stuck to her skin, shifting her shoulders to adjust the un-comfortability. She tugged at her corset, thinking how much she resembled a Mareenian rogue, especially with her cutlass at her side. That may have been the ulterior motive of Nicklaus; *he reads too many of those stories.*

She walked through the dark of the night, feeling the Utopian breeze kiss her. She looked on at the alleys of the capital, feeling the temptation to slip into the darkness and disappear. If anyone saw her, she would lose her credibility as a warrior. *Who puts lavender bows in their hair?* Disgust gripped her; look at what she was reduced to. She only could thank Yehowehel that Nicklaus would be the only one to make fun of her.

"Utopian Rose," the soldier called out to her as she approached the Great General's gates.

"Is dinner ready?"

"Of course, and his highness is already inside."

Natalie brushed her ponytail, threatening to rip the bow from her hair. "Nicklaus is trying to remain discreet. It is advised to cease using his title." The soldiers halted, and Natalie didn't bother making eye contact before asking, "Problem?"

"You should show his highness more respect. Especially for someone in your position."

"My position? Do you mean Seplechuran? If I recall, you are *Pachra*, of old Setas-Lisian betrayer blood. Born to unwilling mothers who were subjugated by Setas-Li when it was no greater than what my home is now." She stepped closer, mere inches from his face. "I am here by choice and by pact. My *position* is more favorable than yours."

A tense pause rent the air then—the soldier nodded before opening the gates. She waited a moment, staring the man in the eyes before entering. "Good evening be upon you."

The lights poured from the windows of the building, each one lit with a candle. She almost felt averse to the light. She thought about the myths her father would read to her about the creatures of the night; she was so scared of them then, and now she felt like them.

The view never grew old. The walls were wooden, adorned with medals and spoils from Johannus's past victories. There was even a Seplechuran banner he ripped from a Seplechuran *Tentagren* or teacher. The same *Tentagren* Natalie trained with as a child. *Pity.*

She followed the scents to the dining table, knowing the path well enough without her sight. She heard Nicklaus's voice; *he must already be here.* There were some things she wanted to discuss with him about her home.

"Nicklaus—," she paused; two other guests eyed her as she walked in.

Right away, she was drawn to the giant, who wore clothes familiar to her, but she couldn't place where she'd seen them. His skin was of a strange texture. Some Kutoans, Mareenians, and even Utopians were of a darker complexion, but these two before her, their skin was—strange, foreign. The people of the desert had tawny, sandy skin that was very noticeable even from a distance; however, their skin was maybe slightly lighter than coal. Their hair was the biggest confusion, dark like her own but thick and spun like a rope or a braid of a vine, and the style didn't lean toward the peoples she familiarized herself with. *Who are they?*

"Natalie," Nicklaus greeted, "these are my guests, ambassadors from the Desert Kingdoms."

She bowed. "Pleasure." *Desert Kingdoms?* There is no such thing; most of the desert kingdoms disseminated into smaller towns for easier management and, then, eventually dissolved away, but of course, Nicklaus would not know that, as Setas-Lisians would not teach about such kingdoms anyway.

"Natalie, you are analyzing again," Nicklaus broke her glare, "please sit. My elfather is in the kitchen."

She sat between Nicklaus and the one with an exquisite piece of black finery, a golden vine design sewn into his fabric. To her, the clothing did fit the ambassadorial look. But then, he held a sword.

"I know what you're thinking," he chimed.

"And what would that be?" She replied nonchalantly.

"How stunning I am; I know. The maidens get speechless."

Natalie cocked her head in amusement. "No." *He is flirty ... wonderful.* Natalie rolled her eyes, facing Nicklaus.

"Okay, let's see ... what about the fact that you can't tell where we're from because we don't look like anyone from this continent."

She stopped for a moment, slowly making her eyes look at him. Only to see him smirk.

"Got you that time, didn't I?"

"Isn't that a bit obvious, Aidan?" The giant spoke, casting his eyes in Aidan's direction. Turning his full attention back to Natalie, he shrugged. "Eh, just wanted to see the look on her face."

Flirty and unfunny, definitely less than ideal. Natalie tried to ignore him, paying attention to the dining hall instead. Aunt Eleanor seemed to outdo herself; the dining hall still remained the coziest part of the house despite it being barely able to hold a dining table. The room lacked any decorations, and Aunt Eleanor made quite sure of that. She hated the stuffiness that they brought, and that was a decision most guests could agree with.

Then there was the boisterous laugh from the kitchen. "Ah! There we go!" Johannus exclaimed loudly, "Food's all ready!"

From the door in the back, Uncle Johannus stepped forward with his tall, stocky frame carrying out large meals in each hand. He twirled with the meals, dropping them on the table before blowing on his fingers. "Oi, everyone's here! And we have guests! Grand!" He stopped when he saw the white-cloaked man, his eyes discerning and wide. "Caesar?"

The boys visibly jumped upon hearing the name; even Nicklaus did so somewhat. That was the name of the man who, with his wife, aided the Utopians against the Seplechuran invasion around twenty-one xantem ago. Rumors spread that the heroic couple came to save their—son.

"Not quite," corrected the white-cloaked man.

"... Jace?" Johannus asked in more reverent awe.

In reply, Jace awkwardly smiled with a nod. Uncle Johannus grew a grin on his rigid face, which was only emphasized by his fading beard. "ELLIE! COME IN HERE!" he yelled.

There were a couple of shuffling steps that didn't sound like they were in any rush. Aunt Eleanor strode in, keeping her grace, hands intertwined in front of her. Her hair, which had grayed from the stress of wartime, had somehow retained some of its brown, golden locks. Despite the wrinkles, one could still see the joy of youth in her tanned skin and hazel eyes.

"Johannus, what is the commotion?" she asked. Uncle Johannus pointed to Jace, and her eyes grew just like her husband's. "Caesar …?"

Johannus corrected this time. "No, Jace."

Aunt Eleanor clasped her hands over her mouth, breathing a sigh of relief and excitement.

Natalie could remember the story quite well: Eleanor took care of Jace after he was taken. She had a special bond with him since her own child disappeared. Seeing him now must have been like seeing a long-lost child finally return home.

Jace spoke, "Hi, Eleanor—*Miss* Eleanor,"

"It's been nearly twenty-two xantem." She held his face, the memories flashing by in her eyes.

Uncle Johannus piped up, "What are you doing here?"

"I—we—have an urgent request for our home. We were hoping to ask for your aid."

"Anything for you, Jace; I still haven't paid your parents back for their assistance. How are they?"

Jace's brow knitted itself into a curl as his eyes scanned the room, yet when his eyes found Natalie's, the crease in his brows thickened. It was a familiar sight. "We'll talk about them over dinner." Jace said, "There's a lot we have to tell you."

Johannus's eyes lowered, glancing at Eleanor before he turned for the kitchen, "I'll get the rest of the food. Eleanor, please take a seat." He pulled out the chair closest to the head of the table, and she sat, eyes meeting Jace's.

"Way to kill the mood, Jace." Aidan yawned. "If I wanted that, we should have brought Natasha from the desert."

Desert? I was right! The flash of steel flourished in one simple motion; Natalie held her blade to Aidan's neck.

"Natalie!" Aunt Eleanor yelled.

"No, no, please." The 'ambassador' mocked. "I want to see how she fights."

Jace ran his hands down his face. "You did this on purpose."

Aidan smiled and shrugged at the accusation.

Natalie moved her blade in closer, the tip of it grazing his skin. Yet, the boy didn't move; he smiled, in fact. *Who are they?* "How do you know my mother?" she growled.

Jace stood, calming Natalie. "Like I said, we have a lot to talk about."

29

Talks at Dinner

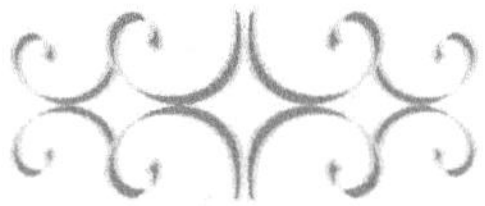

I can't believe he did this.
—The Protector

J ACE WASN'T SURPRISED Aidan was of no help, but for him to make things sour so quickly was a record Jace didn't know his brother could break.

Natasha's daughter stood across from him, glaring, while the scholar looked at them with a skeptical eye. *This amount of tension can choke someone.* Fortunately, the Great General and his wife consoled Jace with easy looks, pushing the tension at bay. He couldn't believe he didn't remember Mister Johannus; the man made his father look small, and that aura—so imposing, and yet he had one of the purest smiles on his face for a man of war. And his wife, Miss Eleanor, had flawless green eyes with hints of brown; his mother told him that Seplechurus and Setas-Li occupied and enslaved the original Utopian people at different points in time. Miss Eleanor's eyes were one of the few beautiful things to make it out of foreign subjugation. They almost glittered, unlike her husband's, which were a darker brown.

"So, explain how you know my mother," Natalie glowered.

"Natalie," Johannus warned.

Jace reached for a roll of bread, biting into its buttery, crunchy substance. "Aidan?"

"From the beginning?" his little brother replied.

Jace nodded. "And don't make things worse."

Aidan sighed into a chuckle, then, in a quick second, the air grew solemn. "Ten xantem ago, Seplechurus massacred the people in our home."

Johannus and Eleanor were shocked, and yet Natalie did not move.

"My parents allowed Jace and me to escape, but at the cost of themselves." Aidan looked to Jace, then back to the others, somber. "Jace believes our parents, dead. I believe them, captured. Either way, they're absent."

Jace continued, "For ten xantem, my brother and I did what we could to survive, that included building a name for ourselves as local sellswords. Then we aimed to take back our town."

Natalie scoffed, "You two? Alone?"

"We're here, aren't we?" Aidan retorted.

"We didn't do it alone," Jace interjected, "we had *her* help. A Delfizcani girl from the desert, known as Aurora the Thief."

Mister Johannus jerked out of his seat. "The Grim Reaper of Bhall-Duraht, she's real?!"

Aidan nearly spat out his food. "They actually call her that?!"

I suppose we are not the only ones making a name for ourselves. Jace continued, "She's been working with Natasha Voshkovik to undermine the Seplechuran Empire." He stared at Natalie, tipping his head sarcastically. "I'm sure you are familiar with her."

"My mother?" Natalie questioned with a fold of her arms. However, whatever intimidation factor she had was lost to the dress she wore. "Why would she help you?"

Aidan tapped his chin, chuckling, "What did she say, 'Our current leader is child, and I will treat him as such.' Yeah, that's it."

Natalie turned away, hiding a faint smile on her face; she regained her composure and faced the brothers. "She told you to come here, why?"

Aidan took a roll of bread. "We're getting to that."

Jace continued, discussing how they encountered Aurora, leaving out the bits about their *antagonistic* relationship. Soon, the faces at the dinner table were enthralled by the tale of the oncoming Sov and the perilous plan they undertook. Jace found himself enunciating his words, calmly but surely acting as if he were telling a story to a young Aidan all over again.

"Then what?" Johannus asked, eyes wide as a child's.

"The Sov rushed at me, and I called upon the mysterious voice that spoke to me earlier. If it wanted me to be strong, I needed help."

Nicklaus pushed himself forward, eyes sparkling with wonder. "And then …?

"There I was, a plane between mind and body, physical and spiritual. I heard a booming voice that was somehow distant. It spoke words to me, then gave me a name …" Jace's breath hushed and turned cool. Those who were not in the desert that day shuddered as the chill circulated the room. Jace picked up his blade, whispering, "Breathe … Nevrence."

Jace couldn't feel the chill, but he saw the wind swirl around the room, causing a torrent of snow and ice. The patrons of the table, Aidan excluded, could only look in wonder as the reason for their war was encompassing them now. The candles hushed with a sizzle, and the lights of the algae lamps faded above.

Only the Blade glowed.

"With this," said Jace, "we defeated the monster, Sov."

The seraph wings of snow fluttered, filling the Blade with a cold mist that did not blow away. Only when sheathed, Jace hushed its mighty form. "Afterward, Natasha told us to come here to get Utopia to occupy our town before Seplechurus gets wind of the situation."

But there was silence in the dark, and for a moment, Jace wondered if he had taken it too far. But when the algae's light returned, all he could see were tears in the eyes of Johannus and Eleanor. "Yehowehel ... finally answered," the Great General muttered.

Eleanor could only clasp her hands over her mouth, completely frozen by the revelation.

"Our war will soon end ..." Natalie awed. "Xantem of bloodshed will finally be over."

Johannus left his chair, toppling it before he got on one knee and bowed before Jace, "Lord Keerie O' Theos."

Nicklaus, Natalie, and Eleanor soon followed. Taken aback, Jace looked to his brother for an answer.

"I'm not bowing," Aidan mouthed.

Jace shrugged. "So, our request about Bhall-Duraht, what can you do about it?"

"Permission to speak," Mister Johannus asked.

Jace raised a brow. "Uh ... proceed?"

"If you can accompany me to the castle tomorrow, I can speak to our monarch about it. Of all the people, our king would be happy to see one of the Blades of Yehowehel."

"If I may add," Nicklaus interjected, "the godly weapon you possess is the absolute center of this war. You could change the tide of the battle with it!"

Jace sighed, eyes weary. He knew that someone would mention him going to war—it may have sounded selfish—but he just wanted Bhall-Duraht to be free; the world started this mess, he felt; *the world can fix it themselves.* Bhall-Duraht established itself to be a personal haven, *his* personal haven, a home away from the politics, the war, the differences of the kingdoms—*why would I want to save that?* "Let's handle Bhall-Duraht first."

"Let's eat first, I'm starved," Aidan complained.

The scholar jerked up, face fervently red. "Do you fully realize what is happening? The Blades have been sought for xantem! War, death, all for the sake of acquiring one of them! And you wish to simply discard that fact, and eat?"

Aidan lowered his eyes, clutching a napkin over his chest. "You're right, sorry. I should have been more mindful—" He looked to the hosts, "—and drinks too."

Nicklaus's mouth hung open, and Aidan's did, too—until it bit into a slice of bread. *Only if Nicklaus knew Aidan, he wouldn't be surprised,* Jace thought. "I'm with Aidan; I say we eat and then discuss afterward. The food is getting cold."

Aidan mumbled between bites, "That's your fault in two ways."

The others removed themselves from the floor, returning to their seats while Eleanor relit the candles.

Eating felt as stressful as the explanation. The others watched him so carefully, their eyes filled with anticipation as if something supernatural would take place during his bites. The scholar looked as if he had more questions.

With a sigh, Jace chewed slowly, keeping his eyes to his food only. Was he taking this seriously enough? The way they bowed just for him, showing them the weapon? A knot began to form in his stomach, and his head nearly got lighter than his bread. This task—this had to be bigger than Bhall-Duraht, maybe bigger than Jace, himself.

"Jace, a word," called Aidan.

Jace rose speedily, pinching a roll of bread from the table, and Aidan did so as well. Once the door opened, a cold blast of wind hit him, filling him with a fresh feeling of comfort. "What did you want to talk about?"

Aidan bit into his roll. "Nothing."

Jace raised a brow. "You said you wanted to speak."

"No, I said, 'a word'. And 'nothing' is a word."

Jace closed his eyes, feeling the refreshing breeze once more. Something about the night breeze made something inside him jump, more so now than before. "Thank you."

"You're welcome. I thought you were going to have a heart attack."

Jace dropped to the grassy floors, groaning exasperatedly. The pressure on him was starting to return, and it felt worse. He massaged his temples, shaking his head. Maybe the scholar was right; Jace argued with himself, maybe he needed to go to the battlefront and save more lives.

"No," Aidan exclaimed.

"No, what—?"

"You're considering fighting their war."

"I have to save those lives."

"Says who?"

"Aidan, it's the right thing to do."

Aidan threw up his arms, face contorted into a sneer. He shuffled his legs and folded his arms, squeezing tight. "You can't be serious! What have they done for us, Jace!? They knew about Bhall-Duraht and did nothing! You heard him! You saw his face, he knew! They're acting like the Setas-Lisian nobles who wanted Bhall-Duraht wiped from the face of the land!"

Aidan ran his fingers through his hair, threatening to make himself bald with the pulling he was doing, and honestly, Jace couldn't blame him. He, too, saw the look on Johannus' face; he did know. He left them to fend for themselves. Was it that he had faith in their parents? If so, why didn't he check on them? He knew about Aurora, so he must have known about the Seplechurans. Jace rubbed his temples again, this time his own skin in jeopardy. "Aidan, I know, but I have to do this."

"Why?!" He shouted like he never had before. "He said you can talk to the monarch tomorrow; he has *that* much power. He could have saved our parents, Jace, and he did nothing." A moment of silence passed. Aidan, realizing his tone, took a deep breath before he started pacing. "Why?" he asked quieter. "We lost everything, Jace, everything. Why do you want to help them?"

Jace knew why. He knew why, and the *why* haunted him. He had to be real with himself as much as his brother. "It's because I couldn't do anything then. I couldn't save a soul then; I have to now. I have the means, I have the power, I have to do something. I just can't let another Jace lose his Bhall-Duraht—or lose his Serenity. Please understand."

Aidan stabbed Jace with his finger. "Are you forgetting? You saved a soul, unless I don't count," Aidan sighed. "Listen, I think you're one of the worst decision-makers in history, and I haven't been a fan of your choices."

"And?"

"That's it."

Jace chuckled, grabbed his brother's head, and wrapped him in a hug. "I'm going to miss you."

"Miss me?" Aidan pulled away. "I'm going with you."

"Who's going to take care of Bhall-Duraht?"

Aidan jabbed Jace playfully. "Natasha."

"Aidan, you have to go back."

"No." Aidan sighed. "We're brothers in blood and twice over in arms; letting you do this alone would be breaking my moral code. We're bound by blood, battle, and our contracts."

Jace chuckled a little bit more, feeling a minuscule warmth inside against the coldness of the breeze. He knew Aidan still had the flame of anger kindled against the kingdoms, but even he knew what had to be done. He wouldn't forgive himself if the world burned like Bhall-Duraht.

Jace smirked, pushing his hand toward Aidan, "If you're sure."

Aidan took it and shook his brother's hand. "Of course, I'm sure."

There was always an adventure on the horizon, always something to reach. Maybe now, they could reach it together. Jace took a look at his brother's smiling face in the candlelight as he settled in his heart; *the journey continues.*

30

Intention

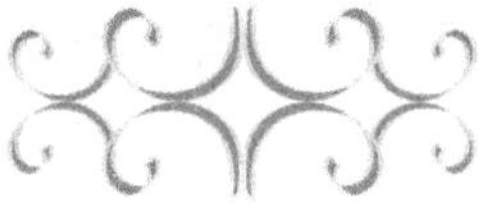

A Warrior of Yehowehel who doesn't want to save his world?
—The Prince

*H*OW CAN ONE *be so reluctant to help the world? The people of the desert were so enthralled in their own reality that they forget the others around them. They were a delusional sort, thinking distance would allow them to escape,* Nicklaus recalled as he tasted the buttery bread from his plate. He tapped his fingers on the table, pondering what those people from the desert could be planning. One of them had a legendary Blade—*the* Blade—which Nicklaus claimed to have been researching all his xantem. *Was he of noble blood?* He pondered further. No, he would not resort to associating himself with a thief, especially a Delfizcani thief. *How fervent was he in serving Yehowehel? Clearly, if he were chosen, he must be a descendant of a priest.*

"Nicklaus, stop tapping. It is disturbing me." Natalie bit into her chicken.

"You are aware I do that when I am nervous."

"I know, I can feel it from here."

Nicklaus sighed, unconsciously tapping away at the table.

The cold air from the door made its way to the kitchen. Nicklaus watched the candles flicker before they once again stood resolute.

"We'll do it." Lord Jace said sternly.

"'We?'" Nicklaus retorted as he turned. "Unless your companions are harboring the other Blades, I suggest they stay in the desert."

Aidan sat down, grabbing his uneaten venison. "And despite that, the war is still going on. Remember, your warmongering kingdoms brought this to *our* doorstep."

"He has point; it will be better to allow him to fight alongside people he knows, yes?" Raven commented, sipping her tea.

Nicklaus paused for a moment, thinking that *maybe it would help him fight at conducive strength; he did say his power surged from the desire to aid his brother.* "Fine then," Nicklaus finished a loaf, "we should head for Setas-Li."

Aidan swallowed some food. "And you have the authority to order us around because ...?"

The loaf nearly caught in Nicklaus's throat when he realized he had never told them about his true identity. Nicklaus swallowed the loaf, thinking back to a proper excuse if such a question came up. "I, uh, have done extensive research on the Blades; my papers are there."

Aidan pressed for more. "Then why were you heading for the desert? We don't have libraries there, nor any information about the Blades."

Nicklaus took off his glasses, cleaning them with the hem of his shirt before setting them back on his face. There was a chance he would die with these questions. Aidan may have spoken foolishly; however, his perception seemed to bypass others. Nicklaus uttered his half-truth, "I have gathered knowledge from many areas, but the desert remains enigmatic; I only hoped to see what was hidden there."

Aidan just continued eating, speaking no words to assure Nicklaus of success or failure. The silence made Nicklaus's chest become hollow.

"Great General," Jace moved on, "I will accompany you to the castle. I really hope something good will come from this."

"As do I," Uncle Johannus let out a boisterous laugh. "Now let's eat, I'm sure you have stories to tell of your travels!"

The food was disappearing as fast as the tension, but the underlying pressure refused to dissipate.

Nicklaus ate his food, but his mind pondered other things. The legendary weapon—the key he needed for him to be a proper king. He would have to learn what he could from this Jace. There was something he was leaving out that could be the key to unlocking the power. The future would look brighter for Setas-Li if the Blade were in the Prince's grasp.

For now, he listened to Johannus ramble about a story he told a million times before, and a couple thousand before that. Nicklaus put on his best princely smile and laugh, though his heart stirred at the center. *If a person like Jace, from an unruly town in the desert, can possess a Blade, then why can't I—the prince of the greatest kingdom?*

31

BETTER ALONE

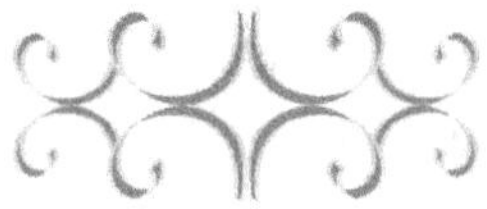

I'll pretend this trip never happened.
—The Thief

EARLIER ...

The three pairs of footsteps were a sign that the boys had gone with their escort. Now, she was alone to ponder her own next steps. She could disappear, never to be seen again. The boys would eventually return to the desert. It was just as well, she felt, because she was not in the mood to explain to them why she would leave. She managed to pick herself up from the floor. Her tears were finally dried. She stared at herself from the night-backed reflection of the window. The glossy night beckoned her closer. It was then she knew she needed fresh air. She grabbed her daggers, then bolted through the window.

The night—always so luscious and captivating, the playground of thieves and hunters, the place where she could be free, and no one knew of her presence. She avoided the lights, inching ever closer to the dark areas of alleys and shadows. But even thieves, especially thieves, hungered for the things in the light.

In the distance, she saw a woman walking with a basket of fruit in hand. Aurora jumped into an alley, turning the corner as soon as the woman began to walk past. The two collided, and Aurora put on her best fake smile. "Oh, I'm sorry, miss, let me help ya." The woman smiled as Aurora returned her bagged goods, little did she know that Aurora charged for her assistance. "There ya go."

The woman showed gratitude and left. After a moment, Aurora began biting into one of the lady's fruits. Aurora smirked. *See? I don't need those boys; I thrive on my own. Natasha is smart, but smart doesn't mean right.* Aurora had all the experience, but what did those brothers bring? *Just pain, judging, and headaches.*

She ambled through the shadows, seeing what else she could get her hands on. *This is Utopia, right?* She heard their daggers were exceptional here. Taking it from the smiths would be too easy, but if she stole it from soldiers? *Now, that would be good.*

Regardless of where they hailed, soldiers were soldiers. A night off was a night off; they were either at a tavern or playing games in the barracks. She climbed some houses for a vantage point. Up there, above everything, the city seemed so beautiful. Everything became so much more beautiful when distant, except gold, of course, which was beautiful up close, too.

Aurora found her pathing, moving from roof to roof, swinging from those house trees. The wind brushed back her reddish-brown locks, letting her feel the kiss of nature once more. Nothing was better than the wintry chill of night air. She lightly touched down on a building, but instead of continuing, she saw something that caught her eye. A young couple, probably a few xantem older than her, sat on the stumps of some trees. They were giggling joyfully. Clearly, by the way the man fiddled with the item behind him, he had planned to propose.

Aurora scoffed. She jumped down from the buildings, inching closer and closer to the couple. They were under one of those Utopian lamps made from bioluminescent algae, or so Natasha had once said. Aurora made her way around; the shadows masked her presence. She knocked on buildings, barrels, wheelbarrows, anything she could to give the illusion of natural noises. Each time, the couple skittered but were not afraid. Little by little, the man's attention drew further away from his precious betrothal item. After one more, louder distraction, the couple held their gaze to the shadows even longer. Aurora swooped in, taking the necklace in a tight fist and bolted into the darkness.

She waited, a devilish grin attached itself to her face, tempted to see what the poor man would do. She watched him panic once he had noticed his necklace had disappeared. *See, how she's going to love ya now.*

"What is wrong?" The woman asked in Elyssi, the Utopian language.

"I … I," the man stuttered.

"Go on, say ya lost it," Aurora muttered from her hiding place in the distance.

"I was … going to propose."

The woman jumped ecstatically, holding her lover in her hands. He seemed less enthused, of course, now all he needed to do was break it to her.

"Yes, thank Yehowehel, yes!" But she saw his face. "What has caused you to be troubled?"

"I," he gulped, "cannot find your betrothal gift."

There it is. Aurora bore an impish grin, waiting for the woman to smack the man in the face and refuse to talk to him. Aurora knew the world too well—*that's exactly what people do when they don't get their way; their true colors are revealed.* There was no such thing as trust or even interest; she was certain of it. In her estimation, the world was, she muttered to herself, "What can I get and who will give it to me?"

"Mikel, I do not need a silly trinket. I know you love me."

"Are you certain? If you give me some time, I can get you another one!"

"Mikel! You worry yourself. Yes, I accept your proposal."

Aurora clenched the necklace in her hand. Sticking to her mantra that people are cruel and distrustful by nature, she shouted in her bruised ego that *they are better alone. I was better alone.*

She dropped it and left, but she heard in the distance, "Thank Yehowehel! Here it is!"

Aurora found herself on the rooftops again. She didn't need a stupid necklace; the weapons were what she wanted to steal anyway. Her steps slowed until they came to a full stop.

Fighting to prove her inner demons right, she grunted to herself, "All that was acting, they didn't truly believe that mush they were spouting. He *lost* the necklace, their symbol of trust; he lost her trust—end of story." However, while still in her moment of disbelief, she was forced to briefly counter her demons, *but he didn't lose it; ya took it.* Aurora clenched her fist, feeling the sharp rage of her bloodline reach her eyes. "Well, the two of them can be weak together ... I don't need anyone."

Aurora turned around. She was going to leave the stupid city; she was going to go anywhere she wanted. No one was going to tell her that she needed anyone because she knew she didn't. As long as the night fell, she would always have a place among the shadows. She was better alone. No one else.

32

BETTER TOGETHER

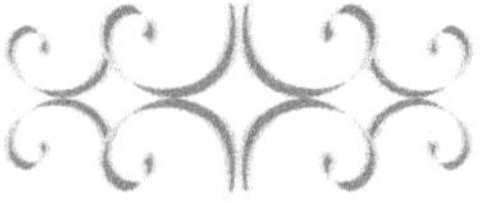

This gotta change.
—The Wildcard

UTOPIAN HOSPITALITY—A TRULY *unparalleled kind of love.* Aidan held his stomach as he wobbled through the streets back to the inn, still catching the careful gazes of the Utopians. Jace stayed behind to talk with the others, but Aidan knew sleep was going to hit him harder than Brand Voshkovik did.

The streets were primed for walking, at least: the crisp breeze chilled every part of his body and through every strand of his hair. He removed the tie that bound his dreads, letting them fall, tickling his chin. "Oh, El, I need to groom myself." His fingers laced his hair as he walked the streets of the town. The temptation to stay in such a historic place, accompanied by the people and the Utopian nightlife, left him torn, but he had a brother to help and a job to do. Besides, it was too cold there anyway.

He pushed the inn's doors, nearly running into someone in the process. He apologized before hobbling up the stairs. Though his eyes looked to his room, his heart stared at Aurora's door. *It's been a few hours; maybe she's calmed down enough to talk.* If she wasn't by now, he concluded, maybe there wasn't much he could do. Aidan knocked softly. "Aurora? It's Aidan. I'm just wondering how you're feeling?"

The floors creaked on the other side; she seemed to be awake. Aidan chuckled at his next thought; *maybe she stole something while we were gone.*

The shadows moved under the door, and after a moment, she opened it, face twisted in a near-scowl. "What?"

Instinctually, Aidan said, "Yikes, somebody activated their Jace today." Aurora at once moved to close the door, but Aidan stopped her just in time. "Sorry, sorry. Habit."

She crossed her arms, really mimicking everything about Jace when he got angry. "Alright laddie, what do ya want?"

"Like I said, I just wanted to check in on you."

Aurora gestured to herself. "As ya can see, I'm fine. Ya can go now."

Aidan breathed out a laugh. "Aurora, if the body was the only part of ourselves that we are supposed to take care of, then I wouldn't bother checking in on you."

She looked down. He could see his words entering her brain, forcing a contemplation before she replied, "I'm functional."

"Functional doesn't mean okay."

"Functional is enough."

She continued to be difficult and not the attractive kind that some of the characters in his favorite stories had. She clearly hid some demons, some dark ones. He didn't want to pry, but he wanted to help. The simple look on her face, the hollowness in her eyes, the way her body twitched when her well-being was questioned, he could see it all. She looked like she had already given up on them, but he couldn't stop there. "Aurora, truthfully, what are you looking for in life?"

She returned her gaze to him. "What?"

"You know, life is a journey; you must have a destination, right?"

She furrowed her brows, breaking her eye contact with him. Once again, his words drove her to think, and he didn't know if it was a good sign or a bad one.

"I don't have a destination. I just keep walking."

"What kind of story is that? A book needs a beginning, middle, and end. Development is based on what your goals are."

"Why do ya keep using book analogies? It's annoying."

Aidan leered at her. "It's because, besides Jace, stories were all I had. The only way I decided to become my own man was because of what I read in stories. Every character was different, yes, but they had to find themselves on the journey. They didn't settle for 'functional' if they had a goal."

Aurora jerked back at his tone. "Insulting me, are ya?"

"I'm trying to understand you," Aidan calmed the rage growing in his voice. "What were you looking for by joining us?"

"I wanted something new." The poison laced her next words, "But I was reminded why I can't have it."

Aidan shook his head. "You can. Listen, Aurora, I know you probably had a storied past of grief. I can see it in your eyes. I won't pry, but I do need you to try."

She furiously pointed at him. "Don't act like ya know me! Ya know nothing of what I've been through."

Aidan stared at her finger; brow knitted in frustration. He crossed his arms, channeling the very energies that got them into this mess in the first place. "I never claimed to know you, but that's what I want to do. However, I refuse to babysit you and Jace." He brushed her hand away. "The desert showed me that you both can work together, and if you refuse and decide to leave us ..." Aidan turned away. "Figure out a goal before running, or you'll be running forever." The sleep kicked in despite the flames burning in Aidan's chest. He returned to his room, convinced it would be the last time he would see Aurora. He wondered if he was too hard on her. But honestly, he wanted to enjoy his journey. And that may have been selfish of him, but those scenarios hadn't come to him yet.

However, when it was all said and done, if she decided to stay, he was certain that things could get brighter. After all, journeys like this were always better together.

33

Better United

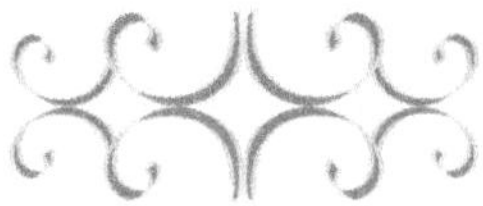

I need a minute to breathe...
—The Protector

THE FOLLOWING MORNING ...

Jace didn't know if the pressure got to him or the honey beer, or *honia burres* as the Utopians called it, was too strong, but he definitely did not feel like himself at all. His head blew any which way the wind took it, yet his eyes and feet weighed like bricks. Despite that, he managed to properly talk to the monarch of Utopia with Johannus; at least, he had hoped he did.

He clutched his head, struggling to keep his steps straight. People started to stare, and with great worry, but no one dared approach; he doubted he would accept the help regardless.

He made his way to an obscure part of Utopia's outer ring. He sat on one of the many cut tree trunks in what seemed to be a storytelling circle. Before he could thank El that it was empty, he clutched his head further, and the more he did, the more he figured out that it wasn't the drinks—it was the pressure.

He drummed his legs before pulling out a small carving knife from his pocket, shakily shaving pieces of wood from a small flute he had begun making ever since they picked up Zania. Something about his old hobby calmed him down, but his hands kept on shaking.

Everything relied on him *again.* Lives, responsibilities, now the whole Elaccursed war. He clutched his stomach, feeling an undesirable churn of worry and doubt.

He thought back to ten xantem ago, a few months before the massacre. He loved hitting the molten steel under his hammer; the sound brought him peace, almost therapeutic; every creation was his best, and if it wasn't, at least he tried.

Then it came down.

"You're going to take over your father's business, right?"

"Family forge is in your hands, yes?"

"Ya have to do better to keep up with yer pa!"

Then nothing was perfect. Nothing was enjoyable. He would destroy the attempts and criticize the "perfections." The overthinking ensued, the headaches became more frequent, and the love for the forge died with the flames at the end of the day.

Jace got up, shaking the nausea out for a moment. He stumbled his way to the inn, trying to keep his breathing under control. He opened the door to his room and rested on it for a moment. He thought about everything again, but his headaches only grew worse and worse. He breathed once more, whispering his little mantra with every breath.

The moments he had to appreciate the calm were rare, mostly because he would stuff his head with things to do. He envied how Aidan could stay so naïve and carefree, thinking about journeying and seeing the world. Life stopped being that easy for Jace xantem ago.

He decided he needed to sleep it off; something told him that he would need energy to break the news to Aidan.

The afternoon blaze peeked through the curtains of his window. The pressure in his head began to cool itself, and his stomach now seemed to be more hungry than nauseous. Two of the few gifts he could ask for. He threw his jacket aside; the metal plates dented the wooden table. He sat up on his bed, resting his head in his hands.

Knock, knock.

Aidan, perfect timing. "Come in." The door creaked open slowly, and that made Jace suspicious. When the reddish-brown curls slowly revealed themselves, Jace was filled with a bit of shock and apprehension all at once. "Aurora?"

Her leg entered first, but the rest of her body didn't make an appearance just yet. Her fingers curled around the door, her eyes absently staring. "I just wanted to let ya know I will be leaving."

Let you know? "I'm surprised you're telling me at all." Jace rubbed his eyes.

Her eyes drifted to the wall. He followed her gaze and understood. *It must've been Aidan.* He sighed to himself; she could leave right now; there wouldn't be any problems. That would be one less person to worry about, especially in this ever-evolving quest. But—maybe he thought about only one aspect of it. As Aidan said, they defeated a Sov together; not many people can say they'd done that. He pondered if he should confess, truly confess, to why her presence bothered him so, but it wouldn't be too believable now, *would it*? "I would agree with your decision; however, I don't think that would be useful."

Her eyes reached his. "Excuse me?"

Jace sighed, gesturing for Aurora to sit in the chair near the bed. Many questions were in her eyes; he could see it. She settled for sitting in the chair, being sure not to touch his jacket.

With a weary groan, he explained everything that they discussed at dinner, about the future and what it could hold.

Aurora crossed her arms, leaning forward in thought. "So, ya need bodies to throw at this?"

"Not quite. I need allies. Listen, I don't trust any of the kingdoms, even my parents' so-called "friends" knew about the Massacre and did nothing."

She nodded hazily.

"So, I want to treasure what I already have. I know we haven't exactly been friendly, and I'm not asking for that. But if we are going to work together, and I want us to work together, we need to be civil. That's only if you decide to stay."

Aurora scratched her head; her eyes settled on the wooden floor. A moment of silence marked the scene, a long moment that made the room pungent with anticipation.

With his behavior, she had no reason to stay, and with her *personality*, Jace didn't know if he could stomach it. If she said yes, they would need to establish a level of civility. The problem would be if they could establish it before their next fight.

"Why would ya want me to stay anyway? I get Aidan is the optimistic one, but ya ..."

He wanted to laugh but silenced himself by clearing his throat. "Has Aidan ever talked to you about our parents at all?"

Aurora shook her head. "Barely."

"They told us to keep friends, reliable ones. Ironic since my father wasn't very sociable."

"We aren't friends," Aurora corrected.

"But we don't have to be enemies," Jace hastily replied. He flexed his thick biceps as he crossed his arms, yet loosened his body as he leaned back on his bed. "There are more serious things to worry about than our squabbles. We have something to protect, a mutual interest, let that unite us, for now."

He could read her like a rock. Her facial expressions didn't move during the entire time they were talking. He unfurled his arms, tapping his fingers on his knees, eyes narrowing at every movement she made. He held in a sigh, trying not to sound or look impatient.

Aurora rubbed her arms, still not looking at him in the eyes. It seemed like she used her curls to hide herself before her next words. "Give me some time to decide, aye?"

"That is perfectly fine. Despite how you are on your feet, I don't expect all your decisions to be made quickly."

Aurora nodded. She stood, looking into his eyes for the second time that day and the first time that moment, yet she turned just as quickly.

"Also," Jace halted her, "if you don't mind calling Aidan, I need to let him know about Bhall-Duraht."

"Aye. I should stay fer that, too."

Jace nodded. Aurora left the room, and Jace finally let go of the sigh he was holding. All of this became so hard to deal with: Bhall-Duraht, Aurora, the war, everything. He had to keep it together, but honestly—he didn't know how much he could take.

However, if he had a team he could trust, maybe the pressure could ease off him. After all, they were better united.

34

A Path to the Golden City

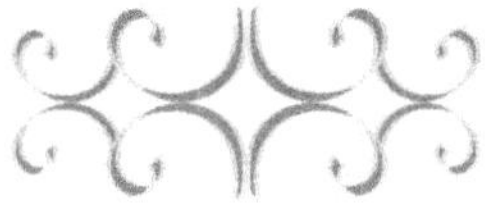

This was all so confusing.
—The Thief

AURORA CLOSED THE door, keeping her back to it. She found her fist clenched around the knob, reddening at the knuckles.

Figure out a goal before running or you'll be running forever. Aidan's words still echoed in her mind from the night before.

She didn't want to run forever, and the path had never been clearer. If Yehowehel really did exist, this must have been a sign. However, this felt—easy. Yesterday, Jace hated her very core; now he wanted to be civil. A catch usually follows these things; there's always a catch. She knew it. And she worked her brain to reason out the logic: *Honestly, if there wasn't, how could I go to Setas-Li? Those people were monsters, no matter what they told themselves. I can't go back.*

She held her wrists tight, muttering words in her native tongue, followed by a shallow sigh. She finally let go of herself, letting her stresses flee from her lips. "I should get Aidan first."

Aurora moved a door over, giving it a hard knock. At first, there was no answer, but when those uncalculated steps made their way to the door, she stopped her knocking rampage.

"Yeah?" Aidan spoke through the door.

"Wake up."

"Aurora? You're still here?"

Aurora pressed a hand to the door, eyes lingering at the floor. "Aye, I'm still here ... fer now. Jace wants to talk to ya."

Aidan chuckled. "Oh El, am I in trouble?" He paused. "Are *you* in trouble?"

"Aidan, it's serious. It's about Bhall-Duraht."

He paused, sighing, "Uh, sure, sorry."

The door creaked open. Aurora's face contorted into a frown of concern. Aidan's body was drowned in sweat, eyes bloodshot, and a face gone pale. She nearly jumped at how ghostly he looked. "Aidan! Are ya okay?"

"Shhhh! Not too loud, I don't want Jace to worry."

Aurora placed a hand on his forehead; it nearly burned her palm— just like in Bhall-Duraht. Immediately, Aurora herded him to his bed, she opened the blinds, letting the sun fully fill the room.

"Aurora, I'm—"

"Shut up," she quickly silenced him.

Aurora thoroughly checked Aidan for a fever, even picking up his arm to check his pulse.

"I just had too much to drink, relax."

She checked his eyes again, hoping it really was the drinks. Aidan removed Aurora's hands, clasping them between his. With a sincere smile, he repeated that he was okay. Aurora hurriedly removed her hands to continue her inspection.

"Let me wash up, I'm sure I smell awful," Aidan joked. Aidan walked to the entrance of his room; Aurora's eyes followed him there. "I'm fine, honest."

He's lying. That smile is a mask, she thought as Aidan walked away. And Aurora wanted to follow him, but her dilemma weighed her down. *What do I care?* She countered. *After all, my chances of staying are slim, right? I'll never have to see him again: that goofy smile, that annoying optimism, and definitely not those words that make me want to pull my hair out of my head. Nope ... I'm not gonna miss it.*

Finally, the three of them were assembled. Jace lay on his bed while Aidan stayed close to him in the chair. Aurora kept herself near the door, arms crossed and ears eager. She glanced at Aidan, who caught her staring; he smiled, the genuineness of it returned, but her heart trembled. *No.* She shook her curls, clearing her mind, and like that, he looked away. *Stop caring, Aurora. Just stop.*

Jace's words snatched her back to reality. "The king agreed to temporarily occupy Bhall-Duraht, if, and only if, we help escort some goods to Setas-Li for him."

Aidan groaned, "Great, doing errands for the crown, that's just degrading. The only thing that makes this better is the fact we're traveling to Setas-Li."

"Ya two worked as mercenaries, ya probably worked for the crown indirectly," stated Aurora.

Aidan grumbled, "While siphoning their coffers. *We* made the deal, now it feels like we owe them something."

Jace regained the conversation, "In addition, Nicklaus was there, saying that he has notes dedicated to the Blades. He was thinking I could make sense of old myths."

Aurora asked, "The laddie's notes are in Setas-Li, aye? Seems convenient a scholar didn't bring them with him."

Jace folded his arms. "Precisely. Also, there is a battle plan that was previously rejected by the king of Setas-Li, the Utopian king, thinks I will be able to convince Setas-Li to agree since they have me."

Aidan narrowed his eyes, shifted in his seat, and bit his tongue.

Aurora spoke what they all were thinking. "Now that ... might be harder for ya."

"Yeah, I agree," Aidan chimed in. "Please tell me the plan isn't something stupid at least."

Jace stayed silent; the aches of the day were probably getting to him; he did seem tired when Aurora saw him earlier. He grumbled. It was filled with disbelief and annoyance, and that was enough of an answer for her.

"Tch." Aidan turned the chair around, leaning forward on the backrest. "That's not good."

"Indeed. It's a foolhardy assault on Seplechurus's capital."

Aurora began flailing her arms to emphasize her rage. "Are those laddies crazy? That's suicide! Literally, everyone knows that Seplechurus has natural defenses, and because of those natural defenses, no sizable armies can get through, and no small army would be strong enough."

Jace huffed. "I know." He sat up, looking dreamily at the wall in front of him. "Regardless, we go. When we leave for Setas-Li, he will send troops."

"When will that be?" Aidan groaned.

Jace hesitated. "Weeks."

Both Aidan and Aurora exclaimed in disbelief, Jace mimicked their sentiment with a groan himself. His head fell back on his pillow; his hair flew up before landing like a tickle on his face.

Aidan threw his hands up. "We spent too much time to get here, now we have to wait weeks? This is stupid!"

"I know it takes time to mobilize a force, but I think the laddie can do better. Maybe send some vanguard to meet with Natasha or something, ya know?" suggested Aurora. She pushed herself off the wall, ruffling her curled locks in frustration. The wood groaned underfoot as she paced around the room, arms crossed, mind running. "Can't the old man do somethin'?"

"His hands are tied as well," sighed Jace.

The trio groaned; they were truly out of options. Silence soon fell like a heavy rain, drenching the room in white noise. An occasional sigh passed around but other than that, nothing else.

Figure out a goal before running or you'll be running, forever. Those words reverberated in her mind again, just as loud as he'd said them to her that night. If she went back, she would have a goal. She could see Lulia, Arundel, and Natasha again. She could preserve the town. The young Delfizcani held her heart, feeling—conviction? "I'll go back," Aurora suggested. "I may not have a fancy Blade like ya, but I can hold my own in a fight."

"Absolutely not," Aidan exclaimed, "we've gotten this far together, we're going farther together. Right, Jace?"

Jace sat silently, a sigh escaping his mouth once more, coal-colored eyes snuffed with uncertainty. "It's her choice. However, I already stated, Aurora, I would prefer you stay."

Sheesh, I thought I would get a little praise. She groaned. This new supportive behavior from Jace confused her, but if he did want to get rid of her, now would be the time.

Jace continued, "On the other hand, I would rather you go back because I would want someone I've fought alongside to monitor the Utopians, but Natasha is already present."

Aidan chuckled. "Translation: we're a team."

Jace rubbed the back of his head. "Now, I didn't say that we just have a mutual—"

Aidan shushed his brother. "Teeeeeeeam."

Aurora chuckled, holding her mouth before it got out of hand. It was far too high-pitched for her liking, but it only made Aidan laugh and Jace sigh in defeat. "Great, now there's two of you."

Aurora kept her smile. "Yer assuming I'm going to stay."

Aidan turned to her. "Aren't you?"

Aurora looked between the boys, and thought, at least for that moment, that Natasha was on to something. She would have to see when the laughing stopped and the steel swung in their direction, but for now. "Oh alright," she groaned, "aye, I'll stay."

"YES!" Aidan wrapped her in a hug, easily lifting her off her feet. He let her down quickly. "Sorry!"

Aurora stepped back, trying to hide the pink in her cheeks. "It's fine." Jace stood, and she put out her hands pleadingly, "Ey ey, not ya two!"

He stretched out his hand instead; the blackness of his eyes had a level of spark in them now. "Partners?"

She took a heavy sigh, reaching for his hand. "Partners."

"And Aidan!" He jumped to put his hand in.

Jace sighed, but he couldn't help his smile. Aurora shrugged as they let go. No one said anything afterward, which turned the moment sort of awkward.

Thud, thud, thud.

"Who is it?" Aidan called.

"It is Natalie, I have something to discuss with you."

The three traded looks with one another before Aidan reached for the door. Natalie sauntered in, inclining her head to Aidan as she entered. Her careful, shadowy eyes observed the room and its inhabitants.

"Can we help you?" Aidan shut the door behind her.

"No. I am here to help *you*." She gestured to the empty chair. "May I?"

Jace motioned an approval with his chin. He folded his arms as Natalie strode to the chair with authoritative steps.

Aurora carefully observed Natalie; her chin was most definitely her mother's, a bit wide but still curved to a point. The bone structure of her face that made her mother so hauntingly beautiful was also apparent: an enviable pronounced structure, semi-high cheekbones, and collarbones to die for. But she was a soldier and her father's daughter; she had scars from the sides of her face to her lips. Her frame was stocky for a woman, yet curvy. Realistically, it was somewhere between both of her parents. She couldn't hide her wide shoulders, which could be a blessing or a curse, depending on what she wore. And who could forget those Seplechuran eyes, their natural shadow around the eyes, that piercing gaze. Both men and women in Seplechurus were either terrifying or beautiful. Natalie somehow embodied that dichotomy. "So, yer Natalie."

Natalie gave Aurora the careful once-over as Aurora did her. *The boys probably talked about me at dinner,* Aurora thought. Natalie probably wanted to know what the big deal was. "And you are Aurora."

The girls eyed each other for a bit longer. Aurora further noticed that despite being Natasha's daughter, she lacked the grace that essentially made her mother's character, and yet, Aurora could definitely see the resemblance. The eyes were the same, calculating, slightly big, but discerning. However, that outfit caught her attention the most, seafoam green armor plating from shoulder to toe. *Those colors do nothing for your complexion.*

"This must be a Hericonian thing," Aurora heard Aidan whisper.

Natalie broke her gaze from Aurora and sat. "My uncle informed me of your predicament. You need solution, yes?"

The trio nodded.

"I am leader of Nightwatch, my personal espionage unit. I can send them to aid my mother before king's troops arrive."

Aurora glanced at Jace, who seemed to have been rejuvenated by the news. He unfurled his arms, letting his inner Bhall-Durahtian come forward.

"How soon?" Jace asked.

"If you wish it, today."

Jace jerked his head. "That soon?"

"Nightwatch consists of warriors who have no relationships and no true home. I have trained them to be ready on any day unless instructed otherwise. Besides, I had them prepared for another mission, but it seems that our priorities have shifted."

Aurora nodded contemplatively. "That's very Hericonian."

Natalie corrected, "I like my soldiers prepared and with purpose. Regardless, it is satisfactory, yes?"

The trio nodded, giving their own words of agreement. Natalie smiled at their answer. With nothing else to say, she saluted and headed out the door.

"Wait, Natalie, why don't you return when you're done?" Aidan asked. "We could have a thank-you dinner or something."

She spun, a slight pink glow on her cheeks. "That is ... generous, but I must attend to other duties." She opened the door but lingered by it for a moment. "We will speak on trip to Setas-Li. We will have time."

Aurora nodded, "We'll hold ya to it."

"I expect nothing less. Farewell."

"*Syvo-lyk*," Aurora replied.

Hearing the Seplechuran from Aurora's mouth stunned the Utopian Rose only for a moment, but a nod marked her exit along with the creak of the door.

"YES!!! El makes a way one more time!" Aidan jumped.

Aurora sighed in relief. "Finally, it seems like *something* is going right today."

"I think this warrants a celebration! How about breakfast!" Aidan suggested.

Aurora held her stomach. "I didn't eat much last night; I could go fer some grub."

"Then what are we waiting for? Food awaits!"

Aidan hurriedly opened the door and motioned for the others to go before he did. Jace didn't even wait to leave the room, but Aurora held back for a second. She thought to herself, *maybe this isn't going to be too bad*. She could still see the fights in the future, but right now, she would stop running, even just for a bit.

The evening came as fast as the morning did. The orange glow brought out the Delfizcani blood in her, showering her in the fiery blaze of her people's locks.

The best time to watch night rise and the morning fall was always the highest point. Besides, after she got into *another* fight with Jace, about table manners this time, maybe staying in the trees remained her best idea. His heart was in the right place, but interacting with him would forever be her greatest challenge. He said they should be civil, but he had a hard time acting like it. Oddly enough, she expected it, but it didn't make it any less annoying.

"I thought I might find you up there!" Aidan yelled from the base of the tree. "What are ya up to?"

"Watching the sunset."

"Want company?"

Her tongue was already at the tip of her mouth, ready to say "no," but Aidan had been nothing but encouraging of her, patient with her, and seemed genuinely ready to help. Honestly, she wished she had those things in a person xantem ago. She answered, "Why not?"

Effortlessly, he climbed the tree, settling on the branch next to her. The fierce glow reflected in his eyes, capturing the fading sunlight—only for him to turn to her. "So, you really decided to stay. I guess you figured out a goal, huh?" he stated jovially.

She sat back. "Aye, I guess I just needed to hear it out loud. I've been running without a destination fer so long, though it led me to interesting places, interesting people." She caught him smiling at her, and the idiot didn't bother to look away. She could only hold his gaze for a moment, trying to fight the curve in the corner of her own lip. "What are ye staring at?"

"Something, I'm just ... happy." He sat back, his eyes now facing the city in the distance. "Not many things go my way. Ever since I was a kid, I had to live to the beat of someone else's drum, hoping that other people's interests would align with mine."

I know how that feels, laddie, was what her silence said as she prayed that he couldn't read minds.

"I don't even ask for much, too, and yet it seemed more demanding." He sighed. "I always wanted friends, people to rely on, people who get it—kindred spirits."

Aurora looked at him. "Is that why ya wanted me to stay?"

"Part of it—most of it. I look into your eyes, and I see someone who gets it. Whatever *it* is, I couldn't tell you, but the sense is there. I really wanted you to be happy with us, ya know?"

Every time she made contact with those dark, carefree eyes, she saw a genuine character. Her own heart didn't want to admit it, but with every other beat, it spoke a little truth to her. Aidan was real. Everything about him was unbearably naïve, annoying, too. Even his smile grew on her, like a child who doesn't know any better but someone who also does. So, when he spoke, she had trouble convincing herself of the fraudulence. She wanted him to be fake so badly, to prove herself right. Even when he sternly spoke with her, she saw nothing but care. "Aidan, I'm sorry."

"For what? Almost leaving?"

"No. Just—I … haven't been fair to ye, ya've been very accepting of me, and I—" She looked away before her eyes could get misty. "Can we just start over?"

Aidan took a deep breath in. "Oh wow! How did you get up here? Well, I'm Aidan, and you are?"

Aurora tried to hold it in, but the laughter crashed through her lips. "Aidan, I don't mean *that* kind of start over!"

"Sorry. So, what do you mean then?" he chuckled.

"As friends."

"So, I can brag to everyone I know that I'm friends with a reaper?" Aidan placed his hand behind his head, looking on at the sunset.

"Ya do whatever ya want." Aurora laced her fingers over her stomach.

"Dangerous words you will surely come to regret later in life."

She smiled at him. That tear she fought managed to come down her face. As the glow of the day began to fade, she said one more thing with the sun as her witness. "Right now, laddie—I regret nothing."

35

A Heart for Others

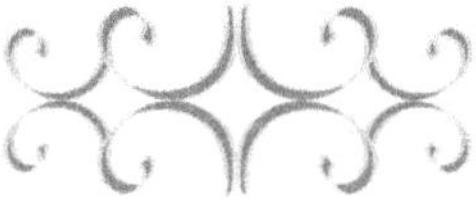

I must find a way to succeed.
—The Prince

A WEEK HAD ALREADY passed, and the thought of going home grew grimmer by the day. Nicklaus stroked Jacques, whispering to him in his native tongue, that was more like venting to someone who could not provide much wisdom. Nicklaus kept on thinking about Lord Jace's story, running everything that happened through his mind: fighting against all odds, protecting the innocent, and bringing joy and happiness. Those were all things the prince himself had done, so what differed? He contemplated.

He continued to ride to the rendezvous point at the East Gate, the lesser of the gates, but its protection of wood and poisonous plants made it quite lethal if one got too close. The path to it was straightforward enough, as it stood on the far eastern point of the multi-ringed city's outer layer. Nicklaus looked on at the sight of the hometrees protecting the various Utopian homes, algae lamps hanging from the trees' branches, and in some cases, children playing in them. He honestly wished to walk the rest of the way, feeling the shaved grass paths under his feet. The desire to walk barefoot as the Utopians did stood ever greatly in his mind, but alas, he had a job to do and a destiny to grasp.

He made it to the rendezvous, and the line of soldiers greeted him there. All the traveling wagons had a substantial guard detail with them; no surprise, traveling in the Contested Lands proved to be a perilous journey even for established kingdoms. However, the path boasted as the quickest route to his homeland of Setas-Li—and to the foolhardy plan his father and the Utopian king set up. *To think they were able to trick Lord Jace with a simple tactic; the plan was always in effect. They just needed a Blade wielder to lead it.* His knuckles grew red at how hard he clenched Jacques's reins; *that should be me leading the army, not anyone else.*

He must not return empty-handed, and the key to his inevitable prize stood by the wagons, accompanied by its companions. With a princely smile, he greeted, "Hello, Lord Jace; a pleasure to see you."

With those simple words, three sets of eyes were on him, one of them less than hospitable. Despite not seeing each other for a week, the younger brother remained hospitable enough, and the Delfizcani, well, she was Delfizcani—she hated him regardless.

"Scholar," Lord Jace greeted, "excited to be returning home?"

Nicklaus leaped off Jacques, bowing before continuing. He approached, but the barrier of tension prevented him from moving forward. "Ah, yes, I cannot wait to return to the libraries."

"Good," Lord Jace said, "we will need your knowledge."

Opportunity strikes. "As a matter of fact, you could help me expand my knowledge."

With one hand, Lord Jace lifted a crate inside the wagon, wiping his hand with a cloth. "I've told you all that I know."

"Are you positive? Maybe there was some ceremony or prayer you may have missed."

The giant man stopped, closing his eyes solemnly. "I stopped praying when my town burned away." He turned to his companions. "Come on, you two."

The others hopped into the wagon and stayed in line, readying themselves for departure.

"Stopped praying?" Nicklaus muttered angrily. "How can a desert dweller *stop* praying and then get a Blade? Yehowehel in the Abode, this is absurd!"

Nicklaus marched back to Jacques, hopping on and grabbing the reins. The hearty laugh behind him startled him but soothed a little bit of his anger.

"I can see the red of your ears from here, Nicklaus; what's wrong?" Uncle Johannus patted him on the back from his own horse.

"Uncle Johannus, can you believe this? Lord Jace just informed me that he ceased his prayers to Yehowehel! A whole decade ago!"

What surprised Nicklaus now wasn't Jace but how unfazed his own elfather was. His oak-colored eyes kept looking on, but he remained unmoved.

"Uncle Johannus?" Nicklaus called out.

The old man dropped his head in thought, grumbling his next words, "I simply don't believe that."

"Exactly! He must be hiding something from me!"

Uncle Johannus gave out a hearty laugh again. "No, not what I meant! I mean—actually, you figure it out, you like puzzles and mysteries, right lad?"

Johannus clapped Nicklaus on the back again, then walked off to address his troops. Nicklaus tapped his chest repeatedly, trying to find the answer to the riddle presented, but the only thing Nicklaus was sure of was the fact that something was being hidden from him. *Why would they hide such important information from me?* He questioned. He wanted to help even more than they did. They simply could not fathom what was at stake. Nicklaus calmed his breath, feeling his heart shift from thunderous rage to soothing calm. He had to remember why this—the Blades—were important. "The prophecy ... I must fulfill it."

The sun blared harshly, but the strong breeze offset it so perfectly as the wagons made their slow advance toward the border town of Cahms, their destination before they reached the more contested lands of the continent. The iquans of different colors and manes trekked with grace across the beautiful Utopian grounds.

Nicklaus kept thinking of what he would do or even say to his parents upon return; he didn't exactly leave with their express permission. However, if he came home with a prize, he would be rewarded instead of reprimanded.

He needed to know more about the Blades if he hoped to be rewarded; thus, he had to make one more attempt at conversation. This time, a different stratagem, one less direct. "Lord Jace," he called, riding up to the wagon. He flipped his blond hair, making sure the strands didn't obscure his sight. "Fine day for a trip, no?"

Without looking at him, Jace replied, "It is."

"Indeed, indeed." He cleared his throat. "I recalled something from your tale the other night regarding your parents. What were they like?"

Jace closed his eyes, only to open them with fatigue. The memories were clearly draining. "My mother was a ray of sunshine that couldn't be blocked by the clouds or frozen by the coldest winter. My father, a strong man who would give his all for his goal, for those he loved, for us." Jace finally looked Nicklaus in the eyes. "They would encourage us to go forward, then they would hold our shoulders so we wouldn't look back."

The glistening pride in his parents shone in Jace's eyes like the sun, unblocked. Such reverence; such respect. It only made Nicklaus feel the hollow pit grow in his own stomach.

"That is ... inspiring. The respect for your parents is apparent; you cherish their memory greatly. I wish I could say the same."

"Parent issues?" The Delfizcani finally spoke to him.

"My parents were not the most ... encouraging, especially my mother." He chuckled ruefully. "I was never good enough for her."

Nicklaus started tapping his chest, blue eyes facing the trees adorning the roadsides. Animals scurrying about with their lives, their own destinies. Though simple, at least they could fulfill it. He cleared his throat. "It does a parent's heart well when their children respect them. Though they are not with us, your parents are smiling at you from the Abode."

Lord Jace nodded hollowly. "Thank you, Nicklaus."

Nicklaus nodded. Maybe the opportunity for pressing was for another time; for now, he slowed Jacques's steps.

"Wait, Nicklaus," this time Aidan called for him.

"Yes?"

"I just noticed your outfit. It was fashioned after Reginald's attire from *The Horror of South Sea*."

A faint smile curled to Nicklaus's lips, "Why yes? You ... can read?"

"And write, yes. I know it's not incredibly common for mercenaries—or anyone who's not noble, for that matter. As for The Horror of the South Sea, I've read the book at least five times."

"Merely five?"

"Merely five?! That Elaccursed book is long!"

Nicklaus flourished his hair, then adjusted his glasses, his body stood straighter now. "Excuses are for the uninitiated of literary culture."

"Did ... you just quote Jasmine from *Clouds Above*?"

Nicklaus changed his posture, shaking his head in an exaggerated manner. "'If you have to ask, then surely you know.'"

Aidan mimicked the pomposity of Nicklaus's stature. "'But a fool like you can hardly keep up with me regardless.'"

Nicklaus felt his inner-Johannus and broke out into boisterous laughter along with Aidan. The others stared, clearly not knowing what was happening. He shifted his weight according to Jacques's new pace on the uneven terrain. "I cannot believe I found another person who read *Clouds Above*!"

Aidan grinned, getting a hold of the reins on the hilly terrain before he opened his mouth, only to repeat it to make sure he was steady. "*Clouds Above* is my second favorite book—good fantastical elements, great character development, and probably the snarkiest person I know besides myself."

"I—yes, indeed! Did you know the author was a Mareenian who traveled with desert storytellers?"

"That doesn't surprise me; a Mareenian gave my mother the book," Aidan said matter-of-factly.

"The benefit of living in such a mixed environment, no?"

"Yeah," Aidan growled jocularly. "How come you couldn't talk about books at dinner? It would have definitely made it more enjoyable."

Nicklaus laughed at Aidan's bluntness. "I simply didn't expect you to be able to read ... talk-less of the books I adore."

"No excuse!" Aidan exclaimed. "You should have tried."

Nicklaus laughed again, surprised at his own tone of voice. He could never laugh that loud in the castle; nothing could make him do so; well, Jasmine could.

He adjusted his glasses, but his laughing offset them every time. To talk with a person who didn't ridicule him for his textile fascinations and instead praised them. It felt so relieving.

"What is going on here?" Natalie rode forward.

"Raven, Aidan here has read *Clouds Above!*"

"That foolish novel you will not shut up about?"

"It is not foolish!" Aidan and Nicklaus defended.

The Delfizcani fluffed her reddish-brown locks before setting them over her shoulders to stroke. "What is it even about, laddies?"

"Aurora! NO!" Lord Jace exclaimed.

Aidan cleared his throat. "Well, you see ..."

For the next few hours, Nicklaus and Aidan explained the plot of *Clouds Above* in—excruciating detail, then transitioned to their favorite characters and themes. A strange feeling arose when someone matched Nicklaus's knowledge concerning his favorite subject matter. Aidan's own fervency settled any unpleasant feelings.

Honestly, seeing the five of them discuss passionate topics with one another was refreshing. The amount of times Raven smiled was more than he could count. Nicklaus knew he should be talking about the Blades, but the journey to Cahms would take days. Nicklaus perished the thought, arguing to himself, *one day of jocular activity would not hurt.*

36

TIRELESS ROSE

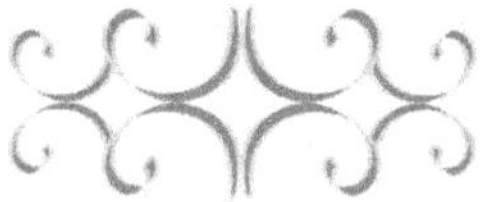

Just Like Home.
—The Rose

THE FIRST OF their many nights fell.

Everyone slept so soundly. They were like children, being rocked by the gentle breeze of the night and hushed by the moving leaves. They felt so at peace despite the war raging around them. It was hypocritical as it was enviable. But the night doesn't sleep; it just lulls everyone else to rest while it watches silently, hiding what may be beyond the horizon. The night, in stories, grew to be synonymous with evil, but it did something that no one seemed to be grateful for—it allowed rest.

Natalie looked on from the branches of her post, watching the Utopians rest on the soft, comfortable mats, dozing off to sleep while she watched.

The night howled a bit, sending a cold chill down her spine. Yet, the breeze reminded her of her home. *Would these Blades finally be end to this war? Or will their manifestation stoke flames of conflict even more?* Nicklaus trapped himself in his own head to even notice, and the desert people were not fully grasping the situation, Natalie thought. She snapped a twig off the tree she sat in, toying with it for a moment. The rugged touch of the twig stimulated her thoughts.

The war would have died off if the Blades stayed hidden a little longer, but even then, she couldn't return home.

Natalie remembered the night she left; it was a night just like this: quiet, breezy, and the smell of animals stuffed her nostrils.

She managed to make it to the forest, the frost tipping the evergreens. The imprints in the snow were deep, and she thought she would never leave any again, but what made it worse was that as she guided Votich, her iquan, through the forest, her mother stood right there to stop her.

"Where do you think you are going?" her mother asked so many xantem ago.

"I am leaving."

"You would abandon Seplechurus right after we charted our course to victory?"

"Abandon? Abandon?! How can I side with murderers and people who abuse my country and her people!"

"Emperor Rastanis is our leader; how is that betraying your country?"

Natalie walked up to her mother, cold eyes looking back at her as their frozen breaths also clashed. "Our emperor is child, and I will treat him as such." Natalie placed a hand on the hilt of her blade. "You are strategist not warrior; if you wish to stop me, you may try."

Her mother stood resolute, face reddened. "You will break your family."

Natalie showed a slight glint of steel before uttering, "My family is already broken."

Her mother moved aside that day, uttering no more words, at least none that Natalie heard. Before she left, she looked her mother in the eyes and remembered seeing tears. She'd never seen her mother cry before.

"I will help Seplechurus from shadows, that is my duty as Heir Kcauss Voshkovik."

She mounted Votich and left, not even looking back.

Natalie snapped the twig in her hand, remembering all from that night. She could still feel the frostbites and her blood turning to ice. And now, they were returning to the place where she made her offer to Utopia, the border town of Cahms.

Now, she flew Utopian colors, but she didn't feel like one of them; they forbade her from stepping foot on the inner rings of the city unless summoned and chaperoned.

She leaned forward, watching the trees rustle outside of their natural, windswept tune. The shadow leaped from the trees to the bushes, steadying itself near the food cart. With her slingshot, she took aim, a small pebble in hand. She launched, hearing a sniveling canine cry. The guard on duty shot up awake, unaware of what occurred.

Like before, everyone slept so soundly, unbeknownst to what happens in the shadows, and right there was where she belonged. Seplechuran or not.

Morning came, and the party was on the move once more. Natalie's eyes burned with the lack of sleep, but she knew she would get over it eventually.

"No animals in the stores, sir," the soldier on guard reported.

"Good," Uncle Johannus clapped him on the back, "time to head out, men!"

Natalie shouted with the others, and she mounted Votich. The Delfizcani girl, Aurora, walked up to her, twirling a dagger.

"So, not going to tell him, aye?"

"Tell him what?"

She smirked as she shifted her weight to one side. "I know fer a fact that laddie was sleeping. Ya were the only other person awake."

Natalie brushed her hair, keeping her eyes forward. "I work in shadows, nothing more."

Aurora looked away, drawing Natalie's attention to her companions as they seemed to be bickering about something. Aurora smiled, crossing her arms. "Yer ma's very proud of ya. Though she says it in very little words."

"That sounds like my mother. How is she?"

"A bit happier ever since she got yer sister."

Natalie raised her brow.

"Adopted."

Her brow lowered.

"Lulia keeps yer mother happy, talkative, almost."

Happy was such a relative term, she felt. *Happiness* for her mother occurred when no one questioned her in court. To think another person could replicate that seemed near impossible. After all, it was one of the reasons her marriage fell apart.

"How is her health?" Natalie asked.

"As healthy as a Hericonian could be in the desert."

Natalie chuckled at that one. She could imagine every Seplechuran being deployed to the desert probably died on the inside. The sun was a rare sight in the cloudy Seplechuran lands, to see it so much as to call it a friend must have been—enlightening.

"You seemed to manage well," Natalie stated.

"It took a few xantem, but I got the hang of it. Though I wouldn't mind a cold breeze."

Natalie looked longingly at the sky. "Wouldn't we all ..." Natalie rubbed her temples, unsure of how to keep the conversation going. She realized, in that moment, how little casual interaction she engaged in. Only Nicklaus could offer such, and he would mix in duty in there as well.

"Aye, ya look tired, I won't talk ya ear off." Aurora waved as she walked away.

Natalie wanted to stop her, but she couldn't find a reason to. Keeping her there wouldn't benefit anyone. "Thank you for your consideration." Natalie sighed, wishing Aurora would come back. *This should be simple conversation, and yet ...* She sighed again, signaling Votich to move forward.

She rubbed her eyes to remove the split visions and the heaviness that came with them. It marked the fourth night she'd been awake, and her body cried for sleep. Unfortunately, being nocturnal remained a grievous habit.

"Raven?" Nicklaus called to her.

"Nicklaus." She shook the sleep from her eyes, just as Nicklaus appeared to her right on his trusted horse. The faint smells of jasmine filled her nose as he appeared, and upon closer inspection, his hair was shinier, partially damp. "Can I help you?" she asked.

"No, not really. I just came to see if you slept; you have already kept yourself alert at night before we journeyed, no?"

"I am fine."

"You look dead."

"Maybe I am."

Nicklaus scoffed, "Hardly, I would know."

She breathed out a laugh; some of the sleep went with it. She sat up straighter and brushed forward her hair, letting the natural shadow of her eyes become even darker. "Not going to ravish our guests with tales from pages?"

Nicklaus chuckled, "In a moment, dear Raven, I just wanted to see if you were doing well."

Natalie massaged her temples. She heard her stomach growl, *did I eat? I had dried meat, no that was yesterday's lunch.* She shook her head, the sleep finally catching up with her. She usually slept during the day but travels such as these were brutal for that kind of lifestyle.

"Get some rest, Natalie; if need be, I can carry your burden."

"I'll rest when we get to Cahms."

"That will be days, Raven. Your stubbornness disfashions you."

"Your nosiness blemishes you."

They both laughed. Nicklaus even patted her on the back.

"I will be fine, Nicklaus. Enjoy your conversation."

He gave a light smile, his shoulders dropping. "Only if you are certain."

Nicklaus rode forward, and Natalie continued to watch from the back, keeping her eyes steady and observant despite how heavy they felt. Every so often, the Delfizcani girl would look back, but Natalie knew better than to befriend a traveler. She just kept her steady pace to Cahms, *only few more days until I can rest.*

The four of them laughed together, and she could see Nicklaus's excitement even from the back. The two of them weren't very social, but somehow, those three from the desert brought the best out of him.

Besides, if she did approach, the words would be lost on her. She's only had superiors and subordinates for all her xantem. The only people who came close to real friends were Nicklaus and Pasha, but she lost Pasha when she left Seplechurus.

What would she even say to them in the first place? The last book she read contained battle tactics; nothing fictional or fantastical about it, *maybe legend of Percivalla? No.* She could talk to the Delfizcani about her mother, but that probably wouldn't last that long.

"Raven!" Nicklaus called.

"Yes?"

"Come hither, we wish to settle a wager."

So, it begins. Votich galloped over, and Natalie kept her face as dignified as someone with four days of no sleep could. Once she made her approach, the younger Camerus kept staring at Votich with curiosity.

Aidan observed, "You're right; they are a different shade of purple; even the stripes look different."

Nicklaus commented, "Yes, Votich is from the northernmost part of Seplechurus, so his fur is darker. That is why they were described as such in the Seplechuran novels. Most Seplechuran writers were from the north."

Aidan nodded inquisitively, "Interesting, haven't thought of that."

Natalie kept silent, unsure of what to say or how to contribute. Aidan looked at her, looked away, then returned to her gaze with a smile. "So, speaking of the Utopian Rose, why do they call you that anyway?"

"Surely everyone knows by now," Natalie replied.

Aidan laughed, "Natalie, I have lived in a cave for ten whole xantem, I don't exactly get the latest kingdom news, and our employers mainly talked about their political enemies, not the latest warriors."

Nicklaus added, "Yes, he didn't even know that *Clouds Above* had two sequels.

"Well, if you must know. I am heir to House Voshkovik's Kcauss Branch. Our house symbol is unfurled black rose. In Seplechurus, I would be referred to as Head Kcauss or Rose."

Aidan's eyes were alighted with wonder, such mundane information made his face become that of a child. With his brother being a literal proxy of Yehowehel, surely her title shouldn't inspire such awe. He baffled her.

"That's so amazing!" Aidan exclaimed. "How many Voshkovik clans are there?"

"Just five, each brandishing flower as symbols."

Nicklaus added, "House symbols are the pride of any clan and a name to a tribe."

Jace lightly breathed as he leaned forward, resting on his knees, "What's your symbol?"

"The golden lo—peacock."

"Wait," Aurora halted, "ya're a Leroza?"

"Why yes."

Aurora cocked a brow and scrunched her lips. Though Nicklaus had lied about his identity, this particular piece of information didn't *necessarily* fall under that category.

"Leroza's are the greedy bastards!" Aurora yelled.

Nicklaus surprisingly guffawed, clutching his stomach as he nearly tipped off Jacques. "That is quite accurate of my clan. Though I would call us ... frugal."

Aurora rolled her eyes. "Ya, sure."

"Well, since you spoke up, what about your clan symbol?" Nicklaus countered her disbelief.

"Oh please, ya already know. Borealis clan's symbol is the eye of the bear, the most ferocious creature in the frigid."

"Except Burnwinter," Aidan interjected.

Aurora jabbed Aidan. "Burnwinter is a fictional creature!"

The rest of them laughed while Aurora grew red-faced, eyes furrowed. "Make fun of my clan all ya want," Aurora tipped her chin at Aidan, "what's yer clan symbol then?"

Aidan's smile faded a little, though he managed to keep it a smirk. "We, uh, don't really know."

Nicklaus scoffed, "Do not know? How do you not know?"

Jace spoke, "Our parents didn't talk about home much. The only thing we have is our names and our blood."

"Oh." Nicklaus shied away from their gaze.

"No, no, we are not about to make this a sad time." Aidan clapped to get everyone's attention.

"I'm sure we'll find out eventually; I just know our parents are alive. We'll ask them then."

Aurora leaned into Aidan. "I'll hold ya to it."

The five of them kept their conversation going for hours, and Natalie was surprised at the fact that words could easily slip from her tongue. Maybe she spent too much time in the shadows, Natalie pondered. Even Votich was enjoying time talking with Jacques and Zania, though superstition, animals coexisting, was a good sign. *Maybe, just maybe, I have reason to look forward to morning.*

37

THE SUBTLE THINGS

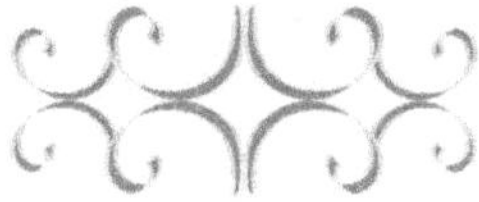

Now, this is more like it.
—The Wildcard

UTOPIAN LANDS LOOKED far different from that of the forests near Bhall-Duraht. The trees in Utopia were dense, barely leaving any room for the sun to pierce through. The soft hum of the glowing flowers reflected the yellow shine of the sun, charging the dark spots with an almost divine tangerine light. Flowers surrounded the base of the trees like children during story time, an array of colors looking at their larger brethren as if to glean from them.

When Aidan asked about the flora, some of the soldiers were skeptical but eventually explained some of the trees to him. Apparently, a type of tree called a Mate Tree was prevalent in the areas near Cahms and Utopia Capital. Two separate trees, that grew at a safe distance from one another, had branches sprouting opposite each other as if they were one tree. Many rare species of birds only made their homes in Mate Trees, and even some rare flowers were known to sprout between them. There was no way Aidan could find such a story anywhere in the desert.

The scenery perfectly distracted Aidan from Nicklaus's droning on about the Blades once again. As much as Aidan liked talking to the Setas-Lisian, once the Blades were a topic of discussion, he became more annoying than a heat rash or when Aidan's old burn scars flared up. Aidan forgot how many times he adjusted his arm ring, a little habit he developed to keep himself awake.

He had to keep the conversation on something else before Aidan crashed them into a tree or something. They already exhausted most of the conversation about the books, so Aidan needed to find another, more long-term distraction. He wanted to let Jace suffer just a bit, but Aidan found himself suffering the most. Guess he had to pray to Yehowehel that he didn't lodge his party into a tree.

Night fell on another uneventful day in Utopian lands. Aidan found his muscles aching for a fight, and yet, he wanted to take back the idea because he had a feeling that would come sooner than he'd thought. For now, he enjoyed the broth that the Utopians began to serve. Made from local game and herbs, the food surprisingly graced his tongue with a splash of salty, zesty flavor. This must've not been the common slop because even the other soldiers patted their fellow on the back as they took more.

Some time passed, and everyone began to talk amongst each other. Aidan was no different. Nicklaus finally stopped talking about the Blades long enough for them to have real fun. Natalie asked them about their mercenary life, and they definitely had stories to tell.

"Wait, wait, the laddie gave ya water?" Aurora asked, shocked.

"Yes, he kept going on about his special spring." Aidan waved his spoon for emphasis.

Natalie stopped eating to truly grasp the concept of what she had heard. "But you defeated armed band of Seplechurans." Aidan could see the wheels turning in Natalie's head, but then they got stuck. "I do not ... never mind."

Jace gave a breathy chuckle as he swirled the still-hot broth. "Trust us, Natalie, it confused us, too."

Aurora jabbed her spoon in her bowl. "I know I'm a thief, but *that* is a real criminal. I would have robbed the laddie blind."

"It was tempting." Jace finally ate his food. "But he really did have poor people in that town; we would have robbed them."

Nicklaus adjusted his eyeglasses. "Then what course of action did you take?"

"Pssh, we just spread his 'bounty' among the people." Aidan grinned, remembering the mischievous act. "Apparently, he was hoarding the spring to himself. I distracted him while Jace led the people to get a drink."

Jace smiled. "I've never seen a person so red in my life."

Aidan slapped Jace hard on the shoulder, nearly making him spill his broth. "Oh El, you should have heard him curse. It was *glorious*."

"Indeed." Jace laughed.

Aidan pointed to Nicklaus with his spoon. "Ironically enough, the people rewarded us with a little something from their houses."

Nicklaus nodded. "That was generous thinking. The gall of people; I would wager he only requested aid so the Seplechurans would not touch his spring."

"Precisely," Natalie shook her head, "such selfishness has no place in this world."

"Yes, I wholeheartedly agree, Raven." Nicklaus turned to the three from the desert. "How did circumstances get so horrid?"

Aidan and his brother exchanged a look. They silently discussed if they should even say anything.

"Setas-Li," Aurora answered, her eyes lingering between the broth and Nicklaus's eyes.

Aidan rubbed the small of his neck. "Yeah ... so, little history and geography lesson. The desert land north of Bhall-Duraht is not where the old land of Termas ends; some of the forests are Termasian, not Utopian."

"That's where most of our bounties took place," added Jace.

"Right. So, the Setas-Lisian crown tried to take over the land for its natural resources. The Termasian people resisted because they knew of the negative things that happened to Utopia under the Setas-Lisian occupation. The crown has been making it hard for us to live ever since I was a kid."

Jace tipped the wooden bowl to his mouth. After finishing the broth, he lowered the bowl below chest level, gazing down into its emptiness. "Setas-Li also sent saboteurs to our lands, putting pressure on us to comply with them. Even Bhall-Duraht was no different. Many people were skeptical of Setas-Lisian immigrants just because they thought they were spies for the crown. Eventually, all of them were turned away."

Aidan chuckled hollowly, "Seplechurus wasn't the only reason why we had so many contracts."

"Yer also forgetting the rampant slave trade," piped Aurora.

"Don't start with me concerning the slave trade," Jace growled, "innocent people hunted down like dogs as runaway criminals only to be shipped off elsewhere." Jace crushed the bowl, pieces of wood splintering through his hefty fingers. He scoffed as he picked up the pieces. "I liked the craftsmanship of that. "

A silence seized the words of everyone present. Aidan wanted to soften the blow with a joke, but maybe Natalie and Nicklaus needed to hear this as it was. They might have meant well; Aidan could give them that, *but the crowns of Dominius are nothing but a bunch of thugs draped in gold*. The war was about power, he knew. He was certain that the minute the countries obtained the Blades, they would use its power to oppress everyone else, *good kingdom or not*.

"I did not realize such things were happening," Natalie muttered in shock.

"Most people don't." Aidan finished his broth before continuing. "I don't know if they turned a blind eye or Setas-Li is just that good at hiding their tracks, but barely anyone knows what's going on."

Despite everything said, Nicklaus had not muttered a word since. Aidan thought of the harsh punch in the face the scholar would get if he silently agreed with everything his country did; maybe that's why he chose silence.

"Setas-Li has its dark history," Nicklaus confessed. "To think we would go so much as to repeat it in the modern day. Unthinkable." He smirked. "I know of people with connections to the crown; maybe we can discuss this."

Jace nodded. "That would be a great idea. Your cooperation will be necessary."

Even Aurora couldn't help but smirk. "Aye, if ya'll really be able to do that, I'll change my mind about ya prissy blonds after all."

Aidan squinted his eyes as if to see through Nicklaus. *Something's not right.* Nicklaus shifted his weight multiple times; his eyes were far more rapid than their usual pace, his fingers tapping around his bowl.

"We can discuss such later, foremost, let me get more broth, excuse me." Nicklaus inclined his head before exiting.

Aidan exhaled a small, barely audible breath from his nose. Aidan's parents gave him stern instructions to be his brother's eyes, and as he looked at Nicklaus, he didn't like what he saw.

38

SIMPLE REVELATION

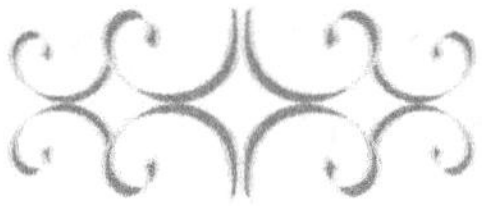

This is dire.
—The Prince

NICKLAUS TAPPED AROUND his bowl; his eyes unable to focus on the world around him. *To think the desert people hated the crown with such vigor. Clearly, there had to be some fallacy in that, the Amoran clan would never do such things; it had to be the work of individual actors.* Regardless, Nicklaus knew one important thing: if they found out he *was* the crown, he would never obtain what he desired.

Nicklaus knew that there was good and evil in this world, and that line often became blurred in war.

His eyes slinked open; rays of blue could cut through the white of his tent, and yet he did not see a sliver of orange light. He stretched before kneeling. His index and middle fingers of his left hand interlaced with the little finger and ring finger of his right, stacked atop one another. The thumb of his right hand nestled against the bridge of his nose.

His prayer: "Yehowehel, Fero auth Vehemi, perosh mon blade inth mumeni, perosh mon ilumi inth afrés-mu, perosh mon stép inth penumi. Perosh mon teng inio je'spe, perosh mon oiu inio j'evet. Omer je poi malio, shuwer in'yu illuminahto. (Yehowehel, Father of the Vehem, guide my blade in the morning, guide my eyes in the evening, guide my steps in the night. Guide my words when I speak, guide my ears when I listen. Keep me from evil. Shower me in your light.)"

Nicklaus kissed the two joints on his thumb before standing. He sighed, grabbed his glasses, and then exited his tent. Some of the soldiers were up and about, checking food stores and getting ready to move out. Others were still asleep, due to their night shifts being longer.

"Oh, you're awake. With how much broth you had last night, I didn't think you would be up," Aidan stated as he approached.

Nicklaus ran a finger through his hair, holding a neutral tone to his voice. "I am more surprised of yourself. You consumed for ten soldiers."

"Eleven, probably. I've been very hungry lately." He pointed to the forest. "Are you about to freshen up?"

Hmm, maybe this will be my chance. Surely, Aidan would have an interesting perspective on his brother's transformation. "I could use a cleaning. I swear dirt gets into my hair easier than most."

Aidan chuckled. "You're telling me. Apparently, all Camerus are born with dreadlocks; maintenance of it is mandatory in our culture. One of the few things our father shared with us."

"Dreadlocks? Is that what that style is called?"

Aidan nodded. "Yep. Comes from some words I don't quite remember." He shook his head. "Anyway, let's get cleaned up before everyone else wakes up."

Nicklaus motioned for Aidan to take the lead. The two of them journeyed deeper inside the forest. Many of the soldiers eyed them. Some of them hinted they would follow.

In the blue light, the forest almost looked mystical, some of the trees still hiding shadows and darkness, acting as corridors to a world beyond. So, captivating the morning hue, it must've been why the Father of the Vehem sanctioned them to pray at such a time. The beauty of the rising dawn. The birds were alighting with music, signaling to their friends that a joyful morning was upon them; the winds whistled through the branches, aiding the birdsong. *How beautiful is such a creation?* Nicklaus mused.

"Nicklaus, I have a question," Aidan asked, cutting the silence.

Nicklaus smiled at his chance. "Humorously, I have some inquiries of my own."

"We'll trade then, yours for mine."

A desert dweller to the core. "Fine with me. Ask at your leisure."

"From your perspective, someone who isn't noble or royal, what are the views of the Setas-Lisian people on Bhall-Duraht? I felt a little bad bashing on your kingdom yesterday without letting you explain."

In an instant, Nicklaus sized up Aidan and an opportunity: *Such a foolish question, but it does have its uses.* Aidan appeared to be the kindest of the group, Nicklaus observed, one whose heart beats with that of a gentle father. Nicklaus further thought that Aidan would make a good king if he weren't polluted by the selfishness of the desert. *Such wasted potential. He truly is the best of them.* Regardless of how he felt about Aidan, Nicklaus was confident that he could use this moment to garner sympathy. *I can divert Aidan's charisma to my cause.* At last, at long last, he could have what he so desperately sought after. "Truly, I pitied the desert; many of us do." Nicklaus lied. "The average citizen sees war as a candidate for chaos and loss. Many of Setas-Li's smaller towns were at the brunt of such catastrophe when the war initiated. Those same people felt the same sympathy for the desert."

Aidan nodded. He lifted a branch, allowing Nicklaus to pass unharmed. "That's interesting."

Before Aidan could continue, the two of them were face-to-face with a small stream, though deep enough to submerge their bodies without issue. Wordlessly, Aidan shed his outfit, throwing it on a branch. Immediately, Nicklaus witnessed the web of ill-colored skin seemingly spinning on Aidan's back, along with small pellets of discolored skin accompanying them.

"By El's breath ..."

"Hm?" Aidan turned around. "You say something?"

"Your back ..."

"Oh, that? I got burned escaping from Bhall-Duraht. I was trapped in my room under a beam. The small marks were from the pieces of flaming rocks that broke off from catapults when Jace and I were running."

He shed the rest of his clothing, leaving only his undergarments. He dipped into the stream, sighing with relief as the water ran past his old wounds. "You coming in?"

Shaking his shock, Nicklaus replied, "Oh, of course."

Nicklaus soon shed his clothes; his body scar-free, unlike the person he sat across. Aidan submerged his body until the water ran right below his nose. He began vigorously washing his hair before completely submerging himself. "What you told me about Setas-Li was very interesting." He began stroking his hair.

"How so?"

Aidan looked directly into his eyes. His pupils unmoving. A strange, almost paralytic touch seized Nicklaus's muscles. The same touch he experienced with his own parents.

"All the casual citizenry of Setas-Li we've encountered have never even heard of Bhall-Duraht. Only nobles and royals."

"That is impossible," Nicklaus quickly retorted. "Many of us commoners heard of your town."

"Commoner?" he repeated dramatically. "Is that the reason why the Utopian soldiers stopped what they're doing to follow us here?"

He noticed them. This was not the first time Nicklaus had been caught in a lie. As always, composure was everything. He neither shifted his gaze nor his body. Maintain the truth by maintaining eye contact, he believed.

"Perhaps they do not trust you yet. After all, they are as ill-informed about the desert as you claim my people are."

Aidan submerged himself again, once more making certain each strand of his hair was cleaned before rising. "Perhaps." He said nothing afterward, including more allegations. Once he was clean, he simply left.

From the start of his journey, Nicklaus knew he needed to be careful of the desert dwellers. However, he thought it may have been Jace or the Delfizcani that he needed to worry the most about. In reality—it was Aidan.

39

BAD BLOOD

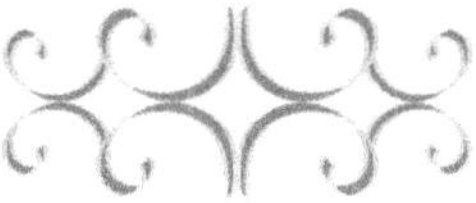

This is Cahms, eh?
—The Thief

AURORA EXPECTED A sea of soldiers to flood her view, marching in unison with their battle cries and battle songs. However, the only thing that flooded her view were quaint houses, all with the Hometrees she saw in the capital. Children were running around with deer and playing in haystacks barefoot. Their parents greeted the party with open arms, singing in their language about the Great General while supplying them with gifts.

Only the imposing wall made from a hardened wood, buffered by roots and thorns, met her serious expectations.

She waited in the trio's wagon, feet kicking off the ends, while the General and his men got the last of their supplies and more troops to hold them. Aidan and Jace went to the weapons shop, she believed. Nicklaus left, hoping to get more books, maybe. The little Setas-Lisian scholar didn't come off as bad as she thought he would; once he got his Jace-worshipping out of the way, he seemed pretty nice and quite knowledgeable. Maybe she guessed wrong about his prissy nature. However, she grew concerned at the fact he was Leroza. They were the ones who had the Delfizcani slaves, and they benefited the most out of this war. However, he seemed nothing like them; he seemed more Amoran, all righteous and pious.

Natalie soon approached, cracking her neck and yawning. Aurora heard the pop as she rolled her shoulder, which sounded sickening. "Ya look like ya slept well."

Natalie nodded. "Yes, though my dreams were less than ideal."

Aurora motioned to Natalie to sit beside her, and it was then that she noticed the Utopian Rose was a whole head taller than her. No surprise, she remembered the Rose's father all too well. "What were yer dreams about?" Aurora kicked her legs off the back of the wagon.

"My father ..." She sighed, "Is he really dead?"

Aurora nodded. "Yeah, the laddie was snowflakes."

Natalie exhaled soundlessly, her shoulders dropping. The sun painted the color of her armor in her hair. She and her mother had the same thinking face, Aurora noticed—a slight tilt to their heads with eyes that went completely hollow and unfocused. "Pity," Natalie concluded her thoughts, "I wanted to talk to him at least."

"Natasha told me yer relationship with yer father was ... pretty bad."

"It was, but I still miss him," she shifted her gaze downward, a slight pink tinge to her cheeks. "I am—was—*paipus da eshka.*"

Aurora convulsed with laughter. "Yer a daddy's girl? HA!"

"Silence yourself!" Natalie pushed Aurora.

"No, no I can't! Ya don't seem like the type!"

Natalie's face got even pinker, though Aurora guessed it was anger mixed with embarrassment. She placed a hand on the hilt of her cutlass, which made Aurora tone it down a little.

"I can't believe this, I gotta tell Aidan." She blinked her surprise profusely after saying that, but Natalie did not notice.

"You will tell no one," Natalie whispered sharply, "This is between us Hericonians."

Aurora traced a square over her heart, then a cross. "Fine, fine, I'll swear on it. But be careful around Aidan. He has a way of making ya speak."

"I can see that."

Aurora kicked her feet around some more. "Alright, then. Let's change the subject. What do ya do when yer not crawling around in the shadows?"

Natalie chuckled. "You say crawling around in shadows as if *you* do not do it."

"I don't crawl! I fly."

"Heh. To answer your question, I mainly amble. Aunt Eleanor has tried to get me to sew, but my fingers would not allow it."

"What did ya do in Seplechurus?"

"Trained with sword and thorn. I did not have much else to do besides plant ..."

Aurora couldn't do much but feel for her. A soldier through and through. On the battlefield, she was an asset, but when there wasn't a war or a fight? No one bothered to help her. Aurora knew too well that a childhood taken is a life stolen. "Then why don't we find something for ya to do? I doubt ya like books like Aidan and Nicklaus do, so why don't we spend time to figure something, ya know, just us Hericonian lassies."

Natalie stared at her incredulously. "Do you mean that?"

"Of course, why wouldn't I help? No one else misses the cold like I do."

Natalie sighed dreamily, "Seplechuran breezes ..."

Aurora hopped off the wagon, a smile plastered on her face. "Aye, why don't we try and find something fer ya here? I've been to a couple of villages; they have the strangest little hobbies."

"Aurora, you will not discover hobby like item, I need to experiment. Find what I like."

"Aye, yer not going to find it by thinking of it. At least look at the hobbies here."

She could see the wheels turning in Natalie's head, and when the Seplechuran girl finally hopped off the wagon, Aurora knew she had won.

"Very well." Natalie placed her hands sternly at her back. "Where to?"

Aurora slapped Natalie's hands down to her sides. "I was smelling some amazing bread over there. Maybe ya could try baking?"

"I have never thought of it."

"Aye, well, baking and cooking are an amazing pastime. I learned a little from my ma, but some other Delfizcani taught me a majority of my recipes."

"Neighbors?"

Aurora locked eyes with Natalie for a moment, trying to weigh her words. She looked down and away. "Aye … neighbors." She plastered a smile on her face, pointing to the direction of the aroma. "Let's go!"

The two girls walked through the town of Cahms, seeing the happiest people they'd ever encountered in their lives. The children ran around in the city sector while horse-drawn and iquan-drawn wagons carried farmers to the open fields that seemed to extend as far as the sky.

Still staring at the town, Natalie asked, "I must ask, Aurora. Barr *confiscation* and *reaping*, what are your hobbies?"

"Confiscation and reaping, huh?" Aurora chuckled. "I cook some-times. I like to make a mental note of the ingredients I see on the road. I enjoy acrobatics; the other kids loved it in Delfizcan, bouncing off barrels, swinging on wooden clotheslines, and running after dobbies. I also *adore* looking at the moon and stars."

"Stargazing?"

"There's a word fer it? I didn't know that."

"Many Dominian languages do not have a word for it, Seplechuran and commontongue being the exception."

"Stargazing is such a beautiful word! But yeah, I adore stargazing. Something about the night makes me feel more alive. That's one of the main reasons why I started ... confiscating. Things are so much more fun at night."

Natalie didn't say anything, and at first, Aurora assumed she wasn't listening, but there was some type of melancholy behind her eyes as she nodded. Aurora also noticed that Natalie wasn't as tall as she thought, maybe half a head. She had a longer torso, it seemed.

"It is lonely place, yes?" Natalie blurted.

"What?"

"Darkness, night."

Aurora shrugged. "It can be. Even if someone was there with ya—"

Interrupting, Natalie finished, "You cannot see them."

She sighed, and Aurora could easily figure there was something deeper going on, but should she pry? They were Hericonian, but they weren't friends. However, if she could try with the boys, maybe she should try to reach out to her.

"Is there something—" Aurora cleanly collided with Natalie's shoulder, quite literally forcing her to eat her words.

"Oh my, that smells delectable." Natalie took in a whiff.

Aurora held her mouth, tasting the bitter, metallic flavor of blood. She wanted to tell Natalie to watch where she was going, but the Seplechuran girl's eyes were closed, her pointed nose in the air as she sniffed the baker's mouth-watering wares.

"I have never smelled anything so fine." Natalie approached the baker, and Aurora followed suit. Aurora couldn't help but admire the architecture of the bakery; it followed the quaintness of Cahms. The bakery had a small triangular roof with three pillars holding it up at the points. In the middle of the open area was an oven that had a door on both sides. In the back of the so-called building was a countertop filled with different utensils and doughs, and the front of the area was lined with the different freshly baked foods that drew Natalie's nose.

The baker used a type of long wooden spoon to place a ball of dough into the oven before turning the spoon around to impale the dough with the three long points on the other side. Afterward, the gentleman wiped his hands and approached the girls with a smile. "Welcome," he carefully observed them before welcoming them again in their mother tongues. "What can I do for you?"

Aurora couldn't hide her surprise. "That was Uniket just now, how? Why?"

The man smiled, a tomato-red tinge to his cheeks. "We used to receive customers from all over before the war. I may not look it, but I was old enough to remember those good days." The man looked around, adopting a bit of a frown. "Some people may not think those days were all that good."

Aurora and Natalie followed his eyes to the groups of people that were standing around, watching the Hericonian girls' every move. They didn't even bother to stop staring once they were caught.

"What are ya staring at?!" Aurora called out. Some people cowered at her tone.

Natalie placed a hand on her shoulder. "No, sister, do not give them another reason to fear us."

"We just want some bread!'" Aurora shouted.

Natalie squeezed Aurora's shoulder, staring in her eyes before returning her gaze to the baker. "We will take two fresh loaves, please."

"Of course. I would give it to you for free for this mess, but war has been hard on all of us."

Natalie shook her head. "I would not ask that of you."

Natalie promptly paid the baker and set course for the wagons. Aurora, on the other hand, lingered, staring at the residents of Cahms.

"Sister, come," Natalie called.

Aurora growled as she turned from the crowd of people, noting the homes they were staying in. If they wanted a villainous Hericonian, they would be sure to get one. How Natalie stayed calm is beyond her.

"I don't know why ya let them treat us like that."

"I have been among Utopians doing good for many xantem, yet they do not accept me. Tell me, what good would fighting do?"

That sounded like something Natasha would have said. Aurora had to stifle her grumble. She tried to look at it from Natalie's perspective. The war had been going on for many xantem, older than even Jace. In addition, Aurora was wearing the colors of her home: orange and yellow; she wasn't even sure Aidan knew that. Still, they were not attacking anyone, and they came with the Great General of all people.

The girls finally made it to the wagon. Instead of jumping inside, they decided to just lean on it, eating their bread slowly. Aurora sighed; she changed the subject before she got too heated. "So, I suppose making peace is a Kcauss tactic your mother taught ya?"

Natalie chewed, then swallowed a piece of her bread. "Yes. Of course, it was mostly my father who spent time with me. He was training me, after all."

"Wait, I thought yer ma was the Kcauss leader? Yer pa never used the thorns."

Natalie scoffed, "He said flowers are for Utopians and children. He was ignorant."

So, he rejected using his clan-ability. Aurora knew how that felt, but for her, it was harder. To stop her blood from boiling, to control her anger after everything she'd been through—the hardest battle of her life. "So, he never used it?"

"He did, just never for combat." Aurora felt a pang of guilt hit her stomach. Natalie gave her a discerning look. "If you feel guilty for his death, don't be. He was not good man."

If only. A different void swirled in the pit of her stomach, one concerning her own people. She kept the name Borealis, and she prided herself on talking about her people and banner, but she stopped caring for her heritage. There were nights when she dared not look at the moon or, at the very least, didn't let the raging green reflect in her eyes. She had slipped up before; she knew the boys saw it, but she could never truly let it out.

"Natalie," Aurora lowered her head, fidgeting with her fingers, "I have a question, Hericonian to Hericonian."

"Alright."

"If ya hated yer own parent, would ya deny yer blood just to spite them?"

"No," she said quickly, "your blood is part of you. It connects you to your parent, yes, but it also connects you to your ancestors, your … kindred, as you might say. Do right by them."

Aurora bit into her bread, eyes looking distant. "Are ya sure?"

"Of course. Your blood *is* you; own it, and if need be, cleanse it."

Aurora sighed, pausing in front of the wagon before hopping inside. "Aye, yer right. It'll still take me some time to get used to it."

"Take your time."

Aurora nodded. "Let's finish this bread before the boys get back."

Natalie smiled. "Very well. Perhaps you can tell me more about the desert while we finish."

"Aye, so ..."

Evening light pierced through, and yet their little army was on the move. Aurora dozed on and off as she kept Aidan company at the front of the wagon. The second her head touched his shoulder, she jolted up, apologizing, only to do it again. With all the food she ate, she could sleep for another century. Though Jace didn't seem happy about her spending so much coin on food, at least Natalie supported her. Nicklaus also joined their merry band, staying in the back of the wagon with Jace. He returned to talking about the Blades, but Aidan would interrupt to shift the conversation when he knew the scholar was pushing his questions.

Aurora, in her food-induced daze, kept on thinking about what Natalie had said earlier in the day. Perhaps, the time had come for her to put down the malice she had toward her own blood—her own father. It would certainly give the team an edge in combat if she did, but holding it back for so long, could she willingly call it forth, the emerald eyes of her people? As night drew near, she knew she had to try.

She waited for night to draw to a close, and everyone slept soundly. The Great General had already made the announcement; they would be entering the Contested Lands in the morning, and nothing made her stomach fold unto itself before. The area was a place of savagery. It lay between Seplechurus, Setas-Li, and Utopia and spanned for miles in every direction; the faint of heart dared not enter. But for now, she walked through the darkness.

The night sky was in full bloom; stars spread like flowers. Aurora's eyes glittered and twinkled as they did. A flash of green filled her pupils as if in a hypnotic trance. It called to her. At first, she felt the feeling of wonder, however it soon was overcome with dread. Someone else drew close.

"He's close ..." she cowered in a hush. "Ya see the moon, the same moon."

In an encampment not so far, a large tent blackens anything its shadow touches, the moonlight pressing against it. In it, a pair of eyes glowing a familiar green stared at the moon, the body of a mountain silhouetted in the dark.

"Here, I thought we would never meet again. Yer close, Bonnie ..."

40

INTO THE LAND OF MOURNING

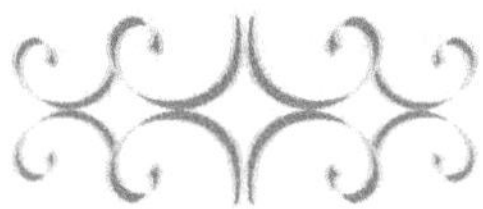

Something's amiss, I can just feel it.
—The Protector

TWO HOURS INTO *the Contested Lands.*

Jace sharpened his weapon, feeling the calm of steel as his whetstone did its work. It also served to overpower Nicklaus and Aidan's rambling in the front. However, the sound of steel did not have enough power to quiet Aurora's silence. Ever since they awoke, she's been distant, wary almost. He could see her micro-expressions with his Songluan eyes, the soft jitter, the twitching arms. He wanted to say something, but he was no Aidan; however, he did want a fighting companion, and by the looks of it, she couldn't fight like that. "Are you alright, Aurora?"

Only her eyes moved, but then she looked away. "No, he's so close."

Jace stopped sharpening. "Who?"

"My …"

Jace clutched his head. Something strange settled in, like pure darkness formed in the pit of his stomach, growling and groaning. Something was wrong, very wrong. The caravans moved slower; everyone looked to gray-leafed forests and charred trees for their enemies to spring their trap. However, Jace had different worries. In the corner of his eye, a shadow moved, but every time he looked—nothing. Something waited in the dark—and it felt like Brand.

Jace grabbed his scabbard and jumped outside the wagon; he marched toward the front, looking around, and Aurora jumped out after him. The area smelled of war.

Aurora stunned out of her trance asked, "Jace, what's wrong?" in her own haunted voice.

"Do you feel that?" he asked to everyone who could hear him.

Aidan looked around; brows furrowed in concentration. He passed Nicklaus the reins and hopped off the wagon. Zania began to thrash about, but Aidan whispered something that calmed her.

The trio from the desert kept their eyes open for any sudden movements, but there were none for now. However, Jace couldn't shake the feeling. Every negative emotion molded itself into a ball and thrusted itself into his stomach.

Aidan gave a half-worried grin. "Please tell me I'm not the only one who feels that?"

"We're not alone," Jace commented.

"Bandits?" Nicklaus asked.

"No," Aurora's voice came out weakly, "Seplechurans."

Something, *someone* stepped closer. This time, the trio wasn't the only ones to feel it. The caravan stopped, and Jace couldn't help but to observe his surroundings. A wide-open area and a large hill perfect for an ambush, several paths extending to the forest where no one could hear a scream. In the morning light, the shadows of the forest were thick like vines, wrapping and strangling all who would dare come close.

They heard Johannus scream from the front, "Men! Arm yourselves!"

Every single soldier armed themselves with staves, swords, bows, axes, and Utopian Antler Hooks, thorny branches that were curved into a semicircle on the end of a large pole. The Great General armed himself with two large war hammers that had meaty heads on them, the sides imprinted with Utopia's Jireh Tree emblem.

The Great General marched toward Jace, beckoning to meet him halfway.

"Warm up, your Blade, lad; this fight won't be natural."

Jace nodded, returning to his friends with the apt warning given to him by Johannus.

"Another beast?" Aidan speculated. "Not sure if we can fight that here."

Jace gripped his blade. "Better trees than buildings."

Aidan silently agreed. He snapped twice, and Chuckle and Snark emerged from his pockets and onto the pommels of his blades. Aidan unsheathed his swords, keeping his eyes mobile on the lookout.

Johannus screamed, "Come on out! OR we'll come to you!"

A few tense moments passed. Any person who wasn't keen in the art of battle would have thought that Johannus had too many *honia burres*.

A tall man, burly in build, slowly approached the crest of the hill. He flew Seplechuran colors, with a drake-like helm with more horns than the usual Seplechuran armor. The wind picked up, letting his cape flutter. "Well, hey there laddies," he greeted, his helmet amplifying his Delfizcani accent.

Aurora inhaled shakily, taking a few steps back. Aidan caught her fear and placed a hand on her shoulder, nodding with a steeled look. "It's okay, Aurora, we have this."

Jace looked at Aidan. "What are we dealing with?"

"Large enemy, about Johannus's height, maybe shorter. I can't see his feet. The claymore on his back is probably heavy, but he's holding it like it's a toothpick. Also, he's not Seplechuran." Aidan looked at Jace, keeping his unnervingly excited smile plastered on his face, "He's a threat. A big threat."

Jace spoke, eyes unmoving, "Any others?"

"Probably," Aidan cracked his neck, "he would be stupid to come alone."

"Or he is a menace," Nicklaus pointed his golden, basket-hilt rapier at the enemy.

"Stay vigilant," Natalie unsheathed her cutlass, "he is flying red cape."

Red cape, burly armor. The feeling Jace received before was right—this guy was an Umbran Sov.

Jace placed a hand on his blade, feeling the true Blade underneath react. The shivering chilled breath bellowed from his lips, filling the air with an unnatural cold.

"All ya laddies are probably wondering why I'm here," the Delfizcani Sov exclaimed. The wagon party let the wind do the talking, and even it had little to say. The figure searched around to find no one catching the bait he had placed. "No one? Bah, ya laddies are no fun, but I'll tell ya anyways." He removed the claymore sheath from his back and unsheathed his blade.

Jace observed the craft of the weapon; from here, he noticed it being of Delfizcani steel, an absurdly heavy metal his dad had him craft once. *A claymore out of that ... that's inhuman.*

The Sov pointed to a random soldier, then scanned the crowd with his finger. "One of ya here has a very special weapon that my emperor wants."

Jace glared as the Sov's meaty finger landed on him. He could feel the Sov's half-smile in response.

"Also, I'm very sure those caravans would be useful to us as well." He sat down on the ledge, his armor echoing in the forest with each word. "This could go two ways: ya surrender, or we clash some metal."

The Great General waved his hammers over his head, then smacked them on the ground with a loud crash.

"Perfect." The Sov motioned to the trees behind him.

Soldiers all flying Seplechuran colors emerged from the dark woods, all carrying different wickedly curved weapons. It was then that Jace felt the blackness in his stomach deepen, and again he started to clutch his head.

Aidan nudged Jace with his elbow. "Come on, brother, no time for a migraine."

"There's something else," Jace replied hollowly.

A heavily armored figure appeared at the Sov's side, sporting no cape but burly armor. The helmet didn't adorn the normal *aquadrig* design. Instead, it seemed closer to a deer's skull.

"Mmm," Natalie grunted, "Seplechuran Berserker. When I captured recent intelligence from Seplechuran scouts, they mentioned such people. They wield outstanding weaponry but are not considered Sovs."

"Well, it was nice knowing all of you," Aidan jested.

Two more soldiers ambled to the sides of the Sovs; they wore blue capes. Otherwise, their outfits were the exact same. One of them stared intently in Jace's direction as if they were sizing him up.

"It's definitely over now."

"Aidan, get serious," Jace commanded.

"Oh, I am."

The Berserker yelled, "Listen, we will not warn you again. Surrender to us now, or we will do battle! The man before me is the Dark General, the emperor's strongest warrior!"

The Great General beat his chest. "Stop trying to scare us and get down here."

The large Sov yelled, "Old man, want to do the honors?"

"*Go-sulki Ebal!*" yelled Johannus.

"*Go-sulki Ebal!*" replied his soldiers.

"Warriors of Utopia!" Johannus pointed his hammers forward. "ATTACK!"

The Utopian soldiers screamed at the highest peak of their lungs, surging forward in a fit for battle.

"HA! ATTACK!" The Sov yelled.

The forest gravely remembered the sounds of war once more as the green of Utopia clashed against the black of Seplechurus. Arrows started to fly from both sides, replacing the birds and falling like stars.

"Take cover!" a soldier yelled.

"Aidan!" Jace called.

"Already on it!"

Lines of golden links started to rise from the ground, intercepting the Seplechuran arrows with relative ease. Some Utopians were taken aback by Chuckle and Snark's presence; Jace couldn't blame them at all. They recovered from their awe and continued their fight without fear of death from above.

Then the air started to ripple.

"Do you hear that?" Aidan barely got the question out before a surge of pressurized air rammed into him.

Aidan, Aurora, and a few soldiers were catapulted back by the awesome power of the rippled air. Those who stood clutched their ears, hoping to get their bearings.

Jace ran to Aidan, "Are you alright?"

"What?!" Aidan shook his head. "Kind of hard to hear!"

Jace clenched his teeth, turning to the person who injured his allies.

It was one of the blue-caped soldiers at the Sov's side. Clearly, Jace could see the figure was a woman with a slender frame.

"Your chains are a nuisance," she spoke, accent unknown. "But they will be a bother no longer."

She seemingly tapped the air in front of her; a mirage-like slit came about before Jace saw a tiny crack form. *Was this her clan's ability? It's sinisterly powerful,* he conjectured.

"Halt your advance!" Nicklaus yelled.

Nicklaus and Natalie jumped at the soldier, slashing away with precision strikes, but missed all of them due to the soldier's deft speed.

"I'm not here for you two," the woman spoke coldly.

"But I am!" A voice called to them. The other blue-caped soldier emerged from the fighting, slashing at both Nicklaus and Natalie with one powerful cut from his sabre.

"I've been waiting a long time to meet you two," he chuckled hollowly, "the traitor and the prince."

Jace glared at Nicklaus, now wondering if that was even his real name. "Prince? You bastard! I should've known."

Nicklaus tried his best to avoid Jace's gaze.

"Oh? What's this?" The newcomer chuckled. "They didn't know? The Amoran continues to tell lies."

"You know nothing of the Amoran!" Nicklaus retaliated.

"I know more than you think, but I guess you will never know." The soldier ran.

"Raven, we must be after him!" Nicklaus commanded.

Nicklaus and Natalie rushed after the man. However, Nicklaus turned around, meeting Jace's heated eyes, then he continued.

"All nobles lie," the woman regained his attention, "it's surprising you look hurt. Though I can imagine why you're angry with him. The constant Setas-Lisian campaigns against desert trade made the free town of Bhall-Duraht little more than adobe and sand."

Jace gritted his teeth. This woman knew where he hailed from and far too much about the situation in the desert. However, he believed it to be a trick to throw him off.

"I will deal with Nicklaus later. As for you, you don't have much room to talk; you're the one who serves a monster."

"Are we so different then? You serve the Utopians; I serve the emperor."

Aidan was some distance away, fending off some soldiers before noticing his brother and somersaulted to his side. The Utopians and Aurora returned to their feet as well; they seemed to still hurt, but they were ready to fight.

Somehow, hearing what the woman said, Aidan interjected, "I wouldn't say we *serve* Utopia." Aidan rubbed his ears, seemingly recovered, "We're just doing them a favor, and trust me, this wasn't included."

The figure chuckled, "You haven't changed much, have you?"

"I like to call it character consistency, but who's asking?"

The woman rolled her shoulder and reached for her helmet, but as a drip of her black locks fell from it, she put it back on. "No, no … that would be too easy; I want you to guess." The woman put on an armored gauntlet that resembled a giant claw of something akin to a bear.

Jace could already tell from the craft that it was a dangerous weapon, and by the size, it could hold a secondary weapon, maybe a dagger. "Aidan, I'll handle her, you help elsewhere," Jace commanded.

Aidan smirked. "Jace, you dog."

Jace smacked Aidan on the back of the head. "Aidan."

Aidan chuckled, rubbing his bruise, "Hey, don't give me a concussion;

I was just joking." He motioned to Aurora. "Want to cause mayhem somewhere else?"

"Ya," she looked at the hill where the Dark General was. "Ya."

As the two ran off, Jace lowered his center of gravity, holding his scabbard with one hand while the other hovered over the hilt of his blade. He glared at the woman, not going to be fooled with mind games. Everyone he knew was either dead or captured. No one he knew would dare join Seplechurus out of their own free will. "Prepare yourself."

"Are you not going to try and find out who I am?"

"No," Jace seethed.

She growled, and the next words seemed to crack, "Just like you, Jace, just like you. Giving up on things like a coward." The woman cracked her neck and stretched out the metallic fingers of her weapon. She came at Jace with incredible speed, but it was not something he hadn't seen before; Aurora was faster.

He dodged her attacks, keeping his blade close to his body when he needed to block. He flourished his cloak to distract her as he went for blunt, powerful strikes, but she seemed to be faster on the dodge than anything.

"You fight like your father," she commented, "cold, blunt strikes."

Jace bared his teeth at her. This lady seemed to know so much, but nothing about her made sense. Not many spent that much time with his father to even know how he moved.

He growled and kept on attacking. The woman's movements were faster now; her gashes were closer and closer to making contact, but she didn't seem to put in the extra effort.

"You're slowing down, Jace."

He stiffened, and she knocked him square in the chest, forcing him to step back. *That ... hurt?*

"I know how strong Camerus skin is; I backed my blows with a subtle push of air pressure."

"You talk too much."

"Not as much as Aidan, you know that. Though Ms. Rosie had more sass."

Jace's eyes widened. "What?"

She hit him again in the chest hard, blood trickled from the corner of his mouth. For once, the mountain toppled over, feeling the cracks on his surface—but that's not what pained him the most.

The pieces were starting to fit together, and Jace didn't like the picture he saw. The fog started to set in. *Hope, regret, hope, regret.* Each word laced the spaces of his brain before puncturing every lobe. His eyes grew narrow, shaken. He stepped back, almost tumbling over. "No ..."

The girl chuckled painfully. "Finally figuring it out, or are you going to ignore this as you ignored my existence? Maybe playing the flute will make you feel better."

She delivered another painful blow that landed right in the middle of his chest. He clutched the bruise as he dropped to one knee.

"You could promise yourself that you'll make it out of this," she laughed painfully, "but that won't matter because you break all of your promises!"

A pressure-backed kick cut Jace across the face, sending him to the ground, grasping for air.

"See how hard you're breathing? That's how I felt when the fires consumed my home. Sick, alone, waiting for you to help me. BUT WHERE WERE YOU?"

She tapped the air, letting a ripple form. Jace coughed up specks of blood, standing up. He could see the vague impression of her face slowly forming on the helmet. But he needed to know.

"Wait." He held out a hand, his eyes growing misty. "Wait … at least let me see your face."

She halted, a shaky finger about to release the air pressure blast, but she held it in. "Okay."

If he was truly correct, then seeing her might have been the hardest thing he had to do. If that woman were *she*, the one person he cared for so much, he knew he couldn't just fight her.

She unlatched her helmet and removed it. The graceful ebon threads unfurled with a gemlike glow. The eyes were familiar, shadowed, and angular, sitting upon the pale skin with an exotic warmness underneath.

She's—alive? "Serenity?"

41

THE (UN) TOUCHABLE

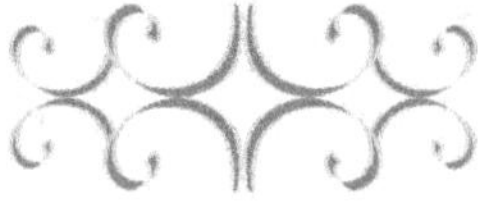

So, this is really war…
—The Wildcard

THIS? THIS IS what was going on in the land for over ten xantem? Man against man, each out for the others' blood. A full-fledged melee where one had to watch their back or risk their head. The opponent, changing faster than a turn of a page, no time to think, no time to breathe.

Aidan downed two soldiers, the ignisium hissing as he pulled both blades from a Seplechuran's body. Before he could see, Chuckle yelled at him, drawing his attention to another soldier who flipped out his blade from his sligek sheath. Aidan immediately brought one blade to guard himself, the ignisium slowly searing through his opponent's weapon.

Then someone screamed.

A soldier pinned to the floor, their hands bleeding as they held a Seplechuran blade inches from their own face, locking eyes with a soulless Seplechuran soldier. Seeing this, Aidan pushed his opponent with his body, severing their blade completely before ending his opponent with a slash.

With astonishing accuracy, he threw his free blade at the Seplechuran pinning the Utopian, giving the Utopian enough of an advantage to get up and finish his opponent. Aidan ran to the soldier, helping him up. "Are you alright?"

"Yes, I …" The Utopian quickly pushed Aidan to the side, taking a sword to his own neck.

Aidan stared wide-eyed, the red liquid spraying from the soldier's wound. In anger, Aidan took the sword that he threw, and without skill, finesse, or anything in between, he brutally overpowered his new opponent until he, too, was a bloodied corpse.

For the first time since the battle started, Aidan felt his heart beating in his chest. It wanted to leave; it wanted to leave the battle. It reminded him of the day he lost his town, lungs yelling to the highest heavens before being cleaved out, rivers of blood formed from lifeless bodies, and the disembodiment—the surreality of it all never truly hit him. He saw the bodies today as he did then. This time, however, he felt the prick of war touch his fingers. *No Jace this time, no, no, only Aidan—and I have to rage.* Aidan rushed through the battlefield, slashing at every Seplechuran he saw. He attracted the attention of several soldiers. Using Snark, he reached for a large tree branch, snapping it from its place and bringing it down upon them.

He only glanced to the side, his body moving before an arrow could graze his skin.

Snark reached for that archer and every other one on that ledge, swiping them down, jingling as they fell from their perches.

More and more soldiers started to notice that the boy with the chains was a priority target. They started to surround him, each of them wary of what he could do. They should, of course, *I am the wild, after all.* Aidan mused.

Chuckle and Snark started to expand and grow, taking out all the soldiers with a single swipe of their golden bodies. The simple sight of cracked Seplechuran armor made Aidan smile devilishly, just a bit, but it wasn't enough; he couldn't let Bhall-Duraht repeat itself, not here, not again.

He continued his crusade. The golden chains stretched across the battlefield, acting as both savior and oppression. Chuckle saved, and Snark had very little reason to play angel. Aidan got into as many melees as he could; anything that overwhelmed him was left up to the chains.

He had to keep moving, so another battle he went into. He jogged to the next fight, painted with sweat and blood. His heart didn't bother to quiet down, and his lungs worked just as hard to sustain him. With heavy hands, he slashed at another opponent. This time, his opponent dodged easily, retaliating with a slash of their own. In his mind, he knew that Chuckle and Snark would help him, but soon, he realized that was not the reality.

Aidan tried to jump back, but the soldier's blade collided with his chest, tearing it as it would cloth. He yelled as he fell on his back. Seplechurans who saw him on the field knew they had to take advantage. He'd never seen Seplechurans run so fast, each of them wanting the opportunity to kill him.

Come on body, move! Aidan pulled himself up, deflecting an attack and immediately making distance. He saw the numbers against him, seeing very little way he could fight them. "Chuckle, Snark, help me out here."

But they didn't. Instead, they jingled lowly, not Snark low, but a new low, one he had never heard before in his xantem of fighting. *They're … tired. Since when could they get tired?*

Aidan continued to retreat. He could wait for them to recover, but he didn't know how long that would take. The second his mind finished those thoughts, his chains went still for a moment. It was a stark reminder that Aidan was on his own.

Up, down, up down. His chest rose and fell, trying to get enough breath to make his next move. He needed to think; he needed to act. Now, he knew, this wasn't a time to be helpless; now wasn't a time to die. Then Aidan heard someone yell, "Attack!" But the accent was off. The Seplechurans turned around to be greeted by Utopians of a great number approaching them. Bravely, or stupidly, the Seplechurans fought, but just as swiftly as they engaged the Utopians, they fell.

Aidan braced himself against a tree, sliding down once the last of the Seplechurans were dead on the ground.

"Are you alright?" A healer came to his side.

Aidan looked down and away. "I'm bleeding because I like the color red," he muttered.

The soldier chuckled, pulling out some salves from her pouch.

"Do you know where my friends are?" Aidan asked.

"The one with the white cloak, I have not seen him, but the Delfizcani lass that was with you is facing the Seplechuran Berserker."

Aurora's fighting a Berserker? And here I am sitting around feeling bad for myself. "Heal me quickly, I need to go."

"Go where?"

"Where else? To the Berserker."

42

Fallen Petals

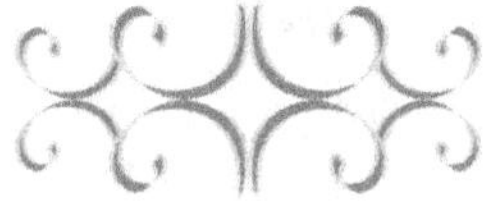

I am NO traitor.
—The Rose

ASWIFT RAPIER CUT past Natalie; only her cheek suffered a graze, adding another scar to the collection on her face. She retaliated with a swift strike of her own, grazing the breastplate of the young male officer. "Impressive style, I can see so much Brand in you," he crooned.

Natalie took a defensive stance, with her cutlass in front of her. Her opponent smiled, taking an offensive posture with his blackened basket-hilt rapier.

Nicklaus came from out of view to stab the man, but the officer sidestepped, causing Nicklaus to recoup and retreat. The man laughed, not even willing to push his advantage. He just allowed Nicklaus to retreat a safe distance.

"What is your name, scourge?" Nicklaus asked.

"Wouldn't you like to know?" He flicked his cape in a taunting fashion, keeping his eyes more on Natalie than Nicklaus.

Either genuine interest or strategy, Natalie didn't know. She didn't care. Right now, she had to understand who this was. His cape color was unused before in the Seplechuran army, and yet he was traveling with Sovs? She wondered. *It is clear he is threat but how lethal?*

"Wow, Brand told me you would do this," he spoke.

Natalie narrowed her gaze. "What?"

He wiggled his finger. "You're analyzing me, aren't you? I came here for a fight, not to be gawked at."

Nicklaus stepped forward. "Reveal yourself and spare us the time."

The man shook his head. "Oh no, that'll be too easy. I guess I'll have to keep you both occupied."

Upon those words, Seplechurans started to emerge from the shadows of the forest, and Nicklaus stuck to Natalie's back in response.

"Now, Utopian Rose," the man pointed his blade at her, "we fight."

The man and his soldiers wasted no time in closing the gap between them. Nicklaus surged forward, using his precise strikes to mow down those who opposed him. Natalie spent time dodging blows, retaliating only when necessary. *These are my people, I cannot …* Her leg suffered a blow. She stepped back, seeing the soldiers crowd her with murder in their eyes.

Had all the lives she preserved become nothing compared to what she had to do now? She could simply incapacitate them, but the Utopians would not let them live. Also, what would stop them from rising up and attacking her once more? She wondered.

She suffered more blows to the body, nothing fatal, but if this continued, Nicklaus would be fighting alone.

Four soldiers decided to gather, in the middle was the officer. She scowled at him; he planned for this. He seemed to know her, which is why he wanted a fight. "Give up," he commanded.

Natalie growled, "Did you not say that you saw my father in me?"

She rushed for a charge; a soldier readied for her; she stopped midway, parrying his blade, grabbing his arm, and with a growl, used his weight to launch him into another soldier. Now, two of them surrounded her, and she did not wait for them to fully mobilize. She aimed for the leg joint of a soldier before slamming his helmet into the ground. The fourth wished to see battle and surprised her with a slash that disarmed her. She kept dodging his continuous slashes until she found an opening. She grabbed his arm, cracking it for him to drop his blade. She removed his helmet and palmed him until his nose flowed with blood, then kicked his abdomen, prepping him for her final move; she got behind him, put her arms around his waist, and suplexed him into the ground.

The officer clapped, and the metallic grinding frustrated her. "Brilliant!" he cheered. "Your fighting style is admirable. It combines the ferocity of Seplechurus with the grace of Utopia."

"Impressed?" She retrieved her cutlass and pointed it at him. She whipped her head, flicking her raven-colored locks from her dark, brooding eyes.

He looked around, nodding at his fallen comrades. "You didn't even kill them? Amazing. You have a force of will equal to your father's."

Natalie shook her head. "No, my strength of will is from my mother." She stabbed her blade into the ground; thorn vines rose from the earth, slithering over the steel. "*This* is from my father." Buds started to bloom from the vines; beautiful roses grew as if the seasons of time were rushed in a matter of seconds. Natalie uprooted her blade with a mighty swing. "Prepare yourself."

Natalie's attacks were wide-reaching and swift, provoking her opponent while keeping him at bay. She left openings which would encourage an attack, but her opponent had a brain, knowing very well the vines had another purpose, presumably covering those blind spots.

"The flowers are quite lovely," he commented, "but they can't be for decoration, no?"

He struck, attempting to sever the vines. Instead, the thorns sundered his blade. Natalie then grabbed his helmet by the mouth, kneed him in the stomach, and ripped the helmet right off.

"Well, I see you have not lost your Seplechuran ferocity." He pulled himself from the ground. He whipped his short hair aside, picking stray pieces of hair from the rest of his locks. His skin seemed to be Utopian, darker than the pale skin of her people, but no, he couldn't be that. His eyes sparkled like Seplechurus's frozen skies, and that pointed nose was unmistakable.

"You are Setas-Lisian," she commented with suppressed surprise.

"Half," he corrected, "from my father's side."

She grumbled. Her hunch was right. The other half could it be Mareenian? Shatersian?

"Observing again," he said sing-songly.

He pointed his broken blade at Natalie, waving it challengingly. He had to be kidding; he could not defeat her, not with that, she reasoned. He must have had a plan; he intentionally separated Natalie and Nicklaus from the others. She observed her surroundings; they were in a pocket of the forest, a small open area that resembled an arena. Since the Seplechurans were here first, he could have planned all this from the start.

"Well then, since you have brought out the roses, I could only do so much alone." He clapped twice, and more soldiers emerged from all sides. They snarled and growled at their blood-kin, as they closed in.

Natalie growled, "I see what you are doing; you want me to slaughter my blood-kin."

The man shrugged, smiling deviously. "I don't know what you are talking about."

Natalie looked around; her eyes swelled with emotion. The numbers of the soldiers continued to grow; she knew she could easily dispatch them, *but ... should I?* "*Evoce*! (Listen!) Can you not see that he is using you?! Sending you to your deaths! How can you listen to his orders!" She spoke the rest in her mother tongue. "Can you not see that Emperor Rastanis treats you as fodder!"

One soldier spoke in the mother tongue, "And where were you? Joining our enemy to slaughter us!"

Natalie roared, "I SLAUGHTERED NONE OF MY PEOPLE."

The soldiers inched closer. "You will have to kill us if you hope to stop us. *Judavek.*"

The tears finally fell from her eyes, her voice shattering like fragile glass. "Stop, please, I beg of you. Look at what you do! Please see Ras for what he truly is!"

"Quiet! *Judavek!* You are all lies!"

Judavek. Judavek. Judavek.

How could they be so blind to this false loyalty? The emperor does not care for their lives; he only moves his agenda at the cost of their own. She looked on at her brothers and sisters who were blinded and refused to see. To them, she was a traitor; she was the blinded one.

She gripped her chest, unable to feel the beat of her aching heart through the armor of people who were not hers. To murder them, to end their lives before they could see, would be inhumane. But she knew she had to lose something for this to happen. And lose she did. The patriot in her went blind.

Natalie whispered with restrained emotion, "You have seen West Voshkovik Gardens, yes? There are many rose bushes there—"

"Attack!" The young man shouted.

She shut her eyes, "—I planted them myself."

The soldiers roared and screamed as they closed in; the little lamb was going to be slaughtered—they thought. They thought wrong.

"*Ogeviz em vrecrum* ... (Grant me purity ...)" The buds of roses started to bloom from the thorns encapsulating her blade; a pale white filled the petals with its shining entirety. "*Uvaya: Witerekcauss.* (Wither: White Rose.)"

Natalie spun, lacerating the armor of a soldier behind her. As the soldier's body collapsed in death, white roses started to bloom, overtaking the body. In a matter of seconds, the body became a lovely rosebush of white roses.

The soldiers came in full force against her, stopping for nothing, fighting with no fear. But why fear? *They would soon become beautiful.*

"*Ameve em O petalia ... Uvaya: Enturukcauss.* (Enthuse me O petals ... Wither: Orange Rose.)"

With speed birthed from the energy of the orange roses, she slashed four more times, four more opponents fell, and four orange rosebushes bloomed. Natalie did neither gloat nor cry. They were hopeless; she was hopeless. She should've known the emperor's clutches would run deep.

She kept on attacking, alternating between orange and white. When she finished, the young man stood alone. She knelt beside a rosebush muttering a prayer of forgiveness to her blood-kin, for they were not to blame, yet they paid the price in full. "It pains me to strike them down," she kissed the petal of the rosebush. "I honor their memory in petals." She turned to the young man; her brows hung low; her face contorted in a ravaging anger. She pointed her blade at him as she stood. "*You*—shall be honored in thorns."

Natalie waved her hand over an orange rosebush; the petals started to blot again, turning a blackish purple. She could see the fear in his eyes; his false ignorance stripped away like the petals she plucked. He knew what was to happen.

But all she saw was the pose. He lifted his sword away from him, pointing to the sky as if extracting power from the very firmament. Natalie's eyes grew wide. She muttered to herself, "Impossible ... he does not know that technique." She hurried, trying to reach for the darkened rose bush, but whatever happened, whatever struck her, was too fast, faster than her hand. All she heard was the rumbling of the earth and terror of the splitting wind. Petals of orange and white moved around her until her vision grew dim.

43

Obstacle

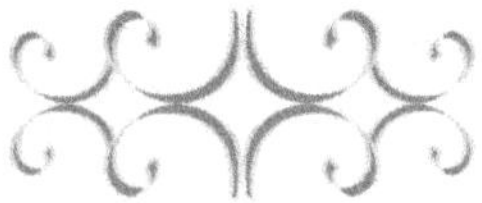

UGH! I HATE FIGHTING PEOPLE LIKE THIS!
—The Thief

SHE BACKFLIPPED SEVERAL times, trying to keep her balance when she finally landed. She rolled her shoulder, and a small dagger of pain rolled with her.

Her opponent was the loud woman who announced her father earlier. Normally, Aurora didn't mind fighting armored opponents, but when they had a giant shield the size of them, maybe, *just maybe,* there was a slight annoyance.

Aurora growled as she circled her opponent, trying to get on her right side, the one that held the shield. Its long rectangular shape, with its spiked appendages on the corners, could offer a proper blind spot that Aurora needed.

"You are a Delfizcani," the Berserker yelled, "just like the Dark General. I have respect for your people. If any of them had half the sense of him, they would have assimilated themselves in Seplechuran units."

"And risk our pride, culture, and honor?"

The woman kept talking. Aurora tuned it out, hoping to get her distracted enough to see an opening. However, the first thing Aurora couldn't help but notice was the woman's accent; she wasn't Seplechuran. In fact, she sounded Mareenian. Hard to tell with her face covered in a cowl.

"—You should join us," Aurora finally tuned the woman back in. "These Utopians do not have love for you. They'll use you, then betray you at a moment's notice. They're Illisian, it's what they do."

Aurora stopped her circling. The creases of her brow knitted in thought.

The woman smiled through her unique helm; the shadows couldn't hide the white of her teeth. "Betrayal," she repeated, seeing its power over Aurora. "I have been betrayed many times before. Seplechurus, despite what it may look to you, hides no betrayal. It provides a comfort you will never know. You are Hericonian, surely you wish to side your lot with us."

Aurora gripped her daggers. Red flowed from her knuckles to her neck. The audacity of the woman in front of her to say something—so deeply steeped in truth. These Utopians would sacrifice her in an instant to save someone like Nicklaus. It didn't hurt to admit it; she just needed to watch her back. If Aurora was staying in the fight for the Utopians, maybe the Berserker's offer would have been tantalizing like her favorite broth, but she wasn't here for them. Aurora smirked.

In seconds, the Berserker lassie put up her shield with a spin; she managed to block someone who was stupid enough to vault off her. Said-stupid-person, using his body weight, specifically jumped on the top part of the shield, tipping the Berserker over, flipping, and landing right beside Aurora.

"Laddie," Aurora greeted.

"Lassie," Aidan greeted. He stretched a little bit, his body jerking as his muscles contorted at a certain point. As she tried to diagnose the problem, Aidan asked, "So, what are we dealing with?"

Aurora looked at him, then at the Berserker who now took to her feet. "Lassie's cocky, but she has the right to be with that shield."

"Can she … you know …?" He threw up his hands and stomped around.

"Haven't seen much of that; she only seems to be good with her weapon."

Aidan pouted. "A bit waste of the name Berserker if she doesn't, you know, go berserk."

Aurora shoved Aidan a little. "Ya sound like ya want her to go mad!"

Aidan shrugged with a little head shake. "Eh, kind of."

Aurora sighed, "Yer unbelievable."

Aidan got low, his swords flaring up for a fight as much as he was. Aurora caught his glance. "We best be careful; we don't know what she could be hiding."

Aurora stretched her legs, twirling her daggers afterward, "I know that."

"Just a reminder," defended Aidan. "Let's get her."

Aidan jumped in front of her, flourishing his blades. Aurora readied her daggers. It seemed that the laddie knew her style by now; Aidan knew that her weapons weren't suitable against a resolute defense.

Aurora split off from Aidan's shadow, circling the Berserker, hoping to find a weak spot. However, the lassie wasn't wearing standard Seplechuran armor; it was thicker, and the pauldrons were rounded and spiked and made to protect her from every angle. She was made to fight people like Aurora, and as much as Aurora hated to admit it, Aidan had to fight alone.

The Berserker blocked every one of Aidan's attacks with minimal effort. Despite the heaviness of her armor, she moved swiftly in it.

Aurora just had to wait. She knew her moment was coming.

"You're stronger than I expected, boy," the Berserker called out.

"And you're weaker than I expected. Of course, I shouldn't expect much from a pseudo-Sov."

The Berserker growled, raising her shield, just in time for Aurora to slide through her legs from behind, delivering a rising kick to the Sov's jaw before retreating. As she stumbled, Aidan went for a vertical slash at her head, severing her helmet.

"Nice!" Aurora cheered.

The perfect orange slit formed right in the middle of her helmet and probably into her skull. But if so, Aurora and Aidan stood there perplexed, thinking, *why does she still stand?*

"Is that ... ignisium?" asked the Berserker. "Curious, we have yet to find a way to forge them into weapons. Maybe we'll take you as a slave and have you do it for us."

Between his heavy breaths, Aidan chuckled, "Surprised I didn't slice your lips."

She chuckled, "Actually ..."

She removed her helmet and the first thing the two of them saw was the flowing white hair and bronze west continental skin, but what stood out the most was the burning slit down her face.

Aurora and Aidan stared at her wordlessly.

"I guess I should tell you, I don't feel any pain." She ran her finger down the mark on her face. "But you will pay for that. But first ... what is your name, child? I'm impressed."

"Well, if you must know, I am the Wildcard of the Desert, Aidan."

The woman lifted her gaze. "Hmm. I'll remember that as I kill you." She raised her shield, then dropped it, kicking up some dust and spreading the ashes on the ground.

So, the lassie doesn't feel any pain, Aurora thought to herself. *That automatically rules me out.*

Almost sensing this, Aidan went for another attack, and the Berserker blocked with ease. She pushed back, forcing him to retreat a couple of steps. She continued to push him further back, overpowering him easily.

The laddie shouldn't be losing this badly; he has the same monster blood as his kin, right? Aurora thought.

The Berserker forced Aidan to one knee, his strength waning faster than Aurora expected.

"Aurora, anytime now!" Aidan yelled.

Aidan left the Berserker's guard open long enough for Aurora to aim swiftly at her hamstrings. Aidan used the opportunity to make some distance. "She may not be a monster like Voshkovik, but she's annoying," Aidan huffed, barely standing on his feet.

"I agree; the lassie's tough; she needs to go."

Aidan glanced at Aurora, trying to force a smile because he knew she was attempting to comfort him while he was trying to feign strength.

"Aidan, are ya alright?"

Aidan winked. "Peachy … just tired."

The Sov stared with a smile on her face, a queasy one that made Aurora feel uneasy, but something made it worse. Her wounds to her hamstrings and her face were—healing.

Aidan yelled, "Oh, come on, that's not fair!"

"Did you think painlessness was all that I brought to the Seplechuran Empire? I think you underestimate the—"

Aidan interrupted, "Hey, Berserker, I like your accent," he took to his feet. "But you sound so much better with your mouth closed."

Her brows furrowed. "Witty remarks and sarcasm are for the desperate and the foolish."

"I will not agree or disagree with that."

Keep her talking, Aurora thought. Aidan's distractions had to be one of the best parts of his strategy, especially since Seplechuran higher-ups loved talking. He subtly glanced in her direction, probably praying that she figured out something.

She could only see a giant shield similar to Brand's unbreakable bardiche. The Berserker's strength may have been on par with Brand's, but that could easily be attributed to the sheer size of the shield. Nothing could help them in this situation, and Aidan clearly wasn't going to last much longer. "I want ya to retreat," Aurora demanded.

"I'm not going to leave you here with her! I'm fine," Aidan lied. His swords were sagging in his already loose grip.

"Yer wound!"

"It's not a big deal. I only started getting tired when I fought her."

Aurora almost retorted, but then she stopped, glancing over at the woman who was waiting patiently. "Wait, ya only got tired now?"

"Drastically tired, yeah."

Aurora reran their entire fight up until now in her mind. She never attacked the Berserker directly; in fact, she mostly threw her daggers, save for that one kick she delivered to her face. Aidan had been attacking her this entire time, and the only difference between the two of them was—

"Her shield!" they both managed to say.

Aidan continued his surmising aloud, "It drains energy and gives it back to her." The two gave the woman a hard stare; now, her choice of weaponry made sense. A shield nearly as tall as herself, her opponents had no choice but to hit it. It was clever. Aidan groaned, "So, how do we beat her?"

"I have an idea, but yer not gonna like it."

He chuckled, "The things I do for you, Aurora."

With every word she spoke, his brows began to furrow. She knew she was asking for a lot, but she also knew that Aidan could take it. He fought to stand and take a stance, but words easily slipped from his mouth, "Let's give'em a show!"

Aidan ran ahead per their plan. Hopefully, the Berserker wouldn't think of something new since they were repeating the same strategy. As Aidan attacked, the Berserker raised her shield. Aidan and Aurora alternated their positions to keep their opponent guessing. Aidan tried to avoid her shield with every slash, instead aiming for her head.

"Oh? So, you figured it out? It won't help you much, really." Quickly, the Berserker used her shield to push Aidan, forcing him to block with his blade. He fell to one knee, and Aurora quickly rushed over, knowing he was on the last of his energy.

"You're going to die here today!" the Berserker yelled manically.

"I would retort, but you've literally taken all my energy to care." He shouted, "Aurora!"

Aurora yelled to draw the attention of their adversary. The stalwart warrior tried to meet Aurora's attack, but Aidan whispered to Chuckle to catch the shield.

Aurora knew daggers wouldn't work; she needed one powerful move. Aurora dropped her daggers and balled her fist. She needed to summon the burning rage that resided in her core, the same burning rage she planned on using to attack her father. She only had a blink, a sliver, a second to act—and act she shall. A soft hum of energy radiated in Aurora's eyes, like in the desert, and when she argued with Jace. When her fist connected with the Berserker's face, the most disgusting crunch she had ever heard filled her ears. Immediately making the hum disappear.

Blood sprayed her face as Chuckle wrested the shield from the Berserker. The lassie skipped like a stone, and her head turned at an unnatural angle. Soon, the nearby Seplechuran soldiers who were once fighting the Utopians gathered.

"That's what ya get," Aurora whispered.

Once Aurora saw Aidan staring, she threw her gaze in another direction. One of the other reasons she tried to avoid using that power was because of those looks.

"Uh, Aurora, what the hell?" he asked.

"I ... will explain later. I have to go now."

Aidan fell to his knees, drenched in sweat. He inhaled before asking a tired, "Why?"

"I have to fight my pa ..."

Aidan nodded solemnly. "I figured you knew that guy."

Aurora shivered as if Jace just walked by. Even her legs started to shake, she didn't want to move, or maybe she couldn't. Aidan stood, placing a hand on her shoulder, but she jumped at the slightest touch, eyes flickering with that same green light.

"I could go with you."

"No, I have to do it alone, I have to fight him."

Aidan furrowed his brow. "Why? Aurora, come on. You can trust me."

Aurora didn't even look him in the eyes, but her clenching fist was all Aidan needed to see as she declared, "I need closure, fer me, fer my ma."

"I can't quite argue with closure." Aidan stopped to break her gaze, forcing her to look around. The Seplchurans that gathered around their fallen comrade decided to shift their attention to the two of them. He continued, "Well, if you want that closure, I suggest leaving now."

"What about ya?"

"I have Chuckle and Snark and the Utopians. The Seplechurans will follow you otherwise."

"But—"

"Get out of here Aurora, oh, and make sure you win."

Aidan's smile was the same, but his eyes lacked that spark. The hesitation in her voice wasn't for herself, it was for him. She could stay but if her father escaped, she would never forgive herself. She nodded, running off into the distance, praying, hoping that her father would still be there—and that she could finally end her xantem-long suffering.

44

HE BLINKED

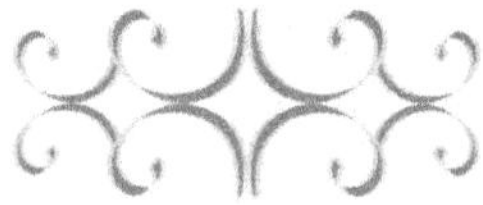

I hope Raven is doing better than I.
—The Prince

THE LAST SOLDIER fell unconscious after a solid hit. Nicklaus had to kill a majority of them, no matter. Blood dripped from the tip of his blade, and even his own cloth was stained. If he had been wearing his armor, maybe he would have felt more merciful, but as the prince, it was his life or theirs, and frankly, he was of the mindset that his life was more important. Raven's merciful tendencies did not have to extend to him; the remaining Seplechurans should feel grateful the prince's mercy reached even their dark hearts.

Nicklaus discarded his glasses because the time for games and facades had passed. His heart mandated that lives were at stake, and the future needed to be preserved.

Rumble, Rumble.

The ground shook under him for a moment. The feeling was all too familiar. A smile crept on Nicklaus's face; surely some Amoran must have found him and joined the fight!

He glanced at the darkening sky; a storm brewed. Hopefully, the fight would be over before they received the brunt of it. He rushed over to Natalie, hoping to see her victorious, however he saw no such triumph.

A half-sundered sword ran through her abdomen, the wielder, the man from earlier unmasked. The fiend's face got close to hers; her eyes glazed in shock. He whispered something, then pulled his sword out, letting her fall.

"NATALIE!" Nicklaus ran to her side, getting to his knees and caressing her hair.

She looked back at him, stunned, scared, hurt. Her body jerked painfully as she coughed, and it looked like she could cease in a moment. Yet, she grabbed his arm, lowering her brow and subtly nodding before her eyes dimmed shut and her arm going limp.

"Oh look, the prince can get on his knees for a commoner," the fiend chuckled.

"What did you do to her?!" Nicklaus roared as he stood.

The fiend chuckled; he actually chuckled. Nicklaus got his rapier and took a massive slash at the man. He dodged, but that didn't stop Nicklaus from attacking again and again. "What did you do to her?!"

"You're Amoran," he answered, "see her wound and tell me."

Nicklaus let the red drain from his face; the coolest of breezes cleansed his anger for a moment. He examined her wound: the precise stab was backed by such force. A perfect slit carved into her flesh with enough power to keep her down. Nicklaus stood, clenching his jaw. His heart skipped narrowly, and his mouth dry as a desert. He watched the man with shaky eyes but never let the trembling get to his blade. "This is Amoran Style Blinkblade."

The man clapped. "How observant."

"H-How do you know this technique? Only Amoran should be able to do this."

A smile formed on the man's face, small and creeping as the dark clouds in the sky. Nicklaus shook his head furiously. "No! No Amoran in their right mind would follow Seplechurus!"

The man cackled, "I was always told that I was a few wheels loose of a wheelbarrow."

Nicklaus pointed his sword away from himself; his body shifted to the side, one leg tilted forward. He saw the amusement in the man's eyes as he did nothing to stop Nicklaus.

A white line, the Blink Rail, formed in Nicklaus's sight. The so-called direction of Yehowehel himself to guide the Amoran, and only the Amoran, to victory. Latching onto it allowed them to perform Blinkblade, a high-speed, forceful attack.

"Blink," Nicklaus muttered.

Nicklaus's body followed the white line at a speed that made the ground kneel before him. Ash and grass on his side as his body soared through the battlefield. His sword stretched forward, aiming for the neck of his aggressor. *This lowly welp thought that siding with his kingdom's enemies was a game*! People's lives were at stake, and he forsook his honor to fly the banner of a different side.

Nicklaus's tunnel vision kicked in, but it didn't matter; once he hit, it would be over.

"Oh, please," the man laughed. He crouched low, awaiting Nicklaus's approach. In the most fluid Amoranian motion, the man caught Nicklaus's arm.

Nicklaus howled in pain; the numbness of his shoulder spread down to his fingers. Small needles of pain stung until a massive jolt surged throughout his body. Nicklaus dropped to his knees, holding his pained area.

The man seethed through his teeth. "Did I dislocate your shoulder? That looks absolutely painful."

An armored leg swept across the back of Nicklaus's head, forcing him into the dirt.

"Oh, look at how the mighty prince has fallen. Tragic, no? At the knees of Seplechurus, no doubt."

"Who, who taught you that? No one can hinder the Blink."

The man deeply chuckled again, this time a Setas-Lisian accent grew thicker on his lips. "Can't believe someone beat you, no? Your pride has been your undoing, just like Athis's."

Athis. Nicklaus's father. The king. The young prince rolled over, looking at the man tiredly. "How do you know my father?"

His smile faded. The man crouched before Nicklaus, staring at him intently. "You really don't know who I am, do you?"

Nicklaus shook his head.

"I don't know if your own hubris is causing you not to see it, or you really are as dull as your pitiful parents." He raised his foot. "Either way, let it be known that you were defeated by a commoner." He brought his boot down.

After that, Nicklaus saw nothing but the void's stare.

45

Never Leave Me Alone

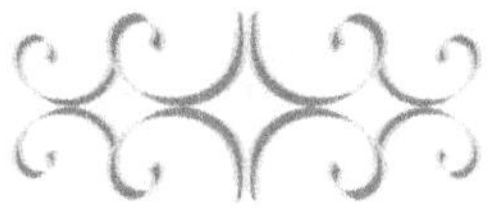

I can't believe she's …
—The Protector

1139 Dominian Xantus, Bhall-Duraht

JACE COULD REMEMBER it all too well; the arid breeze traveling through his desert town caused the sand to act akin to a torch. He finished his training with his father, his brows weary as he saw the line of people forming outside his father's forge. A line of people he would eventually inherit. He ignored the people waving to him—his eyes narrowed. His breaths were labored, and he grabbed his chest, trying to steady himself. Yet, as he remembered where he was going, he managed to catch his breath, regaining himself. He opened his eyes, a smirk gracing his features. Moments later, his joy continued to grow.

"Jace, wait up!" a young Serenity called out.

Jace slowed his pace in the joyful chase that was tag, his feet sinking deep into the sand. As Serenity closed in, she caught her breath, straining

*to breathe. Jace smiled as he pulled out a small cloth. "Sorry, too much?"
the little boy asked.*

*Serenity started hacking uncontrollably, spitting up a little blood. Jace
took the cloth and dabbed the corners of her mouth; a soft smile appeared
on her face.*

*"A little," she smiled, "sometimes ... I feel like you're going to leave me
behind."*

*Jace hugged Serenity tightly. "Don't worry Serenity, I will never leave
you."*

Never

Never

N E V E R

1149 Dominian Xantus,
The Contested Lands of Three Kingdoms

Each strike, each painful strike, ripped their childhood away. With every
slash of Serenity's gauntlet, Jace realized what he had done, what he must
have forced her to do. The high-pitched flares of memories left a deep
gash on his heart. *What have I done?* "Serenity ... please ... let me just
explain," Jace pleaded, his sword hand weakening.

Serenity gave a painful chuckle. "Explain? Explain!? Explain how
you left me! Please, go on, explain to me how you carefully thought of
leaving me behind?!"

Jace stepped back. Flashes of memories of Serenity's sickly face
kept hounding him. By the time he could push them away, he could
see Serenity now, so hurt, so angry. His core beat with a song of pain
and agony. He could see her eyes were so pleading; she wanted to hear
something that would put her at rest—but he had nothing.

"Go on! SAY SOMETHING!!!"

Jace startled backward when she screamed. He knew he couldn't say anything; nothing he could do would remedy what he had done. His hands shook. He dropped his blade—floods of pain cascaded down his face. There was nothing to say.

"I was scared, Jace! Alone!" Her voice quaked, "There was no one ... no one. My mother was gone, I had no friends, no family. I only had you—" she fell to her knees "—and you *left* me."

I should hold her. I want to hold her. But she wouldn't forgive him; he knew it. Jace knew those tears; he cried them before. Those were the tears of someone who stayed strong for so long.

"Tell me," she wiped her eyes, "does Aidan know?"

Jace swallowed a lump. "No. As far as he's concerned ... you died."

Her tears stained her claw when she lifted it up to her face for some solace. Her hair, black and dreary, hid the person whose heart bled.

"You could've come back. I was still there. They let me *rot* for a week; afraid they'd catch my disease." She took a deep breath. "You could've whisked me away, like you promised over and over ... but you gave up on me."

Hope. Something he lost long ago. Sometimes he thought it would cost him, but it didn't, didn't it? It cost *her. If Aidan knew all this, he would stab me for this mistake; at the very least, he would be laughing at how poetic my predicament has become—a full-circle drama where I get my comeuppance.*

Serenity stood to her feet, clicking her pointer finger and thumb together, readying a sound rupture for an attack. "You know, I was in pain for xantem because I thought you were dead. I was going to get vengeance for *you.* They took you from me, and I was going to take everything from them from the inside. I was in pain for you Jace." A small sound generated from the union of her fingers. A faint sound evolved into a rupture. Pressure started to form like a ripple of water from where her fingers pinched, growing like pain. "No more pain. No. More."

Serenity ferociously punched the rupture, expanding it into a blast of air pressure. Jace attempted to pick up his blade to block, but one couldn't block sound, especially one that rushed faster than the raging sea. The ground shook in terror, and the rocks and trees rippled in fear of the power. The oscillating attack threw Jace, sending him skipping like a stone.

"Not going to fight anymore, Jace? You're going to give up?"

Jace tried to get up, but his bones wobbled with weakness and pain. His clothes were slit and torn all around.

"Giving up hope so easily? Just like you," Serenity stalked closer, looking at him on his knees. "You gave up on me; now you give up the will to live. Fitting, you die like this—hopeless." At this point, she was right. He was hopeless, and look where it got him, where it got her. There was no point in fighting her; he would only be grateful that his end would be at the hands of someone he once considered a friend.

She pinched her fingers; the rupture slowly started to form. Jace knelt there, motionless.

"Don't worry, I won't hurt Aidan. However, the General's daughter will not be so fortunate."

General's daughter? Natalie? ... Aurora? It made so much sense now, her trembling, her fear. Fear. Just like Serenity. His hopelessness did cost her, but it should not cost another person he was close to, and, El willing, he should not give up on having Serenity back. Aidan and Aurora, even Natalie. Dying now meant leaving them. After all they had accomplished together—*could*—accomplish.

Jace's body started to grow cold, and so did the air around him.

Serenity's rupture started to collapse on itself; everything shivered. "What's ... happening?" Serenity's voice went shrill.

Jace took a deep breath through his nostrils and let visibly chilling air leave his mouth. "Breathe ... Nevrence."

It soon grew hard to breathe. Serenity's bones started to quiver under the might of the divine ice. People to sculptures, forest to tundra. Jace felt his strength regaining; he heard the frozen call—how mighty his reply.

He wouldn't hurt her; he couldn't hurt her; her predicament marked a fault of his own doing. However, what stirred in the divine winds wasn't going to stop at frostbite.

46

Useless Effort

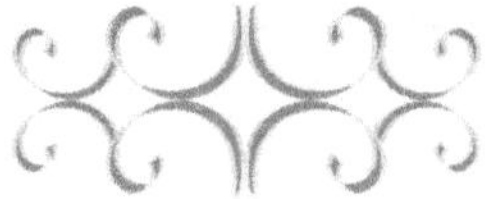

This ... war ain't for me, is it?
—The Wildcard

UTOPIAN SALVES WERE some of the best medicines on the continent. It explained why they were so resilient. Some of the Seplechuran books Aidan read compared Utopian resilience to cockroaches, and after healing up, he could believe it.

He got up, stretching his arms and arching his back, feeling good as new, well, mostly. Even Chuckle and Snark seemed to be more energetic. "Thank you," Aidan said to the Utopian healer who applied the salves. Aidan refitted his tunic, feeling the missing cloth. He barely had enough material to fix his clothes.

The Utopian healer nodded, leaving Aidan to ponder, and ponder, he did. That's when he felt the tear drop from his eye. He reached for it, swiping it away. Nothing here was supposed to happen: the war, the death. The three of them should have been back in Bhall-Duraht, helping the people rebuild with Natasha. He massaged his temples at the thought; he missed the idea—the idea he and the others were invincible. The childish thoughts that he could take on any problem with a smile on his face and a skip in his step. He wanted to be the main character, but now he felt himself drifting to the side of obscurity, only to cheer on others, only to be blissfully irrelevant. This wasn't a story book. He could die; he *could've* died. He questioned. What main character is useless? What main character cannot hold their own against the adversaries that are being thrown their way? Was he destined to be saved every single time, unable to help those he loves?

He leaned on a tree, the weakness setting in. The burdens of his burdensome behavior grew ever heavier.

Chuckle and Snark tried to comfort him, climbing atop his shoulders, whispering soothing chimes in his ears, but there was only so much they could do. His chains were the real heroes before; he could only act as a shield for Aurora, and now the healers had to tend to him like a child.

Would it be a crime for him to say he missed his mother? Or childish that he longed for his father? He never felt more like a child, acting recklessly in battle, acting soberly now. Or maybe—he danced around the word that he truly wanted to call himself.

Useless.

47

IT COMES DOWN TO FAMILY

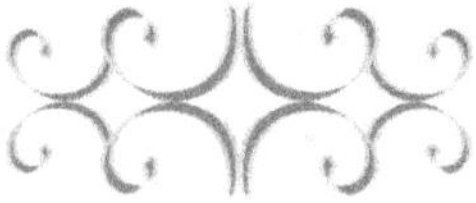

I'm the only one who's gonna beat him.
—The Thief

CLOUDS WERE GETTING gray, and she could swear she felt the tears of the sky fall to her face. It had the right to weep; nothing about war prompted happiness. Dead bodies littered Aurora's way to her father. Blood drenched the grass as some of the soldiers died in the most horrific ways. Aurora held her nose as she ran past. Some of the soldiers even held their own, weeping as best as they could, while others watched their backs. A privilege for sure. She didn't have time to weep when her mother died; she had to run. The only thing she could take with her was the blood-drenched clothes that her father had bought for her. *Ironic, really*, she thought.

Clashing steel shattered her thoughts; she could hear the types of weaponry. The burly hammer of Utopia and the sharpened weapons of Seplechurus wielded with Delfizcani excitement.

She ran into the clearing where the Great General and her father were fighting. Utopian and Seplechuran soldiers alike were strewn about on the ground, dismembered or smashed in. She took a step forward, hearing a metallic groan underfoot. She lifted her foot, seeing a young Utopian archer, barely older than herself, clutching her weapon. Aurora cupped her hand over her mouth and nose, not wanting the waft of blood to come in and her bile to come out.

"Come on, old man!" her father's voice rang out.

Aurora grabbed her daggers, remembering why she was there. She roared. *This has to end!* She abandoned all subtlety, all the sneaking around; her father had to pay! For the Delfizcani, for herself, for her mother! "PA!"

Aurora ran at her father, surprising both him and the Great General. She got several slashes off, which her father dodged, but before she could get more, Johannus dropped one hammer to grip his other with both hands, and he swung strongly at the Dark General, who took the attack to his chest. With that, the Great General grabbed Aurora, much to her protest, and made some distance.

Aurora growled, "What are ya doing? Let's take him! I have to fight him!"

"I'm not going to let you fight," Johannus shouted protectively. "You can't handle him!"

Aurora stabbed her dagger in the ground, locking eyes with Johannus in a bubbling rage, "Ya have no, absolutely *no,* clue what I can handle. I'm going to take him. He killed my ma, I'm gettin' revenge."

Johannus cocked a brow. She knew he could see it in her—the determination or the stubbornness. *If he wants to stop me, he's gonna have to fight both of us,* Aurora thought. Johannus' mouth opened wide, but no words came out. "You really remind me of Eleanor when she was your age, Yehowehel. She was stubborn," Johannus reminisced. With a nod and tug on his hammer, he continued, "You have my permission to fight, but don't get killed."

Aurora snickered, which caught Johannus' attention, "What's so funny?"

Aurora glanced at the tall general, the general who was much, *much* taller than her. "I wasn't asking for permission."

Johannus gave his famous hearty laugh, "Atta lass! That's the spirit."

Aurora and Johannus twirled their weapons before taking stance. "Steel yourself!" Johannus yelled.

"Aye!"

The two of them approached the lumbering Delfizcani. Her father's sense of humor remained intact all these xantem. He was faking sleep as he leaned on his blade. Now that she was truly staring at him, his personality was not the only thing that had not changed. He looked the same as he did all those xantem ago with the minor additions of forehead wrinkles and noticeable laugh lines. Her father was a rugged, wide-faced man with a pronounced jawline and cheekbones. His hair was thin and redder than her own, something she'd always been jealous of. However, she had his button nose and his abundance of freckles that littered his face. He noted that when he was younger, he and Aurora would have looked like twins since he had noticeably slim eyes. "Oh, are ya two done? Ya know, lassie, I don't like to be kept waiting."

Aurora flourished her daggers. "C'mere then."

He laughed, swinging his sword overhead before he charged with a battle cry. Aurora knew her father; he remained a predictable man, but predictable didn't mean beatable. Battle was a game for him, similar to Aidan's, and yet very different. He always chose which game he wanted to play—speed, power, or precision—and adjusted his style based on that. Right now, with his pitiful strikes, but nimble movement, he had chosen speed.

Aurora didn't have time to tell Johannus this, and shouting it now would only make her father change the game. Besides, wielding a giant war hammer versus a man with a nimble claymore would only tire the old man out. If the Dark General—no—*Merek* chose the game of power, maybe Johannus would stand a chance, but her father liked odds.

As they fought, Aurora realized both Borealis were touching a power they hadn't touched in a long time. Something primal that made them faster, each strike timed perfectly as if they were dancing with one another. Aurora spat at it; she hated the synergy she had with her father, but it couldn't be helped; he *was* the one who mostly taught her how to fight. She knew one strike from her father would put her down, so she had to play smart. He kept his claymore on his shoulder, attacking, then putting it back in place. With one strike, however, he went for a wide swing. Aurora ducked in one motion and kicked her father's face in a swift second. Her father easily recovered and went in for a slash but was stopped by the massive hammer of Johannus, which made Merek skid across the ground. Merek stretched, muttering something Aurora couldn't quite hear, before leaping into battle again, shouting, "Come on lassie! Haven't I taught you nothing?"

"Don'tlecturemepapa!" Aurora snapped quickly in Delfizcani.

"I'lllectureyaifIwantto!" Merek snapped back in their mother tongue before pressing his attack.

Shoot, I'm getting too excited, jumbling my words again. Aurora dodged with a clean backflip, spinning her daggers ready to attack again, but this time her father simply stopped.

He placed a hand to his chin, then wiggled his finger at her. "Oi, where'd ya mount my Berserker? She ain't dead, is she?"

Aurora snarked, "We killed her, and you'll be next."

Merek cracked a smile, which made Aurora extremely uneasy. "That's really unfortunate, I just got me one of those. Aw well, I hope you can handle the Shade."

"...Shade?"

"Aye. When you kill a Berserker, the power in their weapon latches onto their spirit, draining it of negative emotions to form a ... ghost of some sort." Her father scratched his neck. "I don't know how it works fully. I think I dozed off when the emperor was explaining it."

"How can I believe ya?"

Merek shrugged, looking off absent-mindedly. "Why would I lie? Yer gonna die anyway."

A loud groaning reverberated in the forest, a ghostly wail. Johannus and Aurora looked around, standing back to one another. The groaning grew louder and horrific, sounding like a banshee in the night.

Johannus spat. "That doesn't sound good."

A dark light started to spin in the sky, accompanied by ghostly wails and a deep vibrating sound. Aurora could barely see it as it disappeared, only to reappear at Merek's side.

As her father described, the Shade appeared to be some sort of ghost. A solid black like Brand's egg that transformed him. However, the form shifted constantly like a flickering flame under a gale. It could have been due to its fading form or, if her father did speak truths, the emotions from the host.

Aurora grimaced at the Shade despite being a bit taken aback. Though Johannus seemed the most perplexed, seeing as he had never encountered anything like that. The trio had experiences with dark powers before, seeing someone like this seemed trivial at best.

"So, this is the power of Seplechurus's darkness. The lengths they would go ..." Johannus held his hammer tighter now. "Well, maybe Eleanor was right about me retiring," he laughed lowly, "however, I'll tell you what I told her, 'til my dying breath.'"

The Shade shifted in place over and over. It screeched again. Despite its strange form, only one thing remained consistent: bloody red eyes that moved like wheels, and right now, they wished to trample the Great General.

In a flash, it rammed into him, launching into a tree. Surprisingly, the old man shot up quickly, giving a powerful smash as the Shade attacked again.

The Shade stretched out two appendages that took the shape of hands, it launched at Johannus again, this time trying to wrestle him for his hammer.

"Lass!" he yelled. "Hold him off! I will try to freeze this shadow over!"

He winked and she immediately understood what he meant. Though maybe she should have been grateful to the Shade, it got Johannus out of the way. And that was all she would see of him. If she were to have her vengeance, she knew that she needed to do this by herself. The thumping in Aurora's chest grew louder by the minute. When she left the desert, surely, she didn't expect to see her father. If she knew the journey would be this much trouble, she would've ... *no, I still would have come.* She may have had to run away from her vengeance, but now—it stood before her.

He took a defensive stance, waiting for Aurora to make a move. She readied her daggers. She knew for a fact she couldn't beat him, but her father played around; if she could catch him slipping up, maybe *just* maybe, she could get him. For now, she had to quiet her heart—the Grim Reaper of Bhall-Duraht does not make a sound.

48

FLUTTERING PETALS

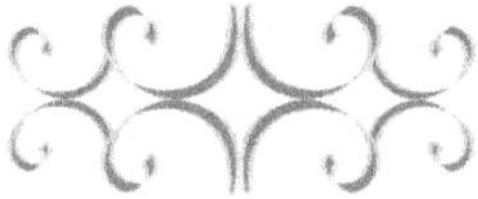

I cannot believe what I have done.
—The Rose

ALISTAIR, HE SAID his name was Alistair. Natalie writhed in pain, her hand covering the wound from that sudden attack. *Whoever this ... Alistair was, he was powerful, but most of all, mysterious; cunning strategist who refused to show all his cards at once, but ... Blink?* That was an Amoran technique, the *royal* Amoran technique.

Natalie fought with her fading might to turn herself over; Nicklaus lay there, face bloodied and beaten. Natalie painstakingly dragged herself over to him. She desired to stay still, but Nicklaus was her friend, one of the few lights at the end of the tunnel. She pressed a hand tighter against her wound and continued.

She quickly removed her gauntlets, pressing her pale Seplechuran fingers on his pulse. She felt it stronger than she had expected. He was going to be okay, but his arm looked terrible. Natalie dug her fingers into the ground, whispering to it, *"Amegred modouveciah. Uvaya: Wumvekcauss.* (Protect those who are loved, Wither: Pink Rose.)" Thorn vines started to rise from the ground, entangling themselves around Natalie's fingers. Buds of pink roses blossomed to embrace the sky that would soon fall with the rain. The thorns pricked Natalie's fingers, filling her with a healing pulse she could feel entering her bloodstream. She cupped Nicklaus's face, letting the vines prick him. She felt her strength return, and Nicklaus started to shake himself awake. Unfortunately, she couldn't do anything about his shoulder.

Natalie managed to sit up. She probed the rosebushes that now littered the fields, her people that she had killed. She tried to swallow her guilt, but it clogged her happiness. She broke her oath. She swore to protect her people, now look at them, victims of her hand. "*Ket ornuc tev do'veree?* (What have I done?)"

She placed a hand over her heart, muttering prayers to Yehowehel for safe passage for her people. Seplechurans were devout followers, but their problem was in how they served him. They thought they should serve Yehowehel through conquest, through power, but in the end, they lost their way to the lust of battle and death. Though it did not make her feel better, she knew, if not by her hand, it would be through someone else's. And yet, why her hand? She closed her eyes. In these times, her parents agreed on one thing, how to cope when things seemed grim—sing: "*Vaza häs uva meri, zudem El a sol ...* (When the night descends, trust in El the strong ...) *Vaza häs uva meri, zudem El a sol ... ort hech tev praed.* (When the night descends, trust in El the strong ...with him I blossom.)"

49

THAT WHICH COMES BEFORE THE STORM

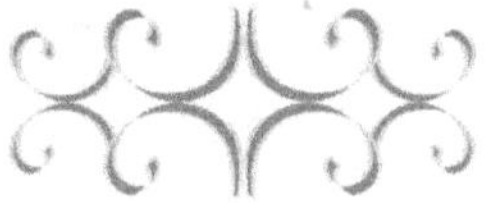

This can't be it.
—The Thief

AURORA HUFFED. HER heart echoed more times than she could count. She didn't think the battle would be easy, but El knew she didn't think it would be this hard. Her daggers were either bent, broken, or shattered, just like she felt. Merek kept smiling, only taking small breaths. How he had that much stamina was beyond her.

"Tired?" Merek asked, his eyes lacking true concern.

Aurora wiped the sweat from her brow, breathing hard but steady. Blood secreted from a wound on her arm caused by a close call that nearly took it off.

"Guess so," Merek sighed, "I guess the fun stops."

Merek, this time, rushed in himself, quickly closing the gap between him and Aurora. He gave quick slashes in swift succession. Aurora dodged, hoping to think of a counter to him, but nothing came to her. She tried to flank him, but his nimble movement prevented that. He protected his weak points very well, too; she didn't expect anything less from him. Before he took on the General title, Merek reigned as an exceptional warrior. His fighting style didn't change all the xantem, but it didn't need to; one doesn't change perfection—*near perfection*, she corrected herself.

Aurora cartwheeled back with one hand, backing into a tree. She dove from her spot as her father aimed for her head, severing the tree clean through. She tried to get enough breath to keep going, but she began to slow, and the blood from her wound still wept.

She had to think, she had to remember. Ironically, her father told her something that she would never forget: *every stance has its weakness. The good ones protect against those weaknesses.* Her father may not have been the brightest, but he had mastered one-on-one combat.

Aurora continued to dodge his attack until he ferociously punched her in the jaw before grabbing her by the neck and throwing her aside. Like a feline, Aurora landed on her feet, but the daze she felt from the blow to her jaw forced her to her rear soon after.

Merek cackled, "Ya know, yer quite the lass, ya get that from yer mother. But ya didn't inherit any of my battle sense."

"Don'tcha know how to keep ya mouth shut, ya dobber!" Aurora barely yelled due to her shortness of breath.

Merek started to laugh loudly, so much so that his head flew back. "Oi, lass, ya got me mouth at least!"

Right there! Aurora called to herself. As Merek's head rolled back from laughter, he left himself open. Aurora removed her last unbroken dagger from her boot and threw it in a singular motion. By the time Merek faced forward, a glint of steel nearly touched the tip of his stubby nose. With little to no time to react, he tried moving his head, but the blade drew too close, and a slit of blood emerged from his cheek to his ear. He held the mark on his face, then stared at the blood on his hands. *Heh, I let ya throw me here on purpose!* She thought to herself as she grabbed a nearby, jagged dagger and threw it. This time, she aimed for his eyes. Aurora smiled as she got him; she caught him off guard long enough for her to get him. She actually injured him!

Or so she thought.

As the blade was about to pierce the eye of her father, he raised his hand in a motion faster than the eye and caught the dagger in mid-air. His cheerful demeanor completely evaporated. "Ya know, I was wrong. Ya exploited my crucial weakness there."

Merek twirled the dagger in his hands. Even doing a few tricks by spinning the blade through his fingers. The sound of his armored fingers made Aurora shiver. She used all her weapons, all she had was the ornate golden dagger in a small sheath in her boot—useless for fighting.

"I'll commend ya, fer sure." Something started to change in Merek. His demeanor shifted, his tone deepened, his posture straightened, and the pressure he exerted nearly doubled. Aurora started to retreat; the queasiness in her stomach made her gag. Merek walked closer; he threw Aurora's dagger behind him as he approached. Aurora swallowed heavily.

"Stayin' strong? That's a Borealis quality." Merek stabbed his blade into the ground. Then, he simply walked over to her with a punch. She fell back in an attempt to dodge, but before she could get far, Merek just grabbed Aurora by the neck with his other hand and slammed her into the ground. He bashed her head multiple times until blood oozed from her nostrils. Tightening his grip around her neck, Aurora begged for air, just a tiny taste of it.

I'm going to die. Aurora admitted to herself mentally. Why didn't she even consider that he would be stronger than his old self? She knew full well that he was a monster, no—a demon. A merciless, overpowering juggernaut.

She felt as if her eyes were going to burst from their sockets. She reached for his claws, but they didn't budge. He just chuckled.

Merek threw her to the side. Aurora didn't catch herself this time. The feline movements had already died their nine deaths. She couldn't come back from this, not now.

Why didn't she bring help? Had she completely forgotten that Jace was chosen by Yehowehel? No, she hadn't forgotten; she couldn't forget. The loom of death made her realize something: she still didn't trust them enough. They were a team, but she hadn't let them fully in. She didn't trust them with this side of her life; she didn't trust them to fight her father, and now she was going to have to pay for her mistrust in full. In a twisted solace, she wanted to smile; at least she was dying the same way she lived.

In a desperate attempt to get up, Aurora managed to roll over, her face looking toward the clouds above. She took a small breath: *it's going to rain.* Aurora pushed herself up to her feet, but her body was softened, weak, and fragile. Merek approached much slower this time. All Aurora could think was that perhaps he wanted to savor the moment.

"Seeing yer body like that, lassie, reminds me of something." Merek stopped his advance, "Do ya remember how yer Ma died?"

Aurora's eyes enlarged when she heard ma. Her face looked shakily at her father, burdened with redness, burning with fatigue. She coughed, choking on blood and saliva, and pleaded with herself to get out one prayer. "Don't."

"Oh? Still touchy about that?"

She sobbed, shaking her head. "Don't."

Merek had a half-smile; he wished to provoke. She knew it—that didn't mean it would stop her.

"It was in the Delfizcani castle, Dupnaught, the name."

A tear streamed from her eye; her voice became as shaky as her body.

She made direct eye contact with the smiling Dark General, "Pa, please, don't," she coughed.

"The king told me to choose someone to kill, ye or my wife."

"I said STOP IT!" Aurora pleaded.

The skies were starting to grow dark; her nose tickled with the smell of rain. Sky tears dropped, and her father lifted his head, allowing a single drop of rain to race down his smiling cheek.

"Do ya remember yer reaction …" Merek smiled sinisterly, "… as yer mother's head rolled?"

With a loud roar, Aurora pulled the golden dagger from her boot and charged at her father. She didn't care about the pain, she didn't care about her life, all she wanted to do was: Kill. That. Man.

She felt the rage build in her veins, the fury coursing through her like her crimson blood. The darkness reached her eyes, clouding her judgment and overcasting the last bit of reason she had left.

She could only see her mother's smiling face and the blade that cut her down. As she stared at the sinister person wielding it—she snapped.

Her father swung his claymore with a decapitating blow, but she raised her golden dagger—stopping the blow entirely.

He exclaimed with a slight gasp.

She, too, hadn't realized her power until the forest green glow of her own hatred and anger reflected in her father's eyes.

He raised a brow. "The Borealis Rage, not a flash of it, but the actual thing, since when did ya …?"

So, this is what it was. She had all but forgotten the name, a power unique to the Borealis Clan, the reason why they were the most feared clan in all of Delfizcan, an ability that turns all anger into sheer power and raises adrenaline to the maximum. She felt the blackness of anger consume the whites of her eyes until she became—

Kill him, her monstrous thoughts yelled at her.

She pushed her father away with an animalistic snarl. With him staggered, she kicked him savagely in the chest, denting his armor.

Kill him.

Aurora didn't aim for the joints as she would normally; she raged at him like a beast, consecutively hitting his armor over and over. He tried again to cleave her head, but her reflexes were like her rage—flawless.

Kill him.

Aurora dove for Merek's legs with a spin. He backed off nimbly, only for Aurora to change her movement and backflip into his jaw. Blood sprayed from his lips, some landed on Aurora's face. The red only sent her into a final frenzy, thrusting forward with her dagger. It wasn't built for combat, but she would make it work. The sound of the gold tearing through his armor rang happiness in her ears. She felt his warm blood dripping from his wound to her fingers, the smell of it nearly forced a smile to her face.

Kill him.

Aurora plunged the dagger deeper. Her father's chuckle cut short like his breathing. Every time he grabbed her hand to fight back, she would only make his pain worse. Merek taunted, "Well, your Rage lasted longer than mine did the first time I used it." He let out a sharp breath before panting rapidly like he had just emerged from a body of water. He gripped Aurora's hand even harder. "Ya did good, lassie. Really good."

Aurora was going to say something, but Merek cut her off, "However, yer going to start feeling a lot of pain right ... now."

As if on cue, Aurora's body tensed up, and she appeared to be out of breath. Her body ached in places she didn't know could ache. Every single muscle started to seize, the slightest movement spelled pain for her. She howled in pain while rolling on the ground.

"Aye, happened to me, too," Merek said, almost jokingly

Merek stroked Aurora's hair in a mocking, father-like fashion. Any movement felt like her bones were snapping. Her eyes blurred with tears. She was crying too hard to even respond to his taunting. The pain was excruciating; it felt as if someone was stabbing a dagger in every part of her being, then lighting the wounds on fire.

Merek pulled out Aurora's dagger, wincing a little, then he threw it at her side. "It'll be over soon, pitiful child." He went over to his claymore, wrenching it from the ground before returning to his daughter, lifting his weapon high in the air.

She grabbed the dagger for solace, watching helplessly as her father brought down his blade like a guillotine. *Of all the ways to end*, she hadn't imagined this. She always thought that she was going to rob the wrong person and get killed, maybe die of old age, or travel the world and die in the most beautiful field ever under the sweet, tender night sky. Either way, she hadn't robbed the wrong person; she was only sixteen, and the sky was cloudy with darkness and rain looming like a bad feeling. Aurora just closed her eyes, finalizing in her heart that with her life, she had done okay. Her thoughts faded into memories like when someone's life flashes before them just before death. Her memories blurred into a dizzying mess. The sounds of rain muted in her agony. She wanted to apologize to her mother; *I failed her.* She wanted to apologize to Jace; *he will be disappointed.* To Johannus, she concluded that she hadn't kept her promise. Lastly, to Aidan, *at least I'd stopped running …*

"Breathe …" She heard the winds whisper.

The icy mist surrounded her, whispering their promises of protection. However, the frozen pillar that had launched her father into the forest whispered something much different.

Aidan and Jace raced to her side. Aidan took her hand, smiling gingerly at her. "And you told me not to do anything stupid."

Jace exclaimed, "No time to joke, Aidan! Aurora, say something!"

Aurora opened her eyes slowly; she saw the boys looking over her. They came for her, saved her—again. Even Jace looked like he cared, in his own special way, she noted. Aurora saw Jace's Blade; it was transformed. He was using his El-given abilities to save her. A smile stretched across her pain-stricken face; she motioned for the boys to come closer. With reluctance, they did. She eked out a breathless, "Thank ya, laddies."

A smile tugged at Aidan's face, which he didn't hide. Jace, of course, showed reluctance; he even went as far as to turn his head as he said to Aurora, "Don't get sappy, just don't die."

Aurora couldn't help but smile at that, even though it hurt. It seemed like the Borealis Rage made her overlook the pain, not give her immunity to it.

"That was a cheap move!" Merek screamed from the forest.

"Aidan, get her out of here," Jace commanded as he eyed Merek.

"Aye, aye captain," he saluted.

Aurora winced and groaned as Aidan picked her up. He looked over at her with a caring eye, trying to find some encouraging words for her. "You'll be safe soon, I promise."

Aurora nodded slowly; her wounds growled. The pain grew far too much for her to tell him to stop talking. All she could do was snuggle closer in his arms, leaning bittersweetly into his chest as if he were carrying her off to some forest wonderland of faux safety.

Aidan laid Aurora on the grass while he rested against a nearby tree. He stared out into the distance for a moment, unsure of what more he could say. *He probably wants to make fun of me fer going it alone,* Aurora surmised. However, when he looked at her, Aurora saw the snark drain from his face, and the only words he could muster were, "I'll be right back."

"Wait," Aurora painfully groaned, "stay with me, please?"

Aidan looked back at the battlefield and then back to the injured Aurora. With a sigh and a chuckle, he sat down next to Aurora, crossing his legs. Aurora smiled, trying to sit up. "Hey, don't hurt yourself now," Aidan exclaimed as he helped.

"Talking is starting to be easier, I think," she strained a reply.

Aidan leaned Aurora on a tree, setting her down as if she were a babe. He kept staring at her wounds, more so her arms. They were covered in blood along with her bruised knuckles. "You're really something, you know that?"

She chuckled plainly, "How so, laddie?"

Aidan looked to the sky, the rain pouring down harder, yet the trees shielded them. As a droplet landed on his face, he wiped it but still kept his eyes toward the heavens. "You really tried to fight a Sov yourself and didn't die. Not only that, but one of the soldiers told me how you led the charge against the Berserker before I got there. You've got quite the talents for a thief from the desert."

Aurora clenched her eyes, holding in her emotions. She silently noted how, yes, Aidan had said all of that, but she clearly wasn't enough to save her mother. For her, it was another example of how she had to run, letting others carry the burdens of her mistakes. "No, I'm nothing, I'm useless. I can't avenge my ma, and I keep bringing people into my mess." She let a tear slip out. "I'm useless, useless, useless."

Aidan rubbed her shoulder. "No, you're not. Honestly, Aurora, I think you could make a difference in this world."

"I can't make a difference in the world! I could barely make a difference in the desert!"

The weakness she had tried to fight all this time was starting to show its head. No matter how much she tried to hurt the person inside, the weakness always came back to haunt her. For all her gloating, for all her skill, she couldn't avenge her mother even though the bastard who took her away stood in the same forest.

"Aurora ... do you remember when I caught you in Utopia?"

She gasped.

"I didn't understand what you were doing to yourself ... but now, I have an idea."

He did notice? She couldn't tell him anything; it was her self-admonishment, *no, no, not anything.* But she knew her face had already betrayed her, solidifying his theory by the hesitation in her eyes and the quiver of her lip.

"I ... don't understand why you do it. Quite frankly, I think that you don't think too highly of yourself." He chuckled ruefully, eyes damp. "I honestly understand not liking yourself. I understand feeling useless, but you have to ask yourself who are you really hurting: the person you think you are or the person you actually are?" Studying her, he took a second to let what he said sink in. "You may think you're nothing, but you may actually be ... a hero."

"Ya don't understand! I couldn't do anything at all! I was weak! I *am* weak! I'm no hero!" She yelled, throwing the dagger in the dirt. "I'm not a hero, I'm not a friend, I'm not a daughter, I'm not anything!!! Everything in life told me that ages ago!"

Aidan's face contorted into a frown. He pointed a finger at her that pierced through her fragile, bruised emotions. Back when they had left the desert, she remembered how she wanted to know where his breaking point began. Now, she had reached it. *He's going to start listing the reasons why I'm forever going to be a terrible person,* Aurora fearfully thought.

Then he spoke, "Life doesn't get to tell you who you are. *You* are Aurora Borealis; you tell me what that means."

Hasty footsteps fell, stepping through the puddled grounds. Natalie and Nicklaus had made their way over, both nursing their fair share of injuries.

"Good," Aidan said, sitting up. "I need someone to watch her while I help Jace."

"I will accompany you. I have a grudge to settle." Nicklaus nodded.

"Don't die; I need someone to talk books with."

The boys ran off, but Aidan turned around, shooting Aurora a grin before disappearing in the rainy mist. She felt a small prick on her arms, and then she noticed that Natalie had vines wrapped around her injuries. "What are—?"

"Voshkovik vines. Hush now, I need to concentrate."

Aurora sighed, silently self-challenging, *Aurora Borealis, what does that mean?* For so long, it meant coward and, at other times, thief. She'd never really defined herself in a positive light. But how could she be more? And why did those two care? It seemed to her that even Jace had grown to trust Aurora even more than she trusted herself. She shook her head. It all seemed hopeless anyway. *I couldn't be anything more than I am.*

"What?" Natalie asked.

"Just thinking."

"You are worrying, not thinking."

Aurora sighed. "Natalie, how did ya do it? Leave Seplechurus, I mean."

"Faith."

"Faith?"

"I do not repeat myself."

Aurora shook her head.

"When you have faith that roses will bud, you will plant. I believed I could help my people." She looked crestfallen, "but now, I am not sure ..."

"What happened?"

Natalie retracted the vines, and the petals of pink roses wilted away. She stood, looking toward the battlefield. "I will assist them. You rest." She ran off without another word. Aurora shook her head; Natalie was just like her mother.

Aurora stood up, giving her fingers a little stretch, then her whole body. *Faith.* Maybe she didn't have any, she questioned, or maybe she had lost it. Everyone around her kept fighting because they had faith, believing that they could win. Natasha had faith that their little group would work out. There was trust. Was that her own problem? That she lacked faith?

She picked up the golden dagger, looking at it intently. Her own reflection: her doubts, insecurities, and pains stared back—but so did her potential, strengths, and courage. She never had faith in herself—that's why trust was so hard, she pondered. She couldn't give what she didn't have, she finalized.

Aurora never thought she could be more than a weak lass or a thief. She never thought she would have friends again, people she trusted. All that she achieved, all that she was, had become her reality. And now, that part of her was threatened.

She ran as fast as her weakened legs could carry her. She stumbled in the dirt, but she refused to stay there.

She ran through the soldiers; it seemed that Utopia had won the day. She continued to the battlefield. *Now, it's my turn for a win.* The air got colder, and sleet stretched across the ground. Jace, Aidan, Natalie, and Nicklaus were all fighting her father, the Shade, and the remaining soldiers. Once her comrades saw her, they rushed to her side, their eyes not leaving their opponents.

"I told you to rest," Natalie snapped.

"Aurora, it's okay," Aidan consoled, "we can handle this."

Aurora smiled, cupping his cheek. "I know. I trust that ya can, but if we're going to do this, I prefer we do it together. She looked at the other three, "All of us."

Her heart fluttered when they nodded in agreement. They turned around and stepped forward, facing their opponents—together. Honestly, she didn't know much about Nicklaus and Natalie, but if they were willing to stand with her now, then there may be something special about them.

"Careful, now," Merek yelled from the other side of the battlefield. "I might kill them, too."

"I doubt you can; we've taken on bigger creatures than you, buddy," Aidan boasted.

"We won't lose to your devices, and we plan to end this war," Jace added.

"Your emperor will not drag any more people to death, not from Seplechurus or anywhere else," Natalie shouted.

"You will fall here, and we will not die trying!" Nicklaus roared.

Aurora breathed in slowly. "Ya have taken enough from me." The thunder crackled in the sky, and rain fell with increased intensity. The lightning flashed and cut the clouds. "I'm not fighting ya alone; we're fighting ya together!"

They had all taken a step forward, but Aurora traveled somewhere else. Her mind drifted to an unknown world, a space inhabited by mind and spirit. She floated in the dark world as if she were coasting on the waves of the sea. Though in a complete penumbral blanket, a light, a yellow moon, that shone in the middle of the space, eliminated the darkness around it. Her eyes remained closed because she refused to wake up from this surreal dream. Aurora knew just where this light was landing. Inside, a booming voice came that sounded distant, powerful, yet comforting. It spoke in a somewhat whisper yet at a perfect volume;

its language was mysterious, yet the words made more and more sense the more it was heard.

"Voice of thunder, hear me.

The enemies of the foul ground they call hell thought they could writhe back to the heavens from whence they came.

You were their first greeter.

You stood there, taunting, waiting; you were the fastest yet the most patient.

With a single flash, they cowered; with a solemn roll, they perished.

Your powers linked the hearts and minds of your kin.

I named it for you ... lightning.

As your bolts struck the traitors, you were witnessed.

My warriors welcomed you; they embraced your presence. Your love knitted them together.

Your movements were swift, your technique flawless, and your blade was all the more. My servant, whose legend echoes in the wind, this is thy name:

Bereka

Tell me, what is the vessel for thy power?"

When Aurora's eyes opened, her hand only held one item—the golden dagger. She raised it in the air, and a bright yellow light swarmed her, crashing into the dagger. After a second passed, nothing happened, but then a great yellow light emerged from her mouth and eyes. The power coursed through her, charging her with energy and healing her wounds.

Then she was back, her first step complete.

She stared at her arms and body; they were healed. *It couldn't be a dream, right?* She looked around at her friends and opponents, and it seemed that not a second had passed by.

"What's going on?" Jace asked. His Blade started to glow brightly. It started to blink with excitement, trembling in its master's hands.

"Jace?" Aidan questioned.

"I don't know what's happening."

Nicklaus looked on. "One of the other Blades ... they are near!" He turned slowly to Aurora, seeing her posture, noticing her healed muscles.

"Don't give them a chance to steel themselves!" her father yelled. "CHARGE!"

The Seplechurans ran forward, yelling their cries of battle.

Aurora hopped in place, feeling the excitement running through her like lightning. "No time to question it, laddies, let's fight!"

They all ran forward with the forest rain drenching them with the dew of the sky. This was not a battle she expected to have, but she'd be darned if she didn't have it.

She leaped for her father, hearing the skies whisper to her to say the name.

With a shake in her voice, she yelled, "BEREKA!" Lightning pierced the sky! Aurora bathed in its bolts, filling her with the divine electricity.

The sound of thunder bellowed through the ears of every living thing for miles, the trees bowed at the power of the sparks. The rolls of thunder played an ensemble of sounds that were deafening. The rain, the lightning, the thunder all bowed to the name that Aurora uttered with a fierce crackle! Her enemies scattered before her, and her allies were left in awe. Another warrior had risen to join the fray.

Aurora, there, one hand in the air, clutched a Blade of divine pro-portions. The hilt was curved and made of a leather-like substance. The Blade itself was gold, lightning dancing on its tip. A single-sided steel with a wicked curve, a crest of a thunderous flower, and a golden ribbon linked the body at the hilt. But what shone the most was the brilliant orange orb in the middle that was surrounded by an onyx crust.

Everyone who witnessed Aurora was in awe of her glorious majesty. She opened her eyes. She stared at her father. *It is time fer a reckoning,* Aurora thought.

A thunderous voice from the heavens issued a warning from the depths of the sky. *Ye, who lies and basks in the darkness, trembles before the shocking light.*

50

Now, The Storm

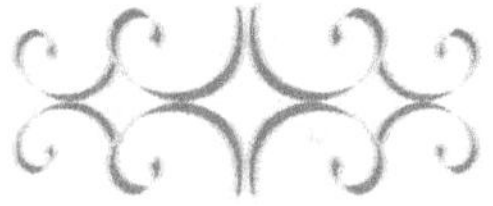

This'll end it.
—The Bolt-Streaked Striker

AURORA FLOURISHED HER weapon, letting the energy crackle. The sky mimicked her movements, following the Blade's intricate step. "Lightning? I always thought I was more of a fire gal."

Her father stood, brushing the mud off his armor, "Oh great, another one. Though, maybe the emperor will reward me twice as much if I bring ya in."

Jace walked to her side, spinning his sword, then taking a stance. "Well, I don't have an excuse to worry about you now. I'll handle the ghost."

Aidan brushed against her shoulder. "And we'll take the fodder." He moved in closer, "I guess Aurora Borealis means something different now after all."

Aurora smiled.

Aidan winked and led Natalie and Nicklaus to the Seplechuran warriors, "Alright, let's give'em a show!"

The thunder boomed above, and the lightning crackled in anticipation. The rainfall acted as the timer before her second battle began.

Aurora called to her father. "Just ya and me, Pa. No more help, no more tricks.

A sinister smile crept onto Merek's face. "Shall we finish this like real Borealis?"

Merek charged his sword in an ebon-coat, a darkness spreading as thickly as ink blotches on parchment. *So, he is hiding some cards up his sleeve,* Aurora observed. Her Blade crackled with a spark of lightning, eagerly anticipating the next steps of their dance. Rain drenched the area, and the sounds of millions of droplets rumbled across the arena. Yet all became quiet; the thick tension of the Borealis battle silenced the field. Good vs. Evil, Light vs. Darkness, Daughter vs. Father. The thunder sounded above. A single lightning bolt crashed, and in that instant, the feet of the warriors started to move. The crackle of lightning, the rumble of thunder, and the shutter of darkness sent intense waves that bent trees and leveled the ground below. Aurora's lightning razed the ground like claws; it trapped and surged through the rush of raindrops around her. Aurora grinned like a mischievous child. This strength, she'd never felt anything like it! She felt as strong as a hundred Auroras, maybe more! It was as if the Borealis Rage blessed her with much more power without the drawbacks.

She gave a strong slash to force her father back, before spinning with a perfect pirouette. She wanted to laugh, the dexterity, the speed! Things she had always wanted to do but could not because her size and strength were all made possible when lightning touched her bones!

She forced the Blade into the ground, sending waves of lightning through the earth. Merek laughed. It was a twisted laugh he let escape his mouth. "Perfect! *This* is a fight!" he declared.

Merek sent his own wave of darkness to combat Aurora's lightning. The elements ran through the ground, up and down; it crashed and rose in movements that made the ocean come to mind; the motion and the ferocity! Both fought for dominance over one another. Aurora roared as she poured more power into her attack; Merek did the same with his guttural scream. The intense waves imploded, destroying trees as if they were mere clay pots.

"More! If ya want to kill me, you have to do better!" Merek howled.

"Oh, shut it, ya bastard!" Aurora retorted.

Aurora recovered from the fierce winds her attack created while Merek ran through the smoke, attacking her like a starved predator. His slashes were strong, fast, chaotic, yet rhythmic. He had somehow combined sophistication and ferocity all at once.

Aurora thought, *How can I beat him? The dobber seems to only get stronger!*

Merek's next attack forced Aurora to the ground. He raised his hand to grab her, but Aurora's body started to oscillate. Her heartbeat was already raised from the battle, but her body seemed to rock like a ship. She didn't have time to even process before she heard the Voice,

"Move."

Aurora heard a crash of thunder, and then—she was behind her father. The streaks of lightning webbed her trail. Pulses of bolts raced across her body and in her veins. "What—?" Before she could say any more, she raced through the rain, cutting the droplets of water into minuscule forms. With a flash of her Blade, her father's armor tore; with another strike, he was brought to his knees. The fulgurous shutter of the bolt-threaded cloak wrapped around her father's arm, pulling him with incredible strength. But her father was no fool; he used the opportunity to try to stab her in the heart. But that only worked once.

Aurora charged her cloth with lightning. With her father stunned, she unleashed a thunderous bolt that blinded before it struck. Aurora recoiled into the trees, her body smoking from the blast. She weakly looked over; her cloth was adorned with six lightning bolt iconographies; the sixth and fifth ones faded fast. *That must be like the laddie's wings. I can't let them all fade away.*

Aurora stood, letting the lightning course through her veins once more. She had to be smart—no senseless attacks and flashy tactics. She had to hit precisely, so she would not have to strike twice.

Her newfound speed gave her an idea.

She thought back to her childhood when her mother decided to train, yet she danced—the movements were flawless, precise, unbridled energy with a centripetal force—it was a beautiful singular point. All this had started because of her mother; yet, even now, among the blazing darkness and the crackling thunder, the thought of her gave Aurora peace.

She asked her mother so long ago, "Ma, what ya doin'?"

"I'm training, sweetie," the brunette dancer replied with a careful step before returning to her original position.

Aurora giggled. "Yer dancin' Ma, not fighting!"

Aurora's mother knelt beside her daughter, looking at the dawning sky of the morning. "I know, but what's the difference?"

She got up and spun, returning to the exact position, "I'm making a fighting style that'll put your father to shame!" She smiled. "Unreadable dance and sharp movements."

Aurora looked at the training dummies, all impaled with a single forceful blow.

"Want to hear the name?" her mother asked, smiling happily.

Aurora nodded energetically. Her mother beckoned her to come closer.

As she did, her mother whispered, "I came up with two; I'm gonna combine them, it's ..."

A slice of energy cut Aurora's memory in two. She kept sending lightning bolts her father's way; her instinctual urge to create distance wore down the bolts on her cloth.

Her father got in close, his blade resting on his shoulder as he gripped the handle tightly with both hands. He kept his weapon straight, controlling the pommel to attack swiftly. Aurora blocked and retaliated with stabs, but if she overextended, then, well, *I'd rather not think about it.*

Her father fought differently, and so did she; though their physical strengths were different, their spiritual powers were even. One wrong move could have killed them both.

The two yelled a mighty battle cry as both their pupils lit up with the green hue of the Borealis Rage; the intensity of their powers grew immensely, firing harsher shockwaves through the battlefield. Regardless of her power, Aurora feared the backlash of the Rage; whatever she needed to do, it had to be done fast.

No more retreating. If she wanted distance, she needed to push forward instead of pulling back. When her father attacked, she parried his blade and then dropped low to trip her father. He growled as he lost his footing, Aurora used her newfound speed to quickly kick her father in the chest.

Aurora didn't celebrate. Now, she needed to end this bout. She remembered her mother's movements and then combined them with the coalescing lightning. She chuckled at how amazing her mother would have been as the Lightning Keerie because it only took one strike in order to finish the job.

Aurora's body started to vibrate again, calling upon her speed. As her father attacked, her body twirled around his blade as if some magnetic force pushed her away.

"What …?" Merek awed.

He attacked again and again, but Aurora danced around his attacks. Her feet glittered like stars, and her body swayed like the sky's lightning. It formed constellations on the ground. The striding steps and arching movements puzzled Merek. He could not attack what he could not catch.

Excitement filled Aurora as she danced around her father; her movements were of a killing grace, a combination of beauty and determination with the fantastical power of illusion. It was a movement created by the mother and mastered by the daughter. *Be trapped,* Aurora thought, *in the Valse of the Highlander.*

Lightning laced the ground, forming a rope tied tautly. They shot out to the four corners of the battlefield, trapping Merek in a web of lightning, and despite the paths reaching out—they all returned to the center. The web completed, and Merek's eyes lit up with the realization. He brought his claymore down, trying to sunder the weave, yet the spider's web had already marked him late.

Aurora leaped into the air, using the rain and lightning as cover for her technique. The spider had come to reap. Merek met the attack, but the lightning web drew his armor down with an unseen force. He could barely lift his blade before Aurora charged her own power and struck once like lightning! Whatever happened became lost in the flash of light and the crack of thunder. Senses masked with the blinding power of inertia and fatigue.

Aurora simply found herself on the ground, trees leveled. Her Blade's cloth harbored one fading bolt. She finally heard the pitter-patter of rain; only then did she realize her arms were immobile.

She quickly turned to her father.

He laid there—somehow alive, but by the looks of it, barely. Whatever dark energies that clouded him faded, protecting most of his body from the bulbous burns that his skin endured. She could end it.

She tried to raise her Blade to attack, but then that strange male from before, who had appeared to be lurking about, the one with the blue cloak, stood at her father's side. Her father shook his head, looking around like a lost fawn. He looked straight at her, and strangely enough, something innocent shone in his eyes. He whispered something to the laddie beside him, then he spoke to her. "It's been fun, Bonnie, but I have to leave," he yelled over the pouring rain, "important stuff, aye?"

The strange young man lifted a dark orb to his chest.

"No!" Aurora yelled as she tried to rush over but quickly tripped.

The orb swallowed her father and the young man faster than her legs could take her. Aurora stood in disbelief; her mother's killer and her vengeance, gone. She roared, and the thunder mimicked her grief.

I finally had him, and now he's gone! Aurora seethed with lividity; she had to calm herself, for the simple fact that she knew her father would return. He worked for the emperor, and he wanted the Blades.

Aurora fell to her knees, then she fell to her back, the rain dripping on her face as she grinned. She saw her Blade, the magnificent surge of power, and the snapping of lightning. "Thank ya Ma ..."

As the lightning bolt faded, a high-pitched chime overpowered the heavy rain, along with faded voices. She could not make out much, but one thing she heard tilted her lips up—just a bit.

"You did good, Aurora," Jace said, "I'm glad you stayed."

51

Forgotten

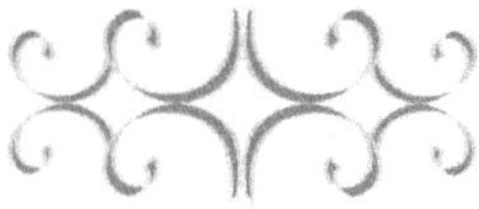

How could this go so wrong?
—The Forgotten

N O BLANKET COULD provide enough warmth to soothe the coldness Serenity felt. Nothing in Seplechurus could be colder.

Explain how you left me! Her mind echoed with the words she yelled. She gripped her head; palms fastened over her ears. She can still hear it, the silence—*Jace's silence.*

Go on! Her mind echoed once more, *GO ON! SAY SOMETHING!!!* "Anything ... please." She curled up against the wooden walls of the wagon. Holding herself and the many layers of blankets. *Jace was supposed to be the one that stayed, the one that never left.* Serenity remembered the trying times of her childhood; the days when she was shunned because of her illness. Death had already marked her for itself.

Paler skin than her part-Seplechuran heritage, bone-dry physique, constant hacking, and the blood—so much blood loss—marked the symptoms of her unique yet terrifying condition. Jace would always have a clean cloth just to wipe her mouth. He defended her when no one else did. He would carve her the most beautiful things, her favorite: the flute.

Now, thinking back on all that, as far as she could figure, her life seemed to have been a lie. When it came down to it, the bottom line for her was that he left. Like everyone else who shunned her, he abandoned her and removed her from his life. She likened Jace to a snake who discreetly found a way to poison her with hope, then left her for dead on the sandy floor. He had made her feel protected, at home, loved—oh, so loved—just to be betrayed. He was no angel, no saint, she knew, *just a filthy liar who got what he wanted.*

Earlier, her eyes were red with sadness now; they showed fury. Yehowehel would burn people like that; she seethed in her mind; there could not possibly be hope for people like *him.*

In the end, he had shown her his true colors. He left her frozen, and left her behind, just as he always had.

"Sere? Are you awake?" Alistair's voice smoothly broke through Serenity's sadness.

"Yes, come in."

Alistair casually jumped inside the moving wagon; he still donned his blue cape. However, he had to shed his helmet. He had told Serenity multiple times he hated the design, calling them useless for travel. He placed his wrist on her forehead. "You seem to be doing better."

Serenity squirmed uncomfortably under the thick layer of covers. "I can barely move."

Alistair threw another blanket over her from the corner, earning himself a dreadful glare from Serenity. "You're mocking me," she groaned.

Alistair slightly bowed. "I'm ensuring your safety."

"I'm fine."

"Your temperature would say otherwise."

Serenity grimaced, but she did not protest. While her heart grasped the coldness of loneliness, her body did not feel alive. The ice Jace wielded was supposed to be of Yehowehel, but to her it felt—unholy. "You needn't treat me like some babe. I'm fine."

He leaned closer, "Oh, silence with that; you know I don't treat you as such."

"Oh, *zilence wiz zat,*" she mocked his Setas-Lisian accent. She could never let go of her friend's voice; Setas-Lisian accented with minor Seplechuran inflections.

"You are a pest, Sere." He whipped his darkened locks.

She chuckled, but it soon faded when she remembered why she shivered so harshly.

"Don't think about him now," Alistair said blankly, "he's not worth your mind."

"He was my friend, Ali; he and I were ... something."

Alistair sighed, "Those feelings were a product of your childish naïveté. They aren't real. The lack of divulgence to his brother is surety of that."

"How?"

Alistair cleared his throat. "He likes to be in control. He will omit anything that keeps him in control. His brother, not knowing, simply means he wants to control the narrative of what happened during the Massacre."

Control. She caught what he was saying. And she thought that maybe it was a strong possibility. But the thought just made Serenity even more furious.

"Jace wanted something that he could control. Alistair was sitting across from her, giving her straight eye-to-eye, emphasizing his point. "*Someone* he could control. And who better than the sickly outcast of the town?"

"Maybe you're right."

"There is no maybe with me. I predict everything, Sere."

She glanced at him softly, countering with, "You didn't predict Nicklaus not knowing who you are."

For the first time, in maybe xantem, Serenity saw Alistair's face fall. He started to brush a finger to his temple, something he did often. "It was … unexpected, but I did factor it in."

"So, do you still hate him? The crown took everything from you. He'll eventually pay like his parents."

Alistair scoffed, "I know that. His ignorance does not absolve him from guilt. In fact, it convicts him more. So, gullible to fall for Athis's deceit. A crown of lies still falls on his head."

Would that convict Aidan? Serenity quickly thought. He did not know; would that absolve him from the guilt? She did not want to bring him into this, not when he could not defend himself from the Seplechurans as well.

"What will you do?" she asked Alistair.

"Currently, the emperor's plans align with mine. I will play his foolish game."

Serenity shushed him, "I implore you to be a bit more discreet."

He rolled his eyes, softly brushing his locks. "The emperor's little mole is gone. I made sure of it. Besides, who here could stop me?"

"I could."

"Not on your best day, Sere," he leaned forward, poking her softly on the forehead. "Get some rest and try not to worry yourself. Your mind is a weapon. Worry is a cancer."

"Alright, mother," she teased.

"Due to your current circumstance, I will turn a blind eye to that."

He nearly made his exit, but his eyes caught hold of the small wooden case that she carried around. He eyed it silently, possibly weighing his words like he always had. "Should I discard it for you?"

"No," Serenity said hastily. "I—I will do it myself." He nodded, his face unreadable, and left.

Serenity soon freed herself from the blankets' clutches, fighting the cold to reach the long wooden box of gold and silver trims. The content shook inside as she picked it up, her moves now turned deliberate. She caressed the box, then slowly opened it. A flute.

She swallowed a lump as she turned the flute over. *J+S*, written in a small, horribly drawn heart. She pulled away the curtain of the wagon, lifting her hand for a mighty throw, yet she trembled. It was not the cold nor the shiver in her bones. Though the hate whispered in her ears seductively, promising the lustful embrace of a stormy calm, she had but one question in mind: was she willing to throw her past away? Was she willing to let the fortunes be memory?

Yes.

Her arm furiously swung with the warrior's cut, but her fingers embraced the flute like a caring mother.

It was settled.

She stared at the flute in her hands, brow furrowing in a vicious motion. Anger would not settle her feelings—not today.

52

All I've Lost

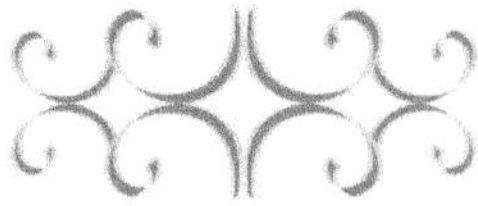

They must be remembered.
—The Rose

I T TOOK ALL her energy to make the roses grow. Natalie did not
have time for weakness when the dead were left without someone to
mourn them. She could not forget them; *no one should forget them.* Her
thorns covered everybody, every soldier who had lost their life to the war.
Utopians and Seplechurans alike had the bushes layered side-by-side for
their sacrifices to Death—for the sake of nothing.

Nicklaus and Aidan tried to grab her, forcing her to rest, but she
threw them aside. *No one will leave until every grave is marked.* Her
breath, laborious. Unconsciousness nearly grabbed her, but before she
could fall, large hands caught her.

"You're not done, lass," Uncle Johannus comforted her.

"Will you not stop me?"

He smiled through the blood that drenched his stubble and the marks
on his armor. "No. It means too much to you."

He carried her to every dead body, even helping her pray to Yehowehel not to judge them so harshly. But would Yehowehel even hear their prayers? No one could blame them for doubting. *Humans have made such mockery of creation and of life; casually bartering it for bragging rights and fleeting successes,* Natalie concluded. Fortunately, she was certain that Yehowehel's love for humanity was far greater than humans' own love for themselves. And that love kept Natalie going.

The next soldier she adorned; she did not know his name. He was one of the first people to meet her after her defection; he had a particular openness about his disdain for her. He spat on her a couple of times too. But to see his eyes open with despair made her heart ache; she reasoned, what satisfaction would she receive for mocking a dead man?

She remembered one time when alcohol claimed his senses; he told her that he respected her work. The following morning, he rescinded his words, saying the beer spoke, not him. However, she felt that she made a difference in the lives she came upon—even his.

She slowly closed his eyes, cutting his cheek with her cutlass. The vines slowly overtook him, wrapping him until he was an orange rosebush.

Her eyes flitted. The bodies became blurry, and her strength was near its end.

"Lass, just one more," Johannus encouraged.

"I – I ..." She laid into him, her body giving out.

"You made it this far, don't stop now."

The weights that held her eyes lightened under her resolve. The last body was right there, a Seplechuran. Her helmet, removed, and body, lifeless. She looked so young, so innocent. Her white hair meant she was of the Luco Clan, and her lack of tattoos indicated that she had never made it to initiation; she was not even a woman yet. *She ... probably was going to it after battle.* "Rest ... sister."

Natalie tried to lift her arm, but she could barely swing it. Her eyes trembled. Did she not have enough strength to adorn one of her own?

"Let me," Aurora called as she suddenly came up behind them.

Natalie felt the hand of fatigue grab her neck. A sharp breath shot from her mouth every time she tried to move.

"Don't bother to look at me," Aurora smiled at her, "it's the least I can do." Aurora grabbed Natalie's weakened arm, making the small cut. White roses blossomed from the girl's corpse along with the vines. Natalie let the smile creep on her face, but the sky dew also found its home on her cheek. The darkness started to take hold, and that which was blurry soon became black.

Two full days later, the distinct sound of wheels crushing rock and dirt woke her. She could not bear to sleep another wink. Her body ached and stung; the fatigue felt mostly gone, but her brain did not agree. She was trapped in a wooden box, just like the day she appeared to the Utopians. She instinctively grabbed her wrists and sighed in relief when she felt her skin.

"Where ...?" she groaned as she sat up. The pain halted her movement.

Her faint howl of pain alerted her drivers. The cloth was removed, and Aidan saw the Utopian Rose clutching her nearly fatal wound. "Welcome back to the land of the living."

Natalie sat up, fighting through the pain. "I do not remember dying." Natalie clutched her abdomen as she successfully leaned up against the wall.

"Ya were close to it," Aurora stated.

Death. It seemed she was fortunate it did not decide to take her, but she could not find solace in death. Not that she craved it, but the fact that Death craved humans. It had taken so many, she felt.

She sighed drearily, "I remember every grave, every soldier who fell … every family I will have to visit."

The silence hung over the group. The tension on its imaginary string nearly snapped, causing the horror and realization of war to plummet into their hearts.

"Where is Nicklaus?" she asked.

"In the front," Aurora replied, "he hasn't said anything since the battle."

So, it is finally time. The uneasiness in Natalie's stomach only grew worse. There would be a great division in their fragile little band. Seeing as she was starting to find companionship, she hoped to Yehowehel that it would not come to a screeching halt.

53

AWESTRUCK

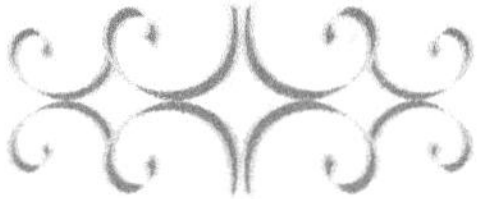

This stupid war could be over any minute!
—The Thief

WHAT A HAPPY time it should have been, a time for celebration and ecstatic behaviors. Jace should have played a flute, Aidan would be dancing, Natalie would be watching with a smile, and Nicklaus *would be doing whatever his people did.*

The sky grinned at Aurora; it now beckoned to her call. Enemy and ally could agree that her mere existence meant that war had drawn closer to its climax, and yet—the atmosphere had grown thick with dread. Heads were down, eyes hollow, and even the horses and iquan seemed distant.

Aurora gripped her bowl of soup tightly. She needed to find a little light. Ever since the party stopped to rest, she had not seen anyone smile. There was only one person who would right now, and he had resigned to the shadows to eat.

Aurora sat beside Aidan. "So, laddie, I thought ya would be fixing yer garments instead of eatin.'"

Aidan sipped a spoonful of soup, muttering his reply, "I don't have enough material."

"What?" she exclaimed for him to speak up.

"I don't have enough material," Aidan said louder, gaze never leaving the soup.

Aurora put down her bowl, looking intently at Aidan. "How? Ya always seemed prepared fer things like this."

Aidan exhaled. "I don't know," he smacked his lips together. "Wait, I do know." Aidan stopped eating for a moment to collect his thoughts. "This is going to sound stupid, but I thought ... I thought we were untouchable. The unbroken few."

Jace and Natalie approached, the latter still recovering from her wounds. They stood nearby, uttering absolutely nothing. *Them too?* At first, Aurora thought it was the death of the others, but something deeper arrested their hearts.

Aidan continued, only looking at his soup instead of her. "I thought we couldn't get hurt beyond minor scratches or little cuts. I know Sov Voshkovik and all, but I still felt ... invincible." He exhaled one more time. "I didn't think we needed more material because I thought we couldn't get *hurt.*" The light in his eyes started to quench, and a grim reality set in for him as it did everyone else.

Aurora had to speak, but seeing Aidan trembling took her words, and her silence only aided his fruitless mood.

"I thought we were the heroic protagonists of this play, but ... this battle showed me something, it showed me a lot ... we aren't as invincible as I thought we were. That's scary, that's really scary," Aidan sharply inhaled, saying one last thing. "Yehowehel gives us these Blades every time we're in trouble; does that mean that things will only get harder?"

Aurora clenched her fist, letting the whites of her knuckles pale,

then swell with red. She would not have this, especially from them. "...
No." Her company looked at her with confusion and with anguish as
well. Aurora rushed to her feet, removing her dagger from the holster
at her back. "Bereka. Her Blade transformed, and lightning crackled on
the tips, sparking and skipping on the edges of her Blade. She angrily
walked over to the party members, shooting a bolt of lightning in the
air to get their attention. "Listen up ya dumb dobbers! Ya have been to
war before; we all have lost something or someone close to us! Did that
stop us from fighting?!"

The soldiers murmured faintly.

"WHAT?!"

"No!" The soldiers yelled with a little more vigor.

"We aren't invincible, I know; sometimes it feels that way." She looked
to Aidan. "But we shouldn't give up if the world hits us back. Shove it
again! Refuse to die!"

The soldiers started to broaden their shoulders and straighten their
backs. Some began to nod and cheer as Aurora spoke.

"There are people who have died, who are counting on us to live on,
fer them, fer ourselves. We can't let them down; we can't let ourselves
down."

A cold wind rushed through, as Aurora heard Jace utter the divine
name of his Blade.

The chill removed the bandages that dared to hold the Blade ordained
of the Abode. The soldiers grew cold in the flesh, but warm in their spirits
when Jace stood beside Aurora.

"We will fly; we will fight," Jace yelled. "Despite the mistakes of the
past, despite the ridicule we have endured ... even from our own."

Aurora smirked at those last words. She caught Natalie raising her
eyes as well. She continued, "We will persist! Though we fight flesh and
blood, we do not fight alone."

The soldiers cheered louder, rumbling the forest of the Contested Lands with renewed vigor and energy.

Jace yelled, "I know death is painful to think about, but if we die on the battlefield, among brothers and sisters, we have lived. And we lived well."

Jace nodded at her, and she cheerfully nodded back.

Raising her Blade high, she sent a bolt of lightning into the sky, steeling her allies and warning her enemies. "So, no matter what we face, no matter what we endure, we fight together, we live together!"

The soldiers cheered, screaming at the top of their lungs at the speech. Aurora and Jace looked around, seeing the faces of the soldiers turn from sad and depressed to full of life. With their spirits lifted, there was only one more thing to shout:

Aurora took a deep breath in. "FER GLORY."

The soldiers yelled back with a deafening cry. Some even threw up their soups, which landed painfully on their heads. They chanted her name like remorseless drunks.

Aurora and Jace snuck off to their group, only to see Aidan dramatically wiping his eyes despite there not being tears. "You really know how to cheer people up, huh?"

Aurora sat beside him, flashing a rising smile, "I guess ... I always had someone to cheer me up."

Aidan raised the corner of his lips. "Anytime."

Jace crashed down beside Aurora, giving them both a happy look. "We all needed it. Thank you, Aurora."

"Awww, no need to get sappy," she playfully mocked their catchphrase.

Natalie inched closer to the group. "You did well, Aurora. Hope is hard to come by. Some find it, but others need to be shown." She bowed before walking off for more food.

Aurora smiled deeply. She never thought she would be in such a position, being what she was, doing what she did. Hope really did bring her far, and friends aided the person that she was. The real battle starts here.

54

Prophesied Heir

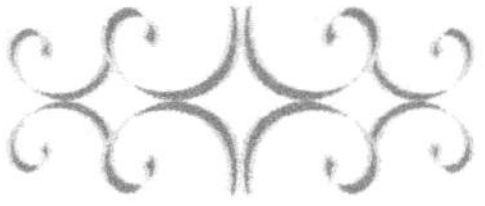

No one makes a fool of me.
—The Prince

NIGHT DREW NEAR. Firelight spread throughout the forest, its smoke moved about and danced to the Utopian folk songs. Those from the desert joined, well, *only the Delfizcani, and that immodest boy,* Nicklaus observed silently. *Raven must have been resting in the trees per her usual vigilance, and Jace is probably somewhere in the forest, lurking perhaps.*

Nicklaus twirled his soup with his spoon. The uneaten meal sent a wave of delicious aromas. Its heat was sensuous and soothing to his nostrils. But such soothing could not penetrate the deepest recesses of his thoughts. He clenched his spoon; his trembling sent ripples throughout his soup. His brows contorted into a scowl as he watched her dance without a care in the world.

How was she chosen? he asked himself. He had been nothing but faithful to Yehowehel, not missing a single mass, praying every morning and every evening. He had followed the sacred texts without hesitation and was able to quote them since he was young. So, why? Why did a godless, immoral *thief* get a Blade when a devout Vessel was standing right here?

Nicklaus could bet all his wealth she could not even say a single scripture by heart. *Can she even read? A Delfizcani, Yehowehel, why would you bestow such power to her?*

Snap!

The wooden spoon broke in two, finding its pieces floating aimlessly in his soup. He threw his bowl aside, then dragged his fingers through his golden strands; blue pupils surrounded by a torrent of red.

I cannot go home a failure. The capital was four, maybe five days out. His mother would mock him, calling him all the names he despised. *Craniilvu projons* (delusional dreamer), *Mal chantoon* (hopeless kitten), and his least favorite, *jamasi appelent,* the translation was spotty in common, but it translated to someone who had no destiny.

But his father would do far worse. His father would snatch his throne, not even looking at Nicklaus as he did it.

Nicklaus buried his face in the warmth of his knees. The redness of his eyes swelled to his face, setting his skin ablaze with enmity. *And she was chosen? A Delfizcani? A gantus? Even that large desert dweller had more appeal, and even he was anomalous.* Nicklaus constricted his fingers as if they were around someone's neck. *Someone from the desert, the unruly "free" town of Bhall-Duraht, no less.* Nicklaus as he rose to his feet, paced in hopes that it would make his thoughts more sensible. *How could Jace possess any positive trait that would make him worthy of Yehowehel's recognition?* If those two could possess Blades, he surmised, why not the prince of the most powerful kingdom?

The prophecies foretold this. Every word was etched into his memory by his father and mother. He ate, slept, and breathed those words. He was supposed to be the Great Leader of Setas-Li, he who unfurled the Setas-Lisian golden flower and led the kingdom into its most righteous age. *Now look at me!*

"Nicklaus?" the Delfizcani called.

"What?" he hissed.

She paused, clearly hearing the poison in his voice. *Any sensible person would leave at the tone of my voice,* he leered at her, but she was Delfizcani, she did not have *sensible* in her lexicon.

"The soldiers are singing Setas-Lisian folks. They wanted ya to start."

His response was slow and toxic. "I refuse." He turned to walk away.

Then all he felt was her hand, which he interpreted as her poisonous touch. "Are ya alright?" she asked.

Nicklaus flailed, pushing her aside. He forgot to activate his princely charm, letting the fullness of his motive shine through in his burning eyes. They locked with hers, and he knew she saw it: the fury, the anger, and in some way, the betrayal.

Her eyes grew in surprise, but her mouth uttered no words. After a moment of contemplation, she worked to keep a smiling face. Aurora turned, shouting to the jovial Utopians that were dancing around the fire, "Nicklaus said he can't remember anything at the moment."

The Utopians groaned in an unfashionable unison before singing their own songs. *The words of Setas-Li should not be uttered, not until I realize my true destiny,* Nicklaus cemented in his heart. By this time, he was used to the disappointment, but that was not going to stop him from finding the truth. If he did find answers on the way, upon his return, he would search every paper, every book, every note, and every prophecy. Another emotion fueled him besides desire—anger. No one would make the prince of Setas-Li look like a fool; he was sure of it. Not the Delfizcani, not the desert dwellers, not Seplechurus, and not that fool, Alistair. *I will become a Keerie-O-Theos—A God Wielder.*

55

Mental Burdens

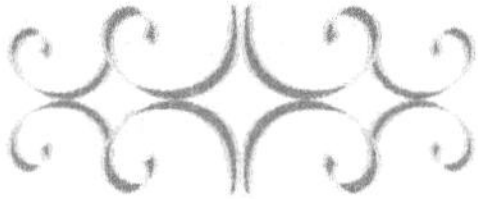

All of this is coming to bite me, isn't it?
—The Protector

LIGHT FILTERED THROUGH the trees, and the shadows that the light produced merrily danced like the Utopians during their jig. The fire, the people, they all looked so warm, and the temptation to join them only grew, and yet—the fierceness of his guilt cut through his happiness. *I have to tell him about Serenity*, Jace thought.

Such a great challenge stood before him as he trotted the dangerous path. Even Brand did not—*could not*—stir his fear as much as this. He had to risk the shame of facing his own brother, the one who stood with him since the beginning of the tale. Jace cursed at himself with a stomp; how could he have lied to Aidan? He wondered. Why hadn't he at least try to find Serenity, even once? Right after Jace found hope again, the hopelessness of his past came to stab him with a wicked grin, twisting the dagger deeper with every thought of her.

Her gentle voice, her soft hair, and her smile that possessed the power to make his problems melt away. *And I left her.* He leaned on a tree, sliding down its coarse bark. "Jace, you betrayed your best friend's trust and lied to your truest comrade." He looked up to the heavens, to the palace above the clouds. "Why did you choose me? You called me protector-borne and yet I abandoned my first charge."

Jace sighed as he rose to his feet. He could rectify one of those things now; he had to.

He carried himself, dragging his body to the camp. The firelight filled the area, and its colors flared to life. His Songluan eyes reflected the colors vibrantly, from the deepest oranges to the brightest of warm hues. They allowed him to feel happy until Aidan approached.

"Hey, where were you?" Aidan lightly slapped him on the shoulder. "You missed Aurora singing! I'd forgotten how good she sounds."

"Aidan."

"There's still more soup left if you want some."

"Aidan."

"Maybe you could play the flute like old times—"

"Aidan!"

His brother, startled, shouted, "What?"

"I need to talk to you," he looked around, "alone." He watched Aidan's shoulders drop along with his smile. It was so fast, he observed, wondering that if his simple request, only hitting a sense of seriousness, caused such a reaction, then what was going to happen when he actually told Aidan the truth?

The soldiers laughed, carrying on their song without a care in the world.

Jace led Aidan through the forest, watching as the light faded from the surrounding area. He walked aimlessly, maybe until he found a spot of power, but no such place existed. Moments like that were made, not found. "Aidan, I have to tell you something." They both halted. Jace gave one more breath, muttering his mantra until he could find the strength to open his mouth. "I—"

Aidan interrupted, "The girl, the Seplechuran lieutenant, was Serenity, wasn't it?"

Jace choked. He wanted to look dead-on at Aidan, but could he stand to see the disappointment in his brother's face? Would other emotions be present? Anger? Sadness? He clenched his fist, arms trembling like the black skies. Did Aidan even see him as a hero anymore? Finally, he mustered up the courage to say more. "Who told you?"

"You did," Aidan stated flatly, "what she said to me was suspicious, but it's the way you're acting now that gave it away."

Jace's arms trembled. He had to face his brother and mount his full apology. He spun on his heels, "Aidan I'm—" Interrupted, his words landed right into his brother's fist. Jace fell off his feet, clutching his face in surprise.

"YOU SAID YOU WENT BACK FOR HER!"

Jace's words choked out into the air between them. "Aidan I—"

"Shut up!!! You broke us apart! We were family! She was a sister to me—I thought you ..." Drowning in emotion, now it was Aidan's words struggling to hit air. "I thought ... I thought you loved her."

Jace used the moment to raise himself, but when he fully beheld Aidan's face, he wanted to slink right back down. Like a shattered mirror, Aidan broke in front of him, each tear like a shard falling—facets of grief. "Why did you leave her?" he asked incredulously before giving in to full sobs.

"I ..." Speechless, again. That was the question Serenity asked, and again he could not produce an answer meaningful enough. His answer was not ready, though he had a semblance of an idea. It was not the time, or maybe it was. Ending his pause, he said, "I wasn't ready to lose someone else." Aidan scanned his brother for a moment. Either way, Jace knew he had to explain. "I lost my parents, my town, my neighbors, and my friends all in one day. You did, too. Now he paused. "But … there was something *you* could never lose—a little brother."

Aidan turned and punched a tree with such intense force that he lodged his fist into its wooden body. With a growl, he wrenched his fist free, pointing a bloodied, accusatory finger at Jace. "Don't you dare use me as an excuse!" he growled. "I'm your brother! Of course, I know what I could've lost! How do you think that makes me feel?!"

Jace felt the heat rise in his belly, and his next words spat like coal. "But I'm your *older* brother, Aidan! You don't understand! If I left to get her, I could've risked losing you!"

The anger on Aidan's face calmed a bit, Jace noticed. Perhaps, he was looking for more explanation than anything. Jace knew that this was his only opportunity to explain fully, and that he might never get Aidan this quiet again, ready to hear him out. "As an older brother, I feel the need to protect you with everything I have. Putting you in danger by going for Serenity, I didn't think it was a fair trade."

"But we could've been together," muttered Aidan. His emotions were exhausted.

"But Serenity was sick. We didn't have the money to get her any of her medication; her death—would have been an inevitability, and I couldn't leave you … not after what Mother and Father said." The realization of the matter caught on to Aidan's face, understanding the gamble. Jace continued, "My regret is that I left her, possibly to die alone. She should've been around us, around friends. I only realized that when I saw her." Before Aidan could react, Jace shook his head. "I'm not blaming you, but I couldn't risk it."

Aidan's face could no longer be read; his eyes neither moved nor did his mouth twitch. Jace needed him to say something, anything, to let him know that saying anything more wouldn't be a mistake.

Aidan's voice was uncharacteristically small, "I want to say you're wrong ... but ... I'm not sure if I could take it ... if I saw Serenity die in front of me." Aidan finally looked up, into his brother's eyes. "But why did you lie to me? All this time, I thought you tried. I thought I could trust you because you *tried*."

Jace sighed. The answer he had to give was far simpler, "The same reason why I didn't want to tell you today ... Aidan, I care about what you think of me. I wanted to be someone you looked up to, like I looked up to Father."

"But you're not Father," Aidan interrupted.

"And I'm reminded of that—of my weakness—every day. I'm just Jace, but I wanted that to mean something to you."

Again, Aidan's face became stoic, unmoving. For someone so outgoing, most could never tell what went on in Aidan's head until he actually said something. Jace knew full well that Aidan could hate someone and still keep a smile around them. It was what Jace feared the most. He did not want his brother to fake his admiration for him. He wanted it to be true. And now, after this night, he may never get it again.

"Let me think about this ..." Aidan said flatly, though some anger was mixed in his words. "I'm not in the mood to deal with this now."

Jace sighed, not even mustering the power to demand an answer. He had been so weary. His eyes felt heavy; his heart had turned to lead. His entire world stared at him with a calculated hatred. If he had to live this life, with his decisions, he could not keep any more secrets—his or anyone else's. "Wait, there's something else I need to tell you." His tone grew solemn.

"Another secret?" Aidan glared.

"Yes. I found this out recently."

"What?"

"It's about ... Nicklaus."

56

HIDDEN SHACKLES

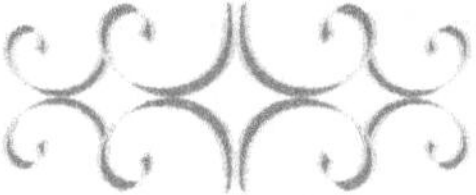

He lied.

—The Wildcard

THE LITTLE BASTARD lied. Aidan knew something was off—the coordinated smiles and the practiced grins. In his favorite books, he'd read enough descriptions of fake smiles, but to see it in action was surreal.

Royalty did not care much for Bhall-Duraht; it had always despised that the desert kept so detached from the war. Some would even say it hated Bhall-Duraht. That is why no one came to Bhall-Duraht's aid during the Massacre. The Illisans, mostly Setas-Li, even tried to interrupt trade between Bhall-Duraht and the outside, something Aidan and Jace's parents complained about constantly. Aidan remembered his mother complaining about Setas-Lisian nobles even killing merchants who traded with the desert simply to put the fear of Yehowehel in those who remained.

The royalty only seized an opportunity when it saw a benefit for them; that's why the Utopians were so eager to help Jace—he drove a bargain.

Now, Nicklaus's presence was not a coincidence. Like every royal, they would have little problem using others as stepping stones. *Mother loathed them so,* Aidan remembered.

Aidan reached the dying light of the clearing. The jolly sounds were not as loud as they once were, and it seemed the soldiers were debating about shifts. He saw Aurora sharpening her golden dagger by the fire; though the light was beautiful, he was startled at the snap of wood. In that moment, he felt dizzy; he clutched his head and stuttered his steps as if in a confused dance. He stumbled into someone. He looked.

"I take it you are recovering from the soup," the snake said with a smile. "It was a little spicy."

"Drop the act, Your Highness."

Aidan had never seen a mask fall so fast. The smile transitioned into a frown, and his body tensed up. How Nicklaus became more imposing so quickly was beyond Aidan's knowledge, but he imagined the royals as such: cold, imposing, and sinister.

"I am assuming Jace told you." Nicklaus's accent seemed thicker.

"I wonder what gave you that idea?"

"I have no time for your prattle."

"And I have no time for your ego, but here we are."

Nicklaus stepped closer, sizing himself up accordingly. Aidan noticed their similar height only at that moment. Which meant, Aidan thought as he cracked his neck, that it would be fun if they fought.

Nicklaus stood straighter before stating, "I have no time to deal with you. Where is your brother?"

"Not in a talking mood with royal scum."

Nicklaus shoved Aidan, his eyes boring through Aidan's soul. A few soldiers nearby started to pay close attention; their hands were dangerously close to their weapons. "Royal scum? I did not come from a backward town that practices irreligious anarchy and paints it as freedom. Combining cultures and towns with no respect for traditions and lifestyle. No respect for *authority*. It is sickening."

Aidan yawned at the soliloquy. Nicklaus scowled. But the princeling paused until Aidan finally closed his mouth. "Don't worry, me yawning is me paying attention."

"Your witticism is a fool's attempt at intelligence."

"Yet it is witticism that fools the intelligent."

Aidan smiled deviously, hoping to tease a rise out of Nicklaus. However, the prince seemed smarter than most. He inhaled deep breaths to prevent himself from getting worked up. He had underestimated how annoying Aidan could be.

"I will not entertain the fruitless tactics of a desert dweller." Nicklaus turned to walk away.

That would be too easy. "You know, you just called people from the desert irreligious, and yet, we have two Blades, and you have ... how many? I'm forgetting ... Five? Six?"

Nicklaus's movement became arrested, and his arms started to shake. The prince wanted power. The thought of him not having it probably must have burned him to his core, Aidan surmised, and he relished in the fact of it all. *To have something the prince wanted but cannot have ... oh what happy day.* Quickly, Aidan prepared himself. *I'm going to get attacked in three, two, one ...*

Nicklaus turned around furiously, punching Aidan, but the Camerus was ready. He dodged, tripping Nicklaus in the process. Nicklaus rose to his feet, enraged, but the fun halted as Natalie and Aurora came barreling through and yanked their friends apart.

"What the hell is going on, laddie?" Aurora yelled in a pointed tone.

Aidan gestured to Nicklaus with his chin. "Ask the prince."

Aurora slowly turned to Nicklaus, seeing the glowing orange firelight play perfectly with his anger. She took a step back, eyeing him cautiously. "Yer the prince ... of Setas-Li?"

Nicklaus let the silence answer on his behalf. Natalie gave a sympathetic glance to the two.

Aurora retreated further, looking in horror at Nicklaus. "Get away from me."

"Sister, please." Natalie reached for Aurora.

Aurora smacked her hand away, glaring at Natalie with the same type of realization Aidan had but a moment ago with Jace. "Ya knew?"

Natalie looked away, not giving Aurora the answer she so desired.

"What happened to being Hericonian sisters, huh? Fully knowing what his people do to mine!"

Aidan turned to Aurora. "Relax, she's not worth the time," he said loud enough for Natalie to hear.

The rest of the three stood their ground, neither backing down as mixed emotions swirled in the air around them, holding their own court. Aidan wanted to growl at all of them. Even though he told Aurora to relax, he wanted to flare his own anger.

The war had been going on for over xantus upon xantus, since the Night Star, the Star of Jace and Serenity's birth. The lack of results stirred unrest, especially in the areas like Bhall-Duraht, who had no say in the war. One would have thought that it would be foolish to blame the Prince, but he did have a say in military affairs—that much was common knowledge. Especially since his clan, if he had not lied, was responsible for funding the war that took Aidan's home.

The blood on his hands was greater than the blood on any soldiers, and for Natalie, a Seplechuran—of all people—to defend him—Aidan could see why her people called her a traitor.

"She will not listen to reason, Raven. Delfizcani never do," Nicklaus dismissed Aurora's plight.

Natalie glared at Nicklaus, which prompted him to roll his eyes. Natalie tried her best to look somber, but she had her mother's stern evaluating look. "Aurora, please, we are all allies here. If we hope to end war, we need cooperation from *all* peoples."

"That's yer excuse?! Do ya know how many Delfizcani his people enslaved? How many men, women, and children his people hold captive?"

She's snapping. Aidan tried to hold Aurora, but every time he touched her, she brushed him off. Raw emotion like this always led to mistakes. Aidan knew what she had already conquered. This might be a door for her to step back in. Aidan lightly grabbed Aurora. "Aurora, hey, calm—"

"Don't tell me to calm down!" she snapped with a brisk interruption, tears welling in her now glowing emerald eyes. "Ya don't know what it's like to wear their sigil on yer skin!" She held her mouth. The fire stopped dancing. Her eyes returned to hazel. Chirping crickets silenced. The night did not simply hush; it went completely dead.

Aidan and Aurora shared the same look, hoping nobody had heard a sliver of what she said, yet both knew that hope was in vain.

Nicklaus looked the most shocked as if staring at a ghost, perhaps realizing how close the sins of his kingdom were. "You were a slave?"

"I think it's time to go," Aidan suggested, grabbing Aurora by the shoulders and pulling her back to the forest.

"Wait—" Nicklaus reached out.

Aidan grabbed Nicklaus's hand, his grip tightening on his wrist. "Hands off, princeling."

The Utopian soldiers grabbed their weapons, but Jace, seemingly appearing from nowhere, swiftly took to Aidan's side. *El, he looks exhausted,* Aidan thought.

"Enough!" Everyone turned to see the Great General, holding a sword with both hands. "Did we not just win a battle together? Did we not see what the power of Yehowehel at work in the very same people you are trying to attack? Were you not galvanized by their words just moments ago? Lay down your arms."

The soldiers looked between each other.

"Now!" Johannus yelled.

Immediately, the soldiers sheathed their weapons. Aidan let go of Nicklaus's hand, still eyeing him.

Johannus approached. "I am sorry for the deceit. As Nicklaus's Elfather, I take full responsibility."

"Uncle—" exclaimed Nicklaus.

"Enough!" Johannus yelled, "You are a prince; learn discretion, Nicklaus."

There was a tense second. Aidan concocted every insult he had in his head. *First, Jace, now this! Can anyone be honest anymore?* He readied himself to fight until he saw Aurora. She was gripping her wrists and looking frantic. *Pettiness can wait.* "We'll ... see everyone in the morning," Aidan retreated.

Aidan held Aurora by the shoulders and led her to the forest path. Jace followed closely behind. Once the three of them made some safe distance, Aidan sighed, anger seemingly dissipated. Because someone had to be calm. "That's not how I expected this day to end."

"Better here than the capital," sighed Jace.

The three sat under a tree, having nothing but moonlight to soothe them. Aidan could only imagine how disturbed Aurora must have been, with the darkness, with her little confession.

"Are you alright?" Jace sat on the ground with a groan.

"No." Aurora confessed with a sob. "I just admitted I was a slave to the Setas-Lisian prince."

Aidan stared at her, measuring his words before asking, "Do you think they'll drag you back?"

Jace twirled a fallen branch in his hand, snapping it effortlessly before tossing it aside. "She has a Blade of El; they wouldn't dare."

"Aye, yer kin is right." Aurora sighed. "Their best option is to make me swear fealty."

The trio grumbled, airing their frustrations to the night sky. It always seemed like things got worse right after they got better, but Aidan was a bit more optimistic. Usually, the things that were bad did not always stay that way; his brother and Aurora were living proof. A couple of weeks ago, they wouldn't have dared to sit next to each other; now, they were consoling one another.

"I guess I might as well tell ya what I was going to tell ya before. With everything ya heard, there's no point in hiding it ..." Aurora leaned against a tree, rendering several deep sighs. Had her renderings been any deeper, her voice would have reached baritone status.

Aidan leaned in curiously, but a part of him wanted her to stop and just relax. She did not need to pressure herself unless, he concluded, confessing would be better for her. He looked at Jace, and he, too, looked interested and made no attempt to stop her. Since Jace's confession about Serenity, Aidan doubted that Jace was the paragon of good decisions right now.

"I guess it started when I was a wee lassie, about six. My mother was beheaded right in front of me ... by my own pa."

Aidan and Jace shared their reaction of shock, mouths ajar and eyes flinching. Before they could say anything, Aurora continued, "I dunno what happened. My pa loved my ma; they were inseparable, and yet, he killed her. The cruel eyes, his crazed stare, that strange purple energy ... and I watched, I couldn't save her."

"Aurora, you were six." Jace came to the defense of the young Aurora. "What could you have done?"

Aurora punched the dirt. "I should've tried! And I stood there like a scared little lass! If my pa wasn't going to save her, then I had to!"

It made a lot more sense to Aidan now; her flustered and desperate reaction to Arundel and Lulia, her desire to work with the boys when people were at stake—she didn't want a repeat of her mother.

Aidan leaned toward her, smiling softly. "Aurora, listen, I know you regret not helping. Trust me, I understand, but if you tried anything, you would've died."

"Better dead than a coward."

Aidan wanted to process those words, but then Aurora inhaled. *There's more?*

"I ... somehow escaped from my home. Finding myself in Shatersus where I met up with ..." Her voice cracked, and she shook herself from the daze. "... They don't matter, or at the very least, I didn't matter enough to them." Her voice became angry. "They betrayed me into the hands of Setas-Lisian nobles who sold me to the Leroza Clan; they put me into slavery."

Leroza, the clan that Nicklaus mentioned, the ones that funded the war. Aidan, hearing that, thought, *Ahhh, so, it seems they had other ventures to attend to, did they not? So, slavery and war. How many evil things did they get their grubby hands on?*

Aurora ruefully chuckled. "It wasn't all bad, though. I did meet other Delfizcani, even learned how to cook Delfizcani recipes. It helped me when I eventually escaped, finding my way to the desert where Natasha took me in, a few xantem later ... we're here."

This time, she exhaled, marking the end of her words. She did not mention the blood from Utopia nor what she did to herself. Everything in Aidan's body screamed at him not to bring it up, and for once, he listened to that voice of common sense. He had gained her trust, at least somewhat. He did not plan on losing it.

Aurora looked at them, probably expecting words to come from their mouths, or at the very least, glances.

Then, Jace groaned, "I'm so stupid." He massaged his temples.

"I know," Aidan added, but his brother didn't retort.

"I acted like them, didn't I? The Setas-Lisians that enslaved you."

Aurora exhaled, not able to bring her words to agree. Jace nodded, taking in the answer. He ran a hand through his locks, a narrow, temperamental look at no one in particular. "It seems that every time I try to mean well, I'm reminded of what I do wrong." Aidan and Aurora glanced at him, silently asking him to explain himself. Jace caught on. "Aurora, do you know why I hated you?"

"Smooth," Aidan once again interjected, and once again was ignored.

"You said something about me being a thief," she answered.

Jace shook his head. "No, that was the cover-up. I –," he groaned again, "I was trying to not get close to you."

"Come again?" She wiped her eyes.

"You were a girl from Bhall-Duraht, you got along with Aidan so well, and your personality was a little like Serenity's."

"Yer dead best friend?" Aurora asked.

Aidan and Jace exchanged a glance. Aidan's eyes were heated. And Jace could not bear the flames.

"She's actually ... alive," Jace informed. "The woman lieutenant that we fought in the Contested Lands was her."

Aurora's eyes widened but simply replied, "Oh ..."

"Anyway," he sighed, "I saw history repeating itself with you. I wanted you to leave. I didn't know if I could deal with losing too many people;

I didn't want to get close to you only for you to just end up … dead. I honestly stopped my grudge with you when you agreed to help us."

The three of them sat silently, far too many confessions happened at one once. Though Aidan felt the unsaid pressure of him confessing something. What would he say? There's only one thing that he felt he truly had hidden: the dreams of fire and death, the demonic beast, and the fevers, or the reality, the reality that he too had a—

"Thank you for sharing your history with us, Aurora. I'm sure it couldn't have been easy," Jace finished.

Aurora shook her curls in a nod, looking at the boys with fresh eyes cleansed by tears. "No, thank ya both fer not giving up on me. I—wanted friends so badly, but I didn't want to risk it, again." She looked particularly at Aidan. "And thank ya, Aidan … fer keeping us together. I know all that fighting must've drove ya crazy."

She held his gaze for a moment, with a smile that reached her eyes. Aidan blinked several times. *Was that a blush on her cheeks? No, no, she just finished crying; that had to be it.* "Uh … yeah, definitely, no problem."

"Really, thank you, Aidan," Jace continued the thought. "I know you're still angry with me that I lied to you about Serenity, but I do want to say that I'm glad you're here, and I'm glad you're my brother."

Aidan groaned, fighting a smile. "No, I'm angry with you, don't get me sappy." He lightly slapped his own cheeks. "Stop it, Aidan, stop it. You're angry."

A lighthearted chuckle filled the forest.

"Fine! You're not forgiven, *but* I will turn a blind eye for now, at least, until we can figure out how to get Serenity back to our side—I just want us all to be together again."

Jace nodded, resolute. "On that, we agree. And Aurora?"

Her hazel eyes perked up from a curl she played with. "Aye?"

"Next time we see your father, we'll make room for you to finish the job."

Aurora suddenly jumped them both, wrapping them in a tight hug. "I love ya laddies."

"Don't get sappy on us now," the brothers exclaimed.

The three of them laughed and talked a little more before joining the quiet chorus of the night. Several yawns from Aidan triggered yawns in Aurora, which forced Jace to give the order for bedtime.

"I'll keep watch," Jace offered.

"Careful then," Aidan yawned and leaned against a tree, "Natalie's already doing it."

Jace shrugged, not even bothering to look up. He curled up against the tree, shutting his eyes faster than anyone else. Aurora was not so quick; she kept on sighing, probably thinking about her old memories before she drifted to sleep. Aidan was the last, for he grew scared of what might happen if he closed his eyes. Despite his laughter, the dizziness still nagged at him. Each night he feared the worst, that harrowing nightmare making its swift return. But the sleep was seductive—

Lustful—

Dangerous—

He was in Bhall-Duraht again. The desert grounds were solid as ice with the cool luster of it. The fire pillar stood larger, closer, and the eyes still pierced.

The eyes hovered over the desert, and the shadow of a smile started to appear. Aidan knew he was being baited, but he had to look. He regretted it instantly.

His parents' bodies, drained of life, burned on the sands, half-flesh, half-skeleton. He tried to yell for them. He wanted to call for them, but his voice went mute amidst the loud flames. His tears began to burn away, and he felt his skin tearing from its seams, turning into ashes and dust.

The sand started to form letters once again: *Fear*

A second word began to appear, but flames spread, tearing apart the town, and sending the bodies of his loved ones to wherever the ashes fell.

As he felt the heat tackle his face, a voice that sounded less than godly called for him. "I'M COMING FOR YOU, BOY."

57

FRAGILE FRIENDSHIPS

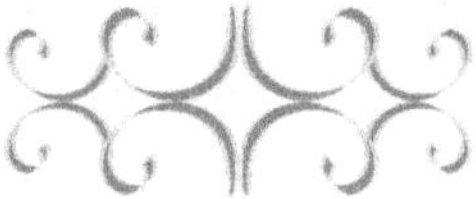

This was inevitable.
—The Rose

ER BODY ACHED, but her heart hurt a little more. Though she watched them all night, they did not even bother to look at her. Were they in the wrong? She wondered because she had hidden such a crucial thing from them, knowing full well of the atrocities that Setas-Li committed in the name of glory and honor. However, those felt so distant. Now, having a case so close to her made it feel so much more real. She should have been honest from the start. So, she could only do what she had always done—watch.

Later, she loaded up the wagons with the other soldiers, though her strength still had not returned. The petals drained more of her power than she had thought, and she could not help but curse herself for the next battle that could occur. She could not help feeling for Uncle Johannus; he had received serious injuries fighting the Shade. To think how he only got up just to make them stop fighting—it made her feel like a disgrace. *I should check on him.* She hefted one last barrel onto the wagon, gesturing to the rest of the soldiers, "Carry on, I will be back."

She walked slowly across the clearing, hoping that her betraying sight would not lead her astray. She could see enough, namely the Bhall-Durahti trio loading up their wagon, glancing at her only to work again. *Just like that, friendship is over.* Natalie did not know why it bothered her so much, but the sinking feeling in her belly had hardly slept since last night. Her eyes dropped, only paying attention to her footing now. The raven-dark streams of her hair draped over her head, and she wondered why she never brought a hair tie; it was quite popular with those from the desert.

She knocked twice on the Utopian green wagon, waiting for a grumble before entering. Per Seplechuran tradition, she kept her eyes to the ground when entering, so as not to see the injuries or vulnerability of a superior officer. "Uncle, I came to check on you." She heard him sip carefully, presumably drinking the tea she had asked a soldier to give him earlier.

"Natalie," his voice returning to him, "lass, you look troubled. Is this about last night? How are you feeling?"

Broken. Distraught. Every negative emotion was brought forth by her recent failures. Her hands were stained red, and her heart crushed like a fragile Aumir leaf. She did not know how one person could so easily destroy what she had built up; how she could fail to realize her own goals. Only one word could encapsulate how she was feeling. "Defeated."

Johannus clapped her shoulder, "You couldn't help them."

"But why does it feel that I did not try hard enough? Why does it feel like I fail in all of my endeavors? Friendship, preservation of my people … all failures."

"A blade cannot be forged without heat, lass. It is the worst times that test our character."

"For how long must I be tested?" Her voice, a whisper.

His burly fingers lifted her chin, revealing her teary eyes. She did not know how she looked to him, but his smile said it all. "Challenges appear on the cusp of a breakthrough. Wounds hurt more when they're healing."

She wanted to ask him what he meant, but he was not Yehowehel, and her tears took the rest of her strength. She only wiped her eyes and saluted. "Rest well."

She exited; her mind filled with even more questions than before. Honestly, she wished to disappear into the darkness, forgetting whatever happened in these Contested Lands. To be rejected by her own people and those she considered—wanted to consider—her friends—all of it was far too much for her mind. Why did war feel easier to her? She drilled her brain for an answer.

She made her way to the wagons, seeing Aidan at the wagon alone. He clutched his chest, and at first Natalie assumed fatigue, but Aidan seemed to be coughing up ... *ashes?*

He immediately collapsed, sending Zania into a panic. She screeched in concern and terror. Soldiers spun, hearing the screech of the iquan.

Natalie rushed over without any hesitation; Aurora and Jace met up with her, and their mutual concern for Aidan was the ink on their fragile treaty.

Aurora slid over to the struggling Camerus; she checked his veins, his head, and everything to give a diagnosis. "He has a terrible heat pitch; he needs a healer!" Aurora bit her lip. "Not again ..."

Jace looked over at her. "Again?"

"He had this same heat pitch—fever—in Bhall-Duraht and again in Utopia; he was fine afterward, so I thought nothing of it."

"He didn't bother to tell me at all."

Aurora placed a comforting hand on Jace's shoulder. "He probably didn't want ya to worry."

Natalie interjected, "We should hurry. We should be coming up on town of Liavesen. Marquise Phillian will help us."

Jace stood to his full height, having the same overbearing presence as Nicklaus, but the feeling was strangely different. "Load him into the caravan, stay with him to monitor his condition. "I'll ride."

Aurora nodded, lifting Aidan's body into the caravan. Chuckle and Snark jumped on Aurora's shoulders as she loaded him in.

Natalie made quick work to inform everyone of the rush order; while they seemed reluctant at first, none of them wished to cross Natalie, especially with Johannus present. It was one of the few benefits of having no friends and only subordinates.

Hooves galloped across the ground, kicking up dirt and grass as they soared through the forest path. Animals fled at the mere sound of the party's approach. Fortunately, Liavesen drew close, and the party arrived before their expected time.

The border town of Liavesen was keenly known as the Leviathan of Setas-Li, with large walls posted for miles around the town; the walls were as thick as four hardwood trees tied together and higher than anything in Seplechurus, which to Natalie was quite the feat.

The Marquise of Liavesen was a woman named Lee-May of House Phillian, a tactical, war-minded soldier who prioritized defense and renewal above all. If anyone could help Aidan, it would be her.

The Great General tried his best to hide his limp as he confronted the gatekeepers. As he did, Natalie used the opportunity to look at Jace, who seemed so distraught. His disdainful, unbothered visage had started to crumble before her eyes. To think, she observed, a Keerie was so—human.

"Alright, lads, let's move in!" Johannus yelled.

The party moved inside, and in no time at all, healers swarmed them. They carried the infirm to the healing yurts in the back of the town. At the center of the command was the tall Marquise herself, flipping golden strands with each order.

"Lee-May," Natalie called.

She turned, flexing her shoulder, letting the golden eagle plate roll. Her eyes were keen, looking past Natalie to observe the cargo. "*Bejuro,* Natalie."

"*Bejuro.* I need your healing expertise."

Lee-May's eyes turned to Natalie. "I escorted the Great General to a yurt. He will be well."

"Not him," Natalie corrected.

She narrowed her eyes for a moment, then said, "Bring them to me."

The stern-faced woman walked with so much pressure that it felt like her steps quaked the ground. Strangely, her lands were quaint with thatched-wood cottages and innocent scenery. The duality of the environment, the wall, and the town was like Lee herself.

"Have you been doing well?" Lee asked.

Surprised, Natalie asked, "Pardon?"

She did not repeat herself, only grunting in contemplation. She was the hardest book to read, always cutting herself short as if she had an epiphany of life. "Never mind." Lee-May furrowed her brow. "That yurt there is for fevers. I will check on them shortly."

Natalie ran into Jace, still feeling the pang of guilt in her chest. She averted her gaze, only pointing to the yurt and relaying Lee-May's orders.

She wanted to speak to them, but their concern over Aidan would outweigh any words she could possibly say. For now, she had to wait, as she had done all her life, and what she would have to continue to do. As she looked at them disappearing into the yurt, she wondered—*for how long?*

58

A Melting Resolve

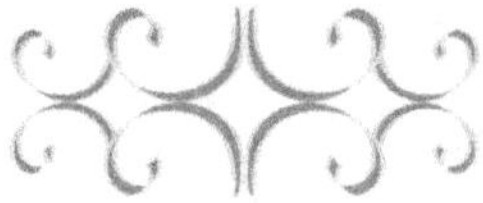

This was exactly what I was talking about.
—The Protector

NO TRUER WORDS came from Jace's mouth than what he said to his brother in the forest. An older brother, seeing a little brother in pain, had a stark contrast that he could not properly describe. The fear of losing Aidan outweighed any negative feelings he had before.

Aidan was lying draped in wet towels and writhing in pain; it made Jace feel helpless. This was not an enemy he could cut down with a sword or a foe whose bones he could break.

A soft hand grabbed his shoulder, yet he did not meet the eyes of their owner. "Go and get some air," Aurora muttered. "I know this can't be easy fer ya."

How about you? He wanted to ask. Aidan and Aurora were obviously close, especially since Aidan protected her from ... *me.* "I'm sure this can't be easy for you, either."

The two shared a knowing look which soon dissolved into Aurora playing with locks of her hair and avoiding contact. "Aidan's not my kin. I'm sure that ya—"

Jace shook his head, interrupting her. "—Let's not compare pains; it demeans both our lives."

Aurora nodded, gently fixing a lock of Aidan's hair. His body seemed to calm at her touch, but never enough to stop the pain. Jace took another cloth and set it on Aidan's body.

"Tell me, what was it like for ya and Aidan living in a cave?"

Jace sighed, fiddling around with his cloak's lapel. He tilted his head, thinking about it. He rarely thought about describing it to someone. "Lonely," he sighed quietly. "Variations of self-pity and nostalgia." He noted Aurora's look of concern. Maybe she expected an optimistic answer, he thought, or perhaps she had forgotten that the conversation was not with Aidan but with him.

"That sounds—depressing."

Everything about our life was depressing. Jace remembered the area of the cave well. They fashioned it like their living room, and when he was younger, he got indignant when Aidan moved a single thing.

One of his most desperate moments was when he tried to shape an image of his mother and father out of wood, but he failed miserably. He could never get the faces right. He had to forget them; he had to remind himself that they died, that everyone died. The worst part about having hope was that when it was rediscovered, it either had to fight stronger doubts or be forced to die. But he knew that without hope, there is no life. That is why he had to focus on living, focus on Aidan. He stood, taking the water bowl with him. "I'm going to replenish this."

"I'll go with ya."

"No, stay with him." His lacquer-black eyes grazed over Aidan. "He needs someone right now."

Aurora stood defiantly, crossing her arms to emphasize that fact. "I don't know who needs more help, ya or yer kin."

He sighed, "Probably both." He left the yurt.

People were scattered about, moving at the behest of the marquise. So much different from Bhall-Duraht; the people were organized here. Everyone seemed to have a mission that did not involve profit, but they seemed not to have any enjoyment in their tasks. Was this how Jace came off the first time that people met him? He wondered.

"You there, desert dweller," the Marquise called. She approached, and immediately her haughty aura blasted Jace in the face. Were all Setas-Lisians so? They were as resolute as their cobblestone paths, but they felt like homes with fragile foundations.

"I have a name."

"Of course, mercenaries such as yourself would like to be known with high officials, I understand."

Jace rolled his eyes, causing the Marquise to raise a brow. "I," she stopped midway to think, "need heavy lifting to be done. I was informed of your heightened strength."

Jace brushed by her. "I need to get water for my brother." He only got a step in before he heard Aurora call his name. He turned in her direction, his face mimicking hers as he witnessed her urgency.

Aurora urged, "Aidan—he started writhing and screaming, and—and we need him to cool down."

He understood the hint. "Let's go."

Of course, Jace relaxed with a breath. He did not even think of using his Blade. *This is going to be easy.*

It was, in fact, not easy. Suddenly, fire rose from Aidan's yurt, filling the sky with a bleak red. The scorching wave tore apart the firmament, looming over the wooden-thatched houses scattered across the field.

"AIDAN!" Aurora and Jace yelled as they ran over to the yurt.

The organized soldiers of Liavesen formed an assembly line to douse the flames that engulfed Aidan's yurt, but their efforts were useless. It was as if they were throwing oil on the fire.

Jace pulled out his blade, unwrapping it with great haste. With a hard exhalation, he roared, "Breathe! Nevrence!"

A blue crack formed, surging throughout Jace's sword. The light underneath wanted to shine forth; its radiance did not want to be held in. The brilliance shone even brighter under the sky of the setting sun. Once Jace's scabbard transformed into its divine silver form, he unsheathed his ice Blade that reflected the sporadic flames in front.

"What in the world?" Lee-May awed.

"Everyone, get back!" Jace yelled.

The soldiers did not wait for their marquise to confirm the order before they separated themselves from the flames.

Jace placed the Blade in front of his mouth, bellowing a mighty breath; the frigid squall doused the flames while forming an ice prison to cool the area. The people cheered loudly as they gathered around Jace, but his focus was not on them. He pushed through the thankful crowd as he and Aurora approached the ice dome.

Listening intently, Jace hushed the crowd with the raise of his hand. A shattering, a spreading ping sounded—like the ones a mistreated blade made after a quench. Something began to warp, and at first, Jace thought it was the ground. As it progressively became louder, he could tell it was the ice.

And Aurora noticed it too. "Is yer ice—cracking? I thought only Sov's could do that."

Jace spun around. "Take cover!"

With a loud roar, an infernal shockwave imploded Jace's dome, knocking him and Aurora back to the crowd. A rushing flame was shot upward, forming a dense pillar of fire. Everyone beheld the two piercing eyes that glowed a blood red. The eyes struck fear in the townspeople. Even the battle-hardened soldiers were shaking in their boots. The worst part of the eyes was not their sinister, ominous gaze; it was the fact that whatever was peering at them rivaled the height of Brand in his monstrous state.

"What in the seven levels of Maserades is that?!" Lee-May exclaimed.

Aurora unsheathed her dagger. "It doesn't matter. Take cover!"

"This is my town." Lee-May unsheathed her rapier and dueler's dagger. "I will defend it with my life!"

Aurora yelled at her. "Ya can't handle whatever that is!"

"And you can?!"

Jace bellowed cold mist. "Yes."

The leer from Jace was more than enough for her. Lee-May looked between the pillar of flames and the two of them. She nodded and sheathed her weapons, placing a hand over her heart. "Fine. Please, save my town."

"Save your people," Jace commanded, "we'll handle the rest."

Lee-May nodded, herding her people to the open fields. The sounds of shouting were faint in the background compared to the crackling flames. In there was Aidan, and something else.

"Laddie, ya ready?" Aurora asked. The sky went completely dark, and the rain followed soon after. A crack of lightning struck before the thunder ended the call; the lightning surged yellow in the sky as Aurora muttered the words that elevated her being to an entirely different plane. "Bereka!"

A canopy of clouds blinked a single bolt, filling Aurora with a new-found power. Jace didn't even stare, but when he felt the tingling of her lightning-cloth he knew she was ready.

Jace repeated the same attack he used to quench the flames before. But his frozen breath could not reach the flames; they were burning too hot for the ice to keep its shape.

"That's bad," Aurora stated.

Jace growled, "Not now, Aurora."

Before they could think of any more ideas, the loud booming voice uttered words to the two chosen warriors. The sudden volume of his voice was intimidating, sounding both grotesque and raspy.

"IS THIS WHAT I AM TO FIGHT?" the voice asked.

Ice and lightning gathered around their masters, trembling at their adversary who commanded the flames.

"What are you?!" Jace yelled. "What did you do with my brother?!"

"WHAT AM I?" A large, reptilian foot stepped out of the flames, shattering the earth beneath its red-scaled toes. "I AM ANGER." Then, a hand resembling a wild feline creature burst through the flames. "I AM HATRED. Its hands began to tear the massive wall of fire as if ripping a veil. Forcing all to watch its awe-striking power. "I AM DESTRUCTION." A loud roar bellowed from the monster's mouth as horns of magma seeped through the veil, dripping with vitriolic heat. "I AM PAIN!"

The rest of the monster emerged from the flames, ruffling its yellow mane. Its entire body was coated in red scales with the exception of its hands, which were burning with magma-like fur. It had the snout of a canine, and its eyes glowed redder than the hellish landscape of Maserades, with no trace of any pupils. The chimeric creature had the body of a human with the carpal legs of an animal. With another roar that was hard to endure, the creature yelled, "I. AM. FEAYRE FIRE."

59

I Am Feayre Fire

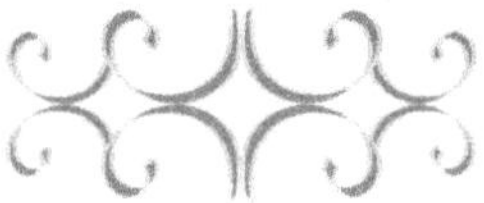

What is that thing?
—The Thief

H ER FACE REDDENED in the presence of the monster; sweat merged the fabrics of her clothes to her skin. Every attack from that demon sent a wave of fear that made her lightning tremble and rain cower into mist. It was the kind of fear that didn't have a logical basis, one that came from a person who simply wanted her dead for enjoyment. Only her father, the Dark General, made Aurora feel such.

"FIGHT! IS THIS ALL YOU HAVE?!" it yelled, conjuring a flame in its hand, and hurled it right at Jace, who barely defended against it with an ice wall.

Aurora rushed by Jace, swooping him up before Feayre Fire could shoot another fireball. Aurora set Jace down behind the beast.

Jace wiped the soot from his clothing. "Thank you."

"Don't mention it, laddie. What's the plan?"

Jace had to come up with something because she surely did not have the energy to. She knew that his hesitancy in combat meant that he was intuitively hatching a next step, or maybe it was something else.

However, Jace's hesitation quelled when the monster ignited its hands and rushed at them. It roared grotesquely, forcing Jace back into the conscious world, and fortunately, with a plan. "Get behind him!"

Aurora let the lightning fill her veins. She bolted in the cover of the steam built by the creature's fire and her rain. Jace formed an ice spear from his Blade, identical to the one he used to fight Brand; with it, he dueled the creature with exceptional prowess. However, the creature's height and human-like physique put Jace at a huge disadvantage, especially if the creature were to grab the Blade.

So, she had to hurry. Lightning trails followed her feet when she flanked the monster. With a call from her Blade and an answer from the sky, she tore into the back of the creature with ferocious bolts. The satisfying pain of its roars made Aurora feel a little giddy. When it tried to retaliate against her, Jace drew its attention back.

"Keep at it!" Jace yelled.

The creature growled, deftly feinting Jace's blow before kicking the ice warrior into the Marquise's beloved wall.

Feayre Fire turned to her, grinning mischievously as he used his hand to block her bolts. *How? They hurt him before. Was it adapting, or maybe it was toying with us?* She gasped. *That's why Jace was hesitant.*

Aurora shifted to mobile offense, running at her highest maintainable speed and shooting off bolts all at once.

Every time Feayre Fire tried to retaliate, Aurora moved. Her quick speed outmatched the fiery giant, but speed could not save her from the radial attack it unleashed. Aurora tried to defend herself with lightning, but her inexperience prevented her from forming a proper protective field.

The fires kept itching her skin as if it would not heal. She had already gasped for air, and if she kept fighting, she knew she would pass out. The fire that thing let off was unnatural, demonic in nature.

The monster laughed, "DO YOU REALLY THINK YOU CAN DEFEAT ME!?"

Feayre Fire raised a fist to the sky. A powerful fireball was forming above its fingers. The fires rose, and the buildings that were not on fire began to drown in the flames. The attack caused the ground beneath it to melt, causing everything around it to shift and kneel. "FEEL MY RAGE! FEEL MY FIRE!"

Aurora's eyes grew; she managed to race over to Jace, trying to pick him up from the rubble.

"Laddie, we have to go—now!"

Jace seemed to have fallen into a trance again, but this time, it felt different. The orb in Aurora's Blade glowed; in fact, the light far outweighed the piercing light of her first transformation.

Jace's breath hit air; it gave off an ice-glittering mist, then completely froze. "Yehowehel, he who called me, give me the power to devour this beast in ice."

A pillar of azure light shot upward through the clouds; the air around the town grew cold and dense. The chill quenched the flames of the nearby buildings; even Feayre Fire grew feeble as the ice weakened its power. Aurora shielded her eyes, unknowing of what was going on.

Jace shivered with power. "Begone—"

Feayre Fire dropped to one knee; the small sun fizzled with a hiss. It grabbed its head and shook it in a frenzy. "NO, I WILL ... I WILL NOT GIVE IN TO YOU!"

"Did ya do it?" Aurora asked Jace.

"I didn't do anything yet."

Feayre Fire roared in pain and anger as he let blasts of fire exude from the bowels of his mouth. "NO, NO!"

A small fire dome enveloped Feayre Fire, and it started to shrink, becoming smaller and smaller until it was the size of a human. It was then that they truly realized—

"... It can't ...," Jace gasped in painful realization.

"Laddie ...?"

Aidan emerged from the flame. He took only two steps before collapsing. Jace and Aurora rushed to his side, yelling his name, but no answer. *So, Aidan did just transform into that thing. Was that real?* The buildings that were now nothing more than ash testified that the battle had taken place. But she had to ask: did this have to do with the Blades? So many questions, and no one to help answer them. Only time would tell what had truly happened, but for that moment, the team had to deal with what was in front of them.

Aidan was lying motionless; one could even assume he had died after all he had been through. Jace got to his knees, shaking his brother. "Aidan, Aidan, wake up."

Aidan groaned. His eyes slinked open, discombobulated. His body shakily moved upward. Jace supported him when it looked like he was about to fall over. Aidan grabbed Jace's arms, feeling his jacket. Aidan's eyes flooded with tears; his breaths were uneven. He looked at Jace; his eyes were childlike and tormented. His once-focused pupils darted around as if he were eagerly searching for something, anything. "I-I ..." Aidan's voice broke, "I can't see." Aidan buried his face into his brother's chest; his voice cracked with fear. Aidan's sobs were sharp; an edge of sadness cut through his core. His shaky hands clutched Jace's clothes, pulling for comfort. His words were lost in the pain; Aidan could barely speak. "Jace, I can't, I can't—I can't see ... Jace, h-help me ..."

Jace grabbed the head of his little brother, holding him close, as close as he possibly could. Jace sunk his face into Aidan's hair, holding back his own tears. He needed to be strong; this was a moment where he needed to be strong. "It's okay, it's okay, hang in there," Jace whispered.

"I—lost them ... I lost my eyes—I lost my mother."

That declaration ripped through Aurora, and it was even worse when she saw Jace shed tears. She dropped to her knees and threaded her fingers through Aidan's thick curls. She whispered in his ear, the only thing she could, "Aidan, we're here."

Aidan let off one more agonizing cry that reverberated through both Jace and Aurora's bodies. The sadness felt so tangible and unbreakable at the same time.

Aurora could not help but think, *How are we ever going to recover from this?*

60

LIVING NIGHTMARE

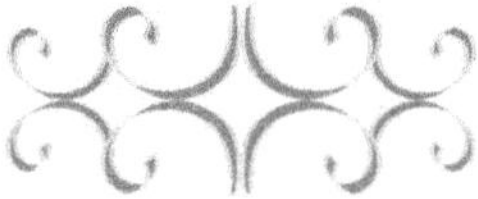

Please tell me it was a dream.
—The Wildcard

HE OPENED HIS eyes—nothing. Not blackness, not dark, just nothing at all. He hoped it was just a demented work of fiction, but reality proved him wrong. Aidan prided himself in seeing the tiniest of details and now, he could not even see the full picture. What would he tell his mother when he met up with her again? He could not bear the thought of facing her as her blind son.

He growled, smacking the straw mat under him, *why not my hearing? My touch? Why my eyes?* He touched the bandages on his eyes, hoping, at least, he could feel if they were still there.

He sat up and felt a strong breeze greet his aching, bandaged body. It seemed as though his rampage had not left much intact.

Out of sheer curiosity, he invoked the one thing that could never burn, he decided to listen to his environment. The soft winds, the creaking yurt along with the smell of smoke were all new yet familiar sensations. However, another sound caught his attention; someone drew close; the steps were unreadable, and they sounded light, almost as if it were a ghost struggling between the ethereal and physical plane.

"Aidan? I brought ya some food," Aurora greeted.

Aurora, of course, Aidan thought. He held his shoulder, paying attention to even more sounds. "I'm surprised I didn't burn down all their crops."

"No, ya didn't do that!" Aurora exclaimed. "That—thing—did."

"Aurora, be realistic, do you think that *thing* would be here if I wasn't?" And like that, he hushed the thunder, for the answer to the sky was as obvious as the smells of smoke.

He heard her churn something, a liquid. From where he laid, he could feel the heat. *Illisians sure love their soups.*

She blew on it before putting the spoon to his lips. "Eat, ya are going to need yer strength."

"To do what? Transform again? Maybe, I'll burn the capital next." *That doesn't sound entirely bad.*

Aurora sighed. "Please, just eat."

Aidan turned his head in defiance, tipping the spoon out of Aurora's hand and right onto his folded arms. Then everything came flooding back: the burning of Bhall-Duraht, the fires he refused to make, the ones he refused to stay near, and, of course, the piercing eyes of that creature. He jerked back, screaming his aggravations while clutching his arm, "Watch how you're handling that, Aurora!"

"Aidan, I'm so sorry." She tried to wipe the burn mark, but he just shoved her away.

Though he lacked sight, he did not lack strength. He heard Aurora hit the ground. Silence hung in the room, and Aidan feared he had done something permanent. Only a few seconds passed before he felt a strange pricking, as if needles surrounded him, prodding at his skin.

"I'm trying to help ya! What is yer problem!"

Help. That was always the problem, was it not? He could not do anything himself, and everyone else just *had* to provide their aid. He clenched his fist, mad at his own uselessness and mad at everyone around him being so capable. His thoughts of frustration caught up with his words, "If I wanted your help, I would've asked!"

"If ya wanted my help?" Aurora parroted with sarcasm, "Laddie, what happened to us being friends and trusting each other? I just want ya to feel better, and that's all ya can say? How selfish and egotistical can ya be?!" Aurora picked up the bowl and tossed it. "If ya want to act like that, then feed yerself!" She stormed through the door, and the strange prickling went with her.

Aidan growled, punching the ground. He brought his knees to his face, hugging his legs, praying for the nightmare of fires and flame to be over.

This was not how he had expected his journey would go; he wished for an experience, one where he would see the sights, but now he'd be lucky to see at all. He whispered, "El, I'll answer your dumb question if you'll just give me something else to wield."

Not even a feeling. Aidan hugged his legs even tighter. Though he was not incredibly religious, he hoped that El would say something—anything.

But he did hear footsteps. They were not as feather-light as Aurora's. No, these were loud, yet all of them were at the same volume and very slow. Metal clanged with these footsteps; someone was wearing armor—of mostly cloth.

"Pardon my intrusion."

"Nicklaus," growled Aidan.

"Bold of you to assume a tone with me, seeing as you destroyed a Setas-Lisian town."

Aidan's heart raced. Jace told everyone how a monster had appeared from nowhere and attacked. Clearly, not everyone bought it. Aidan could not be surprised though; Nicklaus seemed sharper than most.

"So, you came to gloat, *your majesty*?" Aidan taunted.

"No, and please refrain from saying that," sighed Nicklaus, "it does not suit you."

Aidan raised his head. "Then why are you here?"

Nicklaus's hand slapped a book.

By the sound of it, Aidan knew it was hefty. "What's that? Religious text? Come to save my soul before I drown in flames?"

"No, *I do not have that with me currently*. This," Nicklaus cleared his throat, "is the sequel to Clouds Above. I had to forsake my copy here to lighten the load."

Aidan scoffed incredulously. "You want me to read it?" He could just *feel* Nicklaus rolling his eyes. The sigh the prince gave afterward proved it. Aidan could imagine it now, a red-hot Nicklaus with that pompous leer in his eyes. If only he could see it.

"Do you really think me so cruel? To what end do you know of my family and I?"

Easy. "Your family helped keep this war going. Everyone knows how much the Leroza clan benefits from this war and the slaves, you guys have to take. One of them almost grabbed me before Jace got to them first. You're Leroza, aren't you? Unless you were lying about that, too."

There was another sigh; this one seemed defeated, "I am, in fact, Leroza, from my mother's side. I do understand the greediness of my matriarchal clan, but I assure you it is for the best."

"For who's best? Yours? Certainly not mine, certainly not for my neighbors who were slaughtered or my parents and friends who were kidnapped. Certainly not for my friend who was forced into Seplechuran ranks or my brother who had to raise me."

The book was dropped just like the bowl. If Aidan's sole job was to annoy everyone who was providing him with help, he had done an excellent job.

"The Blades will benefit us all!" Nicklaus exclaimed.

"Says who, Nicklaus?! It sounds like you want them for yourself. We don't even know anything about the Holy City or what the Blades truly are. Are you going to ruin so many lives just because of a prophecy we don't fully understand?"

Nicklaus stomped away, keeping himself at the entrance of the yurt. "I tried to be generous, but it seems you people do not understand the concept. So, I will make this clear. If you threaten my lands again with your monstrous transformation—I will end you myself."

The door to the yurt whipped like Jace's cape, and once again the world grew silent. Aidan knew the next person to come in would receive his collective anger, and that was a limit even he did not want to cross. Instead, the familiar sounds of shimmering warmed his ears. "Chuckle? Snark?"

They had slid under the yurt's door, crawling to him with such joy. He could hear Chuckle making a little bit more pace than Snark, which surprised him since Snark had the athletic edge over its sibling.

"You two came just to see me, huh? Sorry, I can't play with you right now." Aidan stretched out his hand, feeling the straw mats that covered the yurt, hoping to find his chains. He picked up his chains and slowly brought them to his knees. "I bet you two were worried."

They chimed energetically, but it soon became a depressing low, even lower than Snark's normal *talking* voice. Aidan tried to keep it together, but his tears were seeping through the bandages. He did not plan for so much of this. He knew things would get bad but even he, who relished in the world of imagination, could have never imagined this.

61

HE WHO WILL NEVER CEASE

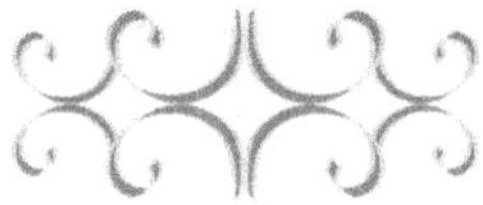

I ... can't do this anymore.
—The Protector

ONCE AGAIN, HE failed to protect something. He failed his town, his parents, his best friend, and now, his brother. He had to ask, hoping someone would answer: was everything he had to protect destined to fall, or did he truly fail at every moment?

He walked through the destroyed town, watching the people weep at their fallen world. *I couldn't even protect that.* He grabbed his stomach, feeling the twists and stabs of the pressure again. He rested on what was left of the city wall, clutching his head. Nicklaus's words came to bite him once more, the words about protecting the entire world. If he could not protect the town, could he truly protect the world? He asked himself: Was he really the protector-born?

The worst part: he couldn't bear to see the fruits of his failure. He couldn't see Serenity's eyes, nor look intently at the town, and certainly, he could not look at how broken Aidan was.

He searched eagerly for his tools; he needed to carve something, anything. But neither his tools nor his flute could ever bring him the necessary comfort.

The eldest Camerus clutched his head harder, fingers sinking deeper into his black dreads. His perceived failures had made him feel the stain of defeat.

"*Be strong,*" he heard the Voice speak.

"HOW?" he yelled out loud.

Those who saw Jace simply moved along, hiding their children and protecting their animals. But he didn't care. To him, those people were irrelevant.

"*They aren't irrelevant. I would have not sanctioned you a Conquest if I did not deem thee ready.*"

"Then—" Jace's voice cracked, "—what do I do?"

In a fading whisper, the Voice replied, "*Breathe.*"

Jace shut his eyes, leaning his head back, sliding down the wall to a sit. Calmly, he inhaled, then exhaled. He repeated. The nausea began to disappear, and his head calmed.

"*Thou wast not made to bear thine burdens alone nor stand in the face of adversity unprepared. I would have not called thee, if thee weren't ready.*"

After that, Jace heard nothing. He kept breathing, remembering the words spoken to him in the desert. He had to stand; a warrior made to be a resolute force, but he felt as if he was chipping.

He rose to his feet, repeating his mantra. The words spoken were somewhat vague, but if he had learned anything from his father, vague messages were for the hearer to fill in.

His greatest fear from past to present remained the same: losing someone whom he held dear. He was a man, not a deity. He could not become omnipresent. So, his allies had to be galvanized, and he could do it the only way he knew how. Helping Aidan would be—problematic, but maybe he could help someone else—he concluded.

He scurried over to the closest townsfolk. "Excuse me, is there a standing forge close by?"

The man looked baffled. "Black ... uh ... smith?" he spoke unsure of his words.

Jace nodded, and the man pointed to the southernmost part of the town. Without a word of gratitude, Jace rushed off. After securing the proper tools and permissions, he began working. He did away with his fashionable robe and put on a smith's apron.

Setas-Lisian smithies were a lot more rustic than he had anticipated. However, the tools were lined up neatly on the wall, and the layout was made so that one person could forge at once. In fact, his father had the exact setup. *Did he learn to smith in Setas-Li? Or did he simply admire the layout?* Regardless, Jace found it easier to work. To this day, nothing proved to be more beautiful than a giant forge that could fit any weapon.

Jace heated the forge, keeping the flames steady. He stared in them, seeing the eyes of that beast. So evil and destructive.

The bladesmith stacked the forge with the sufficient coal. With every move, he heard his father's instructions and the one word that got him through the constant mistakes and feelings of doubt, "Breathe."

The town smiths supplied him with the necessary metals; all he needed to do was bend them. He picked them, heated them, molded them.

No matter how much he held a blade, nothing felt better than holding a hammer and a pair of tongs. He wielded the cold in battle, but in the forge, heat and metal were his weapons. In a forge, he was not a mere smith; no, he felt as if he were a god—and this god had a decree, one written in steel.

He spent hours in the smithy, muttering his mantra as he kept going. Although he would not finish today, he prepared for tomorrow. Every strike had a message for the future; every strike was a reminder of who he was.

With every strike, he remembered the words that Voice spoke to him in the desert: *Stand firm, O protector born, for your winter cometh.* He brought the hammer down.

You stood rigid, not to be stubborn, but to shield. Slam!

You led armies into battle and fought valiantly when all hope seemed lost. Slam!

Not much remains eternal, however ... Slam!

Cold. Slam!

Winter. Slam!

Night. Slam!

You—will never cease. The sparks raised their highest.

The following day, Jace returned to the smithy, putting on his apron and getting to work once more. However, unlike yesterday, he had interruptions. "Lord Jace," Lee-May greeted, "I am sorry to disturb you."

Lord Jace now? Funny. Jace checked the blade he was working on for any stresses, cracks, or warps. "Not sorry enough, it seems."

Lee-May cleared her throat. "The prince wanted me to inform you that our departure is tonight."

He further inspected the weapon. "I'm not leaving until I finish this blade."

"But the prince ordered ..." She trailed off.

Jace took a deep breath in, then exhaled. Cold air bellowed from his mouth as the black smoke did the chimney. Lee-May visibly shivered.

She bowed. "I will inform his highness." She made a swift exit.

Jace spent the rest of those days crafting a blade. Unfortunately, he did not have much time for a scabbard, but it would suffice, hopefully. He personally would not wield a short sword, as it was far too light for his taste, and a fuller in the blade was not his style. Fortunately, he had not made the blade for himself.

On the final day of their stay, Jace spent his time saying goodbye to the other smiths in the town and thanking them for letting him use their equipment. Most of the smiths showed that annoying reverence for him like Johannus and his family did in Utopia, but he still had not adapted to it.

He made his way over to the wagon, where Aurora loaded it with additional cargo since the other wagons were destroyed. "Borealis," he called.

She wiped her brow, greeting him with a tired smile. "Well, hello there, laddie, didn't think ya were going to leave the smithy."

Jace chuckled, effortlessly lifting the last barrel into the wagon, "Sorry, I was going through ... mental trials."

Aurora wiped her hands with a cloth, then removed the hair tie Aidan had given her and stuffed it into her pocket. "It's alright, I can't imagine how hard this is. At least yer time was productive, aye?"

Jace chuckled nervously as he fiddled with the short sword. Only his father and Aidan ever critiqued his work, so this moment had a different kind of value. He brushed his fingers across the fuller of the blade to the black, leather-wrapped grip, and lastly to the silver pommel.

Aurora raised a brow. "Laddie?"

"I saw that most of your daggers were destroyed in the Contested Lands, and I ... never gave you anything when you joined our group. So, here."

Aurora startled as Jace suddenly pushed the weapon in her face but kept her smile. She took the weapon from his hands, swinging it a couple of times to get a feel for the weight. Her enlarged grin validated him already. "Jace, I don't know what to say."

"Just use it, and don't break it too quickly."

Aurora chuckled, "With the way you throw around yer weapon and ya tell me to not break it? Right."

"I'm careful," Jace defended.

"Sure," Aurora called out in disbelief. Out of nowhere, Aurora wrapped him in a hug. "Thanks, laddie, really."

Jace slowly returned the hug. "Uh, sure, you're welcome."

The two poked fun at each other a little more, but they knew the work would only stack up on them if they continued. They had other duties to attend to, and Jace had one more person to talk to. His only hope was that he could stomach the pain.

"Knock, knock." Jace stood in front of the yurt.

"Since when have you ever knocked?" Aidan mocked from the inside.

"Since when have we ever had a door?"

"Good point."

Aidan was partially dressed when Jace entered. Chuckle and Snark were the most active he's ever seen them, too.

"I knocked in Utopia, you know," remembered Jace.

"I remember no such thing."

Jace chuckled. He removed his hair tie, fiddling around with his dreads, hoping it would distract him from seeing Aidan so defeated. His brother lurched up by the back of the yurt, dressed, but lacking in life.

Aidan broke the silence, "So, you haven't visited me in a couple of days."

Jace sighed, trying to keep his eyes away, "Trust me, it's not easy seeing you like this."

"I figured, though, a visit would be nice."

"Sorry."

Jace sat beside Aidan, patting him on the shoulder. Right now, he wanted to wave his hand over his brother's eyes and expect him to be healed, but he knew he did not have that power. However, the Voice did say that Jace was ready; he had to try something.

"Hey, remember that moment when you got stung by that scorpionbee on your knee?"

"Ah yes, mention another time I was completely handicapped."

Jace flicked him on the forehead. "Not my point. Do you remember when you used to call me for everything?"

"Yeah, I remember," Aidan nearly hissed it.

Jace sat back, gathering Aidan's tone. He barely lifted his mouth to smile, nor moved his body to playfully push back. He just sat there, devoid of all his animation, his joy, and his happiness. *Wrong approach, this isn't working.* Jace sighed. "It's time to leave, the wagon is already packed."

"I guess there's no time like the present."

Jace stood, tapping Aidan's arm to help him up, but Aidan refused the help and stood on his own. Jace narrowed his gaze at that gesture; something was clearly amiss. Regardless, he led Aidan out by his shoulder. "Follow me."

The two made their way to the wagon, and soon enough, the entire team set off. Their next destination may prove a golden opportunity or something less than ideal.

62

ACCEPTANCE

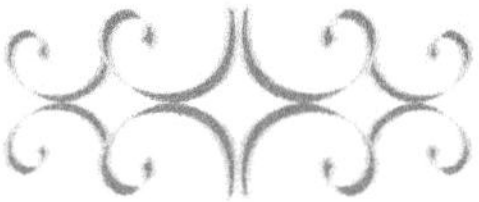

These laddies are something else.
—The Thief

T HE SILVERY SHEEN made her smile grow wider. The fact that Jace made her a blade seemed normal, but a gift? For her? She did not know what had gotten into him. The gift of weaponry felt more important than anything else; a pact etched in steel, a true acceptance, a promise to fight beside one another.

She looked at it again, almost afraid to use it, seeing the amazing detail and feeling the balanced weight. Besides Aidan and now Jace, Natasha was the only person who had ever given her a gift in the more recent days; everything else she had to steal. Unfortunately, Natasha's gift, or gifts rather, were all bent or shattered across her father's armor.

I should get them something. However, she did not know much about their material wants. Honestly, it made her feel awful. Aidan knew her style after a few days, while Jace saw her love for short weaponry, maybe he guessed? She pondered.

Whatever she got them had to be personal. Now, it was her turn to pay attention. While they were finalizing the trade agreement, she could scour the capital to find them something, *and I will pay! No stealing!* She'll drop the coin on the counter and do it the right way; however, the thought of her walking Setas-Lisian streets alone did not bring her comfort. All those eyes looking at her, judging her, wanting her to go back to the life of chains. *No,* she steeled herself, *I got to do this.*

"What's got you all happy?" Jace asked.

She just noticed the smile plastered to her face; *oh no, I hope I aint blushin'.* "Nothing ..."

"I hope you're not planning on stealing anything," he said half-play-fully, half-serious.

"Fer once, no."

Jace nodded, not questioning it further. He focused on the road as he followed behind the others in the wagon train. Ever since Aidan collapsed in the Contested Lands, Zania had been far more receptive to Jace taking the reins. Aurora surmised the iquan was smart enough to know Aidan could not drive, or maybe, she hoped, the beast was truly warming up to Jace.

Aurora shrugged. For now, she paid attention to her surroundings: the air became cooler, and the mountain ranges started to appear in the distance. The trees only shrank as they moved closer to Élurés; somehow, they became less green, but it didn't detract from their beauty. Setas-Li, a kingdom known for its beauty, at least, this part was. She nearly found it hard to believe that somewhere in the kingdom, a camp holding Delfizcani slaves was still active. Life held many hidden monsters; not too long ago, some could not believe the infamous killer of Bhall-Duraht turned out to be a Delfizcani girl.

She leaned back, hoping that the views were as good as they really were, nothing hidden, nothing evil, something she did not have to look too deeply into. But as she yawned, she wondered if the hope for no lies in Setas-Li was as lucid and intangible as a dream.

The wagon shook her awake. The screeching halt made the wood groan, and the chorus of wagons halted stirred her body to movement.

"Wow," awed Jace.

Aurora rubbed the blur from her eyes, only to shield them right after. The intense gleam startled her, but then it was soon replaced with wonder. "Wow," she mimicked.

Golden and gilded, Élurés was an illuminating beacon for all allies, and a flame unquenched to its enemies. The party arrived in a reverential awe; even Natalie, who had seen the sight many times, could not suppress her wonder. Gates of shining metals stood before them, adorned in gold-forged plumes with opals in the gates. If one mistook the gates alone as the entry to the Abode—they would be forgiven a hundred times over.

"This place ... it's amazing," Jace awed, "I've never seen anything like this, such authority."

Aurora hopped off the wagon, taking in the sights more. The entire city was surrounded by a wharf that had water bluer than even Nicklaus's eyes. The mountains in the distance seemed to have fed it, which only added to the stern and beautiful scenery of the city. *To think, this is where Nicklaus grew up,* Aurora thought.

Nicklaus stepped forward to approach the guards at the gate. They exchanged words in Setas-Lisian, some of which Aurora picked up, before the gates squealed open. He stopped near their wagon, eyeing both Jace and Aurora. "Once we convene with my father, the king, we will conclude our business together."

Good riddance. Aurora wanted desperately to sass him, but she held her tongue; soon, she would not have to see the likes of him ever again. Soon, she could see Natasha, Arundel, and Lulia back in the desert. However, the clean, cool air of Setas-Li and Utopia was something she would miss.

Gawking eyes of blue and green followed them like lights as they were paraded through the city streets. Children called, and adults cheered as if they had never seen Utopians before. Maybe, however, the eyes were trained on the desert people as if they were some exotic goods.

Aurora fidgeted with her wrists, thinking about the words those people had for her. No position on her seat remained comfortable for long. Her breath became chopped and distraught, and her eyes could not look away from the ground.

"Breathe," Jace consoled without moving his eyes, "you're not alone this time."

Aurora calmed her breathing but kept rubbing her wrists. "Thanks."

Jace nodded as he continued to observe the area. Aurora tried her best to mimic his bravery, raising her pupils. The architecture clearly differed from Bhall-Duraht; not a single piece of adobe in sight. Instead, the houses were made from a yellowish-gold brick, lined with a wooden skeleton. Even in such a crowded place, they looked orderly, and the golden sheen became far too much for her hazel eyes. Clearly, Setas-Lisians in the capital took their opulence seriously.

Everything in the city was structured perfectly as if the buildings, greenery, and roads were made for the sole purpose of complementing one another, but all that paled in comparison to the castle. Its triple spires scraped the skies, white as the clouds it touched, layered with actual gold that streamed down to the moat surrounding it. In the center of its spires, a hovering, giant golden crystal flooded the entire city with light and resonated with the smaller ones filling the streets—she hated to admit it, but they had the right to be pompous with a castle like that.

Instinctively, her mind went to the treasure vault; could it be broken into so easily? She wondered.

"*Prinz Nicklaus!*" The castle guard shouted in surprise.

Nicklaus silenced him with a wave of his hand, then focused his attention on the wagon and said something in his mother tongue. The guard bowed, then opened the gates for the rest of them to move forward. The long bridge that crossed the moat overlooked the waters beautifully; Aurora looked over to see a waritutu *that was a Delfizcani fish!* The Setas-Lisians loved having their hands on everything.

Later, the maids placed the trio in a small room. It had one bed, which Aidan occupied, and a windowsill where Aurora sat. Jace paced around the room, occasionally gazing into the mirror.

More than twenty minutes sauntered by, and there was still no word from Johannus, Natalie, or Nicklaus. In her experience, twenty minutes could give them enough time to birth a devious plot.

"What's taking so long?" Jace asked.

"I don't know; I can't see what they're doing," Aidan replied.

Aurora sighed, "Stop it, Aidan."

He groaned, turning over on the bed, Chuckle and Snark at his side.

Jace looked over to him, eyes furrowed in worry, but they returned to their stern position. "If they don't come get us soon, we'll leave."

Aurora looked hazily at the city. "What if they come *fer* us?" Aurora asked in a near whisper, slowly turning her head to Jace.

Jace gripped his weapon. "Then we'll fight," he replied matter-of-factly.

Knock, knock.

Jace took a deep breath. "Come in."

Natalie poked her head in before fully opening the door. Her eyes only looked toward the ground as if the shame of her secrets weighed on her neck. "The king would like to see you. Please follow."

Jace and Aurora shared a glance. Aidan stood reaching for his brother, and they all walked toward the throne room. Hopefully, this would not be as terrible as she had thought.

63

MY GOLDEN PRISON

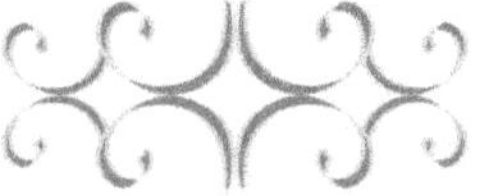

Get me out of here.
—The Prince

BACK IN HIS cell. Substituting iron bars for golden walls did not matter. Nicklaus wondered if the moat that surrounded his jail had the purpose of keeping invaders out or hopeful princes and princesses in. He would have asked his father, but the last time they spoke properly was when Nicklaus was five. He remembered his father telling him stories. Actually, he became the progenitor of Nicklaus's fascination with books, ones where dragons held royals prisoner until a savior came. But as Nicklaus adorned his doublet and golden vambraces and shoulder armor, he felt as if his father might have been the dragon all along.

A knock filled his eardrums.

"*Prinz* Nicklaus," the attendant called.

He walked past, lightly brushing the attendant aside. "I know."

He tromped down the halls, waiting for the ridicule from his parents or the others from court. He would be the talk of the city once again. *Look at the wayward prince* or *look at him chasing fairytales and forsaking his duties,* Nicklaus remembered. He was always being judged, always under the scrutinizing eye of those who never had his best interests at heart. The Blades were the best attempt to shut them up, for him to finally make something of himself. Now, it feels like even Yehowehel now judged him. He continued to walk the cavernous halls, his feet gliding across the golden runner on the white stone of the castle. Giant windows showered him in light from his left side; *only if this light was representative of my predicament*, Nicklaus grieved. "Let me in," he commanded in Setas-Lisian as he reached the doors of the throne room.

The gatekeepers swung the doors open, and he entered with furrowed brows and the weight of his failures on his shoulders. He walked the red carpet without hesitation. "A king's steps should hold power," his father would always tell him.

The desert dwellers were already there, and they eyed him like the devil. He wanted to chuckle; if they hated him, he simply imagined how they would take his parents.

"Nicklaus," Jace greeted neutrally.

"Jace."

"Snake," Aidan greeted.

"Beast. I suggest you not try me in my castle."

"Well, I suggest—"

"Aidan," Jace halted him.

The young man bit his tongue; the prince did not think it possible.

Nicklaus looked around the familiar room, surprised he had to return so soon. The walls were made of gold; the marble flooring resembled the ocean, with black lines curved and contorted as if from a different plane. But, of course, how could Nicklaus forget the portraits of his predecessors who watched every decree and demand that the current ruler made? Now, they all had the distinct opportunity of watching him squirm from the comfort of their graves. "I see you all did not adorn the garbs I sent to your room."

"What garbs?" Jace asked.

"What do you mean, 'what garbs?' You all look drab! If my mother—"

The gates opened. The guards bowed on one knee. Nicklaus closed his eyes, bracing himself for what was to come. He whispered urgently, "Kneel in attention," as he knelt himself.

Of course, they did not listen. *Absolutely no respect for authority,* Nicklaus's thought raced through his mind, confirming the stories he'd always heard about the desert dwellers.

He kept his head low. The smell of lavender invaded his nose before his eyes could see his mother's ostentatious dress; not too far after, he heard the sound of his father's greaves clashing with the marble floors. As they approached, he tried to stand to address them, but he felt his mother's hand push him back down. She patted his head like some kind of cur. Nicklaus clenched his teeth, threatening to mess up his perfect smile.

"So, you are the Keerie?" she asked, feigning joy. "My, my you all look ... rugged."

"Stand Nicklaus," his father commanded.

He obeyed. He hid his hands behind him, hoping no one would catch them trembling.

"Well done in finding us the Blades. You have done Setas-Li proud this day."

His father bore the closest thing to a smile: a minor upturn of his lips that barely made any laugh lines. It seemed he cut his hair short in Nicklaus's absence; it was easier to see his condescending glare, one glare that only deepened when Nicklaus hesitated.

The arrow of guilt stung deep within Nicklaus's heart. "I—uh—did not find them, Father. Jace was already a Keerie when we met, and Aurora received hers on our journey here."

His father's almond-shaped eyes narrowed. He scanned the desert dwellers, then returned to his son. "So, your travel was a waste?"

He gulped, trying to hide his watered eyes. "Yes ... Father."

His mother whispered into her husband's ear, clearly loud enough for him to hear, "I told you he was galavanting uselessly."

"This is ... disappointing." He turned to the desert dwellers. "I hope my son did not inconvenience you. He prattles on about those Blades, but he never gets results."

Nicklaus's chest felt heavy, and his mouth was dry. He wanted to shed his tears, but he had to compose himself, but for whom, he did not know. His arms trembled even further; the faint sound of his armor could be heard. He could see that he had disappointed his parents for the last time. Why would anyone want a son like him, anyway? He gloomed. His mother was right; his galavanting had proven to be fruitless. *A king is as useful as his promises.*

"He wasn't much trouble, really," Jace answered.

"No need to be modest!" His mother giggled. "You desert people are so polite. He's a king. You must be stern with him."

And then, Nicklaus heard something he was not expecting to hear from Jace, "But—he's still your son."

His parents paused. Nicklaus paused. A wave of empathy showered him, nearly making his tears spill out. How could Jace say that knowing—*knowing*—everything that had happened?

Nicklaus's chest contracted, but he sighed to prevent himself from heaving.

"Yes," his mother's tone swayed, "but he will be king, and that's more important."

Jace stepped forward. "With all due respect, I disagree. A king is as strong as his foundations, and the primary foundation of any person is family."

Queen Fahtalia began to shake a little. Nothing could upset her more than someone defying her authority or making her sound inferior. Her style of parenting came into question just as much as Nicklaus's childhood. His mother would *never* admit to ruining her child because she would need regret and shame for that.

"A king is as strong as his wealth and power," she chuckled heinously. "Maybe that's just the Leroza in me. I *am* the head of the clan."

Aidan, Jace, and Aurora all gave a widening glare at Fahtalia, the same one they gave Nicklaus back when they found out he was the prince. The queen smiled, knowing full well what she had done, knowing full well what she had revealed. She continued, "Of course, a desert dweller would think so; you people have no monarch, no respect for authority, and, of course, no power or wealth to call your own."

Jace hid his shock and proceeded to counter, "We didn't have a king, yes, but we had leaders who were chosen from the best of our people. The people we respected and looked up to were our leaders, chief among them being my mother and father. Also, I am quite sure that my mother alone disrupted the Setas-Lisian trade with her clothing."

The queen leered. "You're the son of that woman, Rose—"

King Athis raised a hand. "Enough of politics. Tomorrow night is The Day of Nissi; our founding festival. We would be honored if you would join us."

The desert dwellers hesitated, rightfully so. Nicklaus noticed their hesitation, *of course, they do not wish to stay here, not a single person had their best interest at heart—in fact—no one here had mine.*

After consulting amongst themselves, Jace spoke, "We will be leaving after the festivities. Though, I will be returning later today to discuss the plan the Utopian king proposed."

The king nodded. "Very well then."

Fahtalia clapped her hands together. "Grand! I'll dress you all up. We can do away with these drab, cut-up, bloodstained clothes."

"Hold me back, Jace," Aidan whispered.

They tried to depart, but the king stopped them. The little gold of his locks swayed in his swift motion. With his silver breastplate and the urgency of his movement, it almost seemed he was about to ask for battle. "Nicklaus has been doing research on your weapons. See if he's put his time to good use."

Nicklaus shared a look with Jace. He did not know how pitiful his face looked to make Jace relent so quickly. Nicklaus clasped his hands together, smiling so easily, so practiced. "If you all would follow me to my study." He turned away quickly, strutting through the room. While everyone saw the composed prince, his parents saw a failure, and he did not know what to think about himself.

64

Behind the Gold

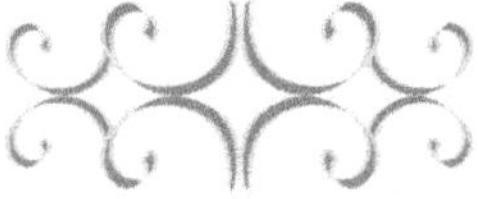

Maybe he's a victim in all this, too.
—The Protector

T*HIS IS A study? Houses in Bhall-Duraht didn't even get this big,* Jace thought. Nicklaus's study did not resemble a study at all; the room was an entire library. Seeing such a place begged the question: how much did he read? The floors were made of marble; the ceilings were adorned with paintings, depictions of great battles and great victories. One character on the tapestry above even resembled King Athis. The walls were lined with pillars that did a wonderful job of separating the bookshelves. However, the coziest part of the study was the desk in the far back of the room, lying under a glass oculus—a perfect area for reading in the sun or basking in the stars. The team sat down in chairs while Nicklaus rummaged through his papers. Natalie joined them, but she silently stood in the corner, hugging the darkness close in case she needed to flee.

"Nicklaus?" Jace called.

Nicklaus did not stop his rummaging. Jace sighed, understanding why Nicklaus did not want to return home. He could see the slightest cues in his face when the capital and his parents were mentioned—they were a complete mess. Nothing made sense, and his notes were as sporadic as his movements. Jace shared a look with Aurora; at that moment, they seemed to be thinking the same thing.

Aurora bit her tongue, looking between Jace and Nicklaus, until she finally opened her mouth and asked, "Nicklaus, are ye okay?"

He lifted his finger, shaking it, punching the desk with his free hand; however, he kept to his princely training. "I am fine."

Jace shook his head, his tone harsh, "Nicklaus, we all heard what happened in there. It's not fine."

Nicklaus yelled, "What do you want me to say to you then!?"

His raised volume shook everyone. It seemed that the last of his composure was used on the smile to get to the study.

His question proved to be a sound one. What did they want from him? He silently screamed in hurt and frustration. He was Setas-Lisian, he was the reason why Aurora was hurt and why the brothers' town received no aid. He was a practiced liar who only wanted to befriend them for information. But for some reason, they didn't see any of that; they saw a hurting boy. Jace knew bottled up grief, what it did to someone; what it did to him, to Serenity, and even Aidan. "Just talk," he said.

"Ah, talk," he chuckled ruefully, "talk about how my parents believe I am useless! Ever since I was young, I had that prophecy looming over my head! When I was a lad, I wanted to frolic with the other children, but my mother would halt me—asking why I wanted to mingle with those who did not have prophecies of their own. I spent my life researching tactics, playing instruments, attending Mass, practicing speeches to be the perfect king!"

Nicklaus's voice cracked, his trained princeliness started to fall like pieces of a shattered mask. He began to reveal who he really was, and it was not at all what Jace expected.

Nicklaus continued, beating his desk with every sentence. "And then my parents, my wretched parents! They were never satisfied with anything I did! Always telling me I was never enough, my researching was never enough, my effort was NEVER ENOUGH! I am the prince of the greatest kingdom in all of Illisia, so many lives on my shoulders, and I had to bear them alone!"

Bear them alone, of course. That's a feeling Jace knew all too well. Nicklaus lashed out, hoping to solve problems on his own merit with parents who did not support him, and no siblings to cheer him on. Natalie was busy in Utopia, Jace bet that meant Nicklaus rarely received any assistance, no one to talk to, no one to share his burdens.

He smiled maddeningly, "When I found out about the Blades, I finally had hope that something would be mine. Something to show for efforts that I could hold onto. I latched on to the fact that Yehowehel would award me for my dedication and pain! But NO!" He growled, pointing an accusatory finger at them. "Two brothers from the unruly desert town and a Delfizcani slave succeeded where I so desperately have tried! Despite being a prince, I had nothing to call my own. Despite being a prince, I was not raised in complete luxury. Despite being a prince, I have nothing! So, what you fail to realize is that THE BLADES ARE ALL I HAVE!"

The last of his words echoed greatly through his study. Nicklaus crashed into his chair, gasping for breath as his rant finally died down. He clutched his head, probably trying to calm the headache he just gave himself with all that screaming.

However, nothing appeared more soul-crushing than Natalie's face. She looked crestfallen, eyes wide and mouth agape. Did she not notice Nicklaus was hurting this entire time? "Nicklaus ..." Natalie reached for him.

"Everyone, get out!" he yelled. "Just get out!"

Natalie tried to reason with him, but he slapped her hand away.

"Come on," Jace told everyone.

One by one, each person left their chairs and made their way to the exit, unsure of what to make of Nicklaus now. He was not a whole prince; he was a broken man stitched together by training and princeliness, falling apart yet still dancing on a string. The moment when reality hit, and the fantasy's image shattered like glass. Jace knew it well.

The door creaked shut.

65

SHARED BURDENS

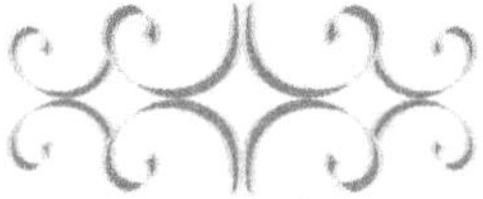

How come I never noticed his pain?
—The Rose

WHY? SHE WONDERED. Why did the only friend she had suffer right under her nose? How come she did not know he felt so broken? How could she have missed a crucial fact about one of the three people who ever considered her an equal?

Natalie walked the streets of the Setas-Lisian capital, unaware of the looks of wariness and distaste the locals were giving her. They did not see the green of her armor, but the black of her hair, and the shadows of her eyes. She was Seplechuran: a fact she had to live with.

Still grieving her lack of observance, she ruminated. Maybe she focused too much on the people of the desert that she did not bother to cherish what she had. She could not remember the last time she had sent Nicklaus a letter or invited him to dinner to talk about his life. They never had a heart-to-heart, though she hated heart-to-hearts oh so dearly. But that court of his was a brood of vipers; if they saw the prince fraternizing with a Seplechuran, they would surely talk.

Nicklaus recommended that they should keep their distance for both of their sakes. Now, she wondered how much distance she had kept, and how much it hurt her friend. He had always felt alone, and yet she could never notice. Maybe the shadows were not where she needed to stay. *I have to make this right,* she steeled herself.

She left the streets of the capital and found herself in the castle once more. Fortunately, the Great General was famous enough to vouch for her casual travel in and out of the castle. As a guest of The Day of Nissi, she was allowed entry. Though Nicklaus's parents may have done so out of bitterness, she thought. After all, The Day of Nissi was when her people had lost to the first Setas-Lisians settlers.

Now, she knew that she needed to focus on Nicklaus. She'd given him the space he needed; now they had to talk, not as soldier and prince, not as Seplechuran and Setas-Lisian, but simply as friends.

She marched through the halls, ignoring the guards who clearly did not approve of her presence. Once she made it to the Royal's floor, the royal guardsmen protested, "You are not supposed to be here."

Natalie stomped. "I want to speak with Nicklaus."

The guards scoffed and spat at her feet, "*Prinz* Nicklaus is unable to see you right now. We will not let you socialize with him."

Natalie stepped closer, and the guards straddled their hands on their weapons. The tension knotted in her stomach; she wanted to disappear into the shadows, but she couldn't—or maybe she could.

Behind the guards, she saw part of the castle; the ledges seemed even. She could scale the outside of the building handily. *It should be no different than scaling tree, hopefully.*

She huffed, turning away from the guards, letting them enjoy their false victory. As a soldier, she knew the importance of giving ground to create a false sense of security.

She hurried to her room, quickly changing from her armor to a cotton tunic and white breeches. She opened the window, feeling the sharp gust of wind smack her in the face.

With every mission, she analyzed the consequences of her actions, so she looked down. Clearly, she would die if she fell. She whispered to herself, "Is Nicklaus really worth risk?" She stepped onto the ledge.

The winds felt much stronger up there; even the smallest breezes threatened to push her off the small ledges. She thanked Yehowehel that the castle was built like Setas-Lisian's old churches, with many ledges. But far too many ramps.

But it was okay, she finalized, it was for Nicklaus, it was for her, it was for friendship. She would not let any of those things down.

66

WHAT WILL YOU DO?

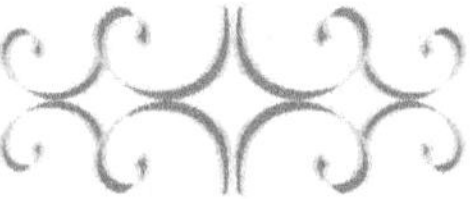

(A long sigh)
—The Prince

AN HOUR HAD passed, maybe two. Nicklaus returned to his life of practiced expressions, and yet, he still stood in awe of his outburst.

Even he did not know he felt such a way; no one had given him an outlet to speak that candidly before. Well, to speak his own mind, that is. However, before he could process it all, his mother had tailors bombarding him with needles and material, so she could at least give the appearance of having a perfect little son.

The tailors bowed before him, but the respect was a formality, not authentic, by now he could tell. The court had already spread their rumors; they must have already known of his failures to bring the Blades home. Either the tailors knew this, or Nicklaus guessed; his face gave it away.

The tailor continued to measure Nicklaus, asking him about his special preferences for his clothing. He answered with feigned enthusiasm, and the smile could barely reach his eyes. "Can we continue this at a later date?" he mumbled.

The head tailor protested, "But your highness, the ball is tomorrow."

"Only for a moment …"

The seamstresses bowed, leaving Nicklaus to his own devices. He walked over to the window; the sunlight blared against his face and his golden doublet. He longed to seek answers from his window when life laughed in his face. Oh, how beautiful his golden city was—its houses aligned in their orderly fashion to match the golden lotus. Even here, he could see the glamstones floating at the crossroads. He chuckled at the memory of him climbing one when the sun went down, retreating right before being spotted by the royal guards. It was the only time he had escaped the castle.

"Setas-Li …" he sighed, despondent, "I have failed you. Forgive me."

Looking at them, his people, he understood what he lacked. He abandoned them for honor; to chase a dream—a selfish dream. Perhaps his parents were right, he conceded; he really was a child in a man's body, galavanting across the continent to chase that which could not be captured.

A tear fell from his eyes as he realized something—Aidan's question. "Who does it benefit?" Nicklaus had answered *everyone,* but that clearly had no bearing. *He* would have been the one to lead the Keerie; *he* would have returned with honor and glory; *he* would have benefited if the war had been won. He did not care for the soldiers who gave their lives, nor his people, nor the others who died. What good was glory and honor if he only surrounded himself with graves?

Nicklaus looked down at the streets, he could see the little dots moving in his vision. So erratic, so playful, they had to be children. Were they benefiting from this? He supposed. Perhaps the Blades were not the answer all along; maybe something else needed to happen. He had to think about his people; he had to think about all peoples.

Nicklaus took in a deep breath. He was not born to be a Keerie, but he was born for something great, something that would change the history of Setas-Li for the better. His mind was enthralled with one grand prospect, a foolish prospect, even though it would not work, he assumed, because he felt far too useless.

He walked over to a quaint lamp in the corner of his room. With a slight tug, it opened to reveal a huge book; its papers fraying the seams. He stared at it, his fingers brushing over the soft, dried leather and the crudely written title: Journal aut Nicklaus, VEGREH! DEDDE AUTH PRINZ! (Diary of Nicklaus, KEEP OUT! DECREE OF THE PRINCE!)

He opened it, chuckling at how terrible his sketches were. On the first page, a light shone in the corner of the page as a terrible drawn Athis and Fahtalia held him to Yehowehel. He skipped a couple of pages: he later gained two siblings, a brother and a sister. He skipped a couple more pages: He was older, holding a sword to the sky. His siblings and parents looked at him with admiration in their eyes, and on the very next page, they hugged him. He tried to read the entry, but the writing had water-damage. He sighed, turning the page. He was a little older now, surrounded by warriors with their own Blades. The entry on the adjacent page was written in decent commontongue. The title: Friends, bound by destiny, not alone, not anymore.

He closed the book, shutting his eyes, along with it.

Tink, tink

He looked over at his window. "Raven?"

He threw the book back in its holding place and shut the compartment. He quickly ran over to the window, helped Raven inside, then shut the window and the curtains.

"Are you mad!? A fall from this height could kill you!"

She brushed her clothes and fixed her hair as if she did not have a care in the world. How she gave an unshakably stout appearance was beyond him. "I had to talk to you," she replied nonchalantly.

"You could have merely walked through my doors," growled Nicklaus.

"Guards."

"Guards?"

Nicklaus scurried to the door, as Natalie informed, guards were posted right at the stairwell. He scowled at them when they saw his face. He shut the door, keeping his voice low.

"What was so important that you needed to risk your life, Raven?"

She shook her hair as she sat on his gold-encrusted bed. She felt the mattress, which was probably unfamiliar to her due to its softness. "Nicklaus, are you truly alright?"

His heart skipped. The anger that swirled in his chest only dropped to his stomach. *THE BLADES ARE ALL I HAVE!* The words replayed in his mind. His face grew somber. "Yes, well, I suppose my … behavior in my study gave you quite the scare. I assure you that …"

He saw her face; now she grew angry with him, but some level of worry shone behind her eyes. *Is this what motherly concern looks like?* It saw past his fake smiles and convincing lies, and it even saw through the deceit he had forced upon himself. He sighed, slumping into his chair. "I am crestfallen. I am tired of my failures, I am tired of my life, I am tired of—I am tired."

Natalie got up, poking him in the chest. "Nicklaus, if you felt this way, how come you never told me?"

That was a good question. Natalie was his closest friend—his only friend. He could have been honest with her, but now, as he thought about it, he knew why. "Fear. Hubris. To seem so …," he held a pause then let it go, "… so broken and unsure in front of you would shatter me. Besides,

I—I did not even know," he drearily looked at his hand, "that I felt so hollow."

She stood, righteous fury painting her pale skin pink. With a strike from the shadows, she slapped him, and he stood in awe, holding his face in pain.

"Do you truly believe that I care if you were uncertain? What friend would I be if I changed my perception of you at moment's notice?" She tried to keep her emotions together, but he could see her growing even more upset. "How could you not be honest with me?"

She truly hit like a Seplechuran; his face throbbed. Though he questioned the need for it, it did, in fact, emphasize her words. "I—I'm sorry."

"No, I do not want apologies," Natalie spoke resolutely, "I want change. I want you to *trust* me. Nicklaus never settles for failure."

"That *Nicklaus* is a farce."

"No, that man is planner, dreamer, and one who never stops trying."

He groaned. He got up as Natalie moved away. He paced in his room, feeling the clutter of the walls bind his thoughts. He faced the wall, hands clasped at his back. "You are right. I have not been true with you, nor have I been true to myself," he sighed. "Aidan asked me an important question in Liavesen, one I truly thought I knew the answer to. Now, I understand, I was being selfish."

"What are you going to do?" she asked.

"I do not know ... but I will think of something, and ...," he turned, smirking with a reddened cheek and a small tear, "... I will consult you about it."

Natalie smiled, rushing to her friend to hug him. Nicklaus immediately held her, unsure if he had done it right. This day marked many firsts for him, a hug from Raven counted among them.

"I must ask," he pulled away from her, "how are you fairing after the Contested Lands?"

Natalie exhaled a quiet breath, likely thinking about the lives that she had taken. No one could claim to be as dedicated as she was when it came to the salvation of the Seplechuran people, even when flying Utopian colors. Nicklaus would never stop admiring that side of her.

"I do not know. It is like my people do not want to be saved. As if they do not want to hear truth."

Her bottom lip quivered, and her eyes shut in remembrance. To her, she committed an atrocity; she took lives. She's been fighting her own people for xantem, without anything to show for her efforts. The story started to become familiar to Nicklaus. However, he would not let the outcome be the same. Not for her. "I do hope you do not plan to surrender?"

She raised a brow. "Surrender?"

"Your ideals, Natalie. You have been fighting for xantem, no? And yet you plan to give up?"

She hooded her eyes, looking away to the wall. "You have no idea what I have been through."

"You are right, I do not, but you do. You are not a failure," *Like me.* "You are a warrior who's held their ground for xantem. As your friend, I will not permit you to wallow in this self-pity."

"Self-pity? Nicklaus, I have been fighting war alone. Tirelessly, pleading for my people."

And they both realized their error. Their combined problem was that they kept fighting alone without letting the other help. Their lives burned hotter than the depths of Maserades, yet they never tried to fight together. No more.

"Did you not just talk about trust mere minutes ago? When I said I would not permit you to wallow in self-pity, I meant I will stand at your side, but that begs the question …" He stepped closer, standing as close as he needed to make his point, "… what will you do?"

67

A Different Kind of Sight

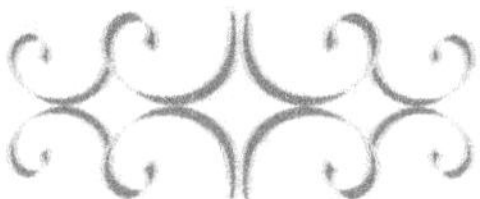

Why me?
—The Wildcard

AFTER NICKLAUS FORCED them to leave the study, Aidan decided to keep to himself in his room. Aurora offered to stay with him, but he refused; he needed time to sort his feelings out—to sort this blindness out. It took a day for that to happen.

Anger and hatred crept at his mind's door, for himself and for his predicament. If useless stood as a problem for him before, then—what was he now? A warrior who couldn't see and couldn't fight.

He chuckled hollowly. His life, his dreams, all reduced to ash; the rest of them went up in smoke. Reading, sewing, fighting, traveling—seeing his parents.

Jace would tell him to calm down; he knew that for a fact. But Jace did not understand because he was closer to their father; Aidan had his mother to rely on. His father saw potential in Jace; he had not neglected Aidan per se, but simply put, their father had not spent as much time with him as his mother did. His eyes: they were a gift from her, Aidan's special gift. He relied on seeing the smallest details and the most vibrant of colors. His mother would tell him that others could not see how they saw; they would not understand what blindness meant. It was not the absence of sight; it was the absence of seeing meaning in all things, including oneself.

He felt the skin over his eyes; it was soft and itchy as if the top layers had been completely removed by the flames. Strangely enough, he didn't know how it had happened. If he became the beast, how did he burn? Regardless, his fingers couldn't help but feel the contrast between his unburnt and burned skin. He felt so ugly.

A character in a terrible novel he read happened to be blind. He ended up that way through similar means; however, he took it well. Aidan attributed that to poor writing.

No, no, Aidan, focus, focus. The character, however, had to adjust. The first step: feel his environment. Aidan copied, feeling the bed under him; it was soft, silky, and thin. Cold steel comforted his palms as he felt the frames.

Then the character listened.

Aidan tuned out his other senses, focusing his attention on his ears. Footsteps were frantic as they moved back and forth. People were yelling, but they were not angry or scared, just in a hurry. Lastly, he heard—*snoring?* Not from a human, but from—Chuckle and Snark. *How come I've never heard them before?* They seemed to come only when he needed help, but other than that, it felt as if they weren't there. Aidan picked them from his pockets, stroking their warm metallic bodies. They squiggled at his touch, but nothing more. Questions still wrapped his mind about what they were, as inquisitive as he was, he never questioned their existence when they appeared.

His thoughts were drowned out by the loud world, however. It baffled him how loud the world seemed to be, but with a quick deduction, he found out that the world did not get louder—he had simply quieted himself.

The world always spoke, and he never felt the need to hear until he had to. He stood, taking a deep breath, a finger to his eyes. *This is my life now.* He had to make the most of it. "Mother would," he told himself. "Come on, Aidan, you know she would start laughing at her predicament, even with tears in her eyes, she would assure you that things would be okay." He laughed as boisterously and loudly as he could; the pain did not go away, not in the slightest, but he laughed anyway. He clutched his eyes shut, laughing as the tears tickled his lips, then dropped to his chest.

Chuckle and Snark shook from their slumber, giving Aidan their most confused jingles. He kept on laughing, and so—they laughed with him.

That feels good ... sort of.

He continued that for as long as his voice could hold.

Chuckle and Snark were playing on the bed, tackling one another, Aidan assumed. The little things had so much more energy when he got happier; honestly, he could ask for nothing more.

"Hey, do you two want to explore the castle? I wanna sneak into Nicklaus's library again."

The low-pitched chime struck his ears before the high-pitched one. The two chains hopped on his shoulder, and then he moved. He had already mastered the layout of his room without feeling, but the hallway, the loud hallway, was different.

Aidan placed a hand on the door, weighing if he should go or not.

He did not feel completely useless, but he knew he could not do things like he used to. "If only I could just see a little …"

Chuckle and Snark wiggled on his shoulder, then they hooked themselves around Aidan's wrists.

"Uh, what are you two doing?"

The two chains shook their bodies slightly, sending a weird tingling sensation through Aidan's body. At first, there was only confusion, but then he started to notice something. He couldn't quite explain it, but he received a weird outline of the room, almost like a picture of pure sound. "Woah …"

Aidan opened the door, directly to his right, knowing that he should have heard two guards marching forward, and he did. Another vibrational message was sent through his body again, and he slowed his steps. He put his hands to the wall, testing the authenticity of the messages. With each test, his movements became braver, and the trust in his chains became more resolute. He could see—sort of. He began seeing with his touch, feeling the area in relation to himself.

"Is this how you two see?"

They started to shake, but the sounds were confusing; a part of him wished they spoke commontongue, that would make life a bit easier.

"Anyway, we should practice a little more. I can't wait to tell Aurora and Jace about this!" He returned to his room, hoping to mess around in a safer environment. As tempting as it was to bolt down the halls, vault off walls, and jump over obstacles, he decided to take it slow—this time.

68

Enough

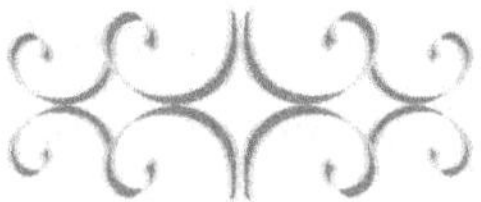

I can't ... I can't empathize with him.
—The Thief

WHAT YOU FAIL *to realize is that THE BLADES ARE ALL I HAVE!* A new day dawned, and yet she could not shake those words from her head. *How could the heir of the greatest kingdom in Illisia even talk like that? He has everything—wealth, security, power, women, fish from other nations—clearly, the laddie is speaking rubbish. He's a spoiled brat,* Aurora convinced herself; nothing more. He wanted things to go his way.

Aurora rolled over, light blaring from the window. She hugged the pillow closer to her face, looking for some comfort in its plush form. Yet, when she did, she just saw Nicklaus's face, his broken face; he had to be suffering, she knew it. That pained look of trying so hard to only fail in the end; she wore that look for so long, too. Perhaps his practiced smiles were not for deceit; maybe he used them to hide.

She shook herself. *No, how can I think like this?* She could not empathize with him. Right now, somewhere on the same soil, Delfizcani cried, bled, and burned as they worked for his clan. *He's a monster!*

However, closer than soil, someone in the same castle had monarchs but never parents, teachers but never guides; people who reared him, loveless, to the point he could turn out worse than them. How could she hate someone who wanted something for himself? Who wanted some recognition for his pain? He just wanted someone, anyone, to love him.

Stop it!

She hated him. She *must* hate him. He's evil, his people are evil. They have done nothing but usher pain to the Delfizcani.

A drip of moisture fell on her arm. She jolted up, staring at the ceiling—nothing. She looked outside, and the rays of the sun were not obscured by clouds. Then, what? She brought her fingers to her eyes; she felt it then.

Aurora punched the pillow at her side. Did she really need to cry for everything? Is this truly the person that Yehowehel chose? Is this truly the girl that Aidan and Jace needed on the battlefield, better yet, the girl that would fight her father? Aurora's mind turned over with so many questions. One thing she knew for certain was, *this* weakness, *this* pain, is what got her shackled in the first place.

She stumbled over to her boots. She pulled out her last, broken dagger. The process, like clockwork, she knew what to do with her weak self, however, it never stopped her breath from catching in her throat. She pulled back her sleeve, showcasing the portrait of her pain and the scars etched into her skin. The painter's knife brushed across its demented masterpiece, waiting for the terrible strokes. She wondered why, even after becoming Keerie, those wounds never healed.

Knock, knock

"Go away," she tried to hide her sobs.

She heard some tut-tutting on the other side. "Well, that's not nice. I was that mean myself not too long ago, but still."

"Aidan?"

"Who else sounds this amazing?" He cleared his throat. "Actually, I, uh, came to talk."

She looked at her knife, then at the door. She did not want to let anyone in, especially not him. No one could see her like this, but Aidan could not see her; he would not judge.

The knife swayed erratically in her hand, indecisively as herself. It either shifted in the boot or on her arm. It had to pick. *She* had to pick.

Aidan sighed, "I could always come back later, if you don't want to chat."

"Wait!" she instinctively called out. She sighed, putting the knife back in her boot. She tried to fix herself up before she opened the door. Surprisingly, Aidan stood there alone. "No escort?" she asked, looking around.

"That's what I wanted to talk to you about," Aidan exclaimed jovially, running a nervous, worn hand through his dark dreadlocks, "among other things."

It seemed he was back to his old self again, and in a way, so was she. She let him in, and he quickly went for the bed, spreading himself all over it like butter. She tried to fight a smile as he muttered something about the texture.

She shut the door, keeping her body leaning against it. Immediately, she noticed the chains: one on his wrist, the other on his shoulder. "Chuckle and Snark, are they why ya don't need an escort?"

"Good eye. Apparently, these little guys can help me see by painting a picture with vibrations that I can feel with my skin."

"What?"

"Uhhh, think of a ripple, like in a river, made of sound. Whatever the ripple touches, I *see*."

"Oh ... Oh! That's amazing." She leaned forward in surprise.

"Right?! These little guys are the best!"

Chuckle and Snark jingled in admiration. Aidan flipped off the bed and landed with only a little bit of trouble. Aurora clapped lightly, and Aidan replied with his signature bow. *He's back.*

"Thank you, thank you. But uh, there was something else I wanted to talk to you about."

He returned to the bed, patting the area right next to him. Aurora brushed her hair forward, obscuring her vision, and took a deep breath as she sat next to him.

"Aurora, I'm very, very sorry for my behavior in Liavesen. I acted rudely to you."

"Aidan, you lost yer sight, it's fine—"

"—No, it's not," he interrupted, trying to control the disdain for his behavior. "I lashed out at you, and worst of all, right after you started to trust me and Jace. That was inconsiderate."

Aurora clasped her hands together, her hazel eyes looking through her vines of locks that obscured them. "I won't lie; ya did hurt me—a lot. I thought ya hated me, and I felt like I couldn't help, and I failed again." She held her head, recounting every moment she had felt that way. From the moments as a lass to where she stood now. Every time, it grew even harder to bear.

"Aurora," Aidan said in a whisper, "you didn't fail anyone. This is my own fault."

"But I could've tried."

"You did. Jace trusted you to fight by his side, and you did." He groaned, "Outcomes are not always going to be what we want."

No, he's wrong; she could not help the thought. If only she had been faster, stronger, something else, things would not go bad. Everyone would be smiling, and she would finally be strong.

Aidan grabbed her hand, lacing her fingers in his. Her eyes hooked on him. *He's smiling.*

"Aurora," he consoled in a low, breathy tone, "there's nothing I could say that could change your mind, that I know. However, I want to say that everything bad that happens isn't your fault. Some things are in your control; others are not."

She leaned into him, resting her head on his shoulder. But suddenly, she felt too tired to continue; at that moment, she wanted to go back to sleep. At least in her dreams, she could be back in Bhall-Duraht, Aidan had never lost his sight, Jace was home, and she was enough.

Aidan pulled Aurora to himself, playing with the locks of her hair. Normally, she would get her knife, but right now, she did not mind. She just wanted to see that smile of his; it truly made her feel as if she had not failed.

"I really wish I could see you right now," he muttered.

She wiped her eyes, then her nose, and chuckled her reply, "No, ya don't."

"Probably," he playfully mocked.

Her eyes were fluttering shut, breathing calmed, and her body was softening. Aidan said a lot of things, but some things stuck out more than others. *Some things are in my control? Hopefully, that is true.*

BOOM!

69

Too Close to Home

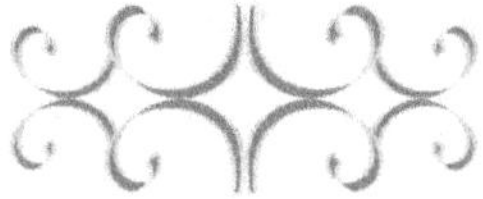

Have I earned no reprieve?
—The Prince

EXPLOSIONS RATTLED NICKLAUS'S senses along with the cries of fear and surprise from his people. His frustration screamed, *Could anything more go wrong? Must I be forced to suffer more humiliation at the hands of the evil and undignified?*

He called soldiers to his side as he ran to the castle gates. Of course, some stayed back to protect the castle and monarchs, the possible real targets. *Perhaps I should let the enemy ... no, perish the thought.*

Once outside, his eyes were immediately hooked on Jace. The desert dweller, with his frozen Blade, ordered unflinchingly as he took command of the soldiers in the streets, escorting the people to safety. The explosions emphasized his gallant stance as a gust of wind kicked up his cloak. The Blade branded him the confidence to walk headfirst into danger, or maybe it was the desert's ignorance that played into his pseudo-courage. Regardless, as the prince, Nicklaus had to act. He ran through the screaming crowds, keeping an eye out for those would-be terrorists.

As Nicklaus ran through the streets, he had noticed two men who were surprisingly calm despite the situation. He spied them posted in the crease of an open corner near a building. He drew closer to them, using the crowd as cover, although he could not easily maneuver through the flow. The men wore the cotton tunic of Setas-Li, but their features forsook them. "Halt!" Nicklaus yelled.

The two men quickly unsheathed their swords, and that's when Nicklaus saw the shadows around their eyes and dyed hair.

They growled as they pressed forward. Nicklaus set aside his eyeglasses on a barrel and engaged them with his own battle cry. The men were using Setas-Lisian short swords, the weight was noticeably different from Seplechuran swords, and he used it to his advantage.

Nicklaus thrust his blade, forcing one of his opponents to choose a side. As one of the soldiers tried to retaliate, Nicklaus threw him off balance into his ally, stabbing him in the chest before the two could get up.

Nicklaus kicked one soldier unconscious while pinning the stabbed soldier with his foot. *These must not be soldiers but simple saboteurs.* "Who sent you here?"

The soldier spoke angrily in his mother tongue. He tried to spit in Nicklaus's face but could not. In retaliation, Nicklaus used his free hand to pop the saboteur in the nose, causing blood to drip from his nostrils. Nicklaus buried his foot harder into the man's abdomen, repeating his question.

"Nicklaus, Nicklaus," a familiar voice crooned from the shadows, "leave the poor man alone."

That voice ... Alistair. Nicklaus turned around, seeing the traitor smiling with a rapier in his hand. The knave looked around. "Is your concubine not with you?"

Nicklaus growled. "Do not speak of Raven in such a manner! She has more important things than to deal with you."

He put a finger to his chin, as if lost in thought. "I admire how you instantly knew who I was talking about. Yes, Raven. You two definitely seem so ... cozy."

"Do not try to avert my attention."

Alistair shrugged, pointing to the soldier. "Let go of my soldiers. Your battle is with me."

Reluctant, but remembering Natalie's own goals, he released the man. The injured man picked up his fellow and retreated as Nicklaus pointed his sword at Alistair, his rival doing the same.

"You may have caught me on the unawares before, Alistair, but I will not be so reckless again."

Alistair smirked. "As if it would hardly take effort to defeat you."

It came to Nicklaus's attention that the two were on a mosaic of the golden lotus, the symbol of the Amoran clan and the entire kingdom. To lose in such an area would dishonor not only him, but also his ancestors.

"*Allévere!*" Nicklaus shouted.

He moved in for a stab, followed by a swift swipe of his rapier. Alistair stayed on the defensive, keeping his eyes locked on Nicklaus like a hawk. Alistair retreated to a pile of small barrels. With impressive strength, he launched them toward the prince. Nicklaus hopped to a stance; blade outstretched and hand overhead. He deftly dodged the barrels while maintaining his center of gravity, though he lamented that his eyeglasses were on one of those barrels. *Ellavi frutois allil!* (Curse it all!)

"You're open!" Alistair shouted as he pressed his attack.

Nicklaus shifted to defense, keeping his overhead hand now behind his back. His blocks were uniform; one step per movement to retreat and advance, as he had been taught by his father. *Never let them think you are running while never letting them think you are overextended.* It did not take Nicklaus's careful observation to know that his defense was superior to Alistair's; however, his opponent's attacks were fluid and relentless. Whoever trained Alistair must have been a blade master. He seamlessly transitioned from one form to another, to attack in several different ways. Nicklaus saw Alistair already catching his breath; such skill brought with it fatigue. Nicklaus had to press his advantage. During a lapse in Alistair's movement, Nicklaus spun around his blade, going for a stab.

Alistair smirked, backing away from Nicklaus's reach, then retaliating with his own attack. An impressive tactic to feign fatigue, but he expected it. Nicklaus descended into a split, whirling his legs defensively to dissuade Alistair's attack.

"Impressive! I was not expecting such ingenuity."

"You face the prince of Setas-Li."

Alistair rolled his eyes, breathing shallowly. "Don't get haughty after one move; I still beat you near death."

Nicklaus furrowed his brow. "Shall we remedy that?"

Now, Nicklaus knew what to expect. The wave of white energy coursed through Alistair's blue eyes, a sign that he was readying for a Blink. Nicklaus charged his eyes as well. Both he and his adversary saw it, the White Rail, the latch that causes one of Amoran blood to Blink.

"Shall we?" Alistair asked, proving he could see it.

Nicklaus and Alistair ran to the rail, assuming the Blink pose; an arm angled high behind him, the other hand resting. The two aspects of the Blink: rest and ravage.

"*Allévere!*" They both shouted the Setas-Lisian word for commence.

Nicklaus had to keep his eyes open, or he would have missed the moment when he silenced the traitor. The ground ravaged behind him, splitting apart as the force of his Blink broke the earth still.

A wave of energy spread from their clashing blades; a hollow white light spread across the area where the clash connected. He did not feel death at the other side of his blade. Instead, he felt a force throwing him away.

He had never felt the absolute torture of the senses that was Blinking into another Blink user. His ears rang, his sight blurred, and his body felt weaker than a newborn fawn. He struggled to move, and only faintly could he hear soldiers calling to him. The chorus of their footsteps shook him from his daze. He strained to see if he had won. Surely, Alistair felt the pain, but when Nicklaus looked on to where his opponent was, he saw nothing but dust. However, something else besides him was in shambles: the homes of his people. Three of them, decimated by the shockwave created by his attack. That was Alistair's plan.

Nicklaus drifted from the world of consciousness, muttering his frustration. "He always has a plan."

Nicklaus slowly drew his wits about him and fought to raise his heavy eyelids. He groaned, pulling himself upward. And immediately, clutched his head, feeling a painful lightness as his cranium bobbled.

"Welcome back," Natalie said.

"Raven? Where—where am I? Where is Alistair?"

"Alistair? He was here?"

Nicklaus got a little of his bearings; the dark, wooded walls and floors were filled with only three beds, etched with the finest linen. He was in the Royal Infirmary. "Yes, he was here. I was fighting him."

Natalie pushed Nicklaus down, then checked the bandages around his head. "You were not supposed to engage him without me."

"I was trying to—"

The doors swung open with a slight screech. The sight of his newest visitor made his head throb twice as hard, and his heart skipped thrice as fast. At this point, he no longer had to feign weakness; his father's presence reminded him of his weakness.

The entourage of soldiers halted behind him, beating down their polearms to signify the king's presence. "Leave us," the king ordered Natalie.

Nicklaus observed how Natalie stood, defying the king, in his presence, with a stare to declare her allegiance to her friend. Nicklaus duly noted that he would soon need to replicate such brave defiance. The king tightened his jaw as his brow rose slowly. Nicklaus knew that look. He squeezed Natalie's arm, motioning her to leave before she incurred his father's wrath.

Once Natalie left, Nicklaus's father yelled in Setas-Lisian, "What in the seven levels of Maserades were you thinking, Nicklaus?"

Of course, he results to screaming first. Nicklaus clutched his head, trying his best to sit up, but when he stared into his father's angry blue eyes, he did not see the ocean blue; he witnessed their unsearched and haunting depths.

"I ... was trying to save the people," he replied in his mother tongue.

"Save the people? By destroying their houses? Injuring the people?"

"I was engaged in combat."

"With whom? No other person was found there."

Nicklaus sharply took a breath, holding his throbbing head, silently screaming—*That should be more than enough proof for you! Why is it not?!* "I was fighting a man of Amoran blood."

His father first looked skeptical, then laced it with indignant anger. "So, you were dilly-dallying with someone from our house when those foreigners were protecting our people?"

"The foreigners?"

"Yes! Even the Delfizcani worked harder, injured as she was, to save the people better than their prince."

Nicklaus sucked on his bottom lip; eyes averted from his father. Aurora hated Setas-Lisians, yet the news he heard from his father contradicted her words. What motivated her to move forward with such resolve? In fact, what moved the three of them? Jace had protected the people, leaving his now-weakened brother to fend for himself. Yet, blinded, Aidan, along with his peculiar chains, helped apprehend the ignisium. Who exactly were these people? He asked himself.

"I expected better from he who was prophesied to be the greatest king of Setas-Li."

"But father!"

"Enough, I do not wish to hear excuses. First, you leave on a senseless adventure to pursue the Blades of Yehowehel, yet you return empty-handed. We made preparations for you to return with honor."

His father kept his arms clasped tightly behind his back, and Nicklaus glanced forward just to see the disappointment and detest in his eyes. Though the feeling was understandable, all the training and hard work that his parents had poured into Nicklaus's education, weapon mastery, kingdom management, and so many other advantages had yet to yield a payoff. The prophecy loomed over him for many xantem, many of the prophets had said he would be the greatest king, the light of Setas-Li.

Athis turned, muttering something to himself, yet Nicklaus was able to hear, "… to believe that Caesar and Roselyn's son and Merek and Lana's daughter would be Keerie …"

Nicklaus turned his head so quickly that a wave of inertia and light-headedness flowed through him, but he had to ask, "You are acquainted with their family?"

King Athis looked up, eyes steady but surprised; clearly, he was not expecting to be heard, "You have no right to ask questions of me." He escorted himself to the exit. "Focus on your recovery, then I want you to resume your tasks. There will be suitors here *tonight.*"

"Suitors! You cannot be serious, Father. We were attacked—in the capital!"

"Are you questioning your king?"

"I am talking with my father," growled Nicklaus.

The tense moment bit into the air and refused to let go. Nicklaus did not understand where his boldness had come from, but he liked it. His father had never fully perceived him, only sizing him up with his stubborn half-cocked glance, "Do as you are told," he growled in commontongue. He opened the door to leave, then paused. "In addition, tell me the name of the Amoran you were fighting; I will deal with them."

Nicklaus sighed, lying back in bed. "You will not be able to deal with him; he aids the Seplechurans. We clashed before in the Contested Lands. He said his name was Alistair."

Athis was a resolute man; Nicklaus had never heard him stutter, had never seen him back down, or even yawn. He was as strong as they came, but then—why did he flinch?

Athis held the doorframe, clutching it with so much might. He visibly shook; his head hung in what seemed to be shame.

"Father?"

"What did you say his name was?"

"Alistair. Father, is something wrong?"

Athis stormed out, slamming the door shut. His steps faded with such pace from Nicklaus's ears. There were so many things about his father that did not make sense. He was violently secretive about his past, but for the first time, Nicklaus felt as though his lack of knowledge had become his greatest liability. His father knew something important, and Nicklaus intended to figure that out.

He clutched his head once. *Alright, I will figure that out after I have had some much-needed rest.*

70

Plans in the Shadows

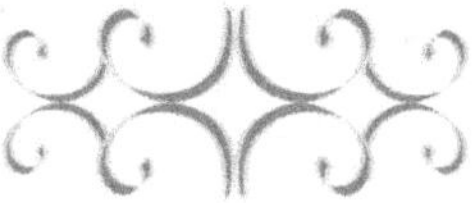

I suppose he's not as incompetent as I expected.
—The Strategist

"**F**INALLY, YOU'RE AWAKE," Serenity stated.

The shadows in the corner of his eyes started to fade away as the faint crackle of wood strummed against his ears. Orange firelight danced in the tip of his vision, blinding yet waking him. He clutched his head when he stood, letting the black strands of his hair drape over his eyes for a moment. Then, only then, he saw Serenity sitting with that gnarled piece of junk in her hands.

"I thought you were going to do away with that," he muttered.

"It's hard."

"I could do it."

She crossed her legs, barely visible against the light. She looked like a sensual demon, or at least, a living shadow. She had always clung to sadness more than anger; it was always a weakness of hers, that Alistair noted.

"Did you succeed?" She changed the subject.

"Did you forget who I am, Sere?"

"No. I saw your face plenty of times when I wrapped you up."

Alistair chuckled. He slid out of bed, the ringing in his ears growing slightly louder, and the lightness of his head forcing him to stumble.

Nicklaus had skill, Alistair admitted. Maybe he should not have held back as much as he did, he pondered over the possibility.

He looked around the room, the dark crept around the fire and the single window. "Is our immaculate leader happy?"

"Yes, I am." A harsh wind halted the fire, poisoning them with blackness. The once orange glow gave off rays of purple and black.

Alistair's heart skipped when the shadows started to contort, and a body made itself known. "Can't use the door like a normal human?" Alistair asked with far too much sass in his voice.

"Alistair, you know I am far from normal." His irises were blacker than night, reflecting the purple light on a dark canvas, emitting a swelling darkness unknown to any Sov. "How many points did you set?"

The rasp in the emperor's accent scratched at Alistair's ears, but he ignored it. "Three, just enough for you and two guests," Alistair replied. He could not see it, but he felt the emperor's smile. It unsettled his soul to *see* his grin, but he would take that over his anger any day.

"I was going to ask Merek, but he's too busy preparing for something else. Why don't you two join me?"

Alistair and Serenity were hushed at the invitation, both marveling at how easy the emperor had managed to make his *suggestion* sound. "You honor us, Your Highness, but wouldn't Nakaye be better suited?" Alistair suggested.

"No. I cannot take Nakaye anywhere. Besides, Merek told me of your …" he paused with a smirk, "… acquaintances."

Alistair's blood boiled hotter than the flames at the lie. General Merek had told the emperor nothing. *That sadistic monarch probably compelled the answer out of him.* Alistair worked to calm his breaths to hold on to his façade for a moment longer. Responding only to the invitation, Alistair replied, "If you truly insist, Your Majesty."

"I do," he chuckled. "Make sure you wear your best, I cannot have you two dragging me down at Setas-Lisian ball, yes?"

"Of course."

He was gone in a snap. The black flames lamented, restored to their natural color and movement. Serenity released a breath, clutching her neck as she gasped for air.

"Are you alright?" Alistair asked.

"No ... he scares me."

Alistair placed a hand on her shoulder, and she jumped at his touch. He tried his best to smile, but he also realized something: his hands were shivering. "Well, it seems I'm not in a place of comforting after all, no?" Alistair tried to play it off, but in reality, he could not. The emperor had the reputation of a faceless entity. And some wondered if he even existed. Some said that he made a contract with a demon, others said that the shadows of war stole flesh and knitted itself a body. Alistair always disdained such superstitious tales. But there was one thing on which he and the emperor, Ras, could agree, and it was that *normal* did not begin to describe the monarch. Alistair could not help but recall Ras's rise to power: The man becomes emperor and suddenly, his armies alone carry the Hericonian battalions to victory. *What mortal man does a thing? Was it divine or demonic insight?*

Alistair removed his hand, noticing that Serenity had dropped her flute. He picked it up, juggling it with insight. The gnarled filth burned his eyes, but he could easily tell it was once beautiful. Though he had never noticed the *J+S* etched onto it before now. "This Jace character, he wasn't just your friend, was he?" he asked.

Serenity's eyes shot up, sparked with anger. She stomped up close, but Alistair held the flute to the fire.

"Alistair, give it here," she commanded.

"No. And before you go making threats, I know you will not hurt me." Serenity looked desperate, again. And Alistair studied her. *What power does this Jace character have that one of my strongest allies turns into a little girl at the mention of his name?*

"Alistair, please."

"I want an answer. Now."

"It's weird … and complicated."

"Sere, you have never been weirder, and *I'm* complicated. Flip that coin."

Serenity pouted as she sat in the chair with her eyes never leaving the fire. "As you know, Night Star is approaching."

"Yes, your birth star."

She played with her hair, twirling the firelit black locks around her calloused fingers, "Jace and I made a promise, when—if—I turned twenty-two …"

Oh no, Alistair could not help but think. *There's only one way—things like this go.* The hurt, the reminiscence, the flute, all of this, he surmised, seemed to be going in one direction.

"… we promised that we would," Serenity's voice got trembly, "… get married."

"So, the flute—it is a sort of—what's the word?" Alistair snapped his fingers. "A promise, engagement of some sort?"

She nodded.

"Then why not throw it away? He clearly broke your heart! He does not remember such a promise!"

"You don't know that!" She held her head as if it ached. "You don't know that …"

Alistair lightly groaned. "When you wake up from this delusion," he threw the flute at her feet, "you throw it away yourself." Then he walked over to the door, opened it, and a mass of light swooped in to bombard his eyes.

"Where are you going?" she asked.

Alistair looked out as the beautiful, golden castle stood strong in the distance. He smiled at its majesty. But his smile got even broader when he thought about what he was about to do to that castle. Alistair turned toward Serenity and simply replied, "Shopping."

71

The Ball Begins

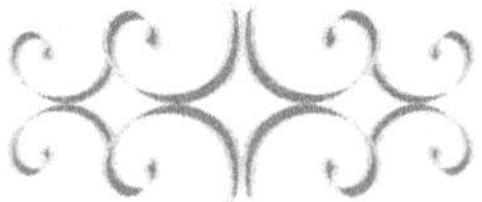

SETAS-LI HAD BEEN nothing short of exciting; only two days in, and they witnessed an attack on the capital. Like Nicklaus when they first met, many people began to honor Jace, but he still sensed their hesitance, especially since he offered his help with the investigation. Many people thanked him, including the lady who had currently fitted him for his ballroom clothing.

He brushed his clothes, gazing into the mirror to see what the Setas-Lisians had made for him. A breeze whipped through the room, letting the velvet texture of his navy-blue outfit flap majestically. The silver chains that held his lapels also shook, reminding him of Chuckle specifically.

They adorned him in a buttoned-up vest that mimicked the same blue as his overcoat. A lupine creature was elegantly stitched on the back of it, in a beautiful shimmering silver.

"This looks good," he found himself saying out loud.

The woman closed the window. "Oh, you … like it?" she asked in a heavier accent than Nicklaus's.

Jace nodded, brushing his sleeves once more. This was the first time he wore anything that was not made by his mother or Aidan. The material felt so different.

His hair was adorned with a silver hair tie, a lupine clip on the side of it. Frankly, he snickered watching the beauticians struggle to understand his hair; they tried to comb it, but the combs broke; they settled on leaving it in an elaborate tie.

"Thank you for, uh … waiting?" The seamstress bowed.

He turned to her, pulling some strands from his bun to drape his face. "Staying," he corrected.

Her cheeks flushed red. "Ah, yes."

Jace quietly groaned, communicating with her proved to not only be tedious but also stale; quite frankly, he would not mind if she had left. Maybe the obnoxious scents the beauticians showered him with had made his aggravation flare.

His concerns were elsewhere, not the Seplechurans, but the Setas-Lisians, more importantly, the king and queen. Something did not add up about them. He heard they were devious, especially the Leroza. As cunning as Nicklaus was, he had to learn it from somewhere.

"Does that conclude business?" she asked.

"Yes—no, actually, what do you know about us … desert dwellers?"

The woman thought for a moment, clutching the basket that held her supplies. She shook her hair, which was wrapped somewhat loosely in a headkerchief. "Unruly ruffians," she said bluntly.

"From whom? Most Setas-Lisians never traveled down south."

"Leroza *esvo*." Esvo, a word Jace heard thrown around a couple of times, a word for the clan leaders.

So, it was the Leroza, "Do you know why?"

"Trade, commerce." The woman trailed off, shaking her head. She fiddled with the basket in her hand. "But, uh, Queen Fahtalia has ... problem? Quarrel? With desert."

Intrigued, Jace inclined his ear as he lifted a brow. "What kind of problem?"

The seamstress looked around nervously. She motioned for Jace to wait. She opened the door, searching nervously before closing it again.

"Royal affair ..." she whispered, even though she checked her surroundings, "I do not know much. My ... mother worked before me."

Jace nodded. "Thank you for the information."

She bowed, before shooting up in exclamation. "Uh, mystery."

"Secret." Jace smirked. "I understand."

She smiled with a bow, letting herself out of the room, leaving Jace to ponder.

The sun decided to rest, letting the moon shine on The Day of Nissi. The reason for its lateness was attributed to the night attack that marked Setas-Lisian victory over their enemies, at least that was what they told Jace.

They gave instructions for the *special guests* to wait in front of the ballroom. While Jace hated walking in the dark, he silently thanked Yehowehel that he had time for peace, and to collect his own thoughts.

The castle looked far more haunted at night, even with the lamps lighting the halls, but actually, that made it worse. The paintings, depicting the rulers of ole, now watched like haunted guardians who had forgotten that their rule had ended.

He made it to the end of the cavernous stretch, lights from the ballroom seemed to melt under the doors, joining the candlelight from the halls. "I'm the first one here?" Jace mused out loud.

"Not quite, dear brother." Aidan emerged from the shadows, suavely moving from one side to the other. He seemed to be moving as if he had sight, maybe the effects of his transformation wore off, Jace thought. He asked, but his brother denied.

"No, actually Chuckle and Snark help me now, I guess, like they've always had."

Aidan gave a long explanation about Chuckle and Snark sending vibrational signals. Jace did not understand most of it, but he knew that his brother could somewhat move freely again.

"Glad to have you back."

"Sorry I left," Aidan laughed. "So, what did they throw you in?"

Jace relayed the information of his outfit to his brother, with every bit of information, Aidan nodded. "That's such a good idea. I always knew you were a vest person. I have to make something new for you when we return to Bhall-Duraht."

"Blind?"

"How else?"

Jace chuckled, taking a gander at Aidan's outfit. It was a jacket overtop a buttoned dress. Unlike Jace, he bore a leonine creature, one with two tails.

"Crimson suits you," Jace commented.

"Crimson? I thought it was black. I told her black!"

Jace smirked, shaking his head; Setas-Lisians did not seem to be good at taking orders. "Just take it off when we're done."

Aidan sighed, "Fine. Speaking of 'we,' where's our resident Reaper?"

"Running late?" Jace shifted his weight to one side as he folded his arms. "That's a surprise."

Aidan chuckled. "Let me see if I can find her."

He knocked on the walls for a moment, leaving Jace baffled at what was happening. However, Aidan smiled. "She's on her way. She must be wearing heels."

Jace shook his head in disbelief, but lo and behold, Aurora arrived wearing heels and a sleek gold dress. They put her in a lace cape of opaque yellow, which may have drawn some inspiration from Aidan's outfit for her.

She did a little spin, and Jace saw the aquiline motif outstretched on her cape, wings extending to her shoulders in stones of onyx. A smaller version of the creature was on her abdomen.

"Well, well, our queen has arrived," Aidan joked.

"Those laddies tried to kill me," she shuddered, "they wanted to comb my hair."

"You too?!" Aidan laughed.

"Me too," Jace groaned.

"Setas-Lisian combs are made from too flimsy and painful a material ..." Aurora chuckled, "I think they learned they can't do that, aye?"

The brothers laughed in unison, allowing the anxiety to leave their stomachs. Once the jolliness died down, Jace's face grew solemn. "Sorry to ruin the mood, but I'm having doubts about our hosts."

"Ya're talking to a Delfizcani, so I never trusted them anyway."

Aidan leaned on the wall. "Did you find something out?"

Jace groaned, relaying the information he learned from the seamstress to them. Aidan could not help chuckling, but Aurora jabbed him every time he did so.

"So, there was some type of royal affair. By whom, I don't know. Apparently, it had to do with Bhall-Duraht," Jace finished explaining.

"An affair? They made Bhall-Duraht suffer because of an affair?" Aidan asked incredulously.

"Not just that." Jace continued, "Bhall-Duraht hampered trade. I remember Father mentioning that most of the southern continent traded with the desert. They—"

The doors swung open, halting Jace's words in his throat. An attendant looked skeptically between the three before walking in with a tray of masks. "You need to wear these."

Jace took the masks, handing them out to his friends. He was not sure if the masks were traditional or was it the fact that they wanted to cover up their *guests* as if they could hide anyway. Regardless of what he thought, it was time for them to enter. Jace and Aurora gripped their weapons, their vessels, as the attendant walked the three of them in.

Immediately, the lights of the room blinded him, and with his advanced vision, it took a little longer for him to adjust. The gaping mouths and the whispering voices were the first to greet him.

Everyone looked professional and noble-like. When Jace finally overcame the blinding lights, he noticed that the masks were optional for some. Clearly, they wished to make themselves known in a room full of important people.

"Here are your seats," the attendant interrupted his thoughts.

Jace stopped short with Aidan and Aurora right behind him. Their table was already occupied, and if Jace did not think the Setas-Lisian monarchs were not up to something before, he knew now.

"I see my mother wishes to play games," Nicklaus commented.

"So, it seems," Jace replied.

Aurora and Jace stared at Nicklaus and Natalie, and after a moment, they all sat down. The sounds of gossip and music washed over their ears, attempting to tune out the awkward silence at the table.

"So, what are your plans after the banquet?" Nicklaus asked.

"Home," Jace replied swiftly and sternly.

"Of course, but what will you do? I am sure the Dark General said he can track you all. Would it not be wise to move elsewhere?"

You have a point. They all knew home would not be safe for their return. Jace saw through Nicklaus's ursine-inspired mask, seeing no ill intent in his eyes. "We'll think of something."

The prince nodded, reverting to silence once more. The food on his plate remained untouched. His eyes almost instantly went to his parents every time he looked up; that's when his eyes grew cold, loveless, and lifeless. Natalie shook him from his trance every so often, but that never stopped his returning eyes.

"Nicklaus," Jace called, "about what you told us in the study."

The prince swallowed hard, driving his fork into his meal. "Ah ... yes. I implore you to simply forget everything you heard."

"Actually, I was—"

"Stand in attention!" an attendant yelled.

The king and queen were about to make their address. The king stood atop the stage, which was at the far right of the room. All eyes were drawn to him; *he was a leader who demanded attention, just like Father,* Jace could not help but think.

With a clearing of his throat, the people silenced. "Thank you all for joining us here, The Day of Nissi. A day where Setas-Li won its greatest victory over the Seplechurans to become the kingdom we are today."

The people cheered, yelling praises in their native tongue. Jace glanced over at Natalie, who was staring coldly with her arms folded.

"Our ancestors adorned themselves in masks of animals to represent different aspects of the warriors. No animal, too small or too weak. Today, we honor that tradition and a new victory that will soon be upon us."

The crowd started to murmur. Jace felt something sink in his stomach; something was afoot, something terribly wrong. He looked straight at the king, who also found his eyes as well. Jace gripped the table, preparing for what the king had to say.

"My son, Prince Nicklaus, found two of the legendary Blades of the Keerie, and the two warriors wielding them agreed to help us march on Seplechurus!"

Snap! A piece of the table fell to the ground.

Jace's breath grew furiously cold. People shuddered when they felt it, but they were not the target of his rage. *That bastard of a king and his smiling queen are to blame.* As far as he was concerned, nothing was going to keep him from his home any longer.

72

Fragile Unities

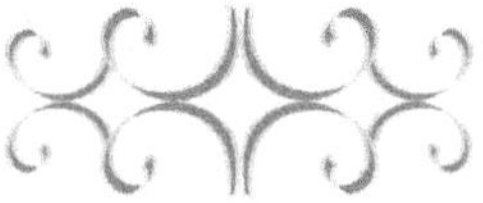

The NERVE of these people.
—The Wildcard

OW. WOW. AIDAN sat motionless at the announcement the king and queen had just made. He knew they were cunning, but this was too far. After hearing the table snap, Aidan knew exactly how Jace felt. The room began to feel blustery cool, and Aidan felt the marble floor take on an icier texture. Should that be possible? He wondered because Jace's powers should not have been able to activate without a Blade. *Are they attached to his emotions somehow?*

Aidan stood, reaching for Jace's hand, which immediately gave him a harsh frostbite. He retracted his hand quickly. "Calm down, we'll think of something. We always do. Also, control that ice, it's getting chilly in here."

Jace inhaled cold air, then exhaled with everything at the proper temperature, and even Aidan's frostbite disappeared. Aidan bellowed a sigh of relief, making sure Jace sat back down before he returned to his seat.

The queen made a joke to recapture everyone's attention. However, her words landed on deaf ears at Aidan's table.

"Nicklaus," Jace's eyes were harshly toned, "did you know about this?"

Nicklaus scoffed, "Do the words of my parents in the throne room align with anything you just heard?"

"A simple 'no' would have been nice, laddie," Aurora sassed.

Aidan chuckled, "In his defense, I would have answered similarly."

Jace growled, but Aidan could not tell if it was directed at him, Nicklaus, or the monarchs.

The table grew more silent than a barren night in Bhall-Duraht. It seemed that everyone was deep in thought, trying to make sense of what had just happened. Clearly, this deception did not feel right to anyone.

"Nicklaus," Aidan called out, "shouldn't you be happy right now? You kept hounding Jace about protecting the world in Utopia."

"*This* is protecting nothing but my parents' reputation and ego. If this was so important, they would not have used deceit."

"Agreed," Jace bellowed.

Natalie finally spoke, "From my observation, war is getting expensive. Leroza would lose profits soon."

"Precisely," Nicklaus agreed, "all the while my parents look like heroes to the public."

"Aye, that would be fer sure," Aurora agreed.

As the team continued, Aidan noticed how the four of them were scheming together, somewhat unified. *So, they could get along if they tried. Albeit from different angles. But it seems possible*, he chuckled to himself. Aidan also felt the presence of more and more people leaning in on their conversation. It confirmed that his books were right about nobles always wanting the newest gossip. "Your highness," Aidan crooned, "is there someplace we could talk ... privately?"

Prying ears were everywhere, and Nicklaus's parents could pin something on them in the long run. That very thing had been done in a couple of novels, Aidan remembered.

"There is a balcony, we should convene there."

The team moved, and frankly, Aidan did not need sight to know that there were eyes looking at them as they departed. Something was wrong with the entire court. No one needed to tell him that every single soul there had to be wise to the Leroza's planning, and that the Leroza was also the face of the problem.

The cold night's air startled Aidan, though compared to what Jace could conjure, it did not have bite. He immediately found the rail and leaned up against it. The stone, gruff under his fingertips, pricked him with chipped pebbles, even though most were smooth and well-designed.

"Aidan, be careful," Jace warned.

"Relax, I got you, Chuckle, Snark, Aurora, the princeling, and the Feather Princess, I'm fine."

"Feather Princess?" Natalie questioned.

"It's because Nicklaus calls you Raven all the time. Though after what I saw in the Contested Lands, Petal Princess might be more suitable."

"We'll discuss aliases later," Jace's stern voice cut through the wind. "What I want to know is what are we going to do about the king and queen?"

Aidan heard Nicklaus make his way to the balcony, pressing his hands to the stone surface of the rail. He sighed, almost sobbing, "There is nothing you can do. My parents are ruthless; they will demean you, make you feel worthless. They will absorb any confidence you have and assimilate it into their inflated egos."

Aurora's heels clacked forward. "I refuse to believe that there's nothing we can do."

Nicklaus growled, "And look where that thinking got your people?"

Aurora retorted, "And look where yer thinking got ya?"

Now they were glaring at one another. Aidan found Aurora and placed a hand on her shoulder. He did the same for Nicklaus, "Enough, you two. I get it. Your people don't like each other, but we have bigger things to deal with."

The two moved closer to one another, but Aidan's Camerus strength pushed them apart. "Nicklaus, do you think this war is wrong?"

"I—absolutely."

Aidan nodded, then he asked Aurora, "Aurora, do you think this war is wrong?"

"Of course."

"Then, on that note, let us be united. The five of us have the knowledge and the power."

"Aidan's right," Jace agreed. "Though I hated to admit it—twice now—we need each other."

"We don't need them," Aurora exclaimed.

"That's what I said about you when Natasha wanted you to join," Jace quickly retorted, "look how wrong I was."

Aurora sighed.

Aidan grabbed her hand and Nicklaus's and united them, with his hand on top. "Alright, everyone, put it in."

Jace's heavy hands rested on Aidan's, and Natalie's hands were on as well. Soon, the chiming of Chuckle and Snark filled their ears. They climbed off Aidan's wrists and bound everyone's hands together.

"We don't have to like each other, but we have to cooperate." Jace sternly told everyone. "We're united for the end of this war."

"To the end of the war," Aidan confirmed.

There was a stiff pause in the air that, strangely enough, Aidan could discern. He knew that Aurora and Nicklaus were glaring at each other. Finally, Natalie yielded her compliance, "To end this war."

Unlike Jace and Aurora's problem, Aurora and Nicklaus had a lot of historical baggage. One did not need to be politically savvy to know how much the Setas-Lisians and the Delfizcani hated each other.

In that moment, Aurora and Nicklaus put aside their differences, finally joining the crew's sentiment in unison, "To the end of the war."

Chuckle and Snark chimed, returning to Aidan's wrists. Everyone backed up to gain some room, though the main question was at hand. "So, what now?" Aidan asked as seriously as he could muster, "If our plan is to end the war, that means we stay with the princeling's parents?"

"Not necessarily," Nicklaus dissented. "If we escape now, we can bide our time and regroup. We have two women who know the path of the shadows. Thusly, an infiltration would be best."

Jace grunted in agreement. "That's right, a full assault will have too many people killed."

"I want my people preserved." Natalie concurred, "So, I also agree with this."

"Good," Jace agreed, "then we—AAArgh!"

Jace and Aurora suddenly cried out, their steps leaving heavy vibrations that startled Aidan. They clutched their heads, dropping straight to the ground. The remaining three tried to console them, but their thrashing made it impossible.

"Jace, Aurora, what's wrong?!" Aidan yelled.

"Laddie—something is coming," Aurora exclaimed.

Jace and Aurora stormed into the monumental ballroom, yelling for everyone to evacuate. Soon, the screams and yells of the people filled their ears. Frantic bodies began to flee in all directions. About a quarter of the guests, either bravely or cowardly, fled the ballroom, while the remaining were too fearful to move from under their tables.

"What is the meaning of this?!" King Athis yelled when the rest of the team entered.

"They know when *true* leader makes himself known," A disembodied Seplechuran voice reverberated throughout the hall.

Natalie shivered. "No ... it cannot be."

A strange, ethereal laugh filled the entire ballroom. All the patrons who were left cowered in fear. Though he had not heard the voice before, considering the level of pain Jace and Aurora were in and the awe Natalie was experiencing, Aidan guessed it could only be one person.

Dark pillars erupted in several locations; Aidan immediately noted the resemblance to Merek, but far superior. Aidan sent out a vibrational wave when the feelings of the dark energy faded, and now, three new guests had been added to the ballroom.

"Athis," the voice called, though more embodied, "I must have lost my invitation."

The man spoke, slowly, suavely, filled with enough confidence that it could crush the entire castle. Maybe he could; the fact that he was able to make himself known so easily was terrifying enough.

"You're not welcomed here, Ras," Athis replied in a yell.

"My presence begs to differ."

Aidan leaned near Natalie, whispering, "Natalie," he tried to hide the fear in his voice, "is it the same Ras I'm thinking of?"

Natalie's voice was mostly muted, but she had enough courage to answer, "That is Rastanis Lekoranoc—The Seplechuran Emperor."

73

THE RESOLVE OF THORNS

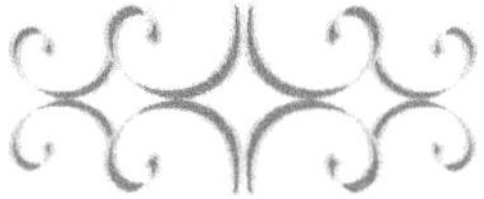

I will end his terror myself.
—The Rose

JUDAVEK! JUDAVEK! JUDAVEK!

It was the name given to Natalie by her own people, by those she wished to call comrades. She had had to run away from her home, renounce her ideals, renounce her life, her family, and her title—all because of *him*.

The emperor taunted her as he spoke jokingly with the Setas-Lisians; talking like he had done nothing wrong. Natalie's arms began to shake, and her eyes furiously twitched. She tried to hold her arm, but the fury was consuming. Her mind wanted her to calm down and plan a strategy, but her body wanted far more. It wanted blood. "RAS!"

She grabbed an idle soldier's sword, running toward the child who called himself an emperor. He turned to her with much disdain, but his disdain did not matter to her.

The crowd parted, and she went straight for Ras's head. She slashed faster than most could blink, but Ras dodged. She slashed again, and he kept dodging; each of his movements was quicker than the last.

She tried again and again, until the emperor raised his hand. Her body became still as if some large invisible hand stopped her. "Oh, I know you." He smiled. "You are Brand and Natasha's spawn, yes?"

She tried to speak, but the force even held her mouth shut. He was so close, though; if she could just get one slash, she could end the suffering of Seplechurus, she could end her own suffering.

"I am not here for you. Goodbye." He merely flicked his wrist, which sent her flying across the enormous ballroom. The streaming lights of the chandeliers became dizzying as the wind rushed through her hair, only stopping when her body crumpled against the wall.

"Natalie!" Nicklaus called, running to her.

The room suddenly got cold again, and strange noises crowded her ears. She thought it was the sound of El's Abode calling, but now she saw movement from the team that gave her hope.

"Aurora, let's go!" She heard Jace yell.

The two zipped from their locations, wielding their godly weapons, ready to strike down the emperor where he stood. However, Ras laughed, "Amusing! Such vigor!"

The shadows crept around his hands, charging them with a devilish glow. With a mere clench, shadow warriors emerged from thin air.

The first wielded a giant sword that was nearly as tall as Jace. With a powerful swing, it cut through Jace's ice barricade and sent him into the wall.

The second shadow attacked with a regal agility, dodging all the lightning bolts Aurora had summoned before slamming a fist into Aurora's stomach, which shoved her to the ground. The shadows disappeared as fast as they came.

Nicklaus set Natalie against the wall and Blinked toward the emperor. Aidan followed suit with his chains ready to attack, but Ras did not even look at them.

A sharp blast of air pressure knocked Aidan and other patrons to the balcony side of the room, while a man, presumably Alistair, Blinked off the wall, intercepting Nicklaus's attack. The two Blinkers skidded to a stop, breaking apart the ground beneath them.

Natalie tried to pick herself up, but whatever the emperor had used left her engulfed in a sauna-like state, almost burning. It also left her void, starved, and weary. She slid down the wall in pain every time she worked to stand. She knew the emperor was powerful, but this pain felt different. Natalie writhed, barely staying conscious, Jace and Aurora were toppled, Aidan was discombobulated, and Nicklaus was still recovering from his prior injury at the hands of Alistair.

"Guards!" Queen Fahtalia yelled.

The guards hesitated but eventually made their way to surround the emperor and his guests. While his two companions were on guard, Ras raised his hands in mock surrender. "Come now! Let us save hostilities for battlefield!" Ras yelled to the crowd. "We eat and drink here, yes?"

King Athis stepped forward, motioning his guards to cease their advance. He looked pensively at Alistair for a long time, then to Serenity before confronting Ras. "What are you doing here, Ras?"

Emperor Rastanis bore a childish grin on his face. "Today is Day of Nissi, yes? I cannot celebrate with you?"

"Do you know the reason for this celebration?" Fahtalia growled at him.

"Yes, yes, it is day my ancestors failed to be rid of Setas-Lisian invaders. I assure you, Mad Queen, history does not always repeat itself."

The emperor made his appearance on The Day of Nissi, the day on which Setas-Li fought against Old Seplechurus to attain kingdom-hood. *Either Ras grew brain to become strategic, or he is choosing to mock Setas-Li this day,* Natalie thought at the emperor's words.

"You are not welcomed here," hissed Athis. He unsheathed his rapier, the edge of his blade glowing.

"This war was started very long ago, and you know it well, Athis. All pieces are in play. We should celebrate like it is our last."

Athis's legs shook awkwardly as his blade teetered from his hands. It was uncertain what the king was thinking, but Ras had shaken him.

Ras motioned to the people and shouted, "People of Setas-Li, I know that war has placed us under much stress; however, I swear on my lineage I will bring no harm for the duration of my stay, yes? I have come with two warriors and unarmed."

Athis scowled painfully at the Seplechuran monarch. "Forswear?"

"What?!" Fahtalia yelled, "You cannot let this rabble intrude in our home!"

"And yet," Alistair's voice rang, as he approached, "you're still queen."

Athis stared once again at Alistair, who was masked. With narrowed eyes, he then turned to Ras. "Enough. Ras, swear on your lineage that you and your subordinates will not harm a single soul here."

"I swear on my lineage *and* on my child's voice."

Natalie raised a brow; such promises were not Seplechuran, but it apparently meant something to the king. He nodded, not even fretting about a retaliation from the emperor. With a wave of the king's hand, his guards stood down, and Ras did the same with Alistair and Serenity.

"Let us continue to celebrate," Athis told his remaining guests, "This is still a day of victory."

Murmurs were running wild now. Some people even departed the ballroom; others were too stunned to move. Ras lingered in the middle of the dance floor before seeking refreshments.

Serenity went over to Aidan, while Alistair made his way to Natalie. "My apologies for the emperor, he was excited to come here." Alistair reached out.

Natalie slapped his hand away. "I should have known your presence earlier was no mere coincidence."

"I am a creature of habit. My father taught me to always have a plan." He reached out again.

She looked reluctantly at his hand; the vow of the emperor was the only thing that made her reach for Alistair this time. Immediately, she felt the hardness of his palms; she could feel the practiced strikes and motions. She questioned him, "Why are you really here?"

"Me? I was forced, same goes for Sere. The emperor ... I do not know. I am not sure why anyone would like to come here." Through his dusk owl-like mask, she could see his brows furrowing. He folded his arms with a groan but softened when he turned back to her. "If you want to know, feel free to ask him."

Natalie glared at Alistair. He chuckled in response. She wanted to grab the rapier at his side and thrust it into his arm for making such a statement. Though part of her strength was returning, she was still too slow and too weakened to do so.

"I only jest," he corrected.

He reached out for her, but she pulled back, "Do not think I forgot what you did in Contested Lands. You made me slaughter my people."

This time he laughed, "You're still on that? I thought you would have noticed ..."

Natalie cocked a brow.

"They were marauders from the eastern lands who were sentenced to death. Working for me was their only salvation. They were criminals."

"They were still Seplechuran."

Alistair shrugged. "See it as you will. Regardless, you did your country a service by disposing of them. They've killed more of your people than any Setas-Lisian."

Footsteps rushed over. "Raven, are you alright?" Nicklaus wedged himself between her and Alistair. It put a deep frown on Alistair's face.

"Of course, I want to have a civil conversation, and you appear. Typical of a little—" Alistair held his tongue. Alistair turned to her. "Well, I will take my leave. Hopefully, I've cleared up any misconceptions about me. Let it be known, Rose, we want the same thing."

He walked off.

She released the breath she held, not from his presence, but from her own guilt. She had handled marauders before; that was one of her tasks as Kcauss Rose. She almost wanted to thank him for clarifying, but his motives still haunted her; he seemed to be always up to something.

"Are you well?" Nicklaus asked.

"Yes ... Alistair was ... resolving something for me."

"Do not be quick to believe him; those like him are capable of great deceit."

She nodded, too tired to say anything more. The emperor was truly frightening, even more so than he was as a child. With such power and a lack of maturity, he was capable of great destruction at the slightest reaction.

Nicklaus beckoned her. "Come, you need to rest."

"Nicklaus," she called, stretching her back, "I am Seplechuran, I do not need to rest."

74

Temporary Alliances

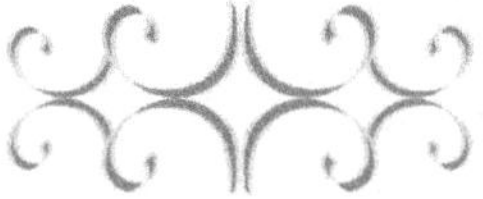

Could this night get any worse?
—The Prince

THE EMPEROR SWIVELED around the room, interrupting conversation after conversation. All eyes were on him, and he drank every second of it. Such an evil man with an immature personality, it sickened Nicklaus to see how welcomed that bastard felt. The Day of Nissi was a day filled with victory over the old enemies of Setas-Li, a monument to a bright new future. *Such a stain on history should not even step foot on Setas-Lisian soil—talk less the beating heart of the kingdom.*

"I can't believe he's actually here," Aidan said, with a hand rubbing one ear. "He doesn't feel so impressive to me."

Nicklaus scoffed, "He is nothing to look at, I assure you."

Jace leaned back, arms folded. His scowl pierced deeply through the crowd, devilishly looking at the emperor conversing. "I want to know why he's here."

"—and how fast can we kill him?" Natalie added.

"Is it not obvious?" Nicklaus nearly slammed the table, "He is here to gloat. Look at him! He thinks he has done no wrong. What manner of man walks around as if he is welcomed?"

Aurora sat silently; her eyes were trained on Ras. Her mouth uttered no words. Was it the fact she had tasted defeat so quickly, or was it another matter? Mulling it over, Nicklaus wanted to broach the topic, but his mind could not shake the fact that the El-forsaken emperor had walked in *his* castle.

"Aidan," Jace called to his brother.

"I know what you're going to say, and I have to tell ya, I don't sense anything wrong with the ground. It seems that he is simply here to party."

That could not be it; a man of his stature should be leading his armies or giving commands for war, not fraternizing with the enemy. A surge of rage filled Nicklaus like the emperor's wine chute. *This man started the entire war, desecrated land and body for his sick ideals, then he enters a Setas-Lisian party with no remorse or dignity. No wonder Raven hates him,* Nicklaus seethed.

Of course, other interruptions had to be addressed as well. "Mind if we sit?" Alistair walked up and asked. The dusk owl mask could not hide Alistair from Nicklaus. After their last duel, his face and features were etched into his mind with a branding iron.

Nicklaus waved his hand dismissively. "Go meddle with your emperor."

Alistair scoffed, adjusting his arm holding Jace's former friend. "Listen, Nicklaus, for once, we agree on one thing. We should not be here—I hate parties."

Nicklaus stood, hatred hissing through his teeth. "Oh, my apologies, I pity that your being here makes you uncomfortable—"

Aidan snickered.

"—then why appear?" Nicklaus continued.

Alistair released the hand of his escort, bringing his face inches away from Nicklaus. "Do you think any of us could say no to him?" He quietly flared. "We're in as much danger as you are being around him!"

Nicklaus cocked a brow, his breath calming. "What do you mean?"

Alistair stared at Ras before lowering his voice to speak, "He is a fickle man with power. The most dangerous person to be around. Every day, there is a different personality or mood. No one wishes to stay around him for too long."

"So, he simply partied today on a whim?" Nicklaus responded, then he stood pondering the absurdity, thinking how this brought up an obvious question—why work with such a man? A man who was a villain in every measure of the word. Nicklaus had read up on his fair share of villains; he even lived with two. Nicklaus shared his ponderings out loud, "Why work with such a man?"

But as he predicted, he only received a scowl and an evasive answer from Alistair, "I needn't explain my motives to you."

"Then you needn't sit with us," Nicklaus replied harshly.

The silence between the seven of them allowed the music to seep back into their awareness, reminding them of where they were. The Day of Nissi marked a day of celebration, and yet Nicklaus grew confident that as long as these *interruptions* manifested themselves, a scowl would be mounted on his face for all eternity.

"Very well," Alistair sighed. "I was hoping we could be civil about this, but it seems we cannot."

Alistair tugged on his friend's arm, but her attention did not reach this reality. Her eyes were locked in a trance with Jace, who could not bring himself to blink.

Then everyone woke from their daze.

"Leaving so soon?" An annoying voice called out to him.

Nicklaus's shoulder dropped, and his eyes immediately rolled. He instinctively mustered a smile as his mother approached the table. The unified scowl that showed on everyone else's face, including Alistair and Jace's former friend, showed how much the queen was welcomed.

"I hope we are not talking about anything too scandalous," the queen crooned.

Alistair hissed, "We weren't discussing anything that concerns you, witch."

Nicklaus tried to bury a smile. Oh, how he had wished to say that to his mother whenever she came barging into his study. His mother snapped a look at him sharply, to presumably invoke his defense of her honor, but he happily remained silent.

So, she retorted, "Of course, you Seplechurans have no manners—"

Alistair and Raven deepened their scowls, arms folded.

"—just like those unruly desert dwellers."

Jace, Serenity, and Aurora all hardened their features when Nicklaus's mother spoke. Aidan turned his head with a slight irritation on his face that grew larger by the second—then he smiled. "You are the head of the Leroza clan, am I right, your highness?"

She puffed out her chest, "Well, of course. I am glad someone recognizes that fact."

Aidan gave a hollow clap. "That explains so much. The only way for you to get money is to drag out this war because if anyone had to pay you for the smart things you say, you'd be destitute."

Everyone gasped. The guards who escorted the queen could only watch in horror because they were unable to protect their monarch from this attack.

"Y—You *insolent* boy! I am *queen*, I could behead you with an order, flay you with a simple command, or rain the wrath of Maserades on your pathetic town! I find your tone—"

Aidan interrupted her quickly, "Then I suggest you stop finding us. You came to *our* table, remember? If you want stimulating conversation with someone on your level," he pointed, "the emperor is that way."

The queen's hand shivered in place. She wanted to race her hand across Aidan's face, as she liked to do often, but with so many people here, she would not dare. Her flawlessly white skin turned red as the first level of Maserades, and Nicklaus wondered if she would implode from anger. "Nicklaus, come," she commanded.

"I apologize, my queen," Nicklaus laced his words with a sardonic tone, "but I must ensure that these *ruffians* have someone to keep an eye on them."

She huffed, marching back to her seat beside the king. Her guards were stunned at first, but eventually they, too, fled from Aidan's assault.

"Farewell, demon," Nicklaus whispered.

A reserved but sharp laugh left Alistair's mouth. "You madman! Do you wish to join the Seplechuran Empire?"

"Someone needed to do it, honestly," Aidan shrugged, "I'm sure there'll be repercussions later, but I'll deal with them. I just know that Jace is gonna—"

"I didn't say anything," Jace interrupted him.

Aurora leaned forward. "I am pretty sure *everyone* was thinking what ya were saying, laddie."

A collective nod circulated around the table.

Alistair bowed his head. "As much fun as that was, we'll be taking our leave, no?" Looking to his left, he gently said, "Serenity?" She latched onto his arm, and the two began to leave. Eyes started moving to one another quickly and intently.

Nicklaus shouted, "Halt." The shock of his assertiveness froze everyone. "If my father can tolerate the emperor's presence, surely we can be civil and procure a temporary truce."

Alistair turned, smiling, which was either a good or ill omen; only time held the answer. Nicklaus's decree stood its ground in the ballroom, and he knew there was no turning back now. And his decree was solidified by Jace's nod of encouragement. So, he continued, "It would be our honor for tonight, and tonight only, that we be allies."

Alistair nicked a drink from a passing server. "To temporary alliances."

Nicklaus raised his drink. "To temporary alliances."

75

CAN WE START OVER?

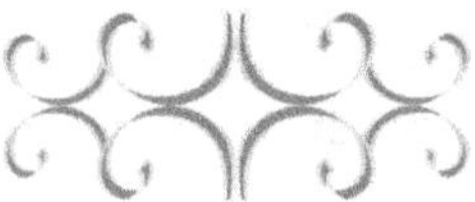

I can't believe Nicklaus let them stay.
—The Protector

JACE'S EYES SHOT up only to find themselves facing the table again. Though she hid behind a mask, the mere fact that he knew Serenity was behind that façade made him quiver. He drummed on his knees, thinking the obvious: she sat right there; he could say something that would make it right. This should not be so hard, and yet when he thought of her face back in the Contested Lands—her voice, the world, everything was so loud. *Why is it so loud? Why is this so hard?* Serenity's hurt and her words reverberated in his head: *Explain? Explain! Explain how you left me? Please, go on, explain to me how you carefully thought of leaving me behind!*

"I need air." Jace pushed himself from the table. He needed time, anything to help him think. He repeated his mantra as he walked to the balcony. He just needed the world to quiet down for a second. Jace peered over the balcony, hands resting on its hard but comforting stone. The coarseness, the rugged yet consistent feeling, it reminded him of the forge; it reminded him that everything takes time. "But how to start?" he whispered to himself.

"Well, well, well, the ice master from a land with no snow. I have been meaning to get you alone," Alistair crooned as he waltzed out onto the balcony.

Jace exhaled a chilled breath. "Just because Nicklaus let you at the table, that does not mean we're friends."

Alistair scoffed, then laughed, "Why would I want to be your friend? I've seen firsthand how you treat those; I would rather be your enemy."

Jace crumpled a piece of the balcony rail under his thrall. A sharp scowl turned to face Alistair. Such a smug man looked unafraid, but one could not hide an apparent emotion like fear from the eyes of the Songlua.

"Don't talk such a big game if you're going to cower, Alistair. I *will* break you."

Alistair chuckled. "So, Sere was right. You do have those annoying little eyes." He placed a finger to his chin. "I also heard your brother had better ones, but they seem to be ... dysfunctional, no?"

Before Alistair could finish getting his chuckle out, Jace's fist closed in on his face. Alistair Blinked away, but Jace's eyes followed him. Not even Alistair could escape the glare of the Songlua. With a swift kick, Jace knocked Alistair into the balcony door before clamping a hand around his neck.

Jace pulled Alistair close enough for him to feel the ice on his breath. "Mention my brother or my friend again and I'll wring every bit of life out of you."

Alistair gurgled a reply. A splash of color boiled up to his face, painting him a shade of suffocated red. Jace dropped the lieutenant, giving him a moment to catch his breath.

Alistair coughed. "For ... the record ... you are ... VERY ... terrifying."

He held his throat, surely feeling the imprint of Jace's veiny hands on his skin.

"What is your aim, Alistair?"

Still rubbing his throat, Alistair stared at Jace in the eyes. "I want to know why you did it."

"Did what?"

"Don't toy with me."

Jace sighed, looking out into the darkness of night. His expression softened from rage to sadness. He could not fool himself; he knew what Alistair meant. What could he possibly say except the obvious? "You know about the massacre. I'm sure Serenity told you."

"Surprisingly, she did not tell me much. She was trapped in her home for the duration of it."

Jace inclined his head. A grave pause halted his words as he thought, *she was really there.* He shivered, continuing. "It was a bloodbath. People, left and right, were dying, cut down by soldiers and ripped apart by war beasts. My parents' last task for us was to make sure that we could take care of each other.

Rubbing the front of his neck, Alistair interjected, "Serenity told me about them. Good lot." He cleared his throat. "They practically raised her when her mother was away."

"Yeah," whispered Jace.

Alistair pondered with an absent-minded gaze, his next words coming out quietly, "So, your final charge was your brother. I'm assuming you escaped through some hidden passage?"

Jace nodded.

"Then?"

Jace ran a hand through his hair, recalling the days when he would try to go back. The nightmares that filled his thoughts of a sickly Serenity getting beheaded, stabbed, ripped apart, or buried all started to come back. He lost faith that she lived, but even worse yet, he could not risk seeing her dead. So, with a heavy heart, he told Alistair just that.

"You were a fool to lose faith. Do you realize what she's been through?"

Jace leaned on the balcony, unable to face Alistair. "No."

"Ask your Raven about the Seplechuran army, about the child soldiers who were left on the ridges of Konkev Mountain." Poison leaked from Alistair's voice, dripping in Jace's ears. "Everything went to the Depths with Ras in power, and Sere was at the brunt of his tyranny."

Jace sighed, crumpling the rail underneath. *No more, I know I failed her ... please stop.* Tiny drips of regret nearly fell from his eyes, a silent wail slipped from his tongue, and the balcony now an ebb and flow of shattered emotion.

Yet, Alistair continued, "And after all that you put her through ... she still kept that dirty flute."

That jab pierced the veil of Jace's deafening emotion, causing him to turn to Alistair, hopeful. "She *still* has it?"

"Unfortunately. I tried to get rid of it multiple times, but she seems bent on keeping that ragged thing. How she kept it this long is a mystery."

Alistair's voice trailed off as his gaze turned to the sky. Jace followed his gaze, the moon glittered along with the stars like children happily clinging to a parent. A specific cluster did catch Alistair's eyes, one that made the corner of his lip move. "Hmmm, it seems Kromopha is out tonight."

"Kromopha?" Jace inquired.

"I swear, you desert people," Alistair said, walking to Jace's side, pointing to the cluster. "Kromopha, the patron Vehem of Forgiveness and Diplomacy?"

Jace shook his head.

"One of the Vehem of the Night Star? The same birth star you and Sere were born under?"

Jace shook his head again.

Alistair took a deep sigh, closing his eyes to hold in his disappointment.

Jace raised a brow. "I didn't take you for a superstitious type. Astrology doesn't seem to match you."

"I find the fundamental forces of the outer world intriguing, nothing more." He walked away. "But ... if Kromopha is smiling tonight—keep her happy."

Alistair returned to the world of light and gossip, leaving Jace in sadness, bafflement, and wonder all at once. The constellation was simple: two crucifix forms met with a single, large star in between them. At first, he did not get it, but the lines seemed to form the longer he stared. It seemed like two people shaking hands in reconciliation.

"Yehowehel, Kromopha, somebody ... give me the strength for what I am about to do." Jace walked off to the light of the party, but not before stopping, staring at the constellation once more. "Thank you." He entered. Unbeknownst to him—Kromopha shimmered, fading into the clouds as fast as she appeared.

Jace walked through the crowd with renewed energy, hoping that what he was about to ask was not going to stab a stake in the heart of the situation. He approached the table, more specifically, he approached Serenity. "Serenity, do you ... want to dance?"

A strange sound stretched from her throat in apprehension; she turned to Alistair, who simply shrugged. She returned her gaze to Jace's outstretched hand and pleading eyes.

"I'm not saying you've forgiven me, but if we can just act like I never failed for one night—I'll take it." Jace's voice was sweet to her, as sweet as she had remembered it—before he let her down.

She lifted her hand shakily, reaching for his grip. Her lace-clasped fingers lightly touched Jace's palm, then slightly drifted back.

Alistair noticed. "If you can keep that Elsdamn flute, you could dance with the man."

Both of them looked at him, Serenity with apparent surprise, and Jace with a silent gratitude. Her fingers welded to his hand. With a force equal to his surety, he picked her from her chair, angling his arm as an invite.

The gossipers around their table started to gawk and whisper. Their breath carried a different tune than the music playing. That did not matter now, however, because he was not there for them; he was there for her. She was the only one who mattered in the dance for her heart.

Once they made their way to the middle of the dance floor, he tried to mimic the simple moves that the men around him were doing. His stance was awkwardly stiff. Now he felt as hopeless as he looked.

"*Misser,*" a servant, holding a wine tray, called out to him as discreetly as he could. "Hands up, left hand on her waist. Sway every second beat, also relax, lower your shoulders."

If Jace was anything, he was a quick study. He followed the commands perfectly, smiling as the servant walked off. *At least not everyone in the ball thinks like the queen.* Once he got ahold of the dance, he knew the hard part was to begin. "You look—beautiful today."

A little smirk crept on her face. "Thank you. Alistair picked out the outfit."

Of course, he did. Amethyst material clasped shoulder-to-toe in a gorgeous gown that even his mother would have been proud of. The purple and white laced around her as if the colors were made just to magnify her visage. It stopped at her shoulders, revealing her structured collarbones and the sensuous dip around her chest area. Serenity had really grown up, he noticed. Jace forced his eyes away. *Yeah, of course, Alistair would pick this.*

She also wore a butterfly mask, one filled with more midnight black than anything else. A few of the other patrons had the same mask on, but no one wore it quite like she did.

"He has good taste, though, but knowing Aidan, he would have a problem with it."

She suppressed a chuckle, just like she used to. "Aidan seams now?"

Jace nodded, "Yes, and he's meticulous about his work. He inherited our mother's eyes for fashion and made Aurora, his, and my clothing himself."

Jace discerned the shock behind Serenity's eyes. "Really?" she replied, "He could quit being a warrior with skills such as those."

"He's planning on it."

Jace breathed out, nearly missing a beat to the step. Without their weapons and a battlefield, Serenity was still Serenity. Her smile whisked away his anxiety. It allowed him to bathe himself in the sound of her voice. "I hate to shy away from a better conversation, but ... what happened to your disease?"

She shook her head. "I don't know. I woke up one morning, cured."

Jace raised a brow. "That's it? Maybe with everything happening around us, I guess I expected more—"

"Flair?" She breathed out a chuckle. "You're starting to sound like your brother."

Jace rolled his eyes; a smirk rose to his lips. "Well, forgive me, my life hasn't been normal in a while."

"I understand that too well," she said absentmindedly.

The two continued their dance when their words began to fade into the crowd. Staring at each other seemed to be more than enough for them. The questions could not get too personal because the unfortunate truth stood—that they were still enemies.

They were grown adults, and yet they wanted to imagine like children, imagine that their past decisions were not so. They both knew that it should have been this way, yes, it should have been him at her side and her at his. This dance should have meant something else, something without the stains and looming shadows in the back of their minds. He should have gone back—the problems he caused her, his own guilt he had to endure—all would not have been if only he had gone back.

"This is how it should have been ..." they both spoke wistfully. Their unified utterance halted them in surprise, and thinking, *did we both just say that aloud?*

"But it could never be this way," Serenity finished the statement.

The pained look Jace gave was enough of an answer. He wanted to ask her why, but he already knew the answer. "Can we just—start over?"

A rueful smile overcame her. "We're not children, Jace, this isn't a game where we can start over because we don't like the score."

"But the game was rigged, and you know it. We were never supposed to be put in a position like that." He paused to regain himself. "You were sick, and I couldn't protect both of you. If I had been a little bit older or had been a bit more powerful, I would have torn through the Seplechuran forces for you."

Serenity did not reply; she just stared, possibly contemplating or judging him. Even with his Songluan eyes, he couldn't tell.

"Aidan and I could only start over; it was the only risk we could take. The slate was wiped completely," Jace retorted in defense.

"And you removed me from your life," she hissed.

Jace ripped off his mask in a desperate anger, drawing the eyes and ire of some around him.

In a tone, part burning with passion and part iced with anger, he asked, "Look into my eyes right now and tell me that I would've not come back if I knew."

As suggested, she looked into his eyes, staring deep into a mirror. There he stood, she could say anything, she could prove that once and for all that justice stood at her side, and Jace had truly abandoned her. Yet, when her words could not find her, Jace knew that she knew—he would've gone back for her.

She turned from him, but he caught her arm, his eyes falling into hers once more. A heart filled with a promise he made audible by speech and touch, "Serenity, please, come back. I will *not* leave you again."

And even though he could see the well fill up in her eyes, he knew that that was the only promise he could give her. He wanted her to turn around to hug her, to forsake the Seplechurans and join their merry little band. But sadly, he knew that if life were that easy, then there would not be war.

She broke from his grip, disappearing into the ballroom, disappearing from his sight. The coldness of his hand—haunting. He stared at the place where her palm had fit so perfectly in his own. He wanted to chase her. But her silence had made it clear that he shouldn't.

The next time the two would meet, it would be on the fields of battle.

76

WHAT THE MOON MEANS TO ME

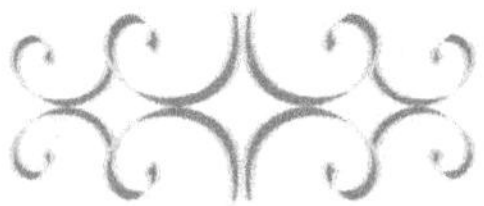

I can't believe I'm missing such an opportunity.
—The Wildcard

EVERYONE WAS HAVING the time of their lives, dancing, swaying, and possibly falling in love. Every good book had a ballroom scene; Aidan knew Nicklaus could attest to that. Alas, the time had finally come for Aidan to have his moment, but now, he could not dance with anyone. While he knew that he surely *could* dance, now, without sight, he was forced into the resignation of, *what good would bumping into others do?* But his brother, oh, his brother. The one who did not read books became the one to have his fairytale dance. Aidan awaited Jace's happy ending with eagerness. "I'm bored," Aidan groaned to no one in particular. "Where's the part where someone starts some juicy gossip? Or a fight breaks out over whose daughter marries the prince?"

No one answered, but for some reason, Aidan could feel Nicklaus's eyes piercing his soul. Aidan sighed, drumming his fingers on the table. While yes, his annoyance continued, he could not help but work to keep track of Emperor Rastanis. The emperor's tangy frankincense scent was pungent and could be tracked along with his heavy, sweeping steps. Aidan homed in on him like a hunting dog as the emperor seemed to walk with no particular intent, in some cases, or just stand in place, probably surveying, Aidan assumed, *but for what?* Did the emperor appear in the castle to party, or did he have another plan? Aidan studied and pondered.

"Can you please stop that racket?" Alistair exclaimed, imploding Aidan's concentration.

Annoyed, Aidan shot back, "Why yes, Alistair, music is blaring at terrible volumes and people sounding like a murder of crows is fine, but for some reason a blind man drumming on a table bothers you."

Alistair sighed, "Fine, do what you wish."

Aidan brandished a quick smile in Alistair's direction before resuming his drumming. And for added insolence, he drummed harder.

Ras seemed to be making a move, but Aidan noticed something; he kept himself in the same area. Each time he did move, he took the same number of steps in every direction. Aidan stopped his drumming. "I don't like it," he whispered to himself. "I don't like it at all." *He's clearly planning something if he's staying still.* The area where Ras entered was where he stayed. *Maybe a quick getaway? But why let Alistair and Serenity linger?* Aidan thought hard on the puzzle Ras was presenting. Did he plan to abandon them there? Hopefully, Jace made more progress by talking to Serenity because right now, Aidan had no leads. Clearly, going up against the guy who had just beaten his friend and brother with one attack was not someone he should be fighting. *I'm wild, not crazy—okay, I'm crazy but not that crazy.*

Aidan stood.

"Where are ya going?" asked Aurora.

"Fresh air, maybe going to start trouble, I'll cross that bridge later."

Nicklaus sighed, "Aidan, please, with the appearance of the emperor, do you truly wish to cause trouble with a mischievous plot?"

Aidan placed his hand on the table, checking for Ras's movement once more. "That's the thing, Nicklaus, he isn't doing anything. If he's playing mind games, he's doing a good job."

Alistair scoffed, "Don't give him that much credit."

Aidan chortled, "You really don't like that guy, do you? I know you won't tell me, but why are you working for a guy you don't respect?"

Silence hung over the group as Aidan guessed that their eyes were probably glued to Alistair. Aidan expected a quick, "mind your own business" since Alistair had earned his title of frequent scoffer. But instead, it seemed like the dark lieutenant was considering the question.

"I have my own personal goals, Seplechurus is the quickest way to make them a reality."

Mildly agitated, Nicklaus asked, "Do these plans of yours involve Setas-Li?"

"Very much so," Alistair answered smugly.

Aidan gawked. "Wow, I'm surprised you even answered me."

"You are the only one of your merry band, I do not take issue with," admitted Alistair.

This time, Aidan scoffed, "I can swiftly and most assuredly change your mind in a few minutes."

Alistair sounded like he wanted to retort; instead, he must have known better. The two of them chuckled. Though Aidan sensed that everyone else at the table was not as jovial. Natalie felt extremely uneasy with the emperor being here, Nicklaus undoubtedly questioned Alistair's motives, and Aurora could not stand the stench of Setas-Lisian people around her.

Aidan proudly took on the role of keeping everyone happy, also proudly knowing that he could just as well keep them insane depending upon his mood. And unless he could make Ras disappear from existence,

Natalie's mood would not change. If he could spill Alistair's guts, then maybe Nicklaus would be happy. That left only one person.

Aidan stretched. "For you, Nicklaus, I won't cause any trouble, for now, but I would still like that fresh air."

"My gratitude," Nicklaus sighed his words.

"Aurora, you coming with?"

"Why?" she asked.

Aidan placed a dramatic hand to his chest. "Oh, I'm sorry, I just assumed you would want my company over everyone else here."

"Bold assumption," Aurora snapped back.

Hearing the smirk in her voice, Aidan extended his hand, saying, "But a correct one."

The touch of Aurora's hand in his sent a small jolt through his arm. She folded herself into his curved arm, letting go a harsh breath.

"Alistair, do you think you can keep his royal highness and resident bird watcher out of trouble while I'm gone?"

"Of course," he drew out his words to annoy them, "it would be my pleasure."

Chuckle and Snark sent vibrations out, helping Aidan navigate the crowd. Everyone seemed to be so bunched together as if to hide their words from one another. It took Aurora to mostly guide the way; he appreciated the help.

She did not have to say they arrived; he knew it when the cold winds filled his pores and dragged him from dream to reality. The breezes were like the ones from their home. Sometimes, Aidan would sit outside, taking in the nature. Jace would join him, only offering his presence as comfort. Now, the visage of the moon, the image of stars, and the lovely green of his home were a distant memory. Strangely, he treasured the memories more than his sight.

As he filled his spirit with the sustenance of nostalgia. He felt something else, a soothing ringing that had no sound but owned a lucid vibration. It reverberated like a church tower's bell and beat like a heart. "Aurora, what are you doing?"

She did not answer, though her arm still wrapped his. He tugged a bit, dragging her attention from whatever she was doing. She patted his shoulder in reply. "Sorry, laddie, I was distracted."

"By what? Ras?"

Strands of her hair swept his shoulder. "No. The moon looks quite gorgeous tonight."

"The moon, huh? Why do you stare at it so often? Is it a Borealis thing?"

She let go of his arm and walked over to the railing. The silent vibrations filled his body once more.

"No—maybe. It's just so captivating, ya know? It's like staring at El, himself."

Aidan chuckled, slowly moving over to the rail. "It kinda is, isn't it? Something so far away, yet it looks right at us every night."

"Ya, it just makes me feel—good, held."

"You know, you're making me feel that way right now." He could tell Aurora was taken aback. He raised his hands in mock surrender. "No, that's not a way for me to flirt. I mean, when you look at the moon, something triggers differently in your Borealis Rage." He placed his hand upward, then he took hers, placing their palms against one another. "It's soft, warm, like a perfect song that doesn't stop."

Aurora replied, her voice was low, childlike, and curious. "A true poet, ya. What does it feel like when I'm angry?"

Aidan took a moment to think. He recalled the times when he focused on her anger. While her anger proved beneficial to defeat their enemies, he questioned who really lost in those fights. "You would think that it feels like spikes," He poked her fingers with his nails. "But it doesn't really feel like that." Then Aidan placed his palm on hers again, this time he spread their fingers as wide as possible to the point she nearly backed off. "It feels like something is tearing apart, worse yet, it feels as if something is separating from its whole."

Aurora pulled her hand away, a growl in her throat. "The Borealis Rage is in my blood, my birthright. Ya cannot tell me it's wrong."

Aidan turned his back to the rail, elbows leaning on the paved gruffness of the stone, he stretched out his arm, detecting that a part of the rail was missing. "No, no, I can't say that. I'm just saying that your birthright seems to be more in line with the moon than with, well, rage."

The balcony became completely silent, and in that moment, Aidan heard a glass cup shatter in the main hall. He hoped he had not said anything that upset her, but the truth could not be denied. The Borealis, at least to him, seemed not only stronger but also less harmful in the presence of the moon. A power that used pure anger could not be healthy, he knew.

"I can't stare at the moon and fight," Aurora said matter-of-factly.

"You'd be surprised what you can do when you need an edge." Aidan shrugged. "Alright, kidding. But yeah, I thought about that. I don't know. I'm sure we can figure out something."

"*We?*"

"Yeah. We're in this together."

She breathed out a chuckle. "I don't know how ya do it, Aidan, helping others so easily, so selflessly. Yer so kind to everyone. Even when we met, ya didn't treat me like an enemy."

"I won't lie, when we met, I was totally smitten by you."

She shuffled, digging her heels into the ground. Her voice sounded so small, "Was?"

He winked. "Hey now, don't sell yourself short, Borealis." He continued, "But now, I see someone who is reliable, mysterious, persistent, driven, and angry. But even that anger is tempered by care—and how deep that care is."

"I don't know who that girl is."

At first, Aidan expected a chuckle from her, but every second she waited, he truly thought she believed that. The softness in her voice did not match her.

"Aurora Borealis, that's who. The girl I've known since Bhall-Duraht."

There she went thinking again—the silence and his intuition told him. Aidan had little problem speaking to her, but sometimes he wondered if she really understood what he said. Did she truly take his words to heart, or did she hear the resident wildcard blabber her ear off? He wanted to help, but his words were his only power now.

How desperately he wanted to rip out any discomfort she had, and honestly, make her see herself like he saw her. *She is not a bad person; yeah, she slit a couple of Seplechuran throats, but everyone did that at some point, right?*

"There ya go again ... helping people. Yer there fer me more than I am fer myself."

He smiled ruefully, reaching out for her hand. Her fingers intertwined in his. "You know, I always thought my kindness was fake? Like, at a drop of a cup, it could disappear."

"What?"

He shrugged. "Yeah. When I lost my sight, I realized how angry I was at everyone around me, everyone who was trying to help me. Heck, even Nicklaus came to help."

"Really?"

"Surprise, right? He wanted to read me something, but I was too angry. I kinda want him to read it now, though. Regardless, I personally don't think true kindness should be able to be dropped like that."

"Not true!" Aurora exclaimed. "Aidan, look at ya. Even with everything ya have been through, you still manage to bring yerself back to this point."

"But with Feayre Fire, if that thing came from me ... was it some inner demon, a true desire? How could I be good or kind when I have *that* in me somewhere?" It had bothered him since the day he transformed, wondering how, if he truly had a kind heart, shouldn't the creature have been different? It would not have been some hulking, fiery beast. It would have been some sweet angel.

"Aidan—" Aurora gripped his arm. "—I want ya to know, ya really are kind. I've met so many people in my life and none of them have yer crazy kindness. At first, when we met, I doubted it, but now, I find myself relying on it. Don't lose it, laddie, *please*."

Aidan felt a raindrop touch the back of his hand. *Aw man, it's starting to rain. I know she controls storms and all, but we shouldn't catch a cold out here.* It was not until his hand brushed across his mask to adjust it that he realized it wasn't rain—he was crying. That realization caused his arms to numb up and his knees to weaken, and yet, nothing stopped his mouth from running. "Well dang it. There go my emotions again," He sniffled. "I suppose we will be seeing a Sad Fire or something?"

"Oh, c'mere ya."

Aurora reached out to hold him. He returned her embrace, head leaning into hers. With a whisper masked in sniffles, he told her, "Thank you."

Aurora did not realize it, but that's what Aidan's mother used to tell him. He thought he had lost her when his vision disappeared, but now, after what Aurora said, he realized that he had never lost his mother—his smile was still intact.

"No. I'm just doing what ya do fer me."

"Hey now, Borealis, we're helping each other out, like real friends."

She grew quiet. Again, she must have been thinking, Aidan concluded. *I swear, she must have been hanging out with Jace more than me.*

"Ya," she finally said, her voice soft again, "*friends.*"

Aidan's eyes widened, realizing the reason for her tone. "Hey, wait—". A scream tore through his eardrums, instinctively forcing him to assume a fighting stance. Aidan chuckled. "And here I thought this ball was gonna be boring."

The two ran in, Chuckle and Snark sending constant vibrational images to Aidan. Immediately, he stopped in his tracks. There was a soft pulse going through the ground; if it were not for his chains, he wouldn't have even felt it. "Aurora, what's happening right now? Ras is doing something real strange with the ground."

Aurora told him everything as best as she could: the three guests were making their exit, something dark and inky swirled around Ras like a whirlpool.

"I don't know what a whirlpool looks like!" Aidan yelled.

"Ah ferget it!" Aurora exclaimed.

Aidan shook his head, trying to shy away from any jokes. They needn't be distracted now. "Strange, usually when dark powers are used, we feel something by now, especially you and Jace."

"It is dark power fer sure, laddie. It's something far more refined than what my pa uses."

"My friends!" Ras shouted. "It has been a pleasure to party with you; however, I must prepare for war."

The harsh metal clang of boots started to swarm like bees. Soldiers surrounded the emperor. Aidan couldn't help the unnerving feeling building in his stomach; Ras had no fear. His heart never sped up or even skipped a beat. Alistair and Serenity may have gotten a little scared, but this man, he was always in control of a situation.

The emperor continued, "I do not like leaving without gifts!"

Athis's growl sliced the air with Blink precision. "You will receive no party favors here, Ras!"

The unnerved feeling in Aidan's gut grew, he could just *feel* Ras smiling. "Aurora, get Jace, get your Blades, I don't know what, but something is about to go down."

"What about ya?"

"I'll be fine, I got Chuckle and Snark. Go, hurry."

Aurora dashed off as quickly as she could move in heels. Aidan turned his attention back to Ras.

"No, friend. I do not want to receive something. I want to give you something." Ras stretched his hands to the crowd. "I want to give you all something!"

The vibrations in the ground were growing even stronger to the point where Chuckle and Snark weren't needed anymore to feel it. As the power grew fiercer, the sounds of terror, a cacophony of screams, blistered Aidan's ears.

Pieces of the castle began to rip apart, careening to the depths of the castle's foundation. The smell of destruction and waft of death circled him like it had once before. People yelled for loved ones and friends. Suddenly, it was a day of celebration ruined by one man's order of rampage.

Aidan cowered. "It's happening again ..."

"Aidan!" Aurora screamed over the storming crowd. "Aidan!"

Aidan clutched his head, people thronging around him for exits or for whatever they could hold onto for security. However, he could not see them; he could only absorb their fear, it pricked at his skin with diamond hardness and lethal precision. Worst of all, it burned, it burned so badly, and he tasted the smoke. His breath tasted of ashes, and his mind thought of nothing but fire.

77

AND IT ALL FALLS DOWN

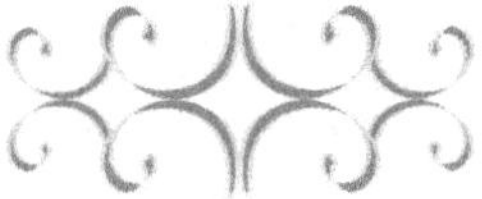

It can't end like this.
—The Thief

"A IDAN!" AURORA YELLED over the large crowd. She pushed her way through the crowd of screaming Setas-Lisians. They were like an endless wave that seemed to only grow the more she moved. Her screams were lost to the abyss of their terror, and she did not know what to do to recover them. She felt a hand on her shoulder. She turned around to fight, but was relieved when she saw the face. "Jace! I lost Aidan; he's transforming!"

His eyes grew wide. "What?! Where is he? We need to find him."

"Nay!" Nicklaus interjected into the conversation by pushing through a few screaming nobles. "I will retrieve Aidan; you need to aid the people!"

People thronged against Jace as he poked a finger to Nicklaus's chest. "You're the prince here, you protect them!"

Nicklaus clenched his jaw. He shut his eyes, admitting something Aurora never thought she'd hear. "I am not strong enough! I was never strong enough to protect them!"

Their focus was drawn by more of the castle tearing away in the presence of Ras's awesome power. Nicklaus's eyes dropped before looking at Jace again. "Please, I beg of you, be strong where I cannot." He groaned. "And let me save what I can save, please."

Jace's eyes narrowed. "No way, am I leaving my brother in your hands to save!"

Aurora shouted, "Right! Ya get yer own people. And we have ours!"

The ceiling further collapsed, the walls tumbling like a rockslide, trapping some people underneath. Seeing this, Jace clenched his eyes. Hating the reality of it, Jace relented with a groan, "Aurora, he's right,"

"What do ya mean 'he's right'?! *We* never asked for this war, the crowns of all these El-forsaken kingdoms did!"

Jace retorted with a damp fury, "When we accepted these powers, we accepted something bigger than ourselves, Aurora! Right now, I'm asking you to trust Nicklaus the same way I trusted you."

Aurora tried to keep the tears in her eyes, but she could not—for in her mind, she feared—and with good reason—that Nicklaus could just betray them; he could leave Aidan to rot while they protected his people. Every moment from the desert to the balcony could turn from moments to memories if Nicklaus turned on them.

Aurora swallowed a lump. "Jace, I can't."

"Aurora, no one is going to love my brother more than me."

More and more of the castle was falling away, some of the granite debris trapped the Setas-Lisians greatest powers under it. She could end the entire slave trade by walking away. Delfizcani, all over, could be freed so easily. But Aidan would never forgive her, and truly, she would never forgive herself for taking *their* way out. She glared pointedly at Nicklaus. "If I see so much as a scratch on him, I will send lightning through yer heart."

Nicklaus nodded. "He will be safe, on my honor ... whatever it is worth."

Jace nodded when Aurora turned to him. "Let's go!" He handed her the golden dagger as he readied his sword.

Frost filled the room, and thunder beckoned with a glance. The elements permeated the atmosphere, knowing that the sovereign names were to be called. In anticipation, they moved, preparing to be galvanized by spiritual energy.

"Nevrence!"

"Bereka!"

Lightning and ice surrounded their respective masters, empowering them with the elements bound by spirit. Before the majestic glow could fade, ice pillars jutted from the ground, holding the walls from collapsing inward.

The people marveled at the structure, almost forgetting that the world around them was literally crumbling.

"Aurora, I'm going to create a ramp near the balcony. See if you can help others in the halls."

She nodded swiftly. "Aye!"

With a growl of effort, Jace shattered the rails with a wave of ice that extended so far down.

Aurora was impressed with how far Jace had come with his abilities; she was going to have to pull her own weight if they were to succeed. With lightning speed, Aurora raced through the castle, entering every room as fast as she could. Anyone in the halls who was far too slow, she picked them up and raced them to the nearest stairwell.

Her veins coursed with enough power to carry her farther than they had before. It was either pride or stubbornness that fueled her action, for she repeated in her mind, *No one's dying under my watch.*

They were Setas-Lisian, so she shouldn't have cared. She could have let a couple of them die; no one would have blamed her. However, she had to admit that Jace was right. The Blades, the war, those things were something far bigger than they were. As long as the lightning beckoned to her call, she had to think bigger than herself. How could she face her loved ones if she aimed too low?

Her heels squealed as she rushed to a stop, turning the corner to see three members of the staff cowering at a crumbling wall. Aurora dashed to their side, hoping to reach them. The second she pressed her foot into the ground, it began to give out. She halted. Her eyes shot up to the people. The wall was going to kill them!

"Do not falter, Keerie! Keep running!"

That voice ... the lassie from Liavesen? Aurora did as she was told; the lightning imprinted her steps when she raced across the rugged ground. Just in time, she caught the workers before the wall could crush them.

The workers thanked her, teary-eyed and red-faced. She smiled at them before sending them to the exits.

Marquise Lee-May was soon at her side, wearing an outfit that was part regal dress and part armor. A fantastic white breastplate that had orange lace around the midriff section flowed beautifully down to her feet. "Exceptional work, Keerie. It seems Yehowehel did not choose a thoughtless woman."

Aurora ignored her comment. "How did ya do that?"

"*Galvan,*" Lee-May explained, "a House Phillian technique. I simply sturdied the ground beneath you. Unfortunately, the wall was out of my reach."

Rocks and dust descended from the ceiling, reminding the ladies that the chat needed to be short-lived.

"Thank ya fer helping me save them," Aurora said with a huff.

"Thank you for saving them. Twice now, you have protected things dear to me."

"Ya knew those servants?"

"No, but they are people of Setas-Li; innocents. As a marquise, it is my job to ensure the common people are protected." The noble looked at Aurora with an intense gaze. "If you can do anything, *anything* to end this war, I beseech you, do it. Commoners should suffer no longer."

Aurora studied the noble's gaze for a moment, and she sincerely felt that her words were true. "Aye, but we start with the ones in the hall."

Lee-May motioned for them to move. "The Eastern Wing has been emptied. The Seplechuran girl, Natalie, makes quick work. Thank Yehowehel that the Great General remained in the city; he also assists."

"Where does that leave the rest of 'em?"

"Just the Southern Wing, the Northern Wing is where the ballroom remains, that should be emptied by now."

"Aye. Jace was helping the rest of them. We should focus on the Southern Wing, then."

Lee-May put her hand up, hesitant to even touch Aurora. "No. You need to help your ally."

"What? I can't leave ya to protect the people, yerself!"

A loud rumbling shook the ceiling once more. Dust and debris flowed from the top like a full hourglass turned upside down, counting down the inevitable fall of the castle. Lee-May shouted, "You both protected my land with great vigor and power; you are stronger together."

Aurora could not deny that; however, from what she saw before, she doubted if they would be enough. Ras had easily overpowered them; now they had to fight him in a crumbling castle.

"Make your mind quickly! Time is of the essence!"

Aurora growled at herself. "Fine! I'll check in on him, then be back quickly. No one die!" She took off, expertly turning corners and weaving through the complex and its degrading Setas-Lisian architecture. Her body moved fast, but her thoughts remained slow: what was Jace up to? How was he handling things on the other side of the castle? She was soon going to find out.

A large tremor shook her from her feet; another threw her up against the wall. The top of the building came down even harder, and she was quick to question the integrity of the castle. She took to her feet, but again, another tremor tipped her over.

These aren't ordinary tremors ... there's a fight going on! Aurora found her footing, then zoomed to the ballroom again. Another shockwave shattered what was left of the left wall, sending pieces of the castle tumbling to the moat below. The wind howled in her ear, along with the screams and cries of innocent victims. She peered over the edge, the strong breeze nearly tipping her over. It was in that moment when she spied the deep descent in the dead of the night that she realized—all of this was no dream.

Ras was here. She was here. People died: battered bodies floated above the moat's waters, and blood filtered downward from under the rocks. The sound of battle only grew louder, and it did not expect to stop anytime soon.

She took a second to catch her breath, a single moment of clarity that would get her through this night, *if* she *could* get through the night. Aurora pinched her eyes closed, hoping that the darkness of the evening was an illusion, but nothing could fix it. Yehowehel, himself, would have to descend and put an end to it all—was her resolve. *If only it were that easy.*

Her eyes opened; she couldn't find the resolve to continue. However, she did come to one realization: *Jace is still fighting, and he expects me to come back.* Her own reasoning for fighting blew with the wind, but she held on to that little notion to keep her going. She moved away from the cliff, finding lightning in her step once more.

The entrance to the ballroom was caved in, the sound of Jace grunting, followed by a shattering clash, was enough for her to know something was afoot. The lightning thrummed through her feet, charging her heart, sending a tickle of sparks to her fingertips. "Jace, ya better move," muttered Aurora. From the tip of her Blade, lightning shot clean through the debris, scattering it with a thunderous force. She rushed in, immediately finding Jace and taking to his side.

"I hate to sound like Aidan, but it's about time you showed up." Jace grabbed his arm. Cuts and blood marked his skin and clothes.

"Sorry, laddie."

Jace breathed out a chuckle but was too pained to smile. "At least you got them."

"Them?"

Shadows that swirled like mist but with a far more sinister purpose twisted around the debris that Aurora had blasted through earlier. Soon, they formed into shadowy figures like the ones that had knocked them away before. However, it seemed that one more had joined their ranks.

"Did ya try to hit Ras?" Aurora asked.

"No good, they protect him almost instantly."

Aurora threw off her heels and cut her dress short with her Blade. "That's just a bother, ya know?"

The shadows were still, only bits of them were hazy like gray smoke. One shadowy figure held a large sword, another held two short swords, and the third had two strange semicircles hovering around it. Ras watched in the back. Alistair and Serenity were still at his side.

The cloth from Aurora's Blade swirled and hovered around her arm, charging electricity from its fibers. She glanced at Jace, who only had three wings left; he couldn't strain himself.

The Shade with the large sword attacked, Jace instinctively moved to block, but it was smart, moving the pressure to Jace's injured side. Aurora jumped over Jace, kicking the Shade, but her attacks passed straight through it. When she landed, she shifted her weight, now slashing with her Blade. The Shade's body fizzled, exploding into the wall in a puff of smoke.

The other Shades attacked; they were far more agile than that last one. The one with the floating semicircles jumped over Aurora. The lightning Keerie tried to shoot a lightning bolt, but the short sword wielder slashed at her. Aurora dodged, quickly trying to retaliate, but in a moment, the Shade appeared right at her side.

"What the …?" Aurora blinked.

The Shade kicked her aside. Aurora tried to reach out with the cloth, but the Shade dodged again. *It's like I'm fighting myself!* Aurora rolled to a stop, just in time to send lightning at the Shade attacking Jace. "Ugh, so they could kick us, but we can't kick them, what a bother."

"Aurora, make it rain!" Jace yelled.

Clouds formed inside the crumbling building, darkening the remaining lights that held inside the castle. Ras gave a cold smile when he saw the clouds. And it unsettled Aurora. Rain filled the room. Its close thunder caused her eardrums to quiver.

Jace waited for the water to fill the area before he exhaled. The Shades' movements soon became hampered as water turned to ice.

Aurora sent lightning through the ice, making the Shades scream with a strong gurgling noise before dissipating into smoke.

Nothing but the pitter-patter of frozen raindrops sounded for a while before Aurora and Jace realized it—they'd won. Aurora shook her head. *No, too easy, far too easy.* Not after what they saw from those same Shades before.

Both Aurora and Jace turned to Ras with a scowl; he clapped. "Very good, very good! Your mastery of your divine powers is impressive, yes? I can now see how you have given Brand and Merek so much trouble."

Brand and Merek, but not ya. Aurora wanted to bare her teeth at him; she felt the rending power of the Borealis Rage in her muscles. *Bastard.* She knew he was only toying with them.

"Now, let us make it a little tougher, yes?" With a snap of his fingers, the Shades reappeared unbothered by the previous damage. Aurora and Jace stayed on guard; their look of surprise must have been apparent because Ras drank up their reaction. He howled in laughter as he bragged, "Why are you surprised? They are shadows! Simple reflections of greater sources."

Greater sources? Did a group stronger than the Sovs exist? Aurora wondered. None of these shapes looked familiar to her, and Jace didn't seem to recognize them either. Maybe they were Sovs, but her father was supposed to be the strongest one.

"Do not lose heart now, let game begin!"

The greatsword Shade heaved the heavy blade, and with one slash, it created a gale so strong it made the dark clouds disappear!

Aurora growled, eyes lit with Rage. She attacked the greatsword Shade, but again, the Shade with the short swords intercepted her. Every slash and lightning bolt sent in the Shade's direction was immediately dodged and countered with a stab. "Stay still, ya darned thing!" Aurora finally wrapped the cloak around it. The lightning caged it for only a second. Either by speed or some other power, the Shade was in front of her.

Before the words could even form, it kneed her in the gut. And as she doubled over, it stabbed her in the back. Aurora howled, punching in anger, but it simply phased right through. The Shade grabbed her by the neck, beating her to the ground repeatedly until the sword protruded through her chest.

A trickle of red seeped from her eyes and nose, and of course, from the gaping wound. The green faded from her eyes, and whatever anger she possessed was replaced by death's blank stare.

Jace, too, was held captive by the greatsword and the semicircle Shade. Ras walked closer to them; the emperor's eyes were a mix of bewilderment and disappointment. "No, no, this is not correct." He looked around. "These Shades should be easy for three Blades." He looked around the bare room, as if waiting for something to happen. "Unless ... there are only two of you?"

Jace and Aurora's silence neither confirmed nor denied Ras's theory.

He shook his head, muttering something, then he spoke aloud. "How could you give Merek so much trouble, along with killing my Berserker and Brand? Either I am underestimating you, or they were weaker subordinates than I thought."

"What are ya getting on about, ya stupid dobber!"

Ras rolled his eyes, flicking his wrist; the shortsword Shade pushed Aurora deeper into the ground, flaring her wound.

"No, do not speak when I am thinking." His smile faded, his mood completely changed, like her father back in the Contested Lands. "I am angry with your merry band, disappointed even."

He turned to Alistair and Serenity, his brows furrowing to a scowl. "You two lost to them? To them!? There's only two of them!"

Alistair and Serenity immediately took to one knee, bowing to their emperor and not daring to look up. He approached them, grabbing them both by the head.

Then Aurora remembered what Alistair said earlier, *Do you think any of us could say no to him?! We're in as much danger as you are, being around him!*

A harsh wind kicked up, commanding everyone's attention. The hands of the Shades holding Jace began to freeze. Jace growled, kicking up another wind so powerful that the Shades backed away.

"Oh?" Ras smiled. "Attached to my subordinates, already? Unless you were attached to one before ... let me guess." Ras grinned a creepy smile that nearly cut across his weather-worn face. He looked at Serenity, forming a dark dagger in his hand. He drew it closer to her neck without breaking eye contact with Jace.

This time, the wind howled. Fractals of ice began to form in Jace's eyes. An ethereal luminescence stared at everyone with the intensity of high heats.

"Oh-ho, I see it now. You, especially, you draw so much power even without resonance."

Resonance? What the hell is that? As if to answer her question, the red orb in Aurora's Blade started to emit a warm glow, Jace's power filled her Blade's and her body's resurgence as well.

A hum of energy replaced the sounds of destruction. It was a sacred tune that aligned with Jace's crystalline energy. He shattered the Shades, forcing them to sink back into the darkness. Aurora, noticing the healing power flowing through her, groaned as she pushed the blade through her chest, watching it clatter on the ground. Before she could truly feel the sting, Jace's resonance began to heal her body. Honestly, Aurora did not realize how cold she truly felt, except for now. She tried to look at him, something about him—ascended.

The glow on Jace's skin was crystalline, reverent, but his eyes coursed with fury as he leered at Ras. "Let. Her. Go." Jace roared.

Ras smiled, releasing Serenity. "Well, well, well. To think mortals can still draw so much power from divine. However, this power of yours ... it is unrefined. No mastery. Shades will be one thing, but True Sovs will test you."

"True Sovs? Who are they? Tell me," Jace growled, his ascended tone reverberated through the crumpled room.

"No. You are too disappointing to receive answers, yes? Get stronger, and I will answer your questions."

Jace tipped his head with a newfound confidence. "That means we will have to beat it out of you."

Ras laughed. "Child. Let me tell you a secret: without more warriors, your powers will always be thin. Never enough to defeat me."

Aurora stepped up. "And what do ya care, huh? It's like ya want us to get stronger."

He gave another disconcerting grin. "There are some things even I cannot do, some keys I cannot obtain. But you … no, I am oversharing. Instead!"

The gooey substance of the Shades started to pull itself toward Ras. In seconds, he was flooded with a dark energy. Tension and pressure circulated around the room, and the ballroom felt it. The last of the foundation waited patiently for a single push of pressure to send the castle over the edge and into the moat.

"Today is celebration." Ras outstretched his arms. "So, here is my toast to you: To getting stronger and for your key ring to … enlarge."

The giant glamstone was the supporting force of the castle and all the lamps of Élurés. The glamstone was more than a light; it was a foundation. It held the castle, or what was left of it, together by way of its own unique gravitational force through the bombardment of Ras's assault.

Ras sent a beam of energy into the midnight-black sky, damaging the giant glamstone. The rumbling threatened a collapse of the castle. Ras waved his arms as a black orb encompassed him and his subordinates. "My final gift: to test your limits, of course." With that, they were gone.

A large Shade came up from the ground, unlike the others before it.

This time, it resembled an armored creature with strange, long arms and disproportionate features.

Jace and Aurora took to stance, readying themselves for their next battle. Aurora shivered at her wounds; she caught Jace staring at the blood seeping from her injuries that were not fully healed. No doubt he intended to try to keep her out of harm's way. However, sitting on the sidelines is not what she had signed up for.

The sound of the castle's walls partly collapsing had rumbled the very foundations of the city. Now, along with the shuttering material, Aurora could now perfectly hear the onlookers from the streets below. But she could not possibly imagine their shock. "Can ya keep this place steady?" she asked, clamping a hand to her wound.

Jace shook his head. The power emanating from him previously, seemingly faded. "Not without sacrificing the last of my wings."

The monster's arms stretched beyond proportion, similar to how Chuckle and Snark moved. The two of them dodged, but the falling debris stopped them from becoming nimble enough. One of the arms caught Jace, squeezing him until Aurora sent a bolt of lightning its way.

Jace couldn't even nod in acknowledgment before the ground began to cave in. The three of them braced themselves as the center floor cracked, drawing them like sand into a pit.

It's one thing after another in here! Aurora anguished.

Jace slashed upward, sending a blast of ice to trail his path and meet the Shade at the center. Upon contact, it burst into a flurry of needles that impaled every part of their tenebrous adversary.

"Jace, careful!"

"We don't have the time to be careful!" he yelled as one wing faded.

Aurora growled at the fact that he was right. She leapt, blasting lightning from her Blade to alter her direction. With a loud yell, she crashed into the Shade with a clap of thunder.

Reckless? Probably. Effective? Definitely. The ground fully caved in, and now the three of them plummeted to the depths of the castle's debris.

Aurora gathered her cloth, latching it onto the creature. A stream of lightning flooded the creature as it groaned in pain.

A wave of agony rushed through her as the backlash from the Rage kicked in again. She realized that she only had a few bolts left; three from what she could see.

Noticing the wane in power, the Shade grabbed Aurora's cloth and swung her into a piece of falling debris.

"Aurora!" Jace yelled.

The pain rocketed through her body as the heavy stones sent reverberations throughout her bones. Blood stained her dress as multiple wounds ripped open.

She had to forget the pain, just for a moment. The ground approached fast, and they were no closer to beating the Shade. Aurora latched the cloth to a piece of debris higher than herself. But—no, the pain was too much. It fell short.

"I got you!" Jace grabbed her cloth, launching her upward.

Ya couldn't at least carry me? Aurora stuck her Blade to a piece of debris, though it didn't help as the entire castle was to be in shambles moments later. Their only saving grace: the golden stone of light above the castle stood resolute; it seemed that it was unaffected by the castle's crumbling architecture. The energy from it caused certain pieces to hover, but not for too long.

"Jace, we need to end this now. Our Blades and bodies are gonna give out soon."

Jace furrowed his brow, shaking his head after a few seconds. "Aurora, I got an idea. Do you have some energy left?"

The debris they were standing on quickly descended, forcing them to brace themselves. Before fully dropping, the piece resumed its suspension.

"Aye ..." she groaned, "I think I have ... something left." Jace shot her a worried glance, but she lightly punched him. "Don't look at me like that. Let's end this, aye?"

Two arms shot up from the shadow of the debris field. Jace formed an ice shield that nearly cost him a wing. He thrust his Blade against the ice, forming several spears from it and shooting them at the Shade. The Shade knocked a few of them away, but some stuck to its structure.

Aurora, understanding the situation, gathered all the lightning that she possibly could. Jace launched more and more of his spears at the Shade.

The Shade detected Aurora gathering energy and tried to redirect its focus. But Jace kept vigilant. In each attack it tried, Jace either repelled it with his sword or redirected his ice shield.

The platform dropped again; the light began to fade from the grains of the wall. Aurora slipped, losing her concentration. She lost sight of Jace, and she slid down the wall into the dark abyss of debris. All she could see was the Shade's hands reaching for her, attempting to cradle her in phantom clutches.

Aurora readied a blast of lightning. But she heard Jace yell out, "No!"

She looked up only to see Jace race by her. He slashed the shadow's arms in a flawless motion and angled himself below her feet. She, in turn, angled herself just above him, causing their feet to meet. They pushed off each other. Aurora rocketed up, and Jace found himself facing the Shade head-on. With what little time she could gather, Aurora harnessed the energy coursing through her veins, her eyes illuminated green, once more.

A flurry of snow kicked up as she saw Jace's glowing Blade slice the Shade. Freezing its movement long enough for her to unleash one blast.

The clouds gathered above her, waiting for their final call before they lay to rest. Lightning eagerly paced in its cumulus cage until Aurora opened the door.

With a yell, Aurora launched an attack that raged like a thunderstorm! The sound deafened the area, grinding small pieces of debris into dust. Lightning sporadically cut through the air and rock, like a knife; light surged in every direction, threatening to blind all who stared.

The forked lightning converged on the Shade, and it yelled in splintering agony. It contorted and convulsed as the remaining bolts on Aurora's cloth faded with the light.

Her eyes flickered like lightning and blinked like a dying star. She fell faster than the remaining pieces of the wall. Her body felt like lead. Her eyes were sealed shut as the dreamscape wished for her presence. Though she understood that she had to stay awake, just enough to touch solid ground. A cold touch gathered her, calming the burning of her Rage-filled wounds. And she could barely muster a smile of relief. "Did we get it?"

"Yeah, we did." Some of the debris finally hit the ground, obscuring Jace's voice.

Her Blade reverted to its normal state in a shimmer of light.

Jace created a construct that would break their fall and give them time to escape. "We need to get out of here and find the others."

Aurora wrapped an arm around Jace as he began to make one last construction that could get them out. She wanted to open her eyes, just to see them make it out of this, just to see their victory. So, she did. But she didn't see victory. "Jace!"

A large hand emerged from the shadows. Jace expertly dodged. However, a second hand came even faster. Jace reacted swiftly enough to cover her with his body. The two of them were launched outside the debris field.

The Shade began to reach for them, but Jace managed to place his Blade between it and them.

Jace and Aurora were now suspended in the air, floating above the moat before the air delivered them to the ground. Wind bombarded their faces as they were about to fall into the bed of sharp rocks and water.

Jace's injured arm let her go, and he turned only to see her slipping away. That was the opportunity that Shade needed; it tried to wrestle Jace's Blade away.

In a moment of sheer weightlessness, before the realization and dread could fully settle, Aurora saw that a choice had to be made, a save was going to have to be made for either her or the Blade. Jace could not reach for both. She knew what he had to choose. After all, this was bigger than them.

It was alright, I had a decent run. The dobber would be fine ... they all would be fine, ya know? Aurora closed her eyes, taking in the final moments of night, and the cold air caressed her skin. It was a fine night to die, she finalized. The dark clouds she had summoned were gone, and the moon glowed bright. *It's okay. Everyone else will be fine.*

But that frigid air was replaced by rigidity, a shadow captured her, and it wasn't tenebrous. A sturdy voice battled against the winds, reassuring her of one simple fact: "You are *not* dying here today!"

THE END ...

... UNTIL IT'S NOT!

About the Author

S.J. Authority introduces himself with his first novel, titled *Vessel for Thy Power*. A writer since the age of eight, he spends his time researching history and, well, writing. When he's not writing, he's engaging in archery, voice acting, and gaming.